CONNECTION

CONNECTION

KIM PRITEKEL

SAPPHIRE BOOKS

SALINAS, CALIFORNIA

Sapphire Books
Salinas, CA 93912
www.sapphirebooks.com

Printed in the United States of America
First Edition – August 2013

Dedication

For Cindy. Here's to new beginnings and the continuation
of our life-long friendship.

Prologue

Silver and shiny. Suffocated light crept in through heavy, dust-covered drapes and bounced off row upon row of quarters glued to the plaster behind them. Like little round soldiers, they marched across the wall, ending at the edge of a calendar heavily marked in small red writing. Nothing discernible, nothing making sense. The sink, a double stainless steel model, was spotted and heavily fingerprinted.

A kitchen. Linoleum tile was old, bubbled up in places, the pattern long since rubbed away by shoe tread and bare feet. The piss-yellow fridge door was covered with alphabet magnets, some forming words mostly just jumbled together into incoherent sentences—no real rhyme or reason, other than they'd been grouped according to color. Red blended into blue, which led to yellow then green, and finally orange, with purple as the caboose. An army of plastic letters, perhaps to go to war against the quarters, all heads up.

Stairs. Wooden, making a hollow thudding sound as someone climbed or descended. A wooden rail worn with wear ran along the left wall, which was painted a muddy orange, though it ended, abruptly and shockingly, in gray, cold cement, the seam edges not entirely smooth. Peaked ridges might prick the hand or fingers of someone not careful. Down the stairs into darkness that was chased away only by a single, naked bulb that shed light on the water-stained ceiling above and dust-riddled air below.

A scream...

ᔥ ᔥ ᔥ ᔥ

With a gasp, Remmy bolted upright, eyes wide as she looked into the images in her head. She could still hear it, that awful, scary, blood-curdling scream. Chest heaving, she brushed sweat-soaked brunette bangs from her eyes as she gulped in several lungfulls of air. Finally she was able to focus on the room around her, a small, smelly motel room. Her fingers fumbled blindly over the bedside table for her pack of cigarettes, belatedly remembering that she had quit the week before.

"Jesus Christ!" She pushed the comforter and the thin, scratchy sheets from her legs as she swung them off the bed, her feet hitting the floor with a reassuring thud. The fabric of the dream was beginning to come apart at the seams, stitch by stitch, until all that was left was the tattered remains. "That was a doozy."

Remmy pushed off the bed and padded to the bathroom, where she switched on the light. Resting her hands on the badly scarred vanity, she leaned forward and studied her face in the mirror. Her eyes were rimmed with red, making the blue color of the irises seem unnaturally vibrant. She looked tired and worn out, far older than her twenty-four years.

The lid of the toilet hit the tank with a loud crack as Remmy sat herself down, face cupped in her hands as she relieved herself. With a heavy sigh, she let the dream images go, and the earlier exhaustion seeped back in. She hoped she'd be able to get back to sleep.

Chapter One

T^{*ink!*}
Julie Wilson was on her feet, cheering for her eight-year-old nephew as he shook himself out of the shock of actually hitting the ball while the crowd yelled for him to run.

"Drop the bat, Skylar!" Julie's brother Matt yelled, hands cupped around his mouth. The boy nodded vigorously, nearly hitting the umpire with the aluminum bat as he took off like a shot.

Julie laughed with pleasure as she watched the man of her dreams round first and head strong for second. She had no children of her own, and the way her love life was going, she wasn't sure she ever would. She tried to shake thoughts of her former boyfriend, Ray, as she cheered for the Little League Brewers.

"Man, that was a great hit," Matt said, his grin huge as he watched his only child give him a thumbs-up, which he enthusiastically returned. "I really wish Lori was here to see it."

"Me too, Matty." Julie wrapped an arm around her brother's waist. Since the death of her sister-in-law four years earlier, Matt had been so lost, trying to raise their son on his own. Julie had stepped in, playing mom to Skylar and confidante to her big brother. It was hard, and sometimes downright heartbreaking watching Matt go through the different facets of being a single dad. She often wondered why he didn't date, didn't even blink when a woman looked his way. She had asked him about it once, and his response was that he had his family and was content. Translated, she knew that meant he was terrified of losing someone again like he'd lost Lori.

As promised, the mini-Babe Ruth was taken out for pizza and Dairy Queen. Skylar sat proudly, cleats banging a happy beat on the booth, hot fudge dripping from the corner of his mouth. Julie didn't have the heart to tell him to wipe his face; he was still basking in the run he had scored for his team. The fact that they had lost to the Yankees didn't matter. He had scored!

"So, are you ready for the new school year to start?" Matt asked, digging his red plastic spoon into the dregs of his Peanut Buster Parfait, trying to scoop as much of the gooey chocolate from the bottom as he could.

"Yeah. I've been going in off and on over the past couple weekends to get the classroom ready."

They ate in silence for a moment before Matt spoke again, his light brown hair falling into his eyes, just as Skylar's did. "Heard from Ray?"

Julie sighed, running her spoon through the soup that was the remains of her sundae. "No," she said finally. She chewed on her bottom lip, tucking a piece of short, blonde hair behind her ear. She'd been debating the idea of talking to Matt about something that was bothering her.

Pre-empting her, Skylar boomed, "Dad, are we still gonna go to the park later and practice my catching?"

Relieved at his unknowing intervention, Julie kept her mouth closed. No doubt she was being paranoid anyway. She rested her cheek on her fist and listened to the men in her life prattle on about baseball, tee ball, and sports in general, all of them subjects that didn't enthrall Julie. Even so, listening to them got her mind off other topics.

~~~~~~

Soft Italian music played in the background, the portable CD player tucked into a corner by the toaster oven. Sergio Venti sang along softly, more of a hum, really. He went over to the fridge, pulled open the door, and grabbed the carton of eggs he had bought with his large grocery purchase the day before. He hoped she liked eggs. They hadn't gotten that far in their conversation yesterday. His grin would have been infectious if he weren't alone in the kitchen, cooking for himself and the beautiful woman waiting for him.

As Sergio chopped up bell peppers and ham to mix into the eggs, he thought about their time together the night before. All night they had made passionate love. He could still hear her cries in his ears, eyes closing at the memory and chills racing down his spine. She had loved it, just as he'd promised her she would.

Sergio heard a thud at the front door. Wiping his hands on the thighs of his immaculate slacks, he headed through the living room. Unlocking the knob and locks, he pulled open the door and waved at the young boy who had delivered his paper. Bending down, he picked up the paper, reading the above-the-fold headline as he stepped back inside his house and closed the door soundly behind him.

ANOTHER WOMAN MISSING IN THE WOODLAND AREA: POLICE BAFFLED

The building inspector shook his head. "How sad." Tossing the paper on the coffee table, he went back into the kitchen, energy flooding through him as his favorite aria came on. He cranked up the CD player, closing his eyes and singing out with Placido Domingo as he sang of his pain and agony at losing the woman he loved.
~~~~~~

"I understand your pain," Sergio said when the song ended. His breakfast preparations finished, he loaded everything on a tray. "Are you hungry, my love?" he called out. Not getting an answer, he smiled and shook his head. "She's deaf sometimes, I swear." Whistling softly under his breath, Sergio grabbed the tray and left the kitchen.

❧ ❧ ❧ ❧

"God, it's hot," Remmy muttered, hitching her backpack higher up onto her shoulders. She turned around, walking backwards down the lonely highway, thumb pointing toward the heavens. She had seen only three cars in the past two hours, and both had rushed past her, leaving her in their dusty wake, just like the pick-up truck that was zooming past. "Asshole!" she yelled, throwing the driver a single-fingered salute. "Damn it."

Turning back to face forward, Remmy began walking again, cursing the empty water bottle she carried. She couldn't bring herself to litter. She tapped it against her leg as she walked, head bobbing to the tune she heard in her head. She had lost her DiscMan back in Phoenix, and hadn't had the money to pick up another one, which sucked. Remmy loved music, any kind at all. She went through phases: one week it was R&B; the next, country with a mix of bluegrass. This week, for some reason, it was Italian opera. She wasn't sure what it was about opera, but suddenly one day she had heard the Three Tenors belting it out. Luckily, today it was Bon Jovi. It would suck trying to keep herself entertained with *Madame Butterfly*.

She was singing "Bed of Roses" out loud when the sound of a car engine pulled up behind her. Glancing over her shoulder, she grinned when she saw a small, white Miata pulling to a stop. The woman behind the wheel had short, blonde hair tucked behind an ear.

"Hey," the driver said, leaning over the passenger seat to look up at Remmy through the window, which was slowly buzzing downward. "Looks like you need a ride." The blonde looked out through her windshield. "Not much around here for miles."

Remmy grinned. "You are all that is holy and good."

The woman smiled. "I don't know about that, but I will give you a ride."

Remmy climbed into the tiny car with relief, shoving her backpack to the floor between her legs. She didn't bother with the seatbelt, a little trick she'd learned along the way: if she wasn't belted in, she could get away faster. She had learned that the hard way.

"Where are you headed?" Remmy's savior asked.

"Anywhere where there's a toilet. I've had to pee for two hours, and," she indicated the barren landscape around them, "there's not much privacy on this highway."

The blonde laughed. "No, that there's not. I know there's a patch of civilization about four miles up the road here. Will that do?"

"That'll be peachy." Glancing at the blonde again, Remmy's smile melted from her face. The blonde's eyes were hidden behind the lenses of her sunglasses. That didn't matter.

Darkness. Cold. Pain. Back was hurting. Water dripping — drip, drip, drip... No! No, please, no! A shadow, dark and foreboding, coming. He's coming. A naked light bulb...

Remmy gasped, her heart pounding out of control. She swallowed, throat and tongue cold from sucking in the cool air in the air conditioned car.

"Hey."

Remmy was startled by the feel of a hand on her shoulder. She blinked several times, face tight from too much sun during her travels. The blonde was looking at her, sunglasses shoved up on top of her head, concern in her green eyes. Remmy realized the car had stopped in front of a convenience store off to their right. When had they arrived?

Remembering the woman's voice, and registering what it had said, she nodded. "Yeah. Sorry. I just..." Her voice trailed off, not sure what she had just experienced. *Am I awake?*

"We're here." The woman gestured toward the gas station. Remmy followed her gaze, then nodded. "Are you sure you're okay? You're pale. Look like you've seen a ghost."

"No. Really, I'm okay." Remmy gathered her bag, grunting as she heaved its weight to her lap, hand on the door handle. She was about to open it, but stopped to glance at the driver. "Be careful. 'Kay?"

The blonde grinned. "This from the woman who takes rides from strangers?" She studied Remmy's face, sobering. "Okay; I will. You too."

Remmy nodded then climbed out of the car. She watched until the little white Miata was out of sight. Looking up into the gathering clouds and rumbling sky, she cursed softly under her breath. Inside the store, she nearly ran to the bathroom, whistling as she came out ten minutes later. Remmy dug into her pockets to see how much money she had left—eight dollars and fifteen cents. It was enough to buy lunch, convenience store style.

The tired clerk behind the counter barely looked at Remmy as she laid out her bottle of Quick chocolate milk and ham and cheese sandwich. He ran nimble fingers over the keyboard of his register, announcing a total and taking the proffered money with diffidence.

"Hey," Remmy said, getting the kid's attention. "You guys hiring here?" Without a word, the clerk reached behind the counter, then slid an application across the scarred surface of the veneered top. "Thanks. Got a pen?" The pen was delivered as rudely as the application had been.

Remmy took her three dollars and ninety-three cents in change, shoved it into the pocket of her jeans. Retrieving her food from the counter, along with the application, she headed for a table near the back of the store. She quickly filled in all the information, just as she'd done a hundred times before. If she let herself think about how many jobs she'd had in the past eight years, she might actually think she was a loser.

Ignoring the clerk's glare as she once again interrupted his magazine reading, she slapped the application and pen on the counter with a victorious grin. "Is your manager here?" she asked.

The kid nodded with an annoyed sigh. He reached for a small walkie-talkie tucked behind the register. Pressing a button, he spoke into the microphone. "Joan, some chick here to see you."

"Thanks." Remmy stepped away from the counter to peruse a display of jerky while she waited for "Joan". Within a few minutes, a plump redhead approached. She was wearing a dark green apron with the store's name and logo stamped in crumbling white ink.

"Can I help you?" she asked, eyes underpinned by heavy bags and topped by finely tweezed eyebrows that were as fiery as the hair on her head.

"Are you Joan?" Remmy asked, extending her hand. Joan took it, nodding as they shook. "I just gave your clerk there an application. See, I don't have a phone, heck, I don't even have a residence yet." She grinned. "Just got into town. I need to know if I've got the job or not. Good worker, ethical and friendly," she assured her potential boss.

Joan stared at her for a moment. "Josh, lemme see the app." She reached toward the counter. She took the piece of paper in her hand and scanned the information on it. "No address," she said, not bothering to look up.

"Uh, yeah, uh, well, I just got dropped off, actually." Remmy grinned. "So, maybe once I begin working, you can point in me the direction of someplace I can stay where I won't have six-legged roommates. I'd be grateful."

Joan looked up at her."How long you plan on staying in Woodland?" she asked.

"As long as I've got a job."

"I see." Joan glanced over at the clerk behind the counter, who had been watching the exchange with mild interest. "Josh, go get me an employment package. They're in the top drawer of my desk." Joan turned back to her. "Okay, Remmy Foster. I'll give you a chance.

Chapter Two

The rain pounded on the rag top of the Miata as Julie pulled into her driveway. She shut the car down and looked out over the landscape, seeing plants pelted nearly to the ground. Squealing, she dashed from the tiny car up the few stairs to her front door; her hair was plastered to her head by the time she got the door open. Two very excited Yorkies met her, barking and whimpering.

"Hello, my babies," she cooed, falling to her knees to surrender to an attack by two tiny pink tongues. "How's my Bonnie and Clyde?" she asked of the brother and sister. The sweetness of her tone got their entire bodies wriggling with the speed of their stubby tail wags. Pushing to her feet, Julie looked down at herself, groaning at her drenched clothing. Tugging her shirt off over her head, she tossed it into the laundry room on her way toward her bedroom. The two dogs followed, growling and playing with each other along the way.

She pressed the PLAY button on her answering machine as she passed the phone/machine combo on her dresser. There was a message from her nephew, thanking her for spending the day with him and for going to his game. Julie felt pride swell her chest as love for Skylar washed through her. She pushed a drawer closed with her hip, a fresh, dry shirt in hand. She was about to pull it over her head when the next message played.

"Julie, this is Ray. I know you're at your nephew's

game, and I know what time you'll get home. I still want to talk to you; I don't care how many times you say you don't wanna talk. We will talk." There was a click as the line went dead.

Julie hurried over to the machine, making sure to save the message, as she had done with the others. Never were they threatening, per se, but they made her uneasy all the same. She pulled the tape from the machine and walked over to her closet, pulling one of the double doors open. On the top shelf was a small box. Inside it were other tapes, pulled from the machine at a variety of times. Each tape contained a message from Ray—some rude and mean, others demanding, like the one she added to it now. All were being kept as evidence, should it become necessary.

Julie decided not to worry about it; instead she'd feed her babies, then get to cleaning the house. She'd intended to do it earlier in the day, but Skylar's pleas for her to go to his game had postponed those plans. No matter. She'd much rather be at the ballpark watching him run the bases than be at home mopping her floors.

The three-bedroom house had been purchased four years ago. It was a ranch-style, decorated in bold colors and contemporary styling. She loved the house on Poplar Street, and planned to live there for the rest of her life. It was large enough and had plenty of storage so that the dreaded clutter wasn't likely to become an issue, yet it wasn't too much house, or impractical, for a single woman with two micro-dogs.

She and her ex, Ray, were together for a year and a half, but she never let him move in, no matter how hard he tried to push her into it. Something just felt... wrong. After their break-up a few months earlier, Julie had felt a relief that was indescribable. She'd grown tired of his demanding, controlling ways; she couldn't take it anymore. The ending of the relationship was messy, to say the least. Ray wasn't used to hearing the word "no" very often, but Julie had to say it. Ray was sucking the life out of her. One day she came home from work, a full day of school filled with rowdy sixth graders behind her, and walked into the house to the sound of some sort of sports on TV, and then tripped over empty beer cans. Ray had been drinking more and more over those last six months, and when he drank, he got mean.

Independent and self-reliant, Julie decided she wasn't going to allow herself to depend on a man—or anyone—ever again. She had a job she loved, home and car payments, and was fine on her own. It wasn't as though she'd exactly found a relationship that really sustained her, anyway. Matt and Lori had been high school sweethearts, and had married on Matt's twentieth birthday. Almost thirty, she had figured she'd be married by now.

She always wondered whether it was something wrong with her. Was she too picky? Was she too independent? Why did men think they could treat her however they felt? It truly made no sense. When her parents were alive, her father treated their mother like a queen, and he and his little girl had been extremely close. Matt was a great guy, treated Lori like gold, treated Julie like gold. Julie often had this discussion with herself, trying to get to the bottom of the reasons she picked the men she did. The basic conclusion she came to was simple: for whatever reason, she wasn't ready for a relationship, so subconsciously she picked men that she knew were bad for her, or would leave or cheat on her, or beat her up. That way she would be kicking them to the curb. No muss, no fuss.

Julie walked into the kitchen, intent on grabbing the broom and dustpan from the small closet when she cried out, hand going to her chest. She would have sworn that someone had just been looking in at her through the back window. She hurried over to the window behind the sink, rising up on her tippy toes to look out in the yard. Seeing nothing, she hurried to the French doors, pulled them open and looked left then right. Though she saw nothing, she thought she heard the squeak of the back gate.

"What the hell?" She closed the doors and locked them. The uneasiness she felt wasn't new to her. Over the past few weeks she'd felt she was being followed on more than one occasion, and two nights ago, when she'd taken the garbage out to the curb, she had the distinct feeling that someone was watching her. Coupled with the messages Ray had been leaving on her phone, Julie reluctantly decided it was time to take action.

❧ ❧ ❧ ❧

Remmy tossed her backpack to the bed, surprised when it rebounded. At least she wouldn't be sleeping on a brick. The room was small, painted in an orange hue that complemented the drawn curtains. 1977 orange; it matched the comforter that had nifty threads of gold and olive green throughout. Bad motif aside, it wasn't an all around bad room. A phone sat on the bedside table and she picked up the receiver, gratified to hear a dial tone. Not that she had anyone to call, but she wanted to make sure it worked, all the same. Placing the handset back in its cradle, she began to hum an aria from *La Boheme*, doing a little jig toward the bathroom as the music swelled in her mind.

The bathroom was typical motel: itty bitty tub with cheap, plastic shower curtain; plain white toilet with the cheapest toilet paper possible formed into a little arrow flap on the roll. A fair number of towels were folded neatly on the rack mounted above the toilet tank, which was good. *Nothing worse than stepping out of the shower and finding no towels.*

Leaving the shower for another time, Remmy went back to her backpack. Unzipping it, she pulled out the contents—her worldly belongings. She set out the framed picture of her and her beloved cousin Monica, whom she hadn't seen in more than seven years. She wondered where Monica had landed. Their early years together had been spent experimenting with everything from alcohol to drugs to sex. Sadly, Monica had never gotten out of the life, and had disappeared from sight.

Deciding not to dwell on something that could be far too easy to dwell on, Remmy finished unpacking and then counted what was left of the advance her new boss had given her. After paying for a weeklong stay at the motel, she had enough left to pay for a modest trip to the grocery store. She was glad that the room had a teeny fridge in it. That would make things easier.

❧❧❧❧

The small grocery store at the end of the block was quiet, with only a few patrons milling about. Remmy pushed her buggy through the aisles, selecting microwavable foods and a few cases of bottled water. She loved water, and besides, soda made her dreams more vivid and strange. She didn't need her sleep to be any more intermittent than it already was.

Groceries in hand, Remmy strode out into the mid-August heat, like a blast furnace on her face. At times like this, she really wished she had a car. She'd had one...once. So, driving at high speeds over a mountain pass wasn't wise. If only someone had told her that two years ago. Ever since then, she hadn't been working or living in one place long enough to afford another automobile. She smirked as she headed back to the motel, remembering the one time when she'd gone into a bank to ask for a loan. That had not been pretty.

With not a trouble in the world, Remmy whistled happily as she crossed the motel parking lot. Juggling her packages to one hand, she dug the room key out of her pocket, inserted it into the lock, and let herself in. The room was exactly as she'd left it. The tune in Remmy's head continued as she played a game of Tetris to fit all her purchases in the tiny fridge. She took the few steps back to the bed and threw herself down, exhausted after a long day: walking, and getting a job, a place to live, and food. She deserved some rest.

As she lay there, eyes closed, her eyebrows drew together as sounds of groaning began to filter through the wall behind her. Blue eyes popping open, Remmy listened, a slow grimace sliding across her lips. Sure enough: the sounds of a quickie over lunch.

"Lovely." She grabbed a pillow, putting it over her head as she turned onto her side. "Not nice to tease someone who hasn't had any in more than a year," she said, her voice muffled by the pillow. Finally, determined to get some much needed sleep, Remmy attempted to just ignore it.

The light flickered. Dizzying. Gray wall, cold, cold against skin. Sharp edges. Blood. A form, shadow, someone coming, hand held out. Something shiny: small, centralized bit of cold on skin.

Pain! Burning pain. It won't stop! No, stop, stop! Please stop!

"No!" Remmy thrashed in the sheets against her nocturnal attacker, finally rolling off the bed. The hard landing shocked her awake, her wide eyes frantically darting around the dim motel room. Outside the sun was going down, bathing the room in an eerie orange-red glow.

Getting to her feet, Remmy ran a shaky hand through her hair, pushing it all back from her face. She was trembling, the fear still clenching her stomach in a vise-like grip. Typically as wakefulness took the upper hand, the fear and images faded. But her heart was still pounding, and no matter how many deep breaths she took, it wouldn't slow. Remmy began to feel fearful. She switched on the bedside lamp, looking around her room for something she could grab to use as a weapon. The fear clung to her and she began to check the room: bathroom, shower stall, under the bed, and behind the curtains. Nothing. She was as alone as she had been when she'd fallen asleep.

"My god," she whispered.

❧ ❧ ❦ ❦

Seemingly sitting patiently, Julie's tapping toe was the only evidence that she was actually quite antsy. Sitting on a hard, plastic chair in the lobby of the Woodland police station, one leg crossed over the other, she watched the goings on in the busy building. At the counter, a handsome black woman stood talking to a uniformed officer. Judging by her clothing—a pantsuit with a badge on a chain hanging around her neck—it seemed that she was either someone in a supervisory position, or a detective. She was listening intently as the officer gesticulated over some papers he was trying to describe to her. Julie couldn't hear what they were saying, but it was obviously important. They were also the reason that Julie was having to wait, as the desk clerk was involved in their animated conversation.

Finally the suited woman patted the officer on the arm and turned away, toward the front door of the station. She glanced at Julie, giving her a small smile before pushing through the double glass doors.

"Can I help you, miss?" the desk sergeant asked.

The small box of answering machine tapes in hand, Julie pushed up from her chair and walked over to him. "Hi. My name is Julie Wilson, and I need to file a report about a stalker." She set the box on the counter. "I have some answering machine tapes here, too."

"Alright, ma'am. Hold on a second and I'll send an officer out to speak with you."

Julie smiled politely and turned toward the lobby to wait a while longer. She was tired of feeling afraid. Less than six months after getting together with Ray, she'd had the distinct feeling that maybe she'd gotten in over her head. After the first year, she knew she was. Afraid of the man she had met through mutual friends, Julie spent the next six months trying to get out of the relationship, until finally she'd managed to force Ray from her life for good. Or so she'd thought.

"Ms. Wilson?" She turned to find a uniformed woman standing not far from her. The redhead smiled when she saw she had Julie's attention. "I'm Officer Renee O'Reilly. I'll be handling your report. Please come with me."

Julie followed, scanning the long halls of the station, officers and staff passing her on their way to one destination or another. Some nodded in greeting, others ignored her completely.

"Here we go," Officer O'Reilly said, pushing open the door for the petite blonde. Inside the small room was a table with a chair on either side. The officer took one chair, indicating the other for Julie. "What do we have here?" she asked, tapping the box Julie set on the table.

"Tapes from my answering machine." Julie pushed them toward the policewoman.

"Okay." The officer had a notebook with her and uncapped her pen, looking up expectantly. As Julie told her tale of the doomed relationship with Ray, Officer O'Reilly took careful notes, asking a few pointed questions to clarify the particulars. After the fifteen minute interview, the officer shook hands with Julie. "Thanks for coming in. Enjoy the rest of your Sunday, ma'am."

"Thank you. You do the same."

As Julie stepped out into the warm day, she pulled her cellphone from her purse, flipping it open and dialing a number she knew by heart. Her brother answered. "Hey, Matty. I'm just heading to the school now, so I'm going to be late."

"I thought you were headed to the school an hour ago," Matt said.

"I was. I got...held up." She unlocked her Miata, tossed her purse to the passenger seat, and climbed in behind the wheel. "I want to tell you something, Matt, but," she held up a finger, unseen by her brother, "before I do, I want you to promise you won't go all crazy on me."

"Okaaay," Matt drawled.

"I'm just leaving the police station. I filed a report against Ray. The police lady also advised I get a restraining order against him, so I'll do that at the courthouse tomorrow, when they open."

"What? Why?" Matt's voice was low, dangerously low. "I've never trusted that son-of-a-bitch."

"I think he's been following me, watching me." Julie glanced around the parking lot, half-heartedly looking for her ex's truck. "He's also left some messages on my machine that were less than warm and fuzzy."

"Oh, Jules." Matt sighed. "Why didn't you say anything?"

"I wanted to be sure. Well, now I'm sure. So, you have nothing to worry about. The report is being filed as we speak, and he'll get served with his restraining order tomorrow. So," she smiled and shrugged, "all's well." Turning her key in the ignition, the engine roared to life. "So, that said, tell Skylar I'll be by around five or five-thirty." She grinned at the thought of her beloved nephew. "I bet he's already packed to go, isn't he?"

"Are you kidding? Spending the night with his Aunt Julie? He's been packed for two days!" She could hear the smile in his voice before he sobered. "Listen, I'm not going to 'go crazy' as you said, but I do worry. I'm glad you're taking care of this."

"I am. Don't worry."

"Okay. See you later then."

Julie flipped her phone shut and pulled out of the parking lot, driving toward the school where she had worked for several years, and which she loved. The new school year would start soon, and she wanted to make sure her classroom was up and ready to go for her new batch of monsters.

❧❧❧❧

Remmy watched carefully as Josh showed her how the cash register worked. She memorized each button and what it did, filing it away in what she'd always referred to as the "filing cabinet" in her mind. Monica used to call her the "steel trap", as Remmy rarely forgot anything once she'd seen or heard it. She was a shark in trivia games.

Still paying attention, she adjusted the nametag that was pinned to her shirt, her name once again stuck to a plastic card with a safety pin attached. The bell above the door jingled, attracting both Josh's and Remmy's attention.

Just outside the large windows and glass doors was a non-descript blue van with some sort of red and yellow logo painted on the side that Remmy couldn't quite read. The dark-haired man who had climbed out of it was now heading toward the coolers at the back of the store. Remmy turned her attention back to what Josh was trying to show her. Within moments, she felt a presence at the counter. Looking up, she saw the man had returned with his purchase. He had dark, neatly styled hair that was tinged with gray in the sideburns. His dark eyes were dancing as he took in the two clerks.

"This, and thirty dollars worth of gas on pump three," he said, his voice rich and slightly accented.

Remmy thought it sounded like Italian. She considered his face, a hint of stylish growth above his lip and on his chin. He was a handsome man. Her gaze made its way up the straight, slightly prominent nose, and she met his eyes, which were on her. He smiled, though the smile did not reach those dark, impenetrable eyes. The air left her lungs at the wave of fear that gripped her; she was thunderstruck.

"Hey, you gonna watch, or what?" Josh asked, irritated that the new hire wasn't paying attention.

"Uh, I..." Remmy backed away, unable to take her eyes off the bewildered customer. "I gotta pee." She hurried out of the bullpen, nearly knocking over a display of candy bars in her haste to get away from the counter.

"Is she okay?" the man asked, looking at the bored teenager.

The kid shrugged. "That'll be thirty-one, ninety-nine."

Sergio Venti passed his credit card across the counter, eyes straying back toward where the pretty brunette had disappeared. He searched his mind, but couldn't remember ever seeing her before, though she had seemed to know him. *Strange.* He signed the card receipt, grabbed his Coke with a smile of thanks, and went on his way.

❧ ❧ ❧ ❧

Julie grunted as she stretched higher, trying to put the last piece of tape in place to secure the poster she'd just put up. Startled by a sound behind her, she cried out as the chair she was standing on rocked beneath her feet. Looking down, she nearly growled at Tommy Rosa, who had been a colleague for two years.

"Damn it, Tommy!" She used his shoulder for support as she stepped down. "You scared the hell out of me."

The seventh grade science teacher chuckled. "Sorry. Couldn't help myself. Saw your light was on, so decided to say hi." Tommy looked around the room, hands on his hips. He nodded. "Looks good."

"I'm glad you approve," Julie said dryly, taking the Scotch tape over to her desk and setting it on the calendar blotter. Tommy was pleasant enough, but she didn't like the way he constantly felt the need to flirt with her, especially since he was married. "How's your room look? Did you end up getting the Salzer twins in your class?"

Tommy nodded with a heavy sigh. "Yeah. I dread that. Those two are evil."

Julie chuckled. "Tell me about it. I had them last year. Hopefully Donald won't send spit wads sailing across your room."

"Yeah, well if he does..." Tommy slammed a fist menacingly into his other palm, leaving no need to finish his sentence.

Julie rolled her eyes. "Good luck with that one."

"Yeah, well a guy can dream." He fingered the tape dispenser on Julie's desk. "So, when are you going to go have that drink with me?"

"How does—never—sound?" Julie raised an eyebrow. "Unless Marcy is planning to come too."

"Eh." He waved her off. "My wife doesn't understand what it's like to be a teacher, you know? Doesn't get how tough it can be."

"Well," Julie said unsympathetically, "I'm sure she would if you took the time to share it with her." She glanced at him. "Ya think?"

"Maybe. Who knows." With a sigh, Tommy stepped back from the desk. "I'm going to head out. Have a good day. I'll see you next week. It sucks that we have to come back a week earlier than the monsters."

"Welcome to Teaching 101." Julie watched him leave the room with a small wave. "What a schmuck," she muttered, turning back to the remaining posters she had bought over the summer. The posters were filled with words of encouragement for her students, as well as amusing little anecdotes for life — sixth grade style.

In less than an hour, the room was completely finished. Julie was pleased that she would be able to enjoy her week with Skylar, a week she very much looked forward to. With this thought in mind, Julie gathered her belongings, shouldered her purse, and snatched her keys from her desk. She flipped off the lights and closed the door, then went to the office to let the principal know she was leaving.

"Hey, Bob," she said, leaning into the office. It was so strange to see him sitting behind his desk dressed in

Bermuda shorts and a tank top, thinning hair covered by a baseball cap. Her boss looked up at her. "Thanks for letting me in, I appreciate it."

"No worries." His pen tapped on the tablet he was scribbling on. "I had some stuff to do today anyway. You outta here?"

"Yeah. See you next week."

"Have a good one," he said, returning to his work.

Julie dug her sunglasses out of her bag as she pushed out through the double doors of Woodland Elementary. Her little white car was one of three in the parking lot. The other was Bob's sedan, and the third, an unoccupied blue van with the logo of a plumbing company. She gave it a disinterested glance, then took the tiny security remote into her hand, the car chirping to life as she pressed the unlock button.

Julie pulled open her car door and the oppressive heat from inside wafted out at her. She tossed her purse inside then suddenly was grabbed from behind. The sound of her cry was muffled by the iron-like hand that covered her mouth. She felt hot breath against her cheek and a strong body behind her.

Feeling herself being pulled off her feet, Julie struggled, kicking wildly, the heel of her tennis shoe making contact with a shin. She heard the short grunt from her attacker, but the grip only got tighter. She tried desperately to peel the fingers from her mouth, but then her arms were pulled roughly behind her, wrists held by a single calloused hand. She was hauled backwards, feet kicking uselessly as she was half-carried, half-dragged the short distance to the van. Her arms were released for an instant as she heard the metallic slide of the van door. Stark fear trickled down her spine and Julie began to kick and thrash wildly, doing everything she could to keep from being put into the van. Pain radiated through her hip when it smacked against the side of the van as she was heaved inside.

Tears sprang to Julie's eyes when the van door slid into place with finality, the hand on her mouth not moving. Arms and hands still free, she began to claw frantically at the arm, reaching back behind her trying to pull hair, gouge out an eye, anything that might free her. Her assailant didn't make a sound, said not one word. Julie's struggling was cut off as a rich, dark pain engulfed her head, her vision going black around the edges. She was having trouble breathing; the hand over her mouth partly covered her nose, as well. She fought weakly, sensing that if she lost full consciousness, it was all over for her. She tried to fight, digging desperately toward the fading light, but to no avail.

Julie was gently laid on the flooring of the van, right next to the plumber's wrench that still had her blood and bits of her hair on it. Breathing heavily, looking at the scratches that bloodied his arm, Sergio made his way up between the front two seats of the van and buckled himself in behind the wheel. Glancing around the parking lot to be certain no one had seen, he started the engine, shifted the van into gear, and carefully signaled before he turned out onto the street.

❧ ❧ ❦ ❦

Skylar looked out the window for the umpteenth time and then returned to his pacing. His bag was packed, filled with all his favorite video games to play with his aunt. His shoes were already on, too. He hated shoes, but his dad told him Aunt Julie would be there by five-thirty, so he was ready.

"Skylar," Matt called from deeper in the house. "Did you grab your toothbrush?"

The boy ran up the stairs, feet pounding as he ran into his bathroom and snatched the Oral-B from its holder on the wall. When he scrambled back downstairs, hoping that maybe Aunt Julie's car would be in the driveway, he saw his father standing at the front window, looking out then glancing at his watch.

Matt met his eyes. "She's still not here." he said. The boy looked disappointed. It was nearing six. He would give it a few more minutes before he called Julie's cellphone. She was notoriously on time, and in fact, usually early. "I'm sure she'll be here soon, buddy," he said, ruffling his son's hair.

Chapter Three

The clock struck seven as Matt flipped his cellphone shut. No answer at Julie's house, no answer on her cell, and no answer at the school. Grabbing his keys from the key board next to the garage door, he called out, "Skylar, lock the front door and get in the car!"

Sharply disappointed that Aunt Julie hadn't shown up and not understanding the gravity of the situation, Skylar did as asked, sulking as he made his way toward the garage door. "She didn't come," he said, throwing himself into the back seat of the car and belting himself in.

"I know, buddy," Matt said, belting himself in behind the wheel. "We're gonna find out why." They drove the streets of Woodland toward Julie's house. Everything looked quiet, locked up tight. "Skylar, run up there and ring the doorbell," Matt said, eyeing his sister's house. The dome light flashed on as the eight-year old climbed out, scurried across the manicured lawn, and bounded up the stairs to the front door. Matt watched him reach up, press the doorbell, then stand bouncing on the balls of his feet. He could barely make out the boyish voice as he called his Aunt Julie's name. Skylar rang again then turned to face his father's SUV, shaking his head. "Come back, son!" Matt called out.

Back on the trail again, Matt drove to Woodland Middle School, where Skylar would be starting classes in two weeks. He drove around the building, looking for something, anything, that might give him a clue. His heart fell when he spotted Julie's white Miata in the teacher's parking lot. Pulling up beside it, he turned off his SUV. "Stay in the car, son," he said tersely, letting himself out.

The car was quiet, hood completely cool to the touch. He tried the door handle on the driver's side, surprised to find it open. That, in itself, was very wrong. Julie loved that car and never left it unlocked. He saw Julie's purse in the passenger seat and nearly fell to his knees. "Oh, god," he whispered, heart sinking.

He hurried back to his car and grabbed his cellphone, having to redial the three digit number four times before his shaking fingers would dial correctly.

"What is it, Dad?" Skylar asked.

"Hang on," Matt said, holding the small phone to his ear. "Yeah, I need a policeman here right now. I think my sister's missing."

The seven minutes it took the police to show up seemed like the longest seven minutes in Matt's life. He sat on the hood of his car, Skylar curled up in his lap.

"Get in the car and stay there," Matt said into the boy's ear, lifting Skylar off his lap as he got to his feet. The squad car pulled to a stop in front of Matt's and Julie's cars. A tall man stepped out of the black and white, putting his hat on as he pushed the door closed.

"Evenin'," he said, walking over to Matt. "Are you Matt Wilson?"

"Yes, sir."

"I'm Officer Barrow. Tell me what's going on."

"My sister's missing." Matt did his best to hold it together as he told his story, starting from the last time he had spoken with Julie that afternoon. The policeman was attentive, writing down the details as they were given. After Matt finished his account, the officer, scratched his chin, re-reading some of his notes.

"Alright. Here's where we stand, Mr. Wilson. Your sister is a grown adult. She's twenty-eight, not some kid. The problem is that so many cases of folks disappearing are nothing more than the person not being in the place they're expected to be. Did she maybe run off with a friend or boyfriend?"

"You mean the one she filed a stalking report on this afternoon?" Matt was growing angry. "That's not Julie's behavior. I'm telling you, she's disappeared, and I want to know what the hell you guys are going to do about it!"

"Sir, I need you to calm down—"

"There's no way I'm going to calm down! My sister is missing!"

"Sir," Officer Barrow said, hands raised in supplication, but he stopped, noting something on the ground two parking spaces away from where Julie's car was parked. In the fading light, he removed a small penlight from his shirt pocket, squatting as he shone the small beam on the anomaly that caught his attention. The droplet had dried, but the beam caught the deep, rich red.

❧ ❧ ❧ ❧

The night was filled with red, blue, and white emergency lights, and the squawk of radios punctuated the air. The parking lot was filled with units, and a tow truck was loading the white sports car to take it back to the station for processing.

Detective Grace Cowan spoke with one of the crime scene investigators, the swirling lights glinting off the badge that hung around her neck. "I remember this woman," she said, looking at the driver's license that was in the purse left in the car. "She was in the station earlier today." The African American woman recalled seeing the petite blonde waiting, as Detective Cowan now knew, to file a report against her ex-boyfriend. She had already spoken with the responding officer who took the initial report from the brother of the potential victim. Looking at the scene now, the white Miata heading down Freemont Street and only a small bit of blood remaining, she couldn't help wondering what had happened in the parking lot. CSI had taken samples of the blood, which would be sent off for testing. Was it Julie Wilson's? Who knew.

"Detective?" one of the officers said, stepping up beside Grace. She turned to him in question. "We're just about done here. Anything else before we head out?"

"Nah," she said, waving him off and surveying the scene one last time. "See you back at the station."

Without another word, the officer gathered up his supplies and crime scene kit, and began to load up.

"So, what do you think of all this, Gracie?"

Grace looked up at her partner, Brian Wong. He adjusted his tie as she turned her attention to him. "I don't know." She took a deep breath, smelling the night air. "Something isn't right here."

Brian chuckled. "You would say that. Personally, I think this chick went off with a new boyfriend. Maybe that's why the old one's following — he's pissed that she's got someone else."

"And the blood?" Grace said. Cops were skeptical by nature, but Brian was downright harsh.

"Could be anybody's." He shrugged. "Some kid riding around the parking lot today, fell and skinned his knee."

"And the fact that Julie Wilson's purse — including her wallet, license, and house keys — are still in the car?

An unlocked car."

"I dunno. I just don't think you need to get your panties in a twist yet." Brian walked toward their car to grab a pack of cigarettes from the glove compartment. That was always his signal that he was finished with an investigation.

Grace could only stare after him, disgust curling her lip ever so slightly. She had lost respect for the man long ago. He had come onto the force as a cocky upstart. In the eleven years since, he had worked his way through the ranks. Seven years his senior and with four more years experience on the job, Grace didn't have much patience with him anymore. She had learned ways to ignore him while still working alongside him. Most had. Brian Wong had few friends on the force, but it didn't seem as if he minded. As Grace watched the slight Asian man light the tip of his smoke, she thought it was quite tragic, really, that he was such an ass. Brian was highly intelligent, but lacked the gut instinct that Grace had. He called it her woman's instinct, but Grace felt it was more a matter of paying attention to what was around her. Things weren't always perceived visually. If Brian didn't see it with his own two eyes, or hear it with his own ears, it didn't happen.

Grace had once gone to a medium at a town fair to have her fortune read. The woman, Mystic Robin, told her that she felt all cops were psychic in their own way. Perhaps…but either way, Grace knew there was nothing more that could be done in the school parking lot. It was time to pack up and head back to the station for the shit-load of paperwork that would keep her late again.

❧❧❧❧

When Matt arrived at Julie's house, everything

was exactly as he knew she'd left it: not a thing out of place, clean, and kid-friendly. Skylar's video game system had already been set out, ready for the insertion of his favorite games. The one thing that troubled Matt the most was walking in to find two desperate dogs. Unable to wait any longer, one had already peed in the corner, while the other nearly clawed through the glass to get out into the backyard as Skylar opened the door to let them out. Both their water and food bowls were empty, something Julie would never have allowed. From the beginning, she had fed them at precisely the same time every morning and every evening. Repressing his despair, Matt loaded Skylar, and Bonnie and Clyde into his car.

Taking one last look at the small, neat house, he started the engine and pulled away from the curb. *Damn it, Julie. Where are you?* Glancing in the rearview mirror, Matt could see Skylar, head leaning against the glass, hand absently petting a needy and visibly anxious Bonnie. He knew his son didn't fully understand what was going on, for which he was thankful. Even so, the disappointment oozing off the boy in waves made Matt feel sad.

"Hey, kid, want to play Mario Brothers when we get home?" he asked, meeting tired hazel eyes in the reflection of the mirror.

Skylar shook his head. "Nah."

"How about some Dairy Queen? Get you one of those cones you like, dipped in the strawberry stuff." Matt offered, hopeful. Skylar shook his head. With a heavy sigh, Matt turned his attention back to the road, his mind abuzz with what he needed to do when he got home. He should probably make some calls of his own to Julie's friends and co-workers, anyone who might know anything. What he wanted to do was go hunt Ray down and beat the living shit out of him. The only reason he didn't was because he couldn't leave Skylar alone, and he wasn't about to take his little boy along to witness that.

As Skylar disappeared upstairs with Julie's two dogs, Matt stayed in the living room, pacing and constantly glancing at his phone, though he knew in his gut that Julie wouldn't be calling. All his own phone calls had been made; no one knew a damn thing. Matt walked over to the front door, staring back at his reflection, the night beyond making the window work as a mirror. He took in the light brown hair that needed a trim, and the dark shadows that were green eyes, just like Julie's.

Stepping out into the warm night, Matt hugged himself, looking up at what could be seen of the stars. It made him think of when he and Julie were young, growing up in the country lanes of Pueblo, Colorado. They would sneak out to the corn silo and climb the narrow ladder up the tall, metal building. They'd find comfortable places to perch at the top and stare up into the night sky, trying to count stars or figure out where a falling star might land. Being seven years older, Matt had tried to explain to his younger sibling just exactly what the night sky was made up of, and that it was not crushed Oreos, as Julie thought it was.

He smiled at the memories, a sad smile. He would have given a lot to have his wife Lori by his side at that moment, putting an arm around his waist and filling him with the logic of her Capricorn mind. Looking up into the heavens again, he sighed. "I need you tonight, Lor."

Chapter Four

The stacks of newspapers had been arranged so that the dates were in order. Chronology was important in collecting. Next, the bottles had all been taken from the shelves and washed with extremely hot water and soap, drained, and dried to perfection.

Sergio sang along with his *La Traviata* soundtrack as he stirred the big pot on his stovetop. The smell was nauseating, but his guests needed protein. His dog scratched and whined at the back door, perhaps to get away from the stink. "Stop it, Romper!" he called to the mutt, who stopped the scratching but not the whining. Turning back to the pot, he smiled. "Only the best for them."

He turned off the heat, continuing to stir with his other hand. After a moment, he brought the wooden spoon out of the pan, brown contents plopping from the spoon as he brought it up to his nose. Wincing at the strong smell, he dropped the spoon back in and removed the pan from the heat.

Sergio scooped one of the cans from the trash and eyed the label. It stated that the contents were full of protein and vitamins, just what every happy, healthy dog needed to live a long life.

Within moments, Sergio had filled a tray with three steaming stainless steel bowls, three neatly folded napkins, and three Styrofoam cups of water. At the top of the basement stairs, he stopped to listen. The aria began to swell, the intensity and passion of the vocals and music blending together to make him feel like his heart would swell right out of his chest. He felt the sting of tears at the sheer beauty of the music. As soon as the song ended, he descended the wooden stairs, careful to keep his forearms and knuckles away from the sharp-edged cement of the walls. He'd been meaning to file that down since he bought the place nine years earlier.

The wooden steps thudded dully beneath the soles of his shoes, the dishes on the tray making a clatter of their own with each step. At the bottom, Sergio balanced the tray carefully on one hand as he reached up and tapped the naked bulb, the sudden light painting eerie shadows across his face. Getting a solid hold on the tray with both hands, he proceeded with his routine.

The first room in the large, unfinished basement was used for storage. Boxes and plastic tubs were stacked neatly, clear labels on their tops and sides to identify the contents. An old, metal dog crate, used to train Romper when he was a pup, sat in the corner, filled with fake, packaged fireplace kindling.

There was a single door in each of two of the walls. One door led to a small, finished laundry room with a washer and dryer, and a hanging rack for those clothes that weren't to be dried with heat. The other door led to another room, this one more primitive than the first, with dirt flooring, a low-hanging pipe-bedecked ceiling, and one window punched into the outside wall, though it had been blacked over for years. Within that room, there was another door. This door was made of thick wood planks, and had a sturdy lock. The door was four and a half feet high, which made entering difficult, especially with tray in hand, but Sergio had yet to spill anything.

The thick wood of the door kept any sounds from within from spilling out into the rest of the basement.

The guy at the hardware store had promised it would. Sergio was glad the clerk knew his stuff.

He set the tray down on a TV table just to the side of the door. The doorknob was there for looks only; it didn't function as a regular knob. It would hold the door shut when he locked it again. The building inspector dug the key out of his pocket and inserted it in the lock. One quick turn of his wrist and the door squeaked open.

No light spilled out when the door was fully open, only the stench of unwashed flesh and damp mildew. The walls had a slight crack down near the floor. It allowed water seepage when the back lawn was watered, hence the mildew in the air. The foundation of the house needed some work, which Sergio intended to do next summer. Unfazed by the smell, he grabbed the tray off the table and ducked down. It took a moment for his eyes to adjust to the darkness of the room. After several long seconds, he reached up blindly, feeling for the chain and then yanking the naked bulb to life. He smiled at the sight revealed by the illumination.

Chapter Five

As odd a character as Remmy was, Joan couldn't help but like her. She'd felt that way from the moment Josh called her to the front of the store the day Remmy had applied. Now she was watching her newest employee carefully stack cans of Hormel Chili—which was on sale—in an ornate display that had already reached about three feet tall. Joan didn't want to disturb her; she didn't want an avalanche of chili scattering across the tile floor, but she wasn't sure what, exactly, her protégé was doing.

When Remmy finally came to a point where it seemed safe to address her, Joan cleared her throat. The young woman glanced over her shoulder at her boss. "Hey, Remmy."

Remmy grinned sheepishly. "Hi."

"What'cha doin'?"

"Uh…" Remmy turned and looked at her creation, hands tucked into the back pockets of her jeans. "Keeping busy." She turned back to Joan.

"So I see," Joan said, hiding her amusement. "Tell you what, Josh comes in at one. When he gets here, why don't you come into the back with me and I'll show you how to do inventory paperwork."

Remmy grinned and nodded enthusiastically. "Okay. Great."

"Great." Joan took in the display again. "This looks great." She grinned widely as she walked away, shaking her head.

Remmy continued building her pyramid, covering the counter whenever a customer came in. As promised, when Josh came in to work, Remmy went to Joan's office in the back, just past the public restrooms. She cringed at the bottle blonde's poor choice of music.

Entering the tiny office, Remmy glared at Joan, who sat behind the desk. "Is it necessary to listen to gangsta rap? I really have no desire to go rape my girlfriend and then knock up my buddy's 'bitch'."

"Well, it's not my fault you have no taste," Joan said dryly, glancing up. "Have a seat." Remmy did as she was told. "So, you've been in town about as long as you've had this job, right?"

"Yep. About fifteen minutes longer, actually." Never able to sit completely still, Remmy tapped her fingers against the scarred wood of the chair arms, eyes darting around Joan's office, taking in every detail.

"Where are you staying?" Joan asked, turning her gaze back to the computer on her desk, the ancient DOS-based system that kept track of the store's business.

"Maple Tree Motel," Remmy said, absently snatching a pen off the end of Joan's desk. She read the words printed in red on the white plastic tube of the pen: DOUG'S AUTO. "Who's Doug?"

"My husband. You feel safe there? At the Maple Tree?"

"Eh." Remmy fiddled with the pen as she shrugged. "I've lived in worse."

"That's a scary thought." Joan turned serious. "Listen, I don't know if you're interested or not, but my husband and I have been looking to rent out the attic. See, I inherited my dad's house a couple years back, and this sucker is huge. Anyway, Dad was a painter and had the attic set up as his studio — water, kitchenette, fully functioning bathroom. So..." She studied Remmy for a reaction.

"How much?"

"We were thinking around three hundred."

"A week!" Remmy nearly flew out of her chair. "I only pay two-twenty-five at the Maple Tree."

Joan chuckled. "No, a month. Three hundred a month. You'd have your privacy. There's an outside door leading up to the upper floor of the house, which is a short staircase away from the attic. It's not huge, but it's not tiny, and it's safe and clean."

Remmy chewed on her bottom lip, head cocked to the side as the offer bounced around in her head. She pictured her motel room, remembering the roaches that scattered whenever she turned on the bathroom light. Grossed out, she had quickly dressed and hurried to work. She brought the pen up, tapping it on the side of her head. "What about a laundry facility?"

"I've got a brand new set from Maytag in the basement."

"I see." Remmy nodded. "Annnnd, your husband would be okay with this?"

"Of course. Hey, we just want to get it rented. If it's not you, it'll be someone else, but I figured I'd give you first crack." When there was still no answer forthcoming, Joan took the pen she kept tucked behind her ear and jotted down her address and phone number. "If you want to come look at it—no pressure—give me a call, or drop by. 'Kay?"

Remmy took the stickie that was stuck to the end of the desk, looking at the address before tucking the paper into her pocket.

"Okay, so, that's out of the way." Joan slapped her palms on the desktop. "Next on the agenda is to continue your training. I like you, Remmy, I'd like to expand your responsibilities here at the store."

"Really?" Remmy was stunned. Typically any meeting she had in the boss' office was to give her her walking papers. She was overjoyed that Joan was happy with her work. But then, she hadn't gotten one of—them—yet; that would interfere with her ability to function.

"Are you interested?"

"Yeah, I'm interested!" Remmy enthused. "That'd be great."

"Oh, good." Smiling, Joan motioned for Remmy to bring her chair around the desk so she could begin to explain and teach.

❧❧❧❧

On her way home, Remmy toyed with the Rubik's Cube she'd bought at the store. She was seriously considering Joan's offer. She didn't like staying at random motels, and the thought of having a place of her own, a real honest to god place, was more tempting and wonderful a thought than anything she'd felt in a long, long time. The life of a drifter was a hard and lonely one. As she walked down the main street of the town, looking at the passersby and the small, quaint businesses, she thought that maybe she had found a home.

Remmy tossed the puzzle game into the air, catching it in both hands as her gaze came to rest on the newspaper dispenser sitting in front of the barber shop. She nearly missed catching her next toss as the lead story caught her eye. Tucking the cube against her chest, she walked over to the box that held the *Woodland Daily Record.*

LOCAL WOMAN MISSING: EX-BOYFRIEND SOUGHT FOR QUESTIONING

Beneath the headline was a small, grainy picture

of a beautiful blonde with sparkling green eyes and an infectious smile. Remmy recognized her immediately as the woman who had given her a ride not so long ago.

Reaching into her pocket, Remmy dug out some change, slipped it into the machine, and snatched a newspaper. Rubik's Cube forgotten, she sat on a bench alongside the paper box. She learned the woman's name was Julie Wilson. As she came to the part of the article that mentioned Julie's ex-boyfriend, and asked that anyone who knew his whereabouts to call the Woodland Police Department, Remmy felt cold.

Looking at Julie's picture, Remmy's entire world became the image off that lovely face. Everything around her disappeared, all sound fading to white noise.

Fear. Horrible fear. Who is this? Where am I? My head hurts, something hard and quick, can't see. Cold. So cold. So cold...

Remmy gasped; the feelings were so strong within her that she actually eyed every person who passed by with suspicion. She could scarcely breathe as she got up on shaky legs. She looked down at the picture of Julie again, making contact with the lifeless eyes of a photograph. For a moment, just a breathless heartbeat, they looked back at her, pleading, a distant scream echoing in Remmy's head.

Shaken, she threw the newspaper to the bench, jumping back from it like it was a poisonous snake. Glancing around, Remmy noted that she had caught the attention of an older couple walking by. She gave them a weak smile. "Spider," she said by way of explanation.

The older man chuckled as he steered his wife past the strange young woman. He patted Remmy on the shoulder, leaning in conspiratorially. "I use household cleaner to kill the little buggers." With a wink, the old couple moved on.

Taking several deep breaths, Remmy went into a coffeeshop across the street. After purchasing a gooey cinnamon roll and a large mocha breve, she sat at a table near the window with the newspaper spread out before her. She re-read the article three times, soaking in every single detail. The story began to unravel in her brain. She had no idea where the teacher was or why she'd been taken; she had no idea who had taken her, but she knew it wasn't the ex-boyfriend. As surely as she knew her own name, she knew it wasn't him.

"She was a cool chick."

Remmy was startled by the unexpected voice, and slightly irritated at the intrusion into her thoughts. She looked up to see a young man, no older than twenty, grinning down at her. Given his green apron, replete with logo, he worked at the coffeeshop.

Pointing at the picture of Julie Wilson, he said again, "She was a cool chick. My little sister had her for sixth grade last year. All we heard the entire school year was 'Miss Wilson this, Miss Wilson that'." He rolled his blue eyes, brushing too-long red bangs out of them.

"Oh, uh, I don't know her," Remmy said finally, shaking herself from her stupor.

"This guy, though," he continued, as though she hadn't spoken. He tapped the word "ex-boyfriend" in the headline. "…is a real dick. Ray is his name. They used to come in here sometimes, and more than once my boss, Tony, had to kick him out. Julie would just sit there, looking for all the world like she wanted to melt into the table." He grinned, but then quickly sobered. "Not at all surprised that something like this happened, really." He looked around the busy coffeehouse. "I don't think anyone is."

"So, you think he did this?" she asked, irritated that he had bothered her, but interested in what he had to say, all the same.

Nodding, he answered, "Oh, yeah. Definitely." Suddenly he stopped, holding out a rather large hand. "I'm Roman, by the way. You work at the Texaco, right?"

"Yeah. Hi. I'm Remmy." She shook his hand and gave him a polite smile.

"Nice to meet you, Remmy. Well, hey, I think you're new in town, so if you ever want a tour, or wanna know the cool places to go and hang out — like, all three of them — just let me know." His grin widened. "I got a car, so…"

"Cool. Okay." Remmy smiled, hoping he'd go away. "Thanks."

"Sure thing." He glanced over his shoulder and saw his co-workers glaring at him as business picked up. Turning back to Remmy, he slowly backed away, nearly knocking over a customer. "Well, hey, it was nice meeting you, Remmy. Take it easy."

"Later." Turning back to the paper, Remmy sipped her coffee, finger tapping on Julie's picture.

Chapter Six

Detective Grace Cowan gently rocked in her desk chair, no longer hearing its petulant squeaks after so many years. A No. 2 pencil twirled in her fingers, diamond wedding ring glinting in the harsh, overhead light. Light brown eyes didn't seem to be looking at anything as she stared off into the unknown. She nearly jumped out of her skin and light gray pant suit when Brian Wong slammed a small stack of manila folders onto her desk.

"Okay, we got some results back, though nothing is even remotely helpful." He perched on the edge of Grace's desk. "The car in the Wilson case has been processed. Found three sets of fingerprints inside, but only one set on the steering wheel, proved to be Wilson's. No blood, nothing suspicious or out of the ordinary." He glanced at the open file in his hand. "Oh, except for two strands of long, dark hair, found on the passenger side headrest. The brother — who has short, light brown hair — says his kid also has light hair, and it's short, and he can't think of anyone with long, dark hair that Julie would have had in the car. He can't recall any of her close friends with dark hair, or colleagues, but come on," he slapped the folder closed, "long, dark hair isn't exactly uncommon."

Grace listened to him, nodding every once in a while as the eraser of the pencil found its way against her front teeth: *tap, tap, tap.* "Okay. Well then, preliminary results indicate the perp was never in her car, I guess."

"I think that's quite apparent," Brian grumbled, flipping through some of the other files on his lap. "Nothing back from the lab yet on the blood found in the parking lot."

"You know," Grace said, still staring off into space, "the principal said he thought he recalled seeing some sort of a work van or SUV in the parking lot when he went inside the building." She glanced at Brian. "Anything more on that?"

Brian shook his head. "Nope."

"Alright." Grace sighed. "I'm going to go over to Ray Lambert's place again. Gotta catch him home sometime."

"Isn't that what the twenty-four hour surveillance is for?" Brian asked, pushing up from the desk.

"I'm sure it is, Brian." Grace also stood, grabbing her keys from the desk drawer and giving him a sweet smile. "But I'm a woman of action." She pushed past him and strode down the hall to the back door of the station.

It was a hot one outside. Grace climbed into the unmarked sedan she and Brian used on the job. She pulled out of the station's parking lot, nearly struck by a large, blue van that was pulling in. "Asshole," she muttered, pressing her horn to alert the driver to pay better attention. The man behind the wheel gave her an apologetic wave and slowed. Glancing in her rearview mirror, she noticed the red and yellow logo on the side of the beast, though she couldn't quite read what it said from her angle. For a split second she remembered the principal's recollection of a work van being in the school parking lot before Julie Wilson's disappearance, then she shook it off. Coincidences like that just didn't happen.

As she cruised the streets of the town where she was born and raised, Grace's thoughts roamed freely.

She'd wanted to be a cop ever since she was a small child. Growing up in the small, sometimes prejudiced town of Woodland hadn't made that dream easy. Not only was Grace black, but she was also a woman. It had been an uphill battle from Day One.

In school, Grace had joined the ROTC, learning discipline and how to use weapons. From there she earned an associate degree in Criminal Justice at the local community college. She'd hoped that perhaps her advanced education would help her get not only into the department, but further ahead. It was not to be. She started as a beat cop, running the streets for more years than her credentials should have required. But, at last the day came when Grace began to rise in rank within the department, and her career was finally heading where she wanted it to.

Now a detective and well-respected within the department, she still had to deal with assholes like Brian Wong every day. Most of her fellow law enforcement workers were good, hard-working people, whom she respected. But others...

Grace sharpened her focus as she neared the street where Ray Lambert lived. It was a nice neighborhood — well-kept houses with huge, old trees lining the street. She knew Lambert had owned his own business for years, and according to those who worked at his lumber supply outlet store, it wasn't unusual for him to be away for days or a week at a time. Even so, it was highly unusual, his employees admitted, for him not to tell anyone he was leaving town, and for him to not answer his cellphone.

Grace had been by Lambert's house twice already, and had tried to call the elusive man several times. As she neared his house, she had the feeling she would be disappointed yet again.

Pulling into the empty driveway, Grace cut the engine and surveyed the seemingly empty home, reviewing what she knew about Ray Lambert. He was thirty-five and had been married twice. The first marriage lasted for three years, producing a daughter when Ray was seventeen; the second marriage lasted for five years, no children. He had a record of domestic abuse, and assault on the boyfriend of his ex-wife, though Ray had never done time.

Grace made sure her revolver was tucked in its holster, and stepped out of the car. She kept a careful eye out for the unexpected, something she had learned the hard way. During her first year on the job, a man had jumped out at her from an alley and nearly killed her. Three stab wounds later, Grace found herself in a hospital room, begging her captain to give her another chance. She recovered far more quickly than her doctors and peers expected, and had won her way back into the fold with dedication and hard work.

With a little bounce in her step, Grace mounted the three stairs that led to the front door. Making sure her badge was visible, she pulled the screen door open and knocked on the wooden door behind it. After three consecutive knocks that went unanswered, Grace was about to leave when she heard the locks being disengaged. The front door opened and a teenage girl looked out through the screen door with questioning eyes.

"Hello. I'm Detective Grace Cowan with the Woodland Police Department." She held up her badge for the girl, who peered out at it. "Is Ray Lambert at home?"

The girl shook her head. "My dad's in Florida."

"When did he leave for Florida?" Grace asked, keeping her voice casual.

The girl shrugged. "A week ago, maybe."

"Do you know why he went?" Grace withdrew a small notepad from an inside pocket of her blazer and clicked her pen to the ready. The girl watched the movements before returning her gaze to the detective's eyes. Grace wrote down the girl's explanation —her father had gone on a short vacation, taking his new girlfriend with him, and she had been checking on the house a time or two for him before she went back to school to start her junior year.

Grace left the residence ten minutes later, wondering why the surveillance officers hadn't spoken to the young woman before. The daughter had also provided an explanation as to why Ray's cellphone was not being answered. Apparently his carrier didn't have nation-wide service. Regardless, when Ray Lambert came back from his sudden "vacation", they'd be waiting for him.

Chapter Seven

A dripping sound was the first thing she became aware of. Something dripping, and not too far away. There was a constant pain in her head, mostly toward the back and a little to the left, by her ear. She tried to get a feel for her body, where she was. She realized she was very cold, something chilling the entire back of her body where she pressed against it. Was she naked? The sting against her butt and upper shoulders made her think so.

Suddenly Julie's chin was grasped in a vise-like grip, her head turned to the right, making her throbbing skull scream in protest. She started when puffs of hot breath, smelling of garlic, assailed her face, making the eyelashes of her left eye flutter.

"Beautiful," a voice whispered, sending more hot air washing over Julie's face. She tried to open her eyes, but stopped with another groan. The action made her head pound even more. "Shh, shh," the voice cooed, soft fingertips brushing over Julie's closed lids. "Get some rest."

Julie fell back into the blackness, the cold disappearing and the pain fading into peace.

❧❧❧❧

Remmy looked up the imposing narrow staircase from the second floor to the closed door at the top. She wondered what her new place and new life would look like. Mounting the stairs, she ignored the squeak of the old wood under her booted feet, one hand reaching out to slide along the wall to keep her balance. The octagon-shaped window at the top of the stairs shone distorted colors down on her, the colored glass etched and random.

Remmy slid the key into the lock, turned it, and pushed the door open. The space was adequate. It was certainly larger than her motel room. With heavily slanted beamed ceilings, Remmy would have to remember to duck in those places. The front wall was lined with small windows, another octagon-shaped window, three times larger than that at the top of the stairs, located in the middle. It sent red, green, and yellow colors shooting across the hardwood floor.

All the way to the right, against the wall, was a kitchen unit complete with a small fridge, two-burner stove, and a sink. Cabinets lined the walls above the sink and stove. Just beyond that was a curtained off area, which further exploration revealed as the bathroom: toilet, pedestal sink, and a stand-alone shower stall.

Remmy turned her back to the bathroom and scanned the rest of the sparsely furnished space. There was plenty of room for shelves on the walls, plenty of room for a bed area and a living area. It was nice, and the rent was a bargain.

"What do you think?" Joan asked, suddenly standing in the open door.

Remmy glanced over at her. "Three hundred, huh?"

Joan nodded. "That includes your heat, electricity, anything like that. If you want a phone, you're on your own, but all other utilities are included. And," she held up a finger, "Doug can wire cable up here, too, if you want it."

Remmy smirked. "That would require me to actually own a TV."

"How much stuff do you have?"

Remmy patted the pack on her back. "You're looking at it."

"Oh. Okay. Well, there's a thrift shop downtown, and I'd be more than happy to take you down there, if you want. Help you get yourself set up."

Remmy sighed, thumbs hitching in the front pockets of her jeans. "I really appreciate all this, Joan, but I don't have the money to do any of that right now." She looked around the space wistfully. "Wish I did."

Joan's footfalls echoed in the empty room. She slung an arm around Remmy's shoulders. "We'll figure something out, kid. You game?"

"You sure?" Remmy said. Joan grinned with a nod. "Okay. You're on."

Later that evening, Remmy sat on her new/used couch, feet propped up on a scarred, but incredibly cheap, coffee table, watching her new television. She squirted some more of the sticky aloe into her palm, gently rubbing it over her badly sunburned face. She hadn't thought that repaying Joan and Doug for her new furniture setup would be so painful. In all fairness to them, Doug had warned her to put on some sunblock before she went out to mow the yard and pull weeds. She hadn't listened.

The deal had been made — Remmy would help around the house and yard for three months in exchange for the thrift store purchases. Looking around her new digs with something like pride, she was glad she had agreed. A bed — full-sized — all her own, with matching dresser, courtesy of the local Goodwill. She also had a small, two-person table at which to eat her meals, and a full living room, complete with a four foot high bookshelf and wooden TV stand to go with her couch, coffee table, and nineteen inch TV. It was even in color! If only she had known that a visit to a thrift store could be so fruitful. Though it wasn't like she'd ever stuck around anywhere long enough to buy anything, and she certainly couldn't lug a couch down the next nameless highway.

Everything she had done today, the work and promises, would maybe allow her to find some peace and happiness for at least three months. She swore to herself that she would not renege on Doug and Joan, two of the most decent people she had met in a long time.

Slopping more aloe onto her fried shoulders and arms, Remmy absently used the remote to flick through the channels, looking for anything interesting. Doug had to go to work, so he hadn't run the cable up to her room yet, leaving only the five local channels for entertainment. She passed by *Wheel of Fortune*, stopping just long enough to guess three wrong letters, then moved on to find the evening news. She was about to flip back to the game show when Julie Wilson's image caught her attention.

"...be reached, though police say they'll keep trying to contact Lambert," the news anchor said, glancing briefly down at her notes. *"If you have any information on the whereabouts of Lambert or Julie Wilson, please call police."*

The gaudy music began, indicating a commercial break. Remmy gazed at the screen, but was no longer seeing it. Chewing on her bottom lip, she came to a decision.

❧❧❧❧

Inside the small room furnished with only a small,

square table and two chairs, Remmy stood in front of the two-way mirror and was looking into the smoky mirror, hands cupped around her face, trying to look through to the other side. She heard someone clear his throat to get her attention.

Remmy whirled around and saw a man in a dark brown suit standing in the doorway to the small room. She grinned. "I uh, I always wondered what was on the other side of those," she said, hitching a thumb over her shoulder toward the two-way.

"Well," the man entered the room and closed the door behind him, "I hope your curiosity has been laid to rest." He slapped his pad of paper down on the table and sat, glancing up at Remmy, nodding toward the chair across from him. "My name is Brian Wong. I'm one of the detectives working the case." He grabbed his pen, removing the cap as he poised the instrument above the pad. "And who might you be?"

"My name is Remmy Foster," she said, getting settled across from the curt man.

"Alright, Remmy. I hear you wish to talk about the Julie Wilson case." He looked into Remmy's face, studying her with shrewd, dark eyes. "Do you know Julie Wilson?"

Remmy shook her head. "Nope. Met her once, though."

"Oh? And when was that?"

"Not long before she disappeared. She gave me a ride." Remmy watched as the man scribbled some notes on the yellow legal pad. Hands clasped primly in front of her, she sat still, waiting for him to stop. After a moment, dark eyes met hers again, silently prompting. "I haven't seen her since."

Brian Wong sat back with a sigh. "So, what have you got for me that was so important for you to take time out of your day, and mine, to tell me? Cuz, I gotta tell you," he tapped his pad with a finger, "this ain't it."

"You guys are going after the ex-boyfriend, right?" Remmy asked.

"We'd like to question him, yes."

"Don't bother."

Remmy had stated this so matter-of-factly that it obviously got Brian's attention. "And why is that?"

"Because he didn't do it," Remmy said simply, as though that would suffice as an explanation.

"He didn't do it," the detective repeated slowly, eyeing her. He took in her ill-fitting t-shirt, disheveled hair, and the torn jeans his gaze had flicked to before she sat down. "Look, Miss Foster, unless you can give me something to actually sink my teeth into, you're wasting both our time here."

"No, you have to listen to me," Remmy said, leaning forward, one elbow resting on the table. "I'm telling you — it isn't this Ray Lambert guy."

Brian's dark brows drew. "You said you don't know Julie Wilson."

"Correct."

"Do you know Ray Lambert?"

"Negative, Houston."

The detective's gaze was so intense, so intrusive, Remmy began to feel uncomfortable. She noted that his focus seemed to stop on her hair, the wheels seeming to turn in his head before finally, he spoke.

"So, you don't know Julie Wilson, you don't know Ray Lambert, yet you're telling me that Ray Lambert isn't responsible for Wilson's disappearance."

Remmy nodded. "That's exactly what I'm telling you."

"Okay," he said, setting his pen down and interlocking his fingers on the pad. "Look, Miss Foster—"

"Remmy."

"Whatever." He didn't bother to hide his irritation. "I'll call you Mother Theresa if you want, as long as you can give me something, anything, remotely concrete or useful."

"And I'll call you Columbo if you want, if you'll pick up your pen and write down what I'm telling you," Remmy said, her own hackles rising. Her gaze was steady as it held the detective's for a long moment in a battle of wills.

With a heavy sigh, Brian Wong finally broke the eye contact and did as she asked. "Alright. And what makes you believe that Ray Lambert isn't involved?"

"I can't tell you that."

Brian let out an angry sigh. He threw the pen down and rose to his full height, fists resting on either side of his legal pad. "Listen, Remmy, this is a woman's life we're talking about here, okay? This isn't some goddamn game I'm playing."

"I know it's crazy, but I'm telling you, Detective Wong, you're going in the wrong direction. See, I get these visions—"

"Visions!"

"Yes. Visions. She's in a place right now that's cold, and she's scared and confused. She doesn't know where she is—" Remmy was on a roll, all her visions and the one dream she'd had rushing out of her in a torrent of words. She stopped herself, however, when she saw the look on Brian Wong's face. *Jesus, this guy's a hard sell!*

"I don't understand 'visions'," he said.

Remmy grimaced. "Hell, buddy, I wish I understood 'em!"

"So, what, you see yourself as some kind of psychic? Some sort of Sylvia Browne?" The detective smirked, but Remmy didn't crack a smile.

"I don't know who that is, and no, I don't."

"You don't see yourself as psychic?" Brian asked, voice dripping with doubt. At the shake of Remmy's head, he probed further. "So, what is it like? You have some sort of TV show playing in your head or something? Is that what these visions are?"

"Well, typically it's more like re-runs, like I pick up on older stuff. I don't know, it's almost like when someone is carrying around some pretty serious emotions — guilt, sadness, fear, whatever — from something that's already happened, I pick up on it, and sometimes it'll form an image in my head. But with this," she shrugged, "it's like live TV. I'm seeing things as they happen, feeling them."

Brian tapped the end of his pen on the table. The doubt and condescension dripped from his gaze. "Well," he said, slapping his pen down, "thanks for coming in. I'll look into this cold, dark, foreign place. See what we can come up with." Brian pushed back from the table.

Am I being dismissed? Remmy's eyebrows drew together. "Alrighty, then." She stood and exited out of the door the detective was holding open for her.

"If you think of anything else, give us a call," Brian Wong said before turning toward his office.

Chapter Eight

Weeping. It was quiet, muffled, but weeping all the same. Julie blinked her eyes several times, opening them wide for a moment to try to get rid of a sticky residue that was acting like glue. The flaky "rocks" that seemed to be sifting into the corners of her eyes led her to suspect the gluey substance might be dried tears. This was the most awake she'd been in what felt like months, though she knew it must have been a smattering of days or weeks.

After a few moments of clarity, Julie took inventory of her situation: cold metal was wrapped around her wrists, which were held above her head, hands dangling over the shackles. She was standing, though her feet were separated by a foot of heavy chain, which clinked every time she moved. Her feet were bare, as was the rest of her. Something cool, yet not solid was beneath her feet. *Dirt?*

Julie couldn't see much. It was very dark, but as her eyes slowly began to adjust, she could see the tiniest blue hue of light off to her left. From the small amount of light, she could tell that there was a tiny crack in the wall near the floor.

Hearing the whimpering again, Julie tried to peer through the darkness to her right. She could only see a dark shape against a velvety black backdrop.

"Shh, Roxie, it's okay," someone whispered from directly in front of Julie, whose eyes were now widened as far as they could go to try to pierce the dark.

"I can't die here," another woman's voice said from the right. "I just can't."

Julie assumed it was the whimpering Roxie. She tried to open her lips, but winced as they cracked from dryness and lack of use. She licked her tongue over them again and again before croaking out, "Where am I?" The sudden silence made Julie even more uncomfortable. It was broken when the woman in front of her spoke.

"You survived." It was a statement, not a question. "You're in hell." That got the whimpering started again. "Roxie, knock it off."

Julie didn't know anything about her two companions, but she couldn't help but think the more talkative woman was being amazingly insensitive. "Is she hurt?" she asked after listening to the quiet whimpers for some time.

"Nah," the still-nameless woman said with a sigh.

Julie chewed on her bottom lip, a habit when she was nervous. She grimaced when a piece of lip skin scraped off under her top teeth. Delicately spitting it out, she closed her eyes and tried to concentrate on her surroundings. There was a dripping sound from somewhere nearby, a dripping she thought she remembered hearing before. And creaking, as though a house or building was settling in for the night. After a few moments, Julie realized she was hungry, and incredibly thirsty.

"Is there…" She cleared her throat as her voice cracked. She tried again. "Is there any water?"

"When he brings food, but he already did today," the woman across from her said. "You were out, I guess."

Julie allowed her mind to flip over this new information, trying to sort it all out, but her weakened, dehydrated state wasn't making that easy. Her head also still ached, though it was fairly dull at the back of her skull now. Silence fell again, except for Roxie's soft crying. Finally, Julie spoke again. "Where are we? Who is 'he'?"

Hearing metal grating against metal, Julie's heart stopped, her stomach roiling. Within moments, and to the sound of Roxie's louder whimpering, she figured out the sound was a lock being disengaged. Suddenly, a bright beam of light from the dim wattage of the naked bulb hanging near the open door blinded her.

❧❧❧❧

The thick, rich sauce of Joan's lasagna was a delight for the palate, and Remmy's eyes slipped closed, the fork slowly leaving her lips as she savored the taste of the individual spices, tomatoes, and garlic. She loved garlic, and any food group that used it. Italian food was a staple in her life, but rarely did she ever get homemade anything, let alone Italian.

Joan watched their new tenant closely, her amused expression changing to sad however, by just how much Remmy savored every single morsel of her dinner. "You look like you've never had a home cooked meal before," she quipped. Remmy was on her second helping.

Joan and Doug's laughter at the comment was interrupted when Remmy suddenly stopped eating, fork halfway to her mouth, almost as though her hand was frozen. Her eyes widened and her face took on a strange expression, her lip curling.

"Remmy? You okay?" Doug took a sip of his grape Kool Aid. He glanced at Joan, but Joan appeared to be as surprised and concerned as he was.

"Remmy?"

Remmy's body stiffened, her five senses, one by one, shutting down. She no longer heard the clattering of flatware against dishes or the evening news in the background. She could no longer taste the garlic on her tongue. She could no longer feel the smooth metal of the fork in her hand or the hard dining chair under her. She could no longer smell the freshly baked rolls that were in a covered basket at the center of the table. She could no longer see Joan's concerned face across from her.

❧❧❧❧

Things were blurry, almost as if they were being seen through the eyes of someone who typically wore glasses but wasn't wearing them now. Bright light shone in from the left, painting everything in a blurry, buttery gold. Across the way, someone was there. Who was it? Flesh color. Are they naked? The form looked like a "T"—arms spread out, body line straight down, one leg bent, almost like a flamingo. Maybe the leg was tired? There was a gray background behind the flesh color.

❧❧❧❧

Julie tore her eyes off the nameless woman across from her, turning terrified green eyes to the man entering what she now could see was a tiny cement wall and dirt floor...cave, it seemed. The light was over his head and slightly behind him, so he was featureless, mostly one big, eerie silhouette. A big, eerie silhouette that was walking toward her.

"You're awake," he said in a voice that was soft and deep. As he got closer, she could smell his cologne mixed with sweat and garlic. "Good, good." He brought a hand up, very soft, almost like a woman's, brushing the side of her face with the backs of his fingers.

Julie was too afraid to move. So close was he that she could see the dark pockets that were his eyes contrasting with the pallor of his face. She could tell he had short-cropped dark hair, but that was about it.

"Here."

Julie was grateful despite herself as a cold bottle of water was raised to her lips. She drank unashamedly, the cold liquid spilling down her chin to her bare breasts, making her pull away from the water in a surprised cry. To her dismay, the man took the bottle away.

"I'm so glad you're awake," he whispered, moving in close again. His empty hand was brought to her breast, a quick caress to the rounded edge that made her recoil. He pulled his hand away, looking into her face. A slow smile spread across his lips. "Our lessons will start later. But..." he leaned in close, inhaling her scent, "...they will begin soon."

He turned to the woman who was chained across the room, red hair matted to her head from lack of washing. She stood with arms suspended, hands dangling limply. Her brown eyes filled with heavy shadows as she watched him approach.

Julie watched in horrified fascination as the man, whose back was now to her, unbuttoned and unzipped his jeans. Julie looked away, not able to bear watching what she knew he was about to do. The woman made not one sound, but he more than made up for it, the obscene slap of his flesh against hers loud in the silence of the cell. His thrusts were short and quick, the assault over quickly as marked by his loud groan. He adjusted his clothing and left as he had come, taking the light with him.

A silent tear made a trail down Julie's cheek and dripped off her chin.

❧❧❧❧

Remmy gasped for air, her hands reaching out blindly to grab whatever was closest. Finding nothing, she cried out in surprise as her hand was taken in a small, cool grasp. She blinked rapidly, a sharp pain slicing through the middle of her forehead. Finally, her surroundings swam into view and she saw that she was lying on a couch, Doug and Joan hovering over her.

"I think she's coming around," Joan said, though in Remmy's ears, the sound was distant, and far slower than typical speech. Doug stood just behind his seated wife, looking over her shoulder. He nodded, brow drawn in deep concern. "Remmy? Remmy, honey, can you hear me?" Joan asked, pressing the cool cloth to the clammy forehead. It seemed to help bring the woman around.

Remmy took several deep breaths, trying to get her bearings. She had no recollection as to when she'd been moved to the couch. The last thing she remembered was sitting at the dinner table, nearly having a foodgasm over the lasagna.

"I wonder if we should get her to a doctor," Doug said.

"No," Remmy said, her voice slurred and thick. "No doctor."

"Honey, what happened?" Joan asked, brushing dark strands of hair away from Remmy's face. "Did you have a seizure or something?"

Remmy's mind raced. *Seizure?* She tried to sit up, but she was too weak. With her host's help, she was finally able to lean back against the arm of the couch. She felt sick to her stomach from the centralized pounding in her forehead. Shaking her head, she finally regained a small measure of control.

"No. No seizure."

"Then what the hell was that?" Doug asked. "One minute you're sitting there enjoying the hell out of your dinner, the next you're damn near frothing at the mouth."

"Doug, she was not." Joan glared at him before returning her gaze to Remmy. "But, it sure seemed like you had...something."

"No. I...I..." Remmy tried to think of something to tell them. She didn't feel safe telling them what she thought it was, what she deep-down knew it was. "I just had a spell. I'd really like to go to bed now, if that's okay. I'm pretty wiped out." That was no lie. Emotionally she had reached her limit, and physically, she felt nauseous. She could only remember ever being hit so hard one other time, and that was a long time ago.

Joan nodded, removing the cloth from Remmy's forehead and helping her to her feet. "Do you need any help up the stairs?" she asked. Remmy shook her head, then gingerly made her way out of the room.

⁂

In the safety and privacy of her own apartment, Remmy locked the door behind her and threw herself on her bed. She lay on her side, curling up in a ball. She felt sick, and utterly frightened. What had she witnessed? What had called out to her so strongly that it had literally taken her from the realm of consciousness?

She remembered another time, about four years earlier, when she had been working as a cashier in a small grocery store. She couldn't even remember the name of the town.

She waited on an older woman, ringing up her purchases and sending her on her way with a smile and a wish for a good day. The man who was next in line set his basket on the roller belt, politely stepping back as he waited for Remmy to empty it and ring up all six items.

Looking into his eyes, Remmy was suddenly struck with a sharp pain in her forehead, seemingly arising from the profound sense of guilt the man was carrying. She was able to see fifteen years into his past, and witness the night he had driven home from a party at work, having had too much to drink to navigate through the rain. His senses had been too numb to react to the two young girls who had stepped off the curb in an attempt to cross the street on a green light.

❧❧❧❧

The next thing Remmy had remembered on that occasion was the sound of the shattering glass jar of pickles as she freaked out at the immense burden upon the man's shoulders — the pain of the girls' last moments on earth, and the loss of innocence for all involved. She had been fired on the spot, the manager calling her crazy and accusing her of scaring off customers. Similar scenes in school, involving a young, immature girl who didn't know how to handle the invasion into her thoughts and dreams, had earned her the nickname of *Remmy the Retard* from her fellow classmates. No longer able to take the isolation and ridicule, she had dropped out of school.

Remmy swiped at the lone tear that made its way down her cheek and tickled her nose. *Am I doomed to be a freak forever?*

Chapter Nine

Grace Cowan sat at her desk, phone to her ear as she listened to the results of the blood test that had been done on the spot found in the parking lot at Woodland Middle School. The lab was behind, so their results had been a long while in coming. Brian Wong sat on the edge of her desk, as usual, waiting for her to relay the information.

"Okay, Cathy. Thanks." She hung up the phone and tossed her pencil to the desktop with a sigh. She glared at her partner. "It's hers."

Dark brown eyes opened wide. "You're shitting me?"

"No, Brian, I'm not. Julie's blood was spilled in that parking lot, and I want to know why." She slammed her fist onto the desk. "We've been wasting time, goddamn it! I want to know where this woman is, and I want to know what happened to her!"

Brian looked at her, arms crossed over his chest. The progress on the Wilson case had been negligible; they had gotten nowhere.

"This isn't all my fault," he muttered. Grace stared at him. "I mean, *maybe* I should've been a bit more forthcoming with the information." Running a hand through neatly cut black hair, Brian cleared his throat and continued. "Ray Lambert came by the station this morning. Said he'd gotten all of our messages, as well as one from his daughter." He met the glaring coffee-colored gaze. "He had a rock-solid alibi for the day

Julie was taken, as well as the days before and after."

Grace Cowan felt a wave of rage. She slammed her fist on top of the desk again, jumping to her feet and shooting daggers at Brian. "Why didn't you tell me this?" She couldn't help but feel a bit of satisfaction as the prick stood from her desk and recoiled.

His mouth opened and closed like a dying guppy, eyes wide. Finally, he cleared his throat and spoke, though his tone was not its usual strong, condescending tone. "There was also someone who came in last week, a young woman. She said she was having visions."

"Visions?"

"Yes. Visions. Of Julie Wilson."

Grace felt the pulse in her neck pounding painfully, the beginnings of a headache. She closed her eyes for a moment, getting herself under control. When she spoke, her voice was deadly calm. "Give me her name, phone number, and address, and then get the fuck out of my face."

ᚾᚾᚾᚾ

"Good morning, my beautiful ladies!" a chipper voice rang out, echoing in Julie's head. She opened her eyes, groaning as she lifted her head from where it rested against her raised arm. Her neck was killing her, so completely kinked that she had a constant headache. Sure enough, the little door had been opened, the light from the bulb blinding as the man entered their hell. "I bring good tidings, and breakfast."

Julie watched as Roxie was unshackled first. The body of the forty-one year old housewife and mother of three collapsed to the dirt floor, muscles too atrophied to hold her up. A stainless steel bowl was placed before her, along with a Styrofoam cup.

"Hurry, my love," the man said, his voice deep and resonant. Roxie nodded and began to cry again. She ate her fare as quickly as possible.

Julie watched in morbid fascination; the smell coming from the bowl in front of Roxie, as well as the other waiting on the tray, made her stomach turn. It smelled like Alpo mixed with tuna. She glanced at the woman across from her, Pamela Beecham, a forty-six year old dental assistant, twice divorced.

Pamela glanced at the tray and the single bowl left, then her gaze met Julie's. Her smile was profoundly sad. "Your turn," she mouthed.

⁂

Remmy had been stocking the beer section all morning and was about to freeze her butt off in the refrigerated part of the stockroom, and she still had the light beers to go. She cursed Josh yet again; he was supposed to have completed this task two nights ago. Luckily, the new girl, Mabel, was working the counter so Remmy could get them caught up. She had the distinct feeling that Josh would be quitting soon; he was not a happy boy.

The chimes announced that someone had entered and she peered between the shelves of beer. She saw a familiar redhead waltzing through the front doors. *Crap.* Remmy hurried to finish the rest of the cooler, trying to get out front before Roman drove Mabel crazy with a million questions about where Remmy was.

"I've got this one, Mabel," she said, hurrying from the backroom, pulling the thin gloves from her hands. Roman watched her, a question in his eyes. "Stocking the coolers," she said, hitching a thumb toward the back of the store.

"Oh," he said with a nod of understanding. "So, um, I was just coming by to see if you maybe wanted to go check out a movie tonight, or something."

He gave her a bright smile, which Remmy found charming, though completely ineffectual. *Wrong tree, big dog.* She had opened her mouth to respond when the chime above the door rang again. Remmy glanced at the black woman entering the store, noting that her navy pantsuit was well-fitted and crisp. The customer walked up to the counter where Mabel met her.

"Hello. I'm Detective Grace Cowan. Could you please tell me if Remmy Foster is working today?" Without a word, Mabel pointed to Remmy.

"You in trouble?" Roman whispered.

Remmy shook her head. Butterflies in the pit of her stomach, she watched the police officer move toward them.

"Remmy Foster?" Grace asked.

"Yes," Remmy said. Her mind was racing as she tried to think of the last time she had screwed up and whether she had already been nabbed for it. *Did that clerk ever turn me in for stealing the loaf of bread in San Francisco?*

"I'm Grace Cowan, a detective with the Woodland Police Department. I'm working the Julie Wilson case along with Detective Brian Wong, whom you spoke with. I'd like to do a little follow up on that conversation, if you wouldn't mind."

Glory be! Off the hook. Remmy nodded. "Sure thing."

❧ ❧ ❧ ❧

Pamela closed her eyes, letting out a soft sigh as her second hand was once more enclosed in the hard, cold metal handcuffs. She could smell Sergio's aftershave as he leaned in and placed a soft kiss on her cheek before his warmth was gone. Eyes slowly opening, she saw him move over to the newest addition to their little fucked up family. She was blonde, pretty cute, nice body, and petite, not an ounce of fat on her, unlike Roxie to her left, who had been plump when she'd arrived but was now pretty much skin and bones, her tits hanging nearly down to her belly button from all the kids she'd nursed. Pamela hadn't even bothered to scrutinize her own body in more months than she could recall. She was scared to see.

❧❧❧❧

Julie watched their captor finish up, two empty bowls loaded back onto the tray, followed by two empty Styrofoam cups. He grabbed the tray from the floor and turned toward her. She was terrified, but her stomach growled almost uncontrollably. She wasn't sure of her expression, but she prayed it wasn't too desperate.

"I'll be right back," the man said to her, backing toward the door, watching her for a moment, then he was gone.

❧❧❧❧

Remmy and Grace sat at a cement table at the back of the store, near the parking lot for employees. Cigarette butts lined the sidewalk, some stuffed in the old, rusted Folgers can placed next to the back door for that purpose. Remmy was nervous. She wished she could pick up the half-smoked butt next to the toe of her shoe and light it up.

"So, according to Detective Wong's notes, you

say that you have visions." She studied the young woman sitting across from her. "Is that true?"

Remmy nodded. "Yep. Had a dream a while ago, and then when I was in Julie's car, I had another one. Vision, not a dream the second time," she clarified.

"You told Brian you were positive that Ray Lambert had nothing to do with whatever happened to Julie, correct?" Grace pulled a small pad of paper from the inside pocket of her jacket. She glanced up at her witness in time to see her nod.

"This is true." Remmy nodded emphatically, watching as the detective's pen raced across the page. "You know he's not guilty of this, don't you?"

Grace looked at Remmy, hearing the statement hidden in the question. She knew she couldn't lay her cards out on the table for this odd woman, so she gave her a casual smile. "Why do you think that?"

"'Cause he's not," Remmy said with a shrug. "Julie doesn't know her abductor, Detective Cowan." The passion in her voice got the officer's attention. "I'm telling you, she's scared right now. Very scared."

"So, you believe she's still alive?"

"Oh yes!" Remmy again nodded vigorously. "Without a doubt. She's alive and she's scared."

Grace decided to lay one card down. "We found her blood at the scene, Remmy." Remmy looked at her levelly, apparently not fazed by the news. "Does that mean anything to your visions?"

Grace wasn't sure what she thought of Remmy Foster, or her visions. The practical, logical police officer in her wanted to say this "witness" was out of her tree, just looking for attention. She did not feel that Remmy was involved, but all the same, had to get as much information from her as possible. Julie Wilson's life might depend on it.

~~~~

Her head pounding, Julie blinked a few times. Groaning, she turned her head, shocked to see a window with the sun shining in. Flimsy drapes hung on either side. She realized she was lying on a bed in a medium-sized room.

"Okay," the despised voice rang out, capturing Julie's attention. "Time to take a shower."

Julie felt like she would throw up as her wrists were grasped and she was pulled to a sitting position. The man from the little room was there, though now she could see him clearly. A handsome man, if she had seen him on the street, but now he looked like Satan himself. She noted the neatly trimmed and combed dark hair with well groomed sideburns tinged with gray. The skin of his face was tan, or he was from a darker complected ethnic background. He was pulling her to her feet, her weakened body leaning heavily against him.

He supported her to a smallish bathroom—toilet, sink with vanity, and a tub with tiled walls and clear glass doors, one side already slid open. He helped Julie step into the tub and turned on the water for her. She gasped as ice cold spray hit her back, her body instinctively moving to the far wall.

The man grinned. "Oops."

The water turned warmer, and Julie was urged back under the spray and given the simple command, "Wash." She couldn't help keeping an eye on the voyeur that sat on the closed toilet lid, watching as she washed her body and hair. She was grateful for the shower, but her skin crawled as the man's gaze devoured her.
~~~~

❧ ❧ ❧ ❧

"So tell me more about you," Grace said, tapping the tip of her pencil on the pad. "Have you always had visions?"

Remmy nodded. "Ever since I can remember. But as I told Perry Mason, they're usually of things that have already happened, something the person is carrying around with 'em."

"So, you pick up on something, a particular emotion or memory?"

"Yeah! Exactly." Remmy grinned. *At least this one's got a brain.*

"Okay." Grace leaned back as she studied the girl. "Tell me something about me. What am I carrying?"

Remmy rolled her eyes. "It's not something I can just call up. I can't just say, 'Abracadabra, Scooby Doo, tell me something about you' and then shazam!" Grace chuckled. "It doesn't work that way," Remmy continued. "I can't control who or what I pick up."

"But for some reason, you picked up Julie Wilson?"

"Yes."

❧ ❧ ❧ ❧

Julie's skin was warm and tingly, but her blood ran cold as the shower door slid open, the man holding out a hand to help her out of the tub. Hand trembling, she took it. He quickly drield her off and brushed her hair away from her face. With a look of steely determination, he led her from the bathroom and back into the bedroom.

Without warning, Julie was shoved to the bed, her body bouncing on the mattress. Like a ravenous tiger, the man was on her, roughly handcuffing her wrists to the brass headboard.

❧❧❧❧

Remmy stopped mid-sentence, her eyes opening wide. Grace watched her.

"Remmy?" She glanced behind her to see what was terrifying the young woman. Seeing nothing, she turned back to look at her. "Hey, is everything okay?"

❧❧❧❧

Julie watched with horrified eyes as her attacker undressed himself, his intent clear as his penis bobbed into view. *Jesus, no...* He climbed onto the bed and forced her legs apart. Stunned, and weak from lack of food and water, Julie couldn't resist. In a brief moment of clarity, she wondered if maybe that was his plan all along.

Sergio moved between her legs, pinning her petite frame to the bed with his own much larger body. He looked down at her, bringing a hand up to brush some drying blonde hair from terrified green eyes. "Such a beautiful face," he murmured, almost lovingly. He caressed her cheek with his knuckles. "Lovely."

❧❧❧❧

Grace moved over to sit next to the witness, the blue eyes wide open, the mouth too. Her face had turned ashen and her body convulsed, almost as though she were choking on something. "Remmy?" Cold fear was beginning to trickle down her spine. She reached inside the pocket of her jacket, cursing silently when she didn't find her cellphone, and remembering that it was plugged into the car charger. There was no way she could leave to get it. "Remmy? Can you hear me?"

❧❧❧❧

Julie cried out in shock and pain as her body was invaded, his breath hot on her cheek as he held her close, his groans loud in her ear. Tears of fear and humiliation streaked her cheeks.

❧❧❧❧

Remmy squeezed her legs closed, trying desperately to get rid of the abhorrent sensation. A sob burst from her throat and tears fell down her cheeks unchecked. She could vaguely hear the sound of someone's voice, a ghostly hand on her back rubbing soothing circles.

❧❧❧❧

Sergio's groan, loud and obscene, signaled his finish, and he rested his body on the woman beneath him. His heartbeat finding its normal cadence, he pushed up on powerful arms and looked down into the tear-streaked face. He smiled, placing a soft kiss on the cheek, ignoring the flinch — this time.

"Don't cry," he murmured. "I know the first time is painful. I tried to go slow." He pushed himself up fully, feet touching the carpeting on his bedroom floor. He grabbed his bathrobe from the back of the bedroom door and shoved his arms into the velvety sleeves. "I hope you like omelets," he said, his smile bright.

Left alone, Julie tugged on the handcuffs,

straining to look up at her bound hands. There was no way she could escape; she was a captive. The tears came hard, her body hurting almost as much as her head and heart. Despair was setting in.

⁂

Remmy eventually came back to herself. She felt the solid warmth of Grace's hand on her back, no longer a phantom touch. She grabbed the tail of her long work shirt and brought it up to wipe her face clean of the embarrassing tears.

After a moment, the detective spoke. "I'm absolutely dumbfounded. What just happened?"

Remmy sniffled then released a heavy sigh. She was unwilling, and unable, to unclench her thighs. "You guys really need to find her," she said, voice low and thick with tears. She turned eyes turned electric blue to the detective. "I think she's been taken by a psychopath."

⁂

Julie lay on the bed; for how long, she wasn't sure. She could hear the mundane sounds of someone cooking in a distant room. Her eyes closed, she tried to forget that person existed, that he existed. Her mind raced, replaying the last day she'd had her freedom. She thought back to that Saturday when she had spent the entire day with Matt and Skylar. Despite her circumstances, she smiled as she thought of Skylar. She had so looked forward to having him stay with her for that last week.

Fresh tears streamed down Julie's cheeks as the realization hit her that she should be in the classroom right now. *The second week of the new school year*, she realized, judging by the calendar hanging on the bedroom wall, each day crossed out with a red X. Who had taken over for her? Where did everyone think she was? Did they think she was dead? Maybe she was. Maybe this was all some elaborate scene laid out for her. Maybe Pamela was right; maybe she was in Hell.

⁂

"You're positive you're alright?" Grace Cowan asked.

"Yes, I'm sure," Remmy said. Taking the business card that was extended, she tucked it into the back pocket of her jeans. "And, as promised, I'll be down at the station tomorrow morning." She met concerned brown eyes. "I just can't leave right now. My boss isn't here and I can't leave the new girl alone." She indicated the store behind her.

Detective Cowan nodded. "I understand. I'll see you tomorrow morning, then. Nine-thirty. And don't be late."

Remmy saluted. "Nine-thirty. I'll be there." She watched the woman stride out of sight, turning the corner at the side of the building. Blowing out a deep breath, she collapsed back down to her seat. "Holy shit," she whispered.

Chapter Ten

At the knocking on her apartment door, Remmy looked up from reading a magazine. "Come in," she called out. Joan peered in and Remmy flapped the magazine closed and tossed it aside. "Hey," she said, leaning back against the headboard, socked feet planted firmly on the mattress.

"Hey." Joan stepped inside and closed the door behind her. "You got a minute?"

"Sure." Remmy pushed herself to sitting, pulling her legs under her Indian style. "What's up?"

Joan sat on the edge of the bed, glancing at the glossy so carelessly tossed before turning her gaze to Remmy. "I want to talk to you about what happened the other night at dinner."

Remmy groaned inwardly. She had hoped the incident would be forgotten. "What about it?"

"What happened? I'm truly worried about you. Nothing's...wrong, is it, Remmy?"

Remmy pulled her knees up until they rested against her chest, arms wrapped around her shins. She was feeling cornered. She couldn't repress the rueful chuckle.

Confused, Joan asked, "What?"

Remmy glanced at her, deciding how she should respond. What should she do? More than likely Joan, like the rest of them, would think she was nuts and send her packing. Why not? She was used to it; it had certainly happened before. Taking a deep breath, she said, "You know, it's funny. I spend my whole life with this thing, trying to figure out what the hell it is, and now suddenly I'm explaining it to three different people, two in one day." She met Joan's gaze, which showed even more confusion. Remmy sighed. "I don't have seizures, Joan. I don't have epilepsy. I don't even have a brain tumor, I don't think."

"Then what *do* you have?"

"Visions. Plain and simple, I have visions. I get these crazy images in my head, and once in a while I get to feel the wonderful emotions behind them." It wasn't difficult to see that Joan wasn't following her. "As I've explained to two cops already — both of whom looked at me very much like you're looking at me right now, I might add — I pick up strong emotion, something someone has been carrying with them. I can't control who it will be or what it will show me, but it does. And, for some crazy reason, I'm picking up loud and clear on Julie Wilson."

Joan stared at her. "Julie Wilson?"

"Yes. Julie Wilson. I have no idea why. She started out by invading my dreams, but now she's invading my waking moments too." She turned away so she wouldn't have to see the doubt or disdain in Joan's eyes.

"So, at dinner the other night, you were having one of these...episodes?"

Remmy burst into laughter, Joan's word choice bringing back her own characterization to Detective Wong that this thing with Julie was like live TV.

"Yeah. I was. And it happened again today when one of the detectives on the case came to talk to me at the store."

"So," Joan said, "are you some kind of psychic, Remmy? Empath, maybe?"

Red-rimmed blue eyes focused on her. "No, Joan.

I'm very tired, that's what I am. Today took a lot out of me. I just want to close my eyes and see inside my own head, not someone else's dungeon."

"But—"

"Please, Joan? We can talk about this later, I promise. I just want to sleep."

Finally Joan nodded, rising from the bed. "Okay. We'll talk later."

Alone again, Remmy flopped back against the stacked pillows. "So tired."

❧❧❧❧

The fields were green and lush, wild flowers waving in the soft breeze. Julie walked along, hands brushing over their tops, the soft petals tickling her palms. She felt the flow of a dress around her legs as she walked. She felt happy; she felt safe. Closing her eyes, she raised her face to the warming sunlight, allowing it to reach inside and touch her deepest parts.

Sensing someone close, green eyes opened and Julie looked around. Standing off in the distance, she saw a lone figure, a woman. She couldn't make out the face or any details of the dress she wore, but a slow smile spread across Julie's features. She's here to help me. The words echoed in her head, even as she began to walk toward the woman. She knew in her soul that the woman would not hurt her, that she was watching over her.

Remmy watched as Julie raised a hand in welcome and greeting. She smiled and raised her own hand.

❧❧❧❧

Breathing hard, Remmy sat bolt upright in her bed, face pale and bangs glued to her forehead with sweat. She could feel her heart pounding, intense pain about the size of a quarter fixed dead center in her forehead. Closing her eyes, she brought her hand up to rub it, feeling the clamminess of her skin. Running a hand through her hair, pushing it back off her forehead, she stared out over her apartment.

"Holy shit," she said. Shoving the covers aside, she stood, stretching her back and arms before padding over to the kitchen area. She grabbed a bottle of cold water from the fridge and quickly finished the entire sixteen ounces by drinking down mouthfuls at a time. Crushing the flimsy plastic, she tossed it into the trashcan, aware that the sun was slowly peeking over the rooftops.

She was due at the police station in a few hours. What was she supposed to tell them? What good was she to Julie Wilson when she couldn't tell them a damn thing that was concrete? She had no idea where the woman was, no idea who had taken her. All she got were tortured visions. *Visions.* Remmy couldn't help but be bitter about them. What was the point of them? They'd never done her a damn bit of good, turning her into a freak in the eyes of society.

She thought about the dream. It had been so real, so vivid. She knew it was Julie Wilson she'd been watching. She'd felt the woman's fear, had felt her relief when she realized she wasn't alone in that field. She had felt her.

"Damn it all," she whispered with a heavy sigh.

❧ ❧ ❧ ❧

Julie gasped as she woke abruptly. Trying to bring a hand to her pounding heart, she realized that she couldn't move it. Contorting as much as she could, she saw that her hand was cuffed to the headboard. *That's right. How could I forget that?* Lying still so as not to awaken the monster sleeping beside her, she squeezed her eyes shut for a moment, praying that the sense of peace and safety she'd had in the dream would come back to her. Sadly, it eluded her at every turn. She was left with a sick feeling in her gut and the stinging pain between her legs.

It was close to two in the morning before she was finally allowed to go to sleep, her captor collapsing to the bed in exhaustion after their extreme sessions of... Julie squeezed her eyes shut. She couldn't even bring herself to give a name to what she'd been forced to endure. To her horror, hot tears leaked from her eyes.

Julie gasped, startled as a large hand suddenly covered her left breast. She didn't dare look as the mattress shifted beneath her. He was awake.

"You're up early," he murmured against the skin of her neck.

Julie squeezed her eyes shut, trying not to be noticeably revolted by his touch, his five-o'clock shadow scratching against her tender flesh. "I need to go to the bathroom," she whispered, barely able to hear her own voice.

Sergio lifted himself to an elbow, looking down at the beauty in his bed. Her eyes were closed, a wrinkle formed across her brow. When he didn't speak, she finally looked at him, pleading in her eyes. He nodded, scooting off the bed and walking naked across the room. He dug the key out from underneath his underwear, sure to use his body to block what he was doing from possibly prying eyes.

Crawling up the bed, he straddled her body, reaching above her to unlock her restraints. He couldn't risk losing her. One wrist free, Sergio took her hand in his, kissing the palm before resting the hand on her chest. He quickly turned to the other hand and released it.

Julie sighed in relief, her hands and arms tingling horribly from being in the same position for so many hours. She brought both arms up to cover her breasts in a moment of modesty.

"Go," the man said, giving her permission.

Julie winced as she stood up, wanting so badly to soak in a hot tub of water to soothe her abused sex, but knew that wasn't an option. She made slow progress to the bathroom, shocked that he wasn't following. Sitting on the toilet, she held her breath, desperately wanting to hold back, as she knew it was going to burn. Need overtook pain, and Julie whimpered softly as her body relieved itself. She couldn't help wondering if her flesh had been torn.

Sitting on the toilet, she looked around the cramped bathroom, noting the window just to her right. She glanced toward the doorway. She couldn't see him, nor could she hear him. Turning back to the window, she studied the latch, then raised up to her tiptoes, trying to see through the frosted glass. It looked as though the window would lead to the side of the back of the house. She couldn't see details, but she could make out the striped colors of what looked to be an umbrella with a patio set.

Julie cried out as her head was yanked back by her hair and then her forehead was slammed into the window, knocking the daylights out of her and causing her to see stars.

"I said you could take a piss, not get stupid," the man said in her ear just before her forehead was slammed again.

Julie was aware of the searing pain just before everything went black.

Chapter Eleven

Remmy arrived at the police station, right on time. She was ushered back to where the detectives' desks were, as Detective Wong hadn't come in yet and Detective Cowan was on a call. The other detectives there kept an eye on her as she wandered over to a case on the wall where various medals and trophies were displayed. They looked like softball trophies.

"Won the league last year," Grace Cowan said from behind her. Remmy glanced at the detective from over her shoulder, nodding acknowledgement of the factoid. "Glad you could come. Come with me, please."

Remmy followed her through the office, into an interview room much like the one she'd been in with Brian Wong. No need to explore this time, she flopped into the chair across from Grace, who sat tapping the tabletop with her fingers and glancing at her watch.

"So, what exactly are we waiting for?" Remmy asked.

"Not a what, but a who. My partner will be here any minute, with Julie's brother, Matt Wilson. He wants to meet you."

Dark eyebrows drew over narrowed blue eyes. "Why?"

"He has some questions for you," Grace said simply. She was saved from explaining further when the door opened and Brian Wong appeared, carrying a bag from a Sonic restaurant. He gestured for a good looking guy to enter ahead of him, a man with sandy hair falling into his eyes. Remmy would have immediately known who he was, even if she had happened upon him on the street. She was suddenly filled with a sense of peace, of pure joy, and knew it was coming from Julie, her energy. For a moment she worried that perhaps Julie had been killed, and was in the room with them. Allowing her senses to stream out, searching with finger-like radar, she felt Julie in the form of a sudden and massive headache that seemed to extend all across her forehead.

Shaking off the ill effects, Remmy concentrated on the group that was making the small room feel downright claustrophobic.

"Well, I guess we're all here," Detective Wong said, setting his bag on the table and pulling out his breakfast, oblivious to the three pairs of eyes that were watching him. He set his coffee and breakfast sandwich off to the side, pouring the container of tater tots onto a napkin.

Remmy was amused by the daggers Grace sent his way. "That we are, Columbo," she muttered, ignoring the glare she got from him. "Why, exactly, are we all here?"

"Brian? Why don't you do the honors?" Grace turned hard eyes on him. He refused to look at her, instead taking his time fixing his coffee—three sugars and a touch of honey.

"That's disgusting," Matt said.

"Don't knock it," Brian said, still not looking at any of them. Finally he sighed and looked across the table at Remmy. "We need help in this investigation and we'd like to ask you some questions. About your... visions."

Remmy held his gaze, not wavering as she reached across the table and snatched a tater tot. Popping it into her mouth, she chewed, swallowed, then spoke. "Okay.

I'll help you."

❧❧❧❧

Grace sat in the recliner where she'd been planted all evening, reviewing the notes she had taken that day. She closed her eyes in pleasure as her husband leaned down and gave her a tender kiss.

"Don't stay up too late," he said, heading off to bed.

She returned her attention to the yellow legal pad, flipping back a couple of pages and re-reading what she'd already gone over:

Another person there—
Chained to the wall—
Cold, gray area, cement-like—
Basement?—
Suspects sexual violation—
Does not know offender—

Grace came back to the first point of more than one person being with Julie. She tapped her pen against the pad, brow wrinkled in thought. *What does that mean? Is the other person alive or dead? Male or female? Remmy felt it was another woman, but wasn't sure.*

Grace sighed in frustration. "Where are you, Julie?"

❧❧❧❧

Matt was nervous, sitting at a table, waiting for the unusual young woman he had met earlier that morning at the police station. The two of them, and the two detectives, had sat in that little room for more than four hours, Grace and Brian grilling Remmy. He could tell that Wong was not entirely convinced by Remmy's information, but Cowan seemed to buy the woman's story hook, line, and sinker. Matt wasn't sure, so he'd invited Remmy to have coffee with him. She agreed to meet him after she got off work, which was just about now.

He sat at a back table, heels of his shoes hooked over the bottom rung of the tall stool, tall enough to reach the bistro table. A young, red-haired waiter stepped up to the table.

"Can I get you a refill, sir?" he asked, nodding at the nearly empty mug on the table.

Matt smiled. "That'd be great, thanks."

"Caramel macchiato, right?"

When Matt nodded, the waiter grabbed the mug and hurried off to get his order. The bells chimed above the door and Matt was glad, albeit anxious, to see Remmy step through. She looked around the coffeeshop until she spotted him waving at her.

Smiling in acknowledgement, Remmy went back to Matt's table and climbed up onto the high seat. "Hey," she said, allowing her light jacket to slide down her arms. It was starting to get chilly out after dark. "Sorry I'm late. My relief was late."

"No worries." Matt waved the redheaded waiter over. The boy held up his mug in acknowledgement, but then his gaze fell on Matt's companion. Matt was amused as the boy seemed to trip over himself to get to their table.

"Hi, Remmy." He smiled, resting his hand on the table, but the table was wobbly, nearly resulting in landing the enamored young man on the floor. He managed to catch himself, but not before his face flamed as red as his hair.

Remmy tried to hide her smile by clearing her throat. "Hi, Roman. How are you?"

"I'm great." He turned to Matt and set the steaming coffee in front of him. Turning back to Remmy, his smile returned full force. "Can I get you something?"

"Just water, Roman, thanks." She gave him a polite smile. The boy scampered off, leaving Remmy and Matt alone.

"I think that kid has a crush on you," Matt said, thoroughly amused.

She rolled her eyes. "I know. He's a nice guy, but damn."

Matt wanted to get directly to the reason he had asked for the meeting. Taking a careful sip of his drink, he wrapped his hands around the large mug. "You never knew my sister, huh?"

Remmy recognized the change in his demeanor. She shook her head, not surprised by the question and certainly not by the topic. "No. I just met her the one time, when she was kind enough to give me a ride into town." She sat back while Roman set a large glass of ice water before her, a lemon slice anchored on the rim. "Thanks, Roman."

The boy hung around, bouncing from foot to foot. "Uh, Remmy?" he said, excitement and nerves making his voice breathy.

"Yes?"

"We kinda got interrupted when I came into the store the other day." He glanced over at Matt with every intention of telling this older guy to back off.

Remmy searched her mind then nodded. *Right, Detective Cowan came in and saved the day.* "Right. I remember."

"Yeah, so I was just wondering if maybe you'd like to go to the movies. With me."

Remmy groaned inwardly, but smiled up at the anxious suitor. "Sure, Roman. We can go as new friends, okay?" she said, putting emphasis on the word friends.

"Friends. Right, yeah, okay." He grinned, nodding excitedly, then hurried back to work.

"Anyway…" Slightly annoyed at the kid's bold move, she turned her attention back to Julie Wilson's brother. "Just the one time."

Matt studied his mug, running a thick finger around the rim. "I don't mean to be rude, Remmy, I think you're a nice girl, but I just don't believe Julie would have given you a ride. It's just not like her."

He looked up at her, green eyes cloudy with a variety of emotions. Remmy couldn't quite dissect what they were. "Well, Matt, if she didn't give me a ride, which she did, how do you surmise I know what I know?" Remmy's voice was soft. She knew it all sounded crazy. Hell, she thought it was crazy.

"I don't know. What proof is there that anything you've said is true? You said you have visions, right?" At Remmy's nod, he continued. "What proof, what concrete proof is there that they're real?"

Remmy shrugged, sipping from her water. "Well, I guess the day Julie comes home and tells her story, we'll know."

Matt studied her. She had beautiful eyes. He hadn't noticed that at the police station. "You think she's alive?" He couldn't keep the hope out of his voice. The whole thing was far too "hocus pocus" for him, but for some inexplicable reason, he felt a sense of peace around Remmy, as if he could somehow feel his sister. If he believed in such stuff, and if he was willing to go there, he would've thought Julie's spirit was with the woman sitting across from him.

"Why don't you tell me about her?" Remmy said, reaching across the table and touching Matt's hand. She could see the war within him, as well as the pain.

Matt glared up at her. "Who's to say you won't use what I tell you—"

"Matt," Remmy said, gently chiding, "just talk to me as a human being."

Matt stared into his cup. The time since Julie had gone missing had been the most painful of his life. Even losing both his parents couldn't compare to losing his baby sister. "My son is struggling with this every day," he said, almost too softly for Remmy to hear. He smiled sadly. "We lost my wife when he was just a little guy, so Julie kind of stepped in, you know?" His tortured eyes lifted, meeting Remmy's unflinching gaze. *If she knew something, or was in some way responsible, could she truly look me in the eye like that? No remorse? No guilt? Just look me in the eye like nothing?*

"I feel that your sister is a really great person. I mean, hey, she stopped and gave me a ride, and I didn't even have my thumb out. Shit, I'd been walking for half the day, and no one, I mean no one would stop. Then poof. There she was." Remmy's grin was blinding.

"She was always so giving that way. Always thinking of others first. You know, she was going to take my son for the week. Man, they loved each other. Skylar looked up to her like you can't believe. Want to spend time with his aunt? Oh yes! But with Dad? Dad, who."

They both laughed at that. Remmy was charmed. "Don't talk about her in the past tense, Matt." As she studied his eyes, so much like his sister's, she felt a surge of energy, a determination like she'd never felt before. "I'll bring her home to you. I swear it."

Inexplicably, he believed her. His smile was genuine. He nodded, and in that moment, felt a connection to Julie that was as strong as ever. "So," he said, clearing the emotion from his throat, "you wanted to know about Julie?"

Chapter Twelve

Her heart pounding in her chest, Grace pressed the phone to her ear. The detective in Beaumont County was prattling off the details of a Missing Person's case that was two years cold.

Pamela Beecham, age forty-six, snatched from her driveway at nine-thirty p.m. after she'd come home from having drinks with a male friend. Just prior to her disappearance, Pamela had filed charges against her second husband, claiming he had started stalking her again, as he'd done right after their divorce, eighteen months before. Pamela lived alone, her only child, a son, grown and going to college in another state.

Next, Grace spoke with Detective Ron Piltzer of Daycum County about a case that was nearly eight months old. Roxie Carmichael, forty-one, married for more than twenty years with three children. A stay-at-home mom, Roxie disappeared during a drive home from a cousin's wedding, which she had attended by herself, as her husband couldn't get the time off work and her children were all in school. Roxie's minivan was found at a truckstop thirteen miles from town.

There had been no trail left in either case, no evidence, just simply a matter of both women disappearing off the face of the earth. Unlike Beecham, Roxie had no enemies, no one at all for the police to look at. The ex-husband in Beecham's case was grilled time and time again, but there was never enough evidence to implicate him. Just like in Julie Wilson's case.

Late in the day, all her phone calls made, Grace sat back in her chair, the information she had absorbed rushing around in her brain like a whirlwind. The three counties covered only a twenty-mile radius, not very large, something that a single perp could easily cover. Grace sat at her desk, the pictures she'd downloaded from the system lying side by side. She eyed all three women with drawn eyebrows, trying to make some sort of connection, something, anything.

At only twenty-eight years old, Julie was the youngest. She was a very attractive woman with short, blonde hair and a bright, friendly smile. From what they'd been told, Julie was widely liked by both faculty and students, and had many friends within the community of Woodland. She was active in the community, had worked with Habitat for Humanity two summers in a row, and was very close to her brother and nephew. Parents dead, the few other living relatives were scattered across the country.

Pamela Beecham had been twice divorced, the second one quite messy, as the ex had been a short-haul trucker, and a vicious drunk with a mean temper. Pamela, a dental assistant for more than fifteen years, liked to drink herself, and was often found in the local bar or drinking heavily with friends. She had a volatile personality, though her friends and family said she had a kind, generous spirit. She was beginning to show her age from a difficult life with two difficult men. Hair, once dark brown, was streaked with gray, and the lines around brown eyes gave away her age. She was not unattractive, but certainly not in the spring of life, either.

Grace's gaze moved on to Roxie Carmichael. The forty-one year old housewife was cute, with pixie-cut red hair and a cherubic face. Her body, though slightly heavy, was not unappealing. Her blue eyes twinkled, and according to her husband and children, she was a kind and loving woman, who belonged to the local church ladies group. She selflessly took her two sons back and forth to soccer practice and her daughter to ballet.

Grace brought a hand up, a single finger tapping her chin. She was trying to draw any sort of parallel between the three women and their cases. Her gut was telling her they were connected, even though the circumstances of their lives and disappearances were different. One had been taken from the parking lot at her work, the second from her own home, and the third from a random truckstop, which the family insisted she would never have stopped at.

"Talk to me, ladies," Grace murmured, eyeing all three women again. "Talk to me."

❧ ❧ ❧ ❧

Remmy had been sitting on her bed for the better part of an hour, looking at the picture Matt Wilson gave her. It was a photo taken the previous year for the school year book. The five by seven was a wonderful shot of Julie, her smiling face and twinkling green eyes captivating Remmy.

She and Matt had sat and talked at the coffeehouse for more than three hours, and she found him sweet, with a brilliant mind. She wondered whether Julie was like him. She knew they were close, and part of her was envious of that, as it was something she'd never had. Especially since Monica had been gone for so many years. All the same, sitting and talking with Matt, learning about Julie, had deepened Remmy's resolve to help in whatever way she could. As she stared at the photograph, looking into Julie's eyes, she felt their connection grow stronger.

Remmy decided to try something. She laid back on the bed and stretched out, getting comfortable. Placing the picture face down on her chest, she began to breathe deeply, relaxing her body and mind. Closing her eyes, she took in several deep, cleansing breaths, allowing her lungs to fully expand, the full rise and fall of her chest slow and measured. Her hand reached up and covered the picture as she felt her awareness begin to slip away.

As her mind began to explore the darkness behind her eyes, the picture seemed to take on a weight of its own, pressing into her, a comforting weight. Images began to flicker, like a light bulb tapped into existence by impatient fingers.

A field. Flowers, purple against the green of their stems and the blue of the sky. Soft, flowing movement from an unseen breeze. Fresh air, cool wind.

Just ahead in the endless field stood a figure, her dress flowing around legs that were screened from view by the height of the flowers. The figure, blonde hair golden against the bright colors of the day, stood with her back to Remmy, though she turned her head slightly, almost placing her in profile.

Remmy felt compelled to walk toward the figure, her bare feet leaving footprints in the rich soil, though she barely noticed, her focus solely on the figure. She knew it was Julie; she could feel it. As she got closer, she could see the design on Julie's dress, the way the material hugged her hips, upper back and shoulders bare.

Julie began to turn, her eyes wide and frightened when she spotted Remmy, not twenty feet behind her. Remmy raised her hands in reassurance. "I won't hurt you," she said, voice soft, whispered on a dream. "I'm Remmy. I'm here to help you."

Julie turned to face Remmy fully, fear still in

her eyes, but there was also curiosity. "Remmy?" she whispered.

Remmy nodded, mustering her best smile. "I'm Remmy."

❧❧❧❧

Julie moaned softly, sleep beginning to fade as the ache in her forehead wrinkled her brow. She could feel the cement against her buttocks and upper shoulders again, her body sore and screaming to move. Dark blonde eyebrows drew together, something echoing through her mind and bouncing unbidden into her thoughts.

Green eyes opened. "Remmy."

"Who's Remmy?"

The question startled Julie. She scanned the darkness, sensing Pamela's presence across the scant space. "What?"

"Remmy. You said that name. Who is that?"

Julie thought for a moment, trying to clear her head, which was pounding. She cringed at the feel of dried blood on her forehead and temple, which she discerned by the tightness in her skin. She thought about the question, then the name, barely remembering having spoken it. "I don't know. I think I was dreaming."

"I can't wait 'til I die," Pamela murmured with a heavy sigh. "Then I can actually sleep in a goddamn comfortable bed." She snorted derisively. "But I suppose that bastard will put me in a pine box and I'll have an eternal headache from the hard wood under my head."

Julie didn't respond for a moment, not sure what to make of Pamela's morbid attempt at humor. "You shouldn't say things like that, Pam," she said, her voice soft in the darkness. "Bad karma."

Pamela snorted again. "Honey, I apparently already royally pissed off someone in this lifetime. Or the last."

Julie was quiet, wondering the same herself. "Tell me about your son," she finally said, needing to get focused on something positive before she allowed the dark fingers of despair and depression to wrap around her, constricting her throat and causing a stinging behind her eyes.

Pamela sighed. "Not much to tell. Patrick was going to school in Austin, Texas. He wanted to be a teacher and a coach. He was in his third year last I talked to him, so…" She shrugged as best she could, anchored to the wall. "I hope he finished." She was silent for a moment. "He looks so much like his dad. Always hated that fact. Has his dad's brains, too. Good kid."

"Were you close?" Julie asked, feeling wistful as she thought of Skylar.

"Sometimes. Again, he is his father's son."

Julie could hear the sadness in Pamela's voice. "Do you miss him?" The silence dragged out for so long, Julie thought Pamela wasn't going to answer.

Finally, barely audible, her response came. "Of course."

"Are you okay, Pam?"

A long, drawn-out sigh. "Peachy keen."

"Where's Roxie?"

"When he dumped you back in here, he swapped."

Julie squeezed her eyes shut, remembering what she had been forced to endure over the past two days, picturing their frail cellmate going through the same thing. She took mental inventory of her body, noting that her abused sex was still burning, a slight pulse clenching and unclenching. She wasn't as uncomfortable as she had been, but still wasn't ready to go out dancing any time soon. "How often does he do that?"

"What? Wine and dine?" Pamela said with a snort. "Let me put it to you this way — if I ever get out of here, I won't be eating omelets ever again. Truly, after two years..." She sighed. "Not sure which I hate more — the omelets or the Alpo."

After a moment Julie asked the question that had been pricking at her brain since she first regained consciousness. "What does he want from us?"

"Wives," Pamela said, her voice quiet and devoid of any expression.

"Wouldn't it be easier and less painful if he just became a Mormon?" Julie asked, serious. She was surprised by the hearty laughter that bubbled up from her companion's throat. She couldn't help but grin herself, finally giving in to the contagious laughter, laughing more for the sake of laughing than because what she'd said struck her so funny.

"Oh, kiddo," Pamela said. "That was good. So good I'm crying and can't even wipe my eyes, you damn bitch!"

"Judging by your cackle, I'm guessing it was." Julie laughed.

"You'd be fun to go have a beer with," Pamela said. She was quiet for a moment. "Man, I miss a good cold one. Me and the girls from work used to hit Saucy's Pub after work sometimes. Had the best tap there."

Julie was amused and slightly disturbed. "Out of all the things you could miss from the real world, you think of beer?"

Pamela grinned. "Shit, I've had two years to think of the important stuff. Now I'm down to my vices."

This brought Julie to giggles again. "I just want a long, nice hot bubble bath." She closed her eyes at the thought. "Alone."

"Yeah. I hear ya."

More silence. Then, "Pam?"

"Yeah, Julie?"

"Is he crazy?"

"I don't know. Would it make any difference?"

❧❦❧❦

Sergio tugged open the sliding door of his van, the privacy of his garage allowing him to make any changes that might need to be made without the prying eyes of the neighbors. Old Man Jones liked to come over to chat, surprising him. Not today—he couldn't have any distractions, or interruptions from nosy neighbors.

Standing just outside the van and looking inside, he quickly realized the overhead light in the garage wasn't going to be very helpful. He needed to see the itty bitty details. Walking over to his impressive workbench, Sergio grabbed a halogen lantern he used during camping trips and brought it back to the van. Crawling in on his hands and knees, he meticulously searched every crevice of the back of the van, looking for anything at all that the painters might think suspicious.

The van had been a deep blue color for the better part of six months; he had changed it after taking his second prize. Now, after the third, it was time to change it again. He would have to search through the phonebook, too, to try and find a place that was local, but not too local. Too bad he couldn't go back to the last place — *Color Expressions,* he thought it was called. They'd done a great job and the cost was reasonable. But, alas, he had to move on.

Sergio focused all his attention on what he was doing, fingers carefully parting the fibers of the light gray carpeting that covered the open space in the back of the van. He was always careful, never knowing what to expect when he made contact with a prize, never sure what would be necessary. Unfortunately with the last one, it had been in a public enough location that he'd had to take prompt action to subdue her. Just as that thought crossed his mind, Sergio gasped. He noticed something over by the edge of the vehicle, near the track where the door slid shut. Crawling over to it, he shone his light. How had he not noticed it before? A dark stain — very small, but there — was spread across the track. Shining his light on it, it was more than apparent it was dried blood.

Hopping out of the van, Sergio squatted down and brought his lantern up to inspect the outside, focusing his attention near the opening of the van. There was the tiniest residue against the paint. He brought a finger to it, rubbing it over the small spot. The dried blood flaked off easily, falling to the spotless cement floor of the garage.

Sergio rubbed his fingers together, sighing heavily, heavy brow drawn in thought. Pushing to his full height, he crawled back into the van, searching even more minutely, combing every square inch of the carpet in the van. He used tarps, but still... If that bit of blood had managed to escape his attention, what else had?

Chapter Thirteen

Remmy felt uneasy as she sat across the table from Roman. She'd made it clear the night of the invitation that they were going as friends, but from the looks he was shooting her way, she thought she might just have to iterate that fact.

They were sitting in a burger joint, where nothing under a pound of beef could be ordered. She waited for her lunch, hands cupped around her cup of hot chocolate. She grabbed her spoon from its napkin cocoon and used it to scoop some of the whipped cream off the top.

"So, where are you from?" Roman asked, playing with the straw in his Coke. "I mean, you're not from here..."

I'm aware of that, Roman, but thank you for the bulletin. "I was born in the backseat of a VW van. My parents were on their way from Boise to Seattle. I'm not exactly sure what town they were in when my dad had to pull to the side of the road."

"Your father delivered you? You weren't born in a hospital?" Roman asked, clearly stunned.

"Yep. 'Bout the only thing he ever did for me." Remmy sipped her cocoa. "He disappeared not long after that."

"And your mom? Where did you grow up?"

"Wherever. She wasn't around all that much, either. Me and my cousin Monica used to troll whatever streets we could find. See, Monica's mom, my Aunt

Stacy, lived with us on and off, leaving Monica with us during the 'off'. We were close."

"Not anymore?"

Remmy shook her head. "Not sure where she's at. We...lost touch."

"What brought you here to Woodland, of all places?"

Remmy shrugged. "Dunno. I was in Albany, New York for a while, and just decided to hop a Greyhound west. I rode as far as my money would take me, which was to Topeka, Kansas, and then just began to walk or hitch." She looked around the small restaurant, with its movie memorabilia and bright, neon signs. "It brought me here."

Roman smiled. "I'm glad you're here."

She sighed, setting her cup down. "Look, Roman, we need to talk about something." She looked across the table at her companion, hoping to find the right words to get her point across without hurting his feelings. "You seem like a truly nice guy, and honestly, I think it would be nice to have some friends here. After all," she grinned, "you can't have too many of those, right?" Roman nodded, studying her intently. "I'm getting the feeling that you're looking for something from me that, frankly, you're not going to get."

Roman blinked several times, hands nervously playing with the discarded paper from his straw. "What do you mean?"

"Let's put it this way—you're not my type, big guy."

"Well, I mean, we can be friends, right? And who knows—" He shrugged.

"What I know is that I'm not into guys, Roman. At least not like that."

Roman's eyes widened in surprise and scandal.

"You mean, you're…gay?" he whispered.

"Yes," Remmy whispered back, blue eyes twinkling.

Roman thumped back against the booth, hope knocked out of him. He tossed the crumpled paper to the table, watching his hands as they grasped the cold, sweating glass of soda. "Oh."

Remmy saw the disappointment written all over his face, and she felt bad. "I'm sorry, Roman. I never lied to you. I told you we were going out tonight as friends, and only friends."

"I know." Roman sighed with a small smile. "Guess I just hoped… Ya know?"

Remmy nodded. "Yeah, I know. I'm sorry. Just wanted to be honest with you."

Their food was delivered and they both sat quietly until the waitress left. "Yeah. I appreciate that."

The silence between them was awkward for the rest of the meal, but as they were offered a dessert menu, Roman seemed to shake off his funk. To Remmy's delight, he was playful, smart, and just a genuinely nice guy. She hoped they could be friends, as she hadn't been kidding — she craved friends, something, or someone to help lighten the burden she was carrying concerning Julie Wilson. There wasn't a moment that went by when there wasn't a reminder or her thoughts weren't invaded with images, whether they were visions or of her own making, she wasn't completely sure.

Perhaps Roman's friendship — light, fun, and seemingly carefree — would help ease the rising tension.

⁂

Sergio was pleased with the new color he had chosen for the van; he had always loved the color red.

Stopped at the traffic light, he glanced in his side mirror, noting the way the setting sun shone against the new paint. It made the van look like a brand new vehicle. There was no logo this time. From the driver's seat, he could smell the new carpet he had installed himself. He was proud of just how handy he was. Now he just had to wait for the new plates to arrive, since the van, after all, had been "sold" to a Mr. Rick Avales. He snickered at his own cleverness.

The light turned green, sending Sergio on his way. He'd had a busy day at work, which kept him late. There had been just enough time for him to run home, shower and change, then jump into the newly painted van, leaving his daily-use Volvo behind.

As he trolled along the streets of the small town of Burrow Key, he studied his surroundings, taking in every street, every route, every home and business. After taking his time winding his way through the town, population 12,000, he eventually found himself on Burke Street. The uneven sidewalks and weed infested yards spoke of the lack of care and love for the old neighborhood. The houses were small and extremely close together. Sergio wondered how anyone felt they had any privacy at all.

The van slowed in front of a small, tan house with brick-red trim. The house had a front porch, the cement painted green, a spiderweb of cracks making their way across it. He studied the windows through open curtains but saw no movement. Checking the clock on the dash, he knew it was coming close to time, so he gave the van some gas and drove toward the end of the block, where he pulled into the driveway of a house he knew was empty.

Sergio pulled the sliding door open. His dog, Romper, whimpered excitedly as the leash was attached to his collar. "You ready for a walk, boy?" He asked, giving his dog some physical attention after a long day penned up in the backyard. The dog jumped around, trying to lick his face, but only succeeded at getting a taste of his shirt. Amused, Sergio locked up the van and they were on their way.

He looked around, checking to see who might be around, who might be paying attention to him. His smile made his handsome face even more handsome, he knew. He and Romper were alone, and hadn't been spotted. He kept to a leisurely pace, watching as his dog navigated the horribly buckled and crumbling sidewalks. Anyone on a bike or rollerskates would kill themselves.

As they picked their way toward the tan house, Sergio scanned the neighborhood with surreptitious glances from his hawk's eyes. To his left and across the street, he heard children's voices and noted two boys, maybe twelve, coming out of one of the houses, neither giving him a second look. They grabbed their bikes from where they'd been thrown on the front lawn and peeled off down the street, shirttails flapping out behind them. His heart was beating a little faster as the boys disappeared down the street. To his right, a dog ran up to the chainlink fence, barking loudly at Sergio and Romper. Startled, Sergio pulled Romper's leash to his other hand, forcing the dog to walk on the other side of him.

Eyeing his surroundings carefully, Sergio strolled along until he reached the house he had come to see. It was a small house, which he pictured as only having one or two bedrooms, both probably tiny. Sergio stopped in front of the house, took a pack of cigarettes from the pocket of his shirt and tugged one free. He didn't smoke, but it gave him an excuse to stop on the sidewalk. It took him a couple of strikes to get the new lighter to work, then he brought the flame to the tip of the cigarette, sucking in a mouthful of smoke and holding it before slowly expelling it between his lips. He tried not to grimace at the god-awful taste. How could anyone indulge in such an unhealthy habit regularly?

He flicked the cigarette between inexperienced fingers, nearly tapping the cherry fire off of the end. He glanced over his shoulder, looking back at the small house behind him. A quick look at his watch told him the occupant would be home in three minutes. Unable to stand on the sidewalk for that long without attracting unwanted attention, Sergio clicked his tongue, letting Romper know that the break was over, a gentle tug on his leash pulling the dog's attention from the grass he was sniffing.

As master and dog continued past the tan house, a small, blue Honda pulled into the short driveway. The engine was turned off and a door squeaked open, a female voice suddenly audible.

"Oh, I know. Yeah. I think so too." The woman paused as she climbed out of her car, setting her backpack on the roof, balancing the cellphone held to her ear while trying to get her belongings settled on her shoulder.

Sergio stopped, allowing Romper to find a place to pee on the neighbor's yard at the corner. While he waited, Sergio glanced over at the girl, watching as she selected the door key from her key ring as she trotted up the stairs to the green cement porch. A burst of laughter filled the early autumn air as the girl reacted to something her caller said. Within moments, the flimsy screen door had closed behind the young woman, her voice closed inside.

Sergio blew out the last mouthful of smoke, threw the cigarette down to the sidewalk, and crushed it underneath his boot with obvious distaste.

"Come on, Romper. Let's get some dinner," he said, urging his dog away from sniffing his own urine.

❧❧❧❧

Julie's head was bobbing, her sleep fitful as her body tried to find a comfortable position. Every time she began to sink down, it put a painful strain on her wrists and arms, waking her up, forcing her to begin the process all over. She didn't know whether she would ever get used to it. It was a particularly cold night, too, and her naked flesh was covered in goosebumps. She wanted to be able to just curl up — alone — and get a good night's sleep. She hadn't had that since the night before she'd been brought to her makeshift Hell.

She shifted again, this time willing her mind to relax, trying to think of something that would occupy her brain enough to send her off to a tolerable slumber. She thought of her home, picturing the hours it had taken to pick out just the right colors for her bedroom and living room, the only two rooms in the house where the decorating had been completed.

Drip...drip...drip...

Julie's eyes flew open, though they stung from lack of sleep. She silently cursed the leaking from wherever the hell it was coming. Inhaling deeply, she evened out her breathing and closed her eyes. She imagined her beloved home, then imagined her two dogs into the picture — Bonnie and Clyde romping through the rooms of the house, chasing each other and growling as they played tug-of-war with one of Julie's socks.

A sob sounded in the silence. "I don't want to die here."

"Shut it, Roxie," Pamela said.

Julie sighed heavily, near tears with her frustration. "Damn it!" she yelled out, startling her two companions. "I'm trying to get some fucking sleep! Is that so goddamn hard!"

Pamela snorted. "Here? You betcha."

"Well fine, whatever. Both of you just shut the hell up so I can try." Julie immediately felt bad about her outburst, but only getting an hour of sleep here, two hours there, was slowly driving her crazy. For a third time, she closed her eyes, trying to recapture the picture she had begun to paint in her mind's eye. It proved to be elusive, almost tugging a sob from her throat. She calmed herself, sucked in more lungfulls of cold, stinking air, and let her mind drift.

She couldn't see the face of the woman standing before her; her image was fuzzy, almost as though she was looking at her through gauze. Even so, Julie could see a smile, whiteness against the skin color of her face. She smiled in return, feeling as though a weight was being lifted from her shoulders, her heartrate slowing.

Green eyes studying the field around her, Julie could see the sun above, even feel its warmth against her face, evoking a sigh of contented relief. Startled to feel a soft touch on her hand, she glanced over to see her companion beginning to walk. Julie walked alongside her. Who was this person? Remmy. The name seemed to float along the breeze, entering Julie's subconscious and bringing a smile to her face.

⁂

Remmy forced her mind to produce a lake, its water calm and inviting. She turned the focus of the dream in that direction, leading the way for her dream companion.

Julie walked alongside her, a soft smile on her lips, much like the one from Julie's professional photo. It wasn't a smile of true, full happiness, but it would do.

"It looks so inviting," Julie said, her voice wistful.

"Enjoy it, Julie. Enjoy this."

Julie turned to her out-of-focus companion. "I think I will."

❧❧❧❧

Julie groaned as she was pulled from the deepest sleep she'd had in weeks. Green eyes blinked open as she tried to figure out what had pulled her back into reality. Then it hit her, hard. She gasped, the cramps twisting her insides into knots.

"Oh, God," she whispered, wishing more than ever that she could curl up. Or die. She grimaced as it suddenly felt like her insides were going to fall out from her very swollen, aching sex. She groaned again. She felt utterly vulnerable and exposed, standing there as a very private ritual of womanhood began. Hot, bitter tears seeped from beneath her closed lids. She hated to feel helpless. Within moments, it was confirmed that her period was right on time. "Fuck," she whispered. It wasn't long before she felt wet and uncomfortable.

Julie knew it was senseless to be upset or grossed out, that all her personal needs had to be taken care of where she stood. But somehow her monthly period was far too personal to not be able to take care of properly, and her cramps were about to double her over where she stood. She would have done just about anything for a tampon and some Advil.

❧❧❧❧

Remmy had been holed up in her apartment for the past day and a half, plowing through the stack of books she'd gotten from the library. The titles read like a spiritualist's bibliography: *Lucid Dreaming for Dummies, Astro Projection: Climbing Into the New World* (whatever that might be), and *The Psychic Connection.* On and on the titles went, old books filled with dry information, none of which seemed to strike a chord.

Since the previous night, she'd been sitting cross-legged on her bed, a volume open in her hands and another lying face down on the comforter in front of her. She read every word, trying to squeeze the last drop of information out of them. The only thing that even slightly resonated with Remmy was the book on lucid dreaming, the practice of controlling the events and characters in a dream. That was all true. It was exactly what Remmy had been doing, but apparently none of the books in the library could tell her how she was able to influence someone else during the dreams. She was reaching Julie, of that she was certain. She could feel her reactions, could actually feel her calming as the dream progressed.

The library books were all stacked in Remmy's backpack, ready to be returned early. They had been of no help. She was resigned to just accepting her phenomenon as it was, just as she always had. She did, however, have an idea, and hoped Matt Wilson would be willing to work with her. In the meantime, she had eagerly accepted Joan's invitation to dinner.

"What's going on behind those baby blues?" Joan asked, chopping vegetables as she glanced over at Remmy, who was so lost in her own thoughts that she was in danger of shredding the cabbage for their salad into coleslaw.

"Huh?" Remmy startled from her thoughts. She

saw Joan smirking at her. Cheeks flushing at being caught daydreaming—again—she turned her attention back to her handiwork. "Sorry. Nothing. Just thinking."

"Well, don't think so hard. You might just lose a finger." Joan gestured at the sharp knife Remmy was using on the cabbage She changed the subject with a grin. "So, what do you think of Mabel?"

"In what way?" Remmy lifted the cutting board and scraped her lettuce confetti into the salad bowl. Moments later Joan added diced tomatoes, carrots, and onions.

"As an employee. Do you think she's catching on?" Joan wiped tomato seeds off of her hands and then turned to the hamburgers that were browning in a pan on the stovetop.

Remmy thought about the question for a moment as she snared a couple of carrots from the bag on the counter. She chewed one thoughtfully, mentally reviewing the performance of the newest member of their team at the store. "I guess," she said at length. "I think she's still a little unsure on entering the cash drawer into the system." She glanced at Joan. "Seems to make her nervous. But other than that," she shrugged, "she's good, I guess. Why?"

"We're one short as of Tuesday. Todd's leaving."

"Really? Hmm." Remmy was surprised to hear one of the night managers was leaving. She didn't know him all that well, but it would make work schedules tight. She wondered why Joan was telling her. Even though it affected the store, she had the feeling Joan was stalling, like she had something else she wanted to talk about. Instead, Joan asked Remmy to get the table set as she flipped slices of cheese onto the patties. Remmy knew Doug wasn't home for dinner; he had gone hunting with his three brothers.

Silently and efficiently, the two women took the food to the table, where plates, napkins, and condiments were set out. Remmy spread a generous amount of Miracle Whip on the top bun, then squirted a goodly amount of ketchup on the meat. She could feel Joan's eyes on her and she glanced up at her in question.

"That's disgusting," Joan said, shaking her head as she piled banana peppers and mustard onto her own sandwich. She looked away before catching the raised eyebrow at her own preparations.

"What's on your mind?" Remmy took a mammoth bite from her hamburger, humming in pleasure at the mixture of tastes on her tongue. She was amused by the surprised look on Joan's face.

"That lady cop came by the store the night you were out with your friend Roman. She was looking for you."

"Why?" Remmy wiped her mouth then sipped from her iced tea.

Joan met the curious blue gaze. "The town is going to have a memorial service for Julie Wilson."

Remmy stared at her. "Why?"

"Because they think she's dead."

"But she's not!" Remmy threw her napkin onto the table.

Joan was unmoved. "Remmy, she's been gone for how long now…two months or more? They found her blood, honey. It's likely she is dead."

Remmy looked at her plate, her appetite gone. She had no idea why Joan's declaration upset her so badly. Julie was alive, damn it. She was! "Well, I think that's crazy. I mean, if it'll make them feel better, whatever. But I think it's just going to make them feel worse."

"That might be, but that's what the detective said. She asked me to pass the message on to you." Joan scooped some salad onto her plate and squirted Ranch dressing on top. "I told her you'd be upset," she said, not looking up.

Remmy remained silent. She was angry at Grace Cowan for acknowledging that they'd given up hope for Julie's return. She was also angry at Matt Wilson. Hadn't she told him she'd get his sister back home safe and sound? With a heavy sigh, she continued to eat her now-tasteless dinner.

Chapter Fourteen

Sergio checked his rearview and side mirrors. He was right where he needed to be. Checking the sleeping neighborhood, he made sure that there were no lights shining in any of the windows. Climbing out of the van, he carefully closed the driver's side door and pulled open the freshly oiled sliding door to the back. Still unnoticed, he pulled gloves onto his hands — lightweight, easy to maneuver — and strolled into the backyard. He knew from earlier inspection that there was no dog, or any other type of pet that might harm him or give away his presence.

The yard was barren, the mark of a homeowner who spent little or no time back there. The only indication at all of habitation was a sheet pinned to the line. He took note of it, in case he should he need it later. Making his way onto the back porch, Sergio's black clothing and dark hair blended with the shadows, making him seem to disappear. He reached into the pocket of his black jeans, removing the familiar pieces of metal as he crouched on one knee. Using the tips of his fingers, he felt the knob and deadbolt, easily inserting the picks and manipulating them patiently until he felt his target. Within a couple of moments, the lock clicked open. The first phase of his plan was successfully completed.

Sergio took it slowly, easing his way through what appeared to be a room that had been added on. A washer and dryer lined the left wall, tall, metal cabinets rose on the right. Straight ahead was an open doorway, which led to an "L" shaped kitchen. He ran his hand along the counter, following the smooth line until it was interrupted by the stove, then over another stretch of counterspace. At last he reached the arched entryway to the room, which led to a larger space. He stopped, looked around, listened. Somewhere a clock ticked, its constant marking of time seeming crude in the perfect stillness. Two large windows at the front of the room let in just enough light to show the top of a console television and the arm of what appeared to be a couch or armchair. Apparently this was the front room of the house. The glass panes in the front door confirmed his assumption.

Sergio glanced to his left, seeing a wall with a window in the center, its shade pulled down. Something reflected the muted light from that window and further inspection showed him a built-in cabinet of some sort. It was too dark inside to tell what was stored within. It didn't matter. His treasure lay elsewhere.

Feeling his way past the cabinet, not wanting to misstep and fall against the glass, he felt another archway just beyond it. This led to a dark hallway with another door directly in front of him, one further down the hall to his left, and one further down the hall to his right. From the smell of Irish Spring soap, he placed the bathroom directly ahead. This left him to choose either right or left. Moving to the left, which took him to the room at the front of the house, he realized almost instantly that he had gone the wrong way. Inside was the muted blue light from a gigantic fish tank. A futon couch sat against the opposite wall, and a desk with a computer on it occupied the area under the large window. The room smelled of furniture polish.

Sergio backtracked, his pulse racing and heart

beginning to pound as he crept into the final room, where he knew his prize awaited. He could feel the excitement rising in his throat and he swallowed reflexively. As he got closer to the room, the door slightly ajar, he thought back to his mother, who always slept with her door closed, no matter what. He thought of the bedroom beyond her closed door — sparsely furnished, with a huge, wooden cross that hung over the bed. He always thought his mother's room looked more like a nun's cell than a bedroom in a house in the suburbs of Chicago. The rest of the house had been almost as devoid of any sort of humanity or indication that anyone inhabited its cold, white walls.

He shook the thoughts away as his hand reached out, barely touching the door as he tested the hinges. They squeaked just enough to make him stop. He tensed, listening intently. Nothing. Slowly pushing the door open a little further, he stopped again, then pushed one last time until the door was fully open. The room was very dark, but he could hear the soft breathing of the woman who lay sprawled in the bed. He waited a frozen moment as his eyes adjusted to this new darkness, eventually able to make out a large patch of light color, which he realized was the light-colored bedding. The floors in the room were wood, unlike the carpeting in the rest of the house. Good thing his boots had rubber soles.

He moved slowly, stopping when he felt the gentle resistance of the edge of the mattress against his knees. He smiled at the woman who was sleeping on her side. One arm was outside of the covers, the hand up by her face. Her long, dark hair was spread out over the pillow. He reached out a hand, yearning to touch it, but stopped when he heard a gasp.

In a heartbeat, Sergio was on top of the woman,

forcing her to her back, a hand tight over her mouth. Huge dark eyes stared up at him in terror.

"Shh," he cooed, his hand firmly in place. "Don't be frightened." The girl began to whimper. With his much heavier body weight, he held her in place while he snagged a t-shirt from the floor next to the bed and then reached into the pocket of his jacket to produce a tiny bottle. With a quick twist of his fingers, he had the cap off the bottle and the liquid on the cloth. The barest bit of a scream was audible as the shirt was pressed over her mouth. The girl struggled for only a moment before she went limp.

Sergio kept the pressure on for a moment, making sure she was indeed unconscious. Reassured, he pushed himself up, breathing hard and sweating profusely. He knew he didn't have much time, so he threw the covers off of her and lifted her in strong arms. Mindful of her legs and head, Sergio quickly went back the way he had come, and out into the chilly October night.

⁂

Pamela felt as though she was about to lose her mind. Roxie had been crying off and on for the past... Hell, she had no idea how long. It was a long time. She was at the end of her rope, and if she hadn't been bound to the fucking wall, she would have gone over there and beat the living shit out of the woman. Pamela could tell Julie was sick of it too. Sure, the cute little blonde had said she felt mean for telling Roxie to shut the fuck up and quit her whining. Now, after far too much of this crap, even Julie sounded like she was tired of it, and often told Roxie to stuff a sock in it.

Pamela's musings were cut short when suddenly the little door swung open and the asshole backed in, grunting. She wasn't at all surprised to see that he was dragging someone inside.

❧❧❧❧

"Evenin', ladies," Sergio said, amused at his own casualness. He dropped the hands of his captive and stood to his full height to stretch his back. He looked at the women — one to his left, one to his right, and the sad sack straight in front of him. His gaze was fixated on her. Her eyes were tear-streaked and swollen, her bottom lip protruding. "What?" he asked, his patience thin after his long evening.

Roxie shook her head. "I don't wanna be here no more," she cried, voice thick from hours of crying.

Sergio took a step toward her. "What?"

"Shut up, Roxie," Julie said, her voice breathy with fear.

"I don't wanna be here; I wanna go home," Roxie said, fresh tears leaking down her cheeks.

Sergio's patience ran out, leaving him cold and irritated. He took another step toward her, his facial features hardened into planes of shadow-chiseled stone. "Stop crying," he said, his voice low. His blood began to warm then simmer as her tears not only didn't stop but increased. "I said, stop crying."

"Roxie, please," Julie pleaded.

Roxie's sobs echoed in the tight space, her head shaking as her eyes squeezed shut, tears still falling. She gasped and cried out as a large, strong hand suddenly gripped her throat.

"Stop crying!" Sergio yelled, his face mere inches from hers. He could feel the smooth, cool flesh beneath his hand, the continuing tears making the flesh wet and slippery. Angered that the bitch wasn't following his commands, his blood raged at the sight of this nobody who was not worth his pity, not worth his spit, not worth his mercy. "Stop crying, you bitch!" he screamed, Roxie's gasping face merged with that of a woman much older, eyes small and dark, looking at him with hatred and disgust. "I said stop! Fucking stop!" She opened her mouth, sharp little tongue waggling at him, telling him what a bad boy he was, what a waste and how pitiful he was. *You're not a man,* she hissed. *You're pathetic. God's castoff.* He tightened his grip, watching in satisfaction as those dark, beady eyes bulged, his hatred burning strong, burning deep.

❦ ❦ ❦ ❦

Julie couldn't take her eyes away from what was happening. Her heart stopped in her chest, fear ice cold and heavy. She could hear the rattle of Roxie's bonds as her body convulsed, as she tried desperately to reach for the hand that clenched tighter and tighter, but impotent to do anything — just like Julie was.

❦ ❦ ❦ ❦

"Stop crying," Sergio whispered, Roxie's wide blue eyes staring sightlessly back at him. No longer struggling. No longer crying. No longer breathing.

Pamela watched in a daze as her jailor let go of Roxie, his barrel chest heaving as he panted. He stepped back from the woman whose head fell forward as soon as it was released. Pam was truly terrified for the first time in many, many months.

❦ ❦ ❦ ❦

He ran a trembling hand through his hair, which hung in his eyes, almost giving him the appearance of a little boy. He looked around, unable to meet either woman's eye.

Sudden movement and noise startled them all as the body he had left near the door moved, the girl groaning and coughing. He hurried over to her, gathering her up in strong arms and quickly reaching into his pocket. He shoved the drugged t-shirt over her mouth again, rendering her unconscious within moments.

The stunned silence was broken only by the sounds of Sergio dragging his new victim over to the wall where Julie was bound. He grunted as he hefted the girl's dead weight, holding her in place with his body as he quickly got her into place. Stepping away from her, he bent over, resting his palms on his bent knees and taking several deep breaths.

"It wasn't supposed to happen this way," he muttered.

Julie was terrified to make a move or a sound, not wanting to attract his attention. She knew Pam had to be thinking the same thing as they made eye contact for a brief moment. Neither could bring themselves to look over at Roxie.

❦❦❦❦

Fear... Couldn't breathe! Shaking, couldn't look, didn't look...

Hot tears ran down Remmy's cheeks in her sleep, which was fitful at best. She tossed, crying out in a loud whimper, her legs scissoring in the sheets.

"No," she hissed. "Let go..."

Heart pounding...couldn't breathe! Couldn't

breathe! No! Can't die!

The image was fuzzy, only colors delineating between objects. A naked form, arms out to the sides. Someone dark, in dark clothing stood before her...

Remmy gasped.

Can't breathe! Hands on the form, squeezing, squeezing, gasping... Can't breathe!

Remmy shot up with a cry, eyes wide and tears streaming down her cheeks. "Oh god," she gasped, hands raising to her throat. "Oh god." She was panting, chest heaving as she sucked in precious air. She felt cold and very afraid.

Shoving off the bed, Remmy ran into the bathroom, barely managing to throw the toilet lid up before losing her dinner. Stomach empty, Remmy slid down to the floor, back against the cold porcelain of the tub. She was breathing heavily, running a trembling hand through her hair.

❧❧❧❧

Sergio looked down at the body that lay on the floor of his garage. The woman's skin was pale, except for a deep bruise on the flesh of her throat. He leaned back against his large, red toolbox, unsure of what to do. He noted with mild curiosity that the woman had a tattoo on her hip, which had become distorted and stretched from the spreading of her hips due to childbirth.

With a heavy sigh, he pushed away from his toolbox, opening the drawers at random, looking for something, anything that would make his job easier. With grim satisfaction, he found it, running a finger over the jagged teeth of the blade. Setting the saw down, Sergio looked through another drawer. Finding a box of dust masks, he grabbed one with fingers that shook slightly. Slipping the cord over his head, he slid the mask into place, pinching the thin, metal bar so it hugged the bridge of his nose.

Sergio's work was grim, but he knew it had to be done. Exhausted, he just wanted to curl up with someone for the night. That would have to wait. He had no idea the strength it would take to perform the grisly task, but he was glad he had it in abundance. It took longer than three hours, and by the time he was finished, he was working solely on adrenaline. Scouring his garage and workshop area, he realized he didn't have the final ingredient he would need. He'd have to get that tomorrow. For the time being, he wrapped each section of the body in newspaper, then carefully stowed all of them in a fifty-gallon drum he dragged from the backyard, which he usually stored his trash in. It would do for now.

Brushing a bloody hand across his forehead to dislodge sweaty bangs, Sergio grimaced. He needed a shower. Clicking off the garage light and heading inside, he locked the house up for the night then stripped on his way to his bedroom, careful of what he touched. He hated a mess.

The water was hot against his skin, making him groan with pleasure as the tension eased from his aching back. It had been a long night. He washed his hair three times and scrubbed his hands with a brush, sure to get underneath his fingernails. His skin felt fresh and new as he stepped out of the stall, grabbing a towel from the rack on the door and drying his hair, then his body.

The clock on his nightstand told him the sun would be rising in less than two hours. It was a good thing he was off the next day. Looking at his large bed, Sergio frowned—it was too big, too empty. Making a quick decision, he threw on some sweats and a pair of sneakers and headed toward the kitchen…and the basement stairs beyond.

It didn't take him long to decide whose company he wanted, and it took him even less time to subdue her with a dosed cloth over her mouth and nose. Julie didn't make a sound as her body was unshackled and she was carried out of the confines of her prison.

Once upstairs, Sergio made sure she was properly bound, then slipped out of his sweats and shoes, and into bed, pulling the covers up over their naked bodies as he rested his still-wet head on her shoulder. He was soon asleep, oblivious to the silent tears that fell onto the pillow.

Chapter Fifteen

Remmy was almost frantic. She lay on her bed, taking so many deep breaths that she was on the verge of hyperventilating. "Come on, Julie. Talk to me," she whispered, reaching out with her mind. She could feel herself — her mind — moving through time and space, emotional fingers reaching out, trying to grasp onto something, anything. But they found only cold. Stillness. Blackness. She couldn't tell whether the sensations were emanating from Julie or rising from her own fear. "Fuck!" she yelled after two hours of frustrating effort.

⁂

Grace started, not sure what had woken her, then she realized her cell phone was warbling "Achey Breaky Heart". She grabbed it off the nightstand and flipped it open. She sat up in bed, ignoring her husband's grumbles behind her.

"Detective Cowan," She listened to the hysterical voice on the other end. "Wait, wait, Remmy, wait. What? Dead?"

Twenty minutes later Grace was pulling up to the store where Remmy worked. The young woman was pacing back and forth in the parking lot, huddled in her oversized jacket and sipping a cup of coffee. Grace pulled to a stop, barely out of her car before Remmy reached her. She was shocked by the ghostly pallor of

Remmy's normally radiant face, her eyes a vibrant blue from crying. The rising sun shone in them, making them look almost scary.

"Hey," Grace said softly, gently gripping Remmy's shoulder. "What's up?" She was truly concerned at seeing the normally confident—albeit strange—woman fall apart. Grace took the steaming cup from Remmy's trembling hand, placed it on the roof of her car then turned back to the girl, enfolding her in a motherly embrace.

"I think she's dead, Grace," Remmy sobbed, holding on for dear life. She had never felt such grief or loss. After a moment she collected herself, pulling away from Grace, feeling stupid. She gave her a sheepish, watery smile. "Sorry," she whispered.

"Are you okay?"

Remmy brought a hand up to wipe at her face. "Yeah. Just hit me really hard."

"Come on. Let's go in out of the cold and sit down."

Remmy dumbly followed Grace inside the store. They slid into one of the hard, wooden booths on either side of the scarred table in a small section of the store near the bathrooms and pay phone. Remmy placed her coffee on the veneer top, raising an eyebrow in offer.

"I'll get my own. You want a warm up?" At Remmy's nod, Grace snatched the cup, and quickly got them both a caffeine fix. Once again sitting across from the younger woman, she waited expectantly.

Remmy swallowed hard, deciding where to start. The fear and cold had not left her. In fact, if the situation hadn't been so serious, she would have considered her journey to the store to be quite amusing. She had felt as if she was stuck in a Cloak & Dagger story, checking around every corner before turning it, walking dead center of the street so no one could jump out and surprise or grab her. When she finally made it, she stayed within the light pool from the store while she waited. Her relief at seeing Grace pull up was unparalleled.

"I had what I thought would be just a basic, garden variety vision, which came in the form of a dream," she said, her voice low. She managed to hide the tremble. "I had connected with her, but then…" Remmy looked down at her shaking hands, which betrayed her calm. "Then it got dark."

"Dark?" Grace asked, almost holding her breath at a feeling of impending doom.

Remmy looked up at the detective with shining eyes. "Someone was killed tonight, Grace. I'm so afraid it was Julie."

Grace's heart skipped a beat. Setting aside her formal training and cop instincts for Remmy the psychic, she'd had her doubts about the woman, and what she said. But in that moment, looking into the most sincere gaze she had ever encountered, she knew for certain that Remmy was telling her the God's truth. "What happened?"

Remmy shook her head, sipping nervously from her cup. "I'm not sure. I think she was strangled. But someone is definitely dead. Given the brutality of what I saw, I'd be looking for a body, Grace. This guy is capable of anything."

"Where did it happen? What did he use?"

"I think he used his bare hands. As for where, I think it was in the basement thingy, where he's keeping them."

Grace sighed, frustration making her short of temper. "We need to know something specific, Remmy. I can't go get this motherfucker if I don't have something concrete! I can't go to every damn house all over the state and knock, asking nicely if they happen to have a 'basement thingy' with possibly three women chained up in it."

Remmy's own eyes lit with a fire from within. "Yeah? Imagine it from my point of view. I'm no damn Clarice Starling, either! I wanna catch this guy as bad as you do."

Regretting her outburst, Grace sighed. "I'm sorry, Remmy, you're right."

❧ ❧ ❧ ❧

Julie had lain in numb silence for what felt like hours. Her brain had shut itself off, her emotions frozen by the image that kept replaying itself again and again in her mind's eye. She kept breathing, occasionally blinking, purely out of her body's natural instinct to do so. She couldn't get the image of Roxie's face out of her mind, eyes open wide as she struggled for breath, her face darkening as she slowly sank into unconsciousness, then finally death. She'd never forget the sight, the murder right before her eyes. She was stunned by his brutality and violence during the murder. He had never shown that side of himself; even Pam had been stunned and terrified.

That same man was cuddled up peacefully beside her. She studied his back, noting the broadness and a few freckles that were sprinkled across his shoulders and upper back. His dark hair spiked in various directions from going to bed with it wet. The bed shifted and Julie's body bounced slightly as he turned over, facing her. She could feel his eyes on her, but she couldn't bring herself to look at him, to meet the gaze of the demon. She wasn't sure what she would see if she did, nor did she have the presence of mind to care.

⁂

Sergio studied the profile of the woman in his bed. She was the most beautiful of his prizes, with delicate features, a wonderful body, and vibrant, green eyes. He wished she would look at him with those eyes. Since she would not, he would make it so. He was the master, the man of the house. With two fingers on her jaw, he turned her head so she was looking at him. Yes, the vibrant color was there, but she wasn't.

He released her face, and she turned it toward the ceiling. He shifted into the position in which they had gone to sleep. He could smell her skin; it wasn't pleasant. She needed a shower. But he just wanted to lie there, indulging in the feel of her skin, the heat of her presence.

"I didn't mean to hurt her," he said, his voice barely audible.

Julie didn't respond.

"I'm not dangerous." Sergio lifted his head, looking down into her face. "What's your name?"

The woman swallowed, and her eyes closed for a moment before she whispered, "Julie."

"Julie." Sergio tasted the name on his tongue, deciding he liked it. "Julie," he said again, resting his head back on the pillow. "I like that name. It sounds very..." He struggled for the word. "...innocent." He smiled, liking the image. "Like a schoolgirl." He slowly pushed down the sheet that covered Julie's naked breasts. With a soft sigh, he smiled. The same fingers he had used to end one life now traced delicate patterns around the rounded underside of one breast. He loved breasts, loved how women had them and men didn't. So beautiful. So mysterious. Much like a woman's heart. His hand slid to her arm. He liked this woman, her beauty, her silence. The firm muscle underneath the soft skin excited him. He wanted her.

Cold dread entering her heart, Julie squeezed her eyes shut. She felt as if she was in bed with a loaded gun, a madman's finger on the trigger. Just as quickly as Sergio's touch found her skin, it was gone. She was relieved when her bonds were removed and she was pulled up to a sitting position. It took all her energy just to hold her head up. She was exhausted, half-starved, and desperately in need of water.

"I've gotcha," Sergio said softly, helping Julie to her feet. She had no choice but to lean against him. In the bathroom, Julie was set on the toilet. She had little in her, so had little peeing to do, though, to her disgust, dismay, and even relief, she did hear a couple of blood clots plop into the water. Sergio never left her side, patiently waiting for her to finish, arms crossed over his bare chest, shoulder resting against the bathroom doorway. Julie didn't look up at him, studying her own bare feet, noting the dark bruises around her ankles from the ever-present shackles.

When she was finished, she was humiliated as her captor wiped her clean then flushed the toilet. She was led to the tub, the water turned on and adjusted. To her horror, Sergio stepped in with her. She flinched as he rested large hands on her shoulders. He reached around her to grab the shampoo from the shower caddy, which pressed his body against hers. She endured him washing her hair, dreading the moment when he would move his ablutions to her body, which wouldn't be long in coming. He looked as though he was enjoying the feel of her flesh beneath his fingers, his tender washing strokes frequently turning into caresses.

※ ※ ※ ※

Though exhausted, Remmy kept searching through the stacks of the Woodland library. She already had a pile of books on the table she had staked out. Deciding that the Spiritual section wasn't going to have anything she was looking for, she moved on to the History section, a passion of hers since she was a child.

Now seated, she was surrounded by books, cheek resting in her palm as she read about the fall of the Ottoman Empire. A soft whisper distracted her.

Her eyebrows drew together as she raised her gaze from the words on the page to scan the tables around her. She saw a small group of school-aged girls dutifully doing homework, but it didn't look like any of them had said anything. Turning her attention back to her book, Remmy shook her head and continued to read.

Remmy.

Remmy shoved her chair back, hopped up, and looked around her. A few nearby patrons glanced at her with mild curiosity before returning their attention to whatever they were doing. Remmy's heart was pounding, fear and confusion painting a thin glaze of sweat on her brow.

Remmy...

Realizing it was coming from within, Remmy sank heavily onto her chair, heart racing. Seeing that she was being stared at by the girls two tables away, she quickly gathered her books into a neat stack and hurried to a study room, closing the door behind her. Leaning against the wall, she closed her eyes, a sharp pain beginning to flare up dead center of her forehead.

White tile, the individual squares blurred together, the reflected light from a light source a splotch of brilliant white. Bottles of some sort...a showerhead. Hundreds of tiny diamonds falling from it, warm on chilled skin.

Remmy almost couldn't breathe. She didn't want to get her hopes up, but she quickly shoved her books aside, making room for her to rest her head down as she sat in one of the chairs. She closed her eyes, trying to relax herself.

Fear. Uncomfortable. Cold tile on hot palms. Hot pain. A word. The letter 'R'. Can't say the word. Forty-one stones.

❧❧❧❧

Forced to bend over as she kept her head from slamming into the wall by bracing with her hands on the wall, Julie gasped and squeezed her eyes shut — no lube, and she wasn't relaxed. The pain was hot, searing, and beyond uncomfortable.

Closing her eyes, she tried to release her mind, send it flying off.

❧❧❧❧

Remmy squirmed on the chair, her legs clamping together, the need to curl up into a fetal position so tempting. She focused, and brought the field into sight, the sky the bluest blue she had ever seen. The water from the previous time, calm and refreshing. All that was missing was Julie.

❧❧❧❧

As Julie braced herself against the thrusts from behind her, she felt herself being beckoned away, her mind flying freely, wandering above treetops and the roofs of neighborhood houses. Gently falling snow frosted the landscape. She flew through the sweet smell of burning logs, the smoke spiraling out of the brick chimneys.

Am I dying?

Finally the houses gave way to an open field, the snowy winter magically turning into spring.

❧❧❧❧

Remmy walked to the water's edge, amazed to feel the cool breeze coming off the water, chilling her skin. She was alone, but desperately hoped Julie would hear her pleas and come to her.

❧❧❧❧

Suddenly the pain and discomfort began to recede, leaving only a sense of peace and a happiness that was right on the tip of her brain—especially as the field came into focus.

Julie's feet touched the ground, and suddenly she could smell the flowers and the lush trees that surrounded the lake, where she could see the silhouette of a woman standing, waiting. She smiled, knowing instinctively it was her savior.

Remmy.

❧❧❧❧

Remmy felt a presence behind her and, with bated breath, turned. Julie stood not five feet away.

❧❧❧❧

Julie was enveloped in a strong, reassuring embrace. She rested her cheek against a soft shoulder, her body relaxing, not feeling, not thinking. The wonderfully gentle hand on her back stroked in slow circles. She felt herself melting into the hug, not wanting to let go.

"This, too, shall pass," floated to her on the breeze. "You're alive..."

Julie nodded, still lost in the embrace. "I'm alive."

❧ ❧ ❧

Remmy gasped as she was suddenly wrenched back into the confines of the small study room in the library. The tiny window over the desk showed that the sun was setting. Remmy was startled again at the insistent knocking on the closed door.

"Excuse me? Is someone in there?"

Remmy pushed the chair away from the table and stood, her head pounding in that central spot of her forehead, but she didn't care.

I'm alive.

"She's alive," she whispered, grabbing the doorknob and yanking the door open. The woman on the other side started at Remmy's sudden appearance. "She's alive!" Remmy grabbed the unsuspecting woman and hugged her, jumping them both up and down in a quick circle. "She's alive!"

Remmy left the librarian staring after her as she ran laughing through the library and burst out into the cold night, where the snow fell on her heated skin. She breathed it in, eyes closing in appreciation. "Julie's alive." Her adrenaline surged at the realization, and she took off running into the night, a victorious hoot echoing in the stillness.

❧ ❧ ❧

"Open up, little one."

Disoriented and confused, Julie blinked several times. She was shocked to find herself in his bed, her right wrist cuffed to the drawer of the side table, her back against stacked pillows. Her left hand was unfettered, sitting in her naked lap. Looking up, she saw that her captor sat cross-legged next to her, a large dinner plate resting on his open palm. A cheese and ham omelet took up a good portion of the plate, and there were two sausage links, as well. Meeting his dark eyes, she saw the expectant expression on his face.

Without word or thought, Julie opened her mouth, allowing the forkful of food to be inserted. She chewed mechanically, grateful for the sustenance, even if it was another damned omelet. She could barely taste the flavors of the sharp cheddar mixed with ham and egg. Any joy she'd felt left her the moment she had come back to herself. She was shocked to see that it was dark beyond the closed curtains, the overhead bedroom light on. She wanted to ask him how long he had been at it, but dared not. All she knew was that she had an extremely sore ass.

Sergio took pleasure in feeding his prize. She accepted the food without question or fuss. He had enjoyed their encounter immensely, and from the soft smile that had been on her lips, he thought that perhaps she had too. He wanted to get her fed; he had plans for their night. He wanted to enjoy it. He watched as Julie accepted another bite, this time of sausage. He noted the way her teeth dragged the meat from the tines of the fork, pink tongue coming into play to pull it into the hot, wet depths of her mouth. He needed a few moments to recover from their first session, but he knew it wouldn't take long.

❧❧❧❧

Remmy wasn't sure which movie she was caught up in—*It's A Wonderful Life,* or *Singin' In the Rain*—as she hurried down the flurry-filled streets, yelping and laughing her way toward the police station. She was thrilled to recognize Grace's ugly, cop sedan in the parking lot.

The desk sergeant, who, according to her nametag, was Renee O'Reilly, looked up expectantly as she breezed inside the lobby.

"Can I speak to Detective Cowan, please?"

"In reference to what?"

"To the Julie Wilson case."

The woman nodded and picked up the phone. "Grace, someone's here about the Wilson case." The officer nodded into the phone, then set it into its cradle. "She'll be out in a minute."

Remmy gave the sergeant her brightest smile. "Thanks." She puttered about the lobby, absently reading public notices that had been posted on a cork bulletin board. After fifteen minutes of cooling her heels, she felt a presence behind her. Remmy turned. Grace looked dead on her feet, face drawn. "Hey, you not get any doughnuts today, or what?"

Grace smiled, mildly amused. "What can I do for you, Remmy?" She dropped her body into one of the uncomfortable plastic chairs.

Remmy's smile was nearly blinding. "She's alive, Grace."

Grace stared at her, dumbfounded. "How do you know?"

"She made contact with me this afternoon. She's alive! Told me so, herself!" Remmy's disappointment was obvious at Grace's lack of enthusiasm at the news.

"What is it?"

"Another woman has gone missing. In Burrow Key." Grace sighed, resting her arm on the back of the chair next to hers. "I was there all day today."

Remmy plopped down in the second chair. "Where's Burrow Key?"

"Maybe twenty minutes from here."

"And you think the cases are related?"

"I do." Grace rested her head against the wall. "I don't believe in coincidences, Remmy."

Remmy thought about that for a moment. "Do you have a picture of the victim? Maybe I can help."

"Not yet. The police in Burrow Key are working with us pretty closely, so as soon as I do, I'll get with you, okay?" Grace slapped her hands on her thighs, ready to return to her desk. Her husband would be sleeping alone again. Though it was after nine p.m., she still had lots of work to do.

"Julie told me something that I can't quite work out yet." Remmy stared at her hands in her lap, looking through them as she tried to remember.

"What?"

"Something to do with..." She concentrated, squeezing her eyes shut. Suddenly she saw it all again. "The letter 'R'. I don't know, but that letter seemed to really upset her. Also something about forty-one... something. Shit!" She sighed in frustration and looked at Grace. "I'm sorry. That's all I can remember. I just hope it helps do...something."

Grace smiled, filing the information away in her memory. She patted Remmy's thigh affectionately. "You're a good egg, Remmy." Groaning as she got to her feet, she stretched her arms high over her head. "Talk to you later."

Remmy watched her disappear back through the

Personnel Only door.

꧁꧂

As the garage door buzzed shut behind him, Sergio climbed out of his van. He walked around to the side door, slid it open, then carefully removed the large drum and slid it across the cement floor until it was against the wall. He walked past his workbench, making a mental note to destroy the large container of liquid lye, too, just as he had the empty containers earlier that day. But for now, he was tired and wanted to get to bed. Work came awfully early in the morning after such a busy weekend.

Chapter Sixteen

As she entered through the front door, Grace pulled on a pair of latex gloves. The house was small, but well-kept and cute, with its own charm. The furniture looked to be all hand-me-downs, though it had been cared for. The ugly, avocado green color of the fabric was covered by red bed sheets.

"Tell me about the victim," Grace said to the detective in charge.

"Cameron Sanchez, age twenty. She's a junior at the college," Detective Dick Robb read from a file in his hands. "Five feet, two inches, brown hair, hazel eyes. She lived alone, been in the house for a year. No known boyfriend, no known enemies, no priors." Snapping the file closed, the twenty-six year veteran looked around the living room, rubbing the back of his neck with a large hand.

CSI had processed the scene the night before; telltale signs of their investigation were visible throughout the small house. Grace wanted a second look-see. Cameron's was the first where there was an indoor crime scene, the others taken out of doors which made her wonder whether this case actually was linked to the others. The MO was just too different.

"This look anything like your case?" Robb asked.

Grace shook her head. "We've never had a home invasion with any of our victims." She glanced at the robust detective, thinking he couldn't be any more stereotypical if he tried: short-cropped, graying hair;

hard lines on his face; and a long trenchcoat over his poorly-fitted brown suit. "What was found?"

"Not a goddamn thing," he said, blowing out a long breath. He had been briefed on the cases that Woodland and the other counties were dealing with. Burrow Key was a small town, and this apparent abduction had left its residents shaken. "No fingerprints, nothin'." He sighed out his frustration.

Grace nodded acknowledgement, deciding to take a little tour, unescorted. In the girl's bedroom, she noted the scattered clothing, as though Cameron had stripped before getting into bed, leaving the day's clothing to be picked up the next morning. Only the next morning had not come. At least not in her bedroom. The bed was left in disarray, the blanket nearly on the floor, the sheet and under sheet rumpled. All evidence of that was gone now. CSI had bagged the bedding and taken it for lab work to see whether any DNA evidence could be found.

The windows were all locked from the inside, and none of them were broken. The front and back doors were intact. As there was no evidence of a break-in, it was thought that perhaps the offender knew Sanchez. As Grace studied the back, she knelt down, groaning as her knees popped – an old volleyball injury. She looked at her pained reflection in the silver doorknob. She touched the cool knob with a latex-covered finger, wishing she could see who had touched it, who had reached out and turned it in the middle of the night. It was assumed the offender used the back door, as he would likely have been seen on the very visible front porch.

As Grace peered at the knob, she blindly reached into the inside pocket of her jacket and grabbed her reading glasses. Sliding them on, she looked closely at the knob. She could just barely see a sort of...residue.

Maybe powder. She ran her fingertip over it, catching a few granules on the tip of the glove. Bringing it close, she could see that they were miniscule metal shavings. Reaching inside her pocket again, she brought out a flip-up magnifying glass, removing the glasses as she placed the magnifier over the keyhole. Just barely visible at the mouth of the keyhole were tiny markings—scrape marks.

"Son of a bitch picked the lock," she said, sitting back on her heels. Pushing up with another groan, Grace looked out at the yard, tucking her magnifying glass away. Detective Robb joined her. She pointed back toward the door. "Picked it. She didn't let him in, nor did he have a key."

They made their way around to the front yard. Grace could see that tire casts had been made in the driveway and was satisfied that the investigation had gone well. Standing on the sidewalk in front of the house, she looked everything over, making sure she had missed nothing, retracing every room in her mind, considering every tiny little detail that she recalled, though it might not have seemed important at the time. Nothing.

Turning toward her car, Grace noticed something at the very edge of the grass on Cameron Sanchez's property. Squatting, she used a single finger to nudge it further into view — cigarette butt.

"That's old, Grace. Prob'ly been there for a week or more."

Though she knew his words were most likely true, Grace felt something clench in her gut and she decided to run the butt in anyway. "You have anything? Baggie or envelope?" she asked, gingerly taking the butt between thumb and index finger.

His expression indicating that he was disgruntled

that the visiting cop wasn't listening to him, Dick Robb walked stiffly over to his car and grabbed a plastic evidence Baggie from the console. He watched as she placed the butt inside, sealed the Baggie, and pulled a Sharpie out of the inside pocket of her jacket.

"How much you got in that pocket, anyway?"

Grace grinned. "I don't carry a purse for a reason, Detective." Grace stood, marked the Baggie with date, time, and victim's name, and slipped the marker back into her pocket. "If it doesn't fit in a pocket, I don't need it."

Dick Robb chuckled. "Good to live by, I s'pose."

"Well, I think I'm all done here." Grace looked at Robb, her eyes asking if he needed her for anything else.

He shook his head, rubbing his neck. "I'll keep in touch," he said, heading toward his car.

⊱✿⊰⊱✿⊰

Both of Julie's wrists were cuffed to the bed. She knew it was daytime, though the curtains and blinds had been drawn on the windows before he left for, she assumed, work. Though dim, it wasn't dark like it was downstairs. That was a nice change. It was also a nice change to be lying down, though she'd been there for hours. He'd made her sit on the toilet for about thirty minutes while he got dressed, then he brought her into the bedroom and bound her. She'd had nothing to drink since their omelet feast the night before, which sucked, but at the same time, she was grateful because she didn't have to pee. She felt like a child, though; he'd stuck an open diaper under her "just in case".

"Bastard," she muttered.

With nothing else to do, Julie took a more careful look around the largish bedroom. The bed was probably a queen — she didn't seem to be far enough away from him during sleep for it to be a king. On the wall directly in front of the bed was a tall eight-drawer dresser. She had watched him go quite often into one of the drawers — always the top drawer, which, given her small stature, was fairly high. His back was always to her, so she wasn't able to see what he was messing with, but seemingly it was not always for clothing.

Atop the cherry wood dresser were a few knickknacks, a couple of bottles of cologne, and a picture frame. The strange thing was that only half a picture was showcased in the five by seven frame; the other half was torn away. In the half that remained, her captor smiled in front of what looked to be a wooded backdrop.

Eyes scanning further, she noticed there were no pictures or decorations on the wall. The walls, painted a plain white, were very clean. She had already noted much the same thing about the bathroom — no decorations, everything in its place, everything neat and very clean. The closet door was closed, so she could see nothing inside. From her vantage point on the bed, she could just barely make out half of what looked to be an upside down cross hanging on the wall. Though not religious by any stretch of the imagination, Julie, who had been conditioned to go to Sunday school every week at the Lutheran church downtown, was chilled by such an obvious hatred of religious dogma. *Who is this guy?*

Every time Julie was brought up from the pit, she'd been drugged, only regaining consciousness once she was already positioned on the bed, so she had no idea what the rest of the house looked like. She turned her attention back to the windows, damning the man for pulling the blinds. She would have done almost anything to see some sunlight. She had no idea why she'd been left upstairs, something that hadn't happened after her other couple of stints upstairs.

That morning before he left for work, he'd gotten up and taken a shower, then padded back into the bedroom naked as a jay bird. She had groaned inwardly when she saw his excitement. He had un-cuffed one of her hands and brought it to his erection, warning her that if she did anything he didn't like, he would kill her. It had taken an agonizingly long time for the bastard to finish, Julie trying her best to not grimace at the stickiness on her hand. She was grateful for the wet towel he used to clean her up. She was also grateful that he left her alone, giving her body a chance to recover. She was still sore from the marathon the day before.

With a sigh, she closed her eyes to try and sleep.

Chapter Seventeen

Though he had decided to skip classes on this particular day, Patrick Rossum was basically a good kid. An eighth grader, he had only ever ditched school twice before, and that was when he and his dad had gone fishing. He was walking along a very familiar trail in the woods in which he'd grown up, just outside of Woodland. He carried the walking stick his grandfather had whittled from a fallen branch, which he had used for years in his hiking and fishing expeditions. The thirteen-year old had been overjoyed when it was passed down to him after the death of his granddad.

He stopped to eat the sandwich his mom had prepared for him, though she expected him to be eating it in the cafeteria at Woodland Middle School. He took a large bite of the peanut butter and peach jelly, cut in half, just as he liked it. His friends made fun of him because his mom still made his lunch and he didn't eat the lunch the school provided. He shrugged it off. He loved his mom's PB&J. Even when he made them himself, they never tasted as good.

He hacked at a couple of clumps of wildflowers, and the tip of his stick struck something hard. Figuring it was a rock, he kept going, chewing contentedly as he enjoyed the crisp day. The frost from a couple of days earlier had melted, but from the looks of the sky and the smell of moisture in the air, Patrick guessed they were due for their first good storm. Halloween was a week away, and that was typically when they got hit hard for the first time.

Patrick's thoughts about the weather died away as he caught sight of something just up ahead, partially sticking out from underneath the dirt. Curious, he tapped his way toward it, using the end of the stick to push away fallen debris.

The freckles on Patrick's cheeks stood in stark relief against the pallor of his face, his blue eyes widening to the size of saucers. Suddenly he wished he were sitting in Mr. Alfredo's English class. His half-eaten sandwich landed in a pile of smelly goop.

❧❧❧❧

Roman walked the two blocks from where he had parked his car, to the coffeeshop where he was due to begin working in seven minutes. Hands shoved into his heavy winter jacket, he was startled as a small army of police cars whizzed by, not one of them with a siren blaring. The police station was just down the street at the corner, so he wasn't surprised. He was, however, surprised by the sheer numbers: one...two...three, four, five...six. Next came a van marked *Coroner*.

"That can't be good," he muttered, turning into the recessed doorway of the coffeeshop and pushing against the wood and glass door. Inside the warm cafe, strong fragrances assailed his senses. There were only a few patrons scattered throughout, sipping a beverage or eating the scrumptious offerings, all homemade. Roman was pleased to see Remmy sitting near the window, even though Matt Wilson was sitting across from her. He recognized the guy from the newspaper articles about his sister. Remmy grinned at Roman and gave him a wave. He waved back then ducked into the back room to get ready to begin his shift.

"This one is of my son Skylar and Julie. That's Bonnie in her lap." Matt pointed to the Yorkie curled up in the snapshot.

Remmy took the picture and brought it up to study it. She scrutinized the boy's face smiling at the huge grin he was directing toward his aunt.

"They're close." She could feel the love emanating from the boy in the picture. It didn't take a psychic to see his attachment.

Matt smiled, pride in his eyes. "Very. When she'd take him for a weekend or for the week, half the time I was surprised she brought him back at all."

"Okay. Show me more."

Matt was against letting Remmy roam around his sister's house. For him, it still held Julie's energy, and he couldn't bear to have that disrupted by the presence of someone else. Understanding and compassionate, Remmy suggested that he show her pictures, providing vivid details of things that meant the most to Julie Wilson.

"This was Christmas last year." Matt chuckled. "You should've seen the look on her face when I threw that snowball." He tapped the glossy that his son had snapped. Julie stood in shock, remnants of snow still clinging to her cheek, green eyes wide with disbelief.

Remmy felt the shocked cold that had traveled through Julie's body at that instant. As she reached out for the print, she shivered; the photo paper felt as if it was about thirty degrees. Her fingertips actually burned from the intense cold.

Matt closely watched the woman sitting across the table. He wasn't sure what to make of her. She had the oddest reactions to things, almost literally responding or reacting to what was in the picture presented to her. She seemed to believe so strongly that Julie was alive.

He wanted with everything in him to believe her, that his sister was alive and would be found, but he feared that if he allowed himself to hold onto hope, when it came out that Julie had, in fact, been dead all along, the disappointment would kill him.

He had recently taken Skylar to a therapist to try and help the eight-year old understand what had likely happened to his beloved aunt. The boy was shattered. It wasn't lost on him that "both his mommies" had left him. It was an uphill struggle every day, but Matt was determined to help Skylar get through it. That didn't make it any easier to get through each day himself.

❧ ❧ ❧ ❧

Brian Wong chewed on a piece of Big Red as he looked down at the discovery at his wing-tipped feet. He had to admit the sight was pretty gruesome. The body had been dismembered, the head found in a thicket of wildflowers, a large portion of the skin gone, either from decomposition or some sort of chemical that had helped it along. Further along the trail, a half-buried arm had been found, hand still attached, fingertips missing. The arm was in the same condition as the head.

"More over here!" one of the officers called out, his voice echoing in the quiet forest.

The detective picked his way over, latex-covered hands shoved into the pockets of his pants. He stepped across the yellow tape barrier two officers were setting up that declared the site an official crime scene. The latest find was the most grisly of all—a woman's torso, amputated just above the hips. Many of the ribs could be seen through a substantial hole in her stomach caused by the feasting of the scavengers of the forest.

The officer, a young rookie just out of the academy,

stood looking down at the remains, a cloth held to his mouth and nose.

"You get used to it," Wong muttered, squatting down beside the torso. He glanced over his shoulder at the sound of footsteps in the foliage. Grace Cowan emerged around the small copse of trees between him and the arm. He turned his attention back to the torso.

"They found the rest about a half mile to the west," she said, standing just behind him and looking over his shoulder. Brian Wong nodded as he stood. Both detectives moved out of the way as the department photographer stepped in, taking photos of the body from every direction and angle. "What's Dave say?" Grace asked.

Brian sighed, looking up into the heavy clouds, pregnant with cold and moisture. "Haven't spoken to the ME yet." He met her tired eyes. "Looks to me like maybe some sort of solvent was used. Dunno, just doesn't feel like typical decomposition here. I mean, look." He pointed toward the torso. "There's been critter activity, but somehow it just feels too fresh."

Grace nodded. "I agree. Has anything else been found? Personal items?"

"Nope. Nothing. Just the other body parts and... this." Brian indicated the torso at their feet.

☙ ☙ ❧ ❧

Back at her office, Grace scanned through all recent reports of missing persons. She had thought that perhaps the woman was Cameron Sanchez, but that had been discounted when the family was asked whether Cameron had a tattoo on her hip. She didn't. Back to square one.

The Jane Doe's fingertips had been removed,

so no fingerprinting could be done, and they had no potential identifications for which to compare dental records. "Shit." Grace ran a hand over her hair, smoothing it back into a tight bun. The patterns on the remaining skin didn't match the typical progression of natural decomposition at all, especially given the cold temperatures, so it was likely that a chemical agent had been used — an acid, lye, or something — to speed the disintegration of the body. That made their task more difficult, because it made it practically impossible to determine how long the body had been there. Also, the cold weather had kept the flies away, which meant that the gestation stage of fly larvae couldn't be used to gauge the time.

Grace looked up into the faces of her four missing women, one already eliminated from the victim pool. That left Pamela Beecham, Roxie Carmichael, and Julie Wilson as possibilities. Pulling the files on the three women for the twentieth time, she read up on them, trying to see whether anything new would jump out at her.

What am I missing? she asked herself over and over again.

Chapter Eighteen

Honey, I'm home." Sergio called out, amused at his little joke as he entered the kitchen through the garage door. He glanced around, eyes narrowed as he studied everything. Nothing was out of place; everything was exactly as he'd left it. He stopped at the fridge, absently straightening one of the plastic magnetic letters that had gotten slightly askew. About to proceed to the next room, he suddenly opened the door and grabbed a bottled water and a beer for himself.

Scrutinizing the living room, Sergio was satisfied that all was well in that room, too. The furniture, covered in plastic and sprayed down with 409 the night before, was perfect. Above the loveseat, stacked neatly on shelving, were dozens of building blocks with colorful letters or numbers on all four sides, the type a child would enjoy. They were made of wood, not of cheap plastic like the ones that were sold now. On the other wall, above the 19" television, was another shelf. On it were neatly stacked rows of TV Guides dating back more than six years.

Walking down the hall toward the bedrooms, he passed the first two—one on his right, the other on his left—a bathroom on the right, then straight back to the third bedroom, his bedroom. Before he even crossed the threshold, he could hear soft, even breathing, which brought a smile to his face. Nothing was changed in the bedroom; all was well. Julie was sleeping peacefully, just as he had left her.

Sergio wrinkled his nose at the pungent smell of female blood and urine. It had been wise to leave her with the diaper. He took in the sprawled body of his prize and decided she needed a shower. Fifteen minutes later, he was leading her back to the bed.

"Um…" She made herself look into his dark eyes. "You mentioned dinner." She trembled in his tight grip. "Is it possible that maybe, well, maybe I could eat with you? In the kitchen, or…" She held her breath. She tried not to sway on her feet, but the lack of nourishment was catching up to her. It took all of her willpower to not wince as he raised a hand and brushed her cheek with his fingertips.

"Do you want to sit down, or is it the change of scenery?" he asked.

Julie's mind raced, trying to figure out which was the right answer. She swallowed reflexively as his fingers trailed down across her throat. A quick image of that same hand on Roxie's throat rose in her mind. Apparently the look on her face expressed her thoughts. A cold sweat broke out on her skin as his face hardened.

"I told you it was an accident." He forced her back onto the bed, falling with her and pinning her beneath his body. He was in her face, the hand still firmly clutching her throat, though not squeezing. "'Judge not, lest ye be judged'," he said, spittle landing on her cheek.

"I'm sorry," she whispered, hoarse with fear.

Sergio was breathing hard, his anger and his pulse pounding in his head. He looked down into the green eyes, seeing the fear within them, the tears beginning to well. A surge of warmth spread through him, compassion lightening his touch back into a caress. He leaned down and placed a soft kiss on her forehead in an effort to soothe her.

"You eat in here today," he whispered in her ear. "We'll talk about the kitchen later."

Julie didn't struggle as she was bound to the bed again, her tears falling as he strode from the room.

❧ ❧ ❧ ❧

Taking a deep breath, Grace entered the interview room. She was dreading this meeting. Placing the file onto the small, square table, she smiled at the two men waiting for her as she took a seat across from them.

"Hello. I'm Detective Grace Cowan. I've been working the cases dealing with the missing women, including your wife." She studied the two men, who looked remarkably alike—deep-set brown eyes and short, brown hair, though the older had gray streaks in his hair. The younger sported a soul-patch beneath his bottom lip.

"Nice to see you again, Detective. This is my son, Trevor." He nodded toward the young man sitting next to him.

Grace nodded an acknowledgment. Getting down to business, she put on the most professional yet compassionate face she could. "Mr. Carmichael," she said softly, "three days ago a body was discovered in the woods outside Woodland. The only way to identify the female victim is by a partial tattoo." She studied the man carefully. His Adam's apple bobbed as he swallowed. "I saw in an earlier statement that Roxie had a tattoo."

Trevor looked at his father. "Mom had a tattoo?"

Mack nodded. "Yes, she did."

"Can you tell me what that tattoo looked like?" Grace tried to get the image of their Jane Doe's remains out of her head. In some ways it was like God trying to tell them something, trying to point a finger of recognition. Of the entire hip and pelvis area, the only remaining flesh was where the tattoo was located.

"It was a small blue fairy, little yellow wings."

Grace nodded. The tattoo on the body was faded with time, as well as the solvent used on the body, and had been stretched with childbirth and weight gain. "I have a photograph that was taken in the Medical Examiner's office. Do you think you could take a look at it and tell me if it's the same tattoo?"

Trevor put an arm around his father's broad shoulders. Mack nodded.

"Yeah. I can do that."

"Okay." Grace opened the folder and pulled out a picture taken during the autopsy. The image was centered only on the tattoo. They didn't want to upset the family any more than need be.

Mack accepted the picture with a trembling hand. It only took a moment for him to break down, clutching the photo. Trevor gathered his father in a strong, one-armed hug, resting their heads together.

Grace fought the burning in her own throat as she struggled to maintain her professionalism. "I'm sorry, Mack," she said at length, reaching across the table and resting her hand upon his much larger one.

⁂

Remmy held up another pack of smokes, her eyebrows lifted in enquiry.

"No, that ain't them, neither. What about the blue and white pack?" the old man said, leaning across the counter to point.

Remmy put the Marlboros away and grabbed the pack the old man was indicating. She held it up for his inspection, trying not to get exasperated with him.

"No, them ain't it, neither."

"Sir, we've been through every brand I've got here. The pack you had last week just may not be here." She returned the blue and white pack to its shelf.

"No, damn it!" He slammed his fist into the counter. "I know I bought it here!"

"Maybe you were at *Smoker Friendly* down on Pike Avenue," she said, hoping he would go away. To her astonishment, and irritated amusement, he looked off into space, as though thinking. Remmy's attention was pulled away from him as the bells above the door rang and Grace Cowan walked in. She gave her a quick nod, then turned back to the elderly gentleman.

"You know," he said, voice just above a whisper, "I think you're right."

Remmy smiled encouragingly. "I'm sure they'd be more than happy to help you out over there, sir."

Without another word, the old man hobbled toward the door, but not before letting out a huge, wet cough. Grace watched him go, disgust clearly written on her dark features as she walked up to the counter.

"Hiya," Remmy said with a grin.

"Hi, Remmy. How are you?"

"Just peachy keen."

"Listen," Grace leaned on the counter, "I've got some good news, and some bad news."

"Okay." Remmy leaned against the opposite counter in the small bullpen, arms crossed over her chest as she studied the other woman.

"If I didn't believe in your 'visions' before, I definitely do now. You were right. Someone was killed, her name began with an 'R', and she was forty-one years old."

Remmy felt as if she'd taken a punch to the gut. Swallowing, she nodded, encouraging Grace to continue.

"Her name was Roxie Carmichael, mother of three and a wife. She's been missing for over eight months. But," she held up a finger, "here's the kicker… she wasn't dead all that time. She was left in the woods, and the ME's office doesn't believe she'd been there for any longer than a week, at most."

"I'm really not sure what to think of this, Grace," Remmy said softly, her stomach roiling.

"I know. Here's the good news. We finally have a link. Tire tracks found near the dump site were compared to the ones in the Cameron Sanchez case, and they match."

Remmy had heard about the young woman who'd been taken from her own bed. That was good news. Any lead was very good news. She met the intense gaze of the detective.

"Remmy, do you feel in your heart of hearts that Julie witnessed the death of Roxie Carmichael?"

Remmy met the gaze dead on. "Without a doubt."

"Okay. Then here's what I need from you. I want you to make a connection, make a mental call, whatever it is you do, with Julie, and get as much goddamn information as you can. I want to nail this motherfucker, you hear me?"

Remmy nodded grimly. "Yeah. I hear ya."

⁂

Pamela glanced through the darkness ahead to where she could hear the soft moans. Her heart went out to the new girl. She knew what kind of a headache accompanied that first day back in consciousness. She had no idea what the bastard used to knock them out, but it was potent. She didn't think it was a run-of-the-mill chloroform. His drug kept them out for days if he wanted it to, which was always the case with the new girls.

As much as she hated seeing another life ruined, she was glad for the company. It seemed as if he had kept Julie upstairs forever. Pamela wondered if she was still alive. Hell, she even missed Roxie's crying and sniffling. Pamela had lived in the dark so long now, her eyes were quite well adjusted. She could make out the girl's face well enough to see that she was just a young girl. Even younger than Julie.

"How are you doing, kid?" she asked, her voice soft.

The girl moaned again before raising her head, blinking several times. "Where am I?"

Pamela gave the standard answer: "Hell."

Cameron looked around before a whimper escaped her lips. "Oh my god! Where am I?!" The darkness began to close. Her breathing became loud and intense, her chest heaving as her eyes grew wider. "Help! Help me!"

Pamela rolled her eyes. "Fuck." She took a deep breath, then let the newcomer have it. "Shut the fuck up!" she yelled above the girl's screams. "Unless you wanna loose Satan himself on your ass!"

Cameron shut up immediately, though still whimpering softly. "Who are you?"

"Your fucking best friend, if you'll shut up." Pamela glanced over at the girl, feeling slight guilt and pity. "Trust me on this — you'll make it worse on yourself if you pull shit like that. No one is coming to help you, okay? *No* one."

❧ ❧ ❧ ❧

Upstairs, Sergio spooned another mouthful of the

fragrant soup into Julie's mouth, nearly giddy at seeing her relishing the new taste. The smile slid from his lips as he had a flashback to another time, a bad time.

He had managed to get her sitting up against the headboard of her simple wooden bed. A blanket of pure white had been wrapped tightly over her short legs; her gown that day was the color of cement. Her small, dark eyes bored into him from cracked, white skin, a map of lines threading out from those hard eyes.

Sergio brought up another spoonful, the smell of the inevitable oatmeal making his stomach churn. As he brought the spoon up to her mouth, he missed slightly, some of the lumpy mess sliding down her chin. Quickly he reached for a napkin to clean it off.

"Can't even do that right, can you?" she whispered. "God rejected you long ago for leaving your mother."

Sergio didn't rise to the bait; it wouldn't do any good. Instead, he dipped the spoon into the bowl again, gathering another mouthful for his mother.

He shook himself free of the memory, looking instead into the clear green eyes that gazed out toward the window as Julie silently chewed the meat and potatoes that had been in the last bite.

Julie savored the warmth that slid down her throat and into her stomach. She was amazed she hadn't gotten sick, wandering around in only her birthday suit. He kept the house reasonably warm — upstairs, anyway — which helped. She had never imagined she would ever feel so blasé about nakedness. She was amused at that, as she freely admitted to being a shy, self-conscious person. Even living alone, she never walked around naked, or even half-naked.

She knew it was silly, but a naked body was always something she equated with the sexual, sensual side of life, and she didn't reveal hers to just anyone. The human body, she felt, was a sacred, beautiful thing, not to be on display. Never again would she see her body the same way. Never again would she be able to give the gift of it to someone. For one thing, she was probably going to live out the rest of her days in her prison. For a second, the human body had forever lost its beauty and specialness for her.

Julie looked at the man who was busy stirring the remaining soup, gathering more of the hearty chunks. She examined him, and for a brief moment allowed the anger she felt to enter her eyes. How dare he take that from her? How dare he steal something so precious?

She hated him.

Chapter Nineteen

Roman's hand snapped out, fingers grabbing onto the "oh, shit" handle. He watched as the scenery whirled by in a circular blur, the engine of his car roaring as the car once again righted in response to the driver's hand.

"Holy shit!" he howled, unable to keep the smile from his face. "How do you know how to do this?"

Remmy grinned, gunning the engine. "Can't tell ya," she said, sending them into another doughnut. How could she possibly tell him that stealing cars over the years had taught her how to be one hell of a driver?

"Well, I don't care how you learned this, you're a blast, Remmy."

She grinned over at him, amused at the child-like glee in his eyes. Remmy slid the car into a perfect parallel to the curb, the car rocking to a stop, a whoop of joy coming from Roman. It was a weekend, so the large, empty parking lot at the school made for the perfect place for fun on four wheels.

Remmy was about to relinquish the wheel to the car's owner when suddenly she was hit with something, a very strong something. For the past two weeks, since Grace had come to see her at work, Remmy had been trying her best to force a connection with Julie. Previously, other than the dreaming, she had only gotten images when Julie had inadvertently sent them her way. Remmy was never able to initiate contact. Only once had she been able to discern quick, very blurry images, then they were gone. It had been frustrating, but she was trying her hardest.

Sitting at the wheel of Roman's car, she suddenly felt her body infused with warmth, her stomach full, content. Even so, she could feel the cold tendrils of the most intense anger and hatred she'd ever felt. She saw nothing. There was no vision to go along with the sensations, only a feeling.

Roman, who had opened his door, cried out in surprise as the car lurched to life. He slammed the door shut, glancing over at her. "Uh, Remmy," he said, "don't you need to go to work?"

Remmy didn't even hear the words spoken from a mere two feet away. She drove out of the parking lot, idling at the corner, not sure whether to go left or right. Or straight ahead, maybe. She concentrated, trying to get a handle on the feelings she was experiencing, trying to feel the strength of that anger. She felt a strong pull toward the left. Hitting the turn signal, she headed south.

As the neighborhoods flew by, Remmy hadn't said a word, but the white-knuckled grip she had on the steering wheel was evidence of her emotions.

Remmy turned right at the stop sign, the anger inside her feeling stronger, burning hotter in her gut. Her jaw clenched as emotion tried to consume her. She was heading toward the highway, the need to be there so strong, she could think of nothing else. She put her foot to the gas, the car speeding along toward an unknown destination. Remmy's jaw muscles clenching and unclenching, she growled at the yellow traffic light ahead, knowing she would never make it.

Pulling the car to a sudden stop—Roman cushioning the sharp forward motion by putting a hand on the dashboard—she seethed. Fingertips tapped steadily on the wheel as the red of the traffic light seemed to mock her. "Come on, fucker!" she yelled, startling her passenger.

The light turned green, but the urge to rocket through the intersection had died. Remmy blinked several times, looking around her in confusion and mild fear. A honking horn behind her alerted her to the fact that she needed to move.

"Remmy, it's green," Roman said, looking over at her.

She blinked rapidly as she got the car moving again, only to pull off onto a side street, then into the parking lot of a hardware store. "Holy shit," she said, hands trembling. She felt empty and cold, the gentle hand on her shoulder making her start. She met Roman's concerned gaze.

"You okay?" he asked tentatively.

Remmy nodded. "Yeah. Fine." She climbed out of the car, walking around the front and waiting at the passenger door for Roman to get out. When he did, she claimed his seat, pushing far down in it, resting her head against the seatback. She had a pounding headache and felt nauseous. *What's happening to me? Do I have a brain tumor?*

༄ ༄ ༄ ༄

Remmy pushed through the glass door of the store, ignoring Josh's glare as she made her way toward the back room, where she grabbed her apron from the peg just outside Joan's office door.

"Where were you?" Joan asked, stepping to the doorway of the small room.

Remmy glanced briefly at her as she pinned her nametag to the apron.

"Sorry. Got...held up."

"Josh needed to leave a half hour ago, Remmy."

"I said I'm sorry!" Remmy snapped, surprising both of them. The events of that afternoon had left her feeling confused and disturbed. She felt as though she'd lost total control of herself during that period of time. She remembered very little of it, other than staring up at the stoplight and wondering how the hell she got there. Her fears had not eased when Roman told her what happened.

Nodding, Joan turned to head back into the office. "We'll talk about this later, Remmy," she said, hurt in her voice. "For right now, we just need to get Josh out of here."

Remmy felt bad as she made her way out to the bullpen. She would apologize later, but for the moment she needed to try and sort things out in her own head.

"'Bout time you showed up," Josh grumbled, handing her the register keys and slipping past her before slamming out the front door, not even bothering to remove his apron first.

Remmy got herself settled in, checking to see what Josh had done during his shift and what would need to be completed during her late shift. It was already after six, and she had until two a.m. She was grateful for the hours that Joan was giving her, but she hated to work nights.

It was already ten, and slow, and Remmy was re-stocking the soda, bringing it up from the back. The Coke or Pepsi guy would come and stock the back room, the employees of the convenience store re-stocking the front as was needed. They were having a good sale on Coke products, so the twelve-packs had sold down to next to nothing. Josh hadn't bothered to refill them. She was grumbling under her breath as she carted out a dolly of the red and white boxes when Joan caught up to her.

"So, you wanna tell me what that was about earlier?"

Remmy didn't look at her as she continued to work. "Not really, honestly."

"And why not? It's not like you to be late, then to be a bitch about it, Rem." Joan helped, moving a twelve-pack of Mountain Dew that someone had set down, probably after noticing that the Coke was cheaper. She opened a nearby cooler, put the soda where it belonged, then turned back to Remmy. She studied her. "Does this have to do with Julie?" Joan asked. "I can't think of anything else that would bother you so much. Never in all my life have I known anyone who can just shrug off the problems of the world like you can." Her gaze bored into Remmy. "Except when it comes to Julie Wilson."

Remmy nodded. She thought she might dissolve into tears right there if she tried to speak. Instead she continued working, building the display, something that had become her specialty in the store. She tried to make each one more creative than the previous. The Coke display was no exception.

Joan stood back and watched. "Maybe you should talk about it, Remmy. You look upset. I don't mean to push—"

"Then please don't," Remmy said softly, getting to her feet and standing directly in front of Joan. Tortured blue eyes looked deeply into Joan's.

Joan sighed. "Okay. I'll leave it be." She held Remmy's gaze. "I don't want to be insensitive to what's going on with you, Remmy, or about your abilities, but understand that this is still a business. I can't afford to give you special privileges or schedules. Okay?"

Remmy nodded, irritated that Joan felt she had to tell her that, but she understood why she had. She watched her walk away, only to return a moment later with her purse and keys in hand.

"Have a good night, Remmy. Call if you need anything."

"Thanks." Remmy turned back to her work.

Chapter Twenty

Sergio rubbed his hands together, warming the lotion between them. His newest prize lay on his bed, still unconscious. He gazed at her firm, perfect flesh, freshly bathed by his own hands. He began his ministrations at her feet, rubbing the lotion into the pads of her toes then working it into the hardened, calloused undersides. He figured she must enjoy being barefoot. His gaze settled on her three tattoos—a mermaid perched atop her right collarbone, a unicorn on her ankle, and the image of an astrological Scorpio sign on her pubic bone just above neatly trimmed pubic hair, which had started to grow back over the past week that she had been his. Sergio couldn't help but wince at the last tattoo—must've hurt, considering there was no fat there, only bone.

He slid his hands up soft calves, squirting more lotion into the palms of his hands as needed. The thighs were thin, very little muscle or definition. Not like Julie's. It didn't matter. He loved all types, shapes, and sizes. He remembered when his first had arrived. She'd been plump, with the belly and sagging breasts of a woman who had left youth behind and hadn't prepared or taken care of herself for middle age. He had quickly taken care of that. She was now thin and streamlined.

Gentle, firm hands made their way up over narrow hips, the hip bones jutting a bit too much. He wondered why the girl was so thin. He would have to feed her a little extra, perhaps. Squirting more lotion, he ran his hands over the concave belly, thumbs caressing the bellybutton and noting the gold ring that hooked into the flesh, then his gaze moved up to her breasts. They were small, the nipples dark and puckered in the cool confines of his bedroom.

As he massaged them, he realized that this one reminded him of her, from very long ago. She had been built much the same way, with similar features, though her skin wasn't quite the tanned shade of this girl's. She was slender, with slightly larger breasts. She had only allowed him to marvel at those breasts just the once, and that was because he had given her all his milk money for a quick peek. At thirteen years old, that's all he'd had, seventy-five cents. She had lifted her shirt, giving him the tiniest flash before turning and sauntering away.

Tossing the memory away, he returned to the prize lying on his bed. Her nipples were responding nicely to his hands, and he liked that. She sighed quietly in her semi-conscious state, but didn't move. He used a thumb to roll over the hardened bud, eyes quickly glancing up at her expressionless face. He noted with mild excitement that her hips moved a bit, readjusting on the bed.

He left her nipples — there would be plenty of time for them later — and continued massaging the lotion into the skin of her shoulders and upper chest, and then her neck. After he finished, he would have to leave her for a bit. He was running low on supplies and would have to go into town. At least shopping on a Sunday morning wouldn't be bad; everyone was in church. He hated to leave her, and just when they were becoming acquainted. With a sigh, Sergio squirted more lotion onto his hands.

The school gymnasium was decorated with flowers, the pull-out bleachers on either side filled with students, community members, family, and friends. A podium had been set up underneath the basketball net on the north side of the large room, the floors polished to a shine. Those that were going to be speaking sat in chairs that were set up along the free-throw line.

Dressed in jeans and a dark blue sweater, Matt Wilson stood behind the microphone, waiting for nine-thirty before beginning, giving everyone a chance to get settled. He smiled at Skylar, who sat at the end of the bleachers. Every seat was taken, and there were also people standing all along the back wall of the gym.

"Everyone," he said into the microphone, voice echoing off the walls in the large space, "if we can get started, please." The quiet murmuring faded. "Thank you. I appreciate it." He stood back, giving them another minute, then he stepped up to the podium. "I want to thank everyone for coming. I know Julie would be extremely pleased and proud that all of you came to rejoice in her memory. This is truly a testament to the kind of person she is. I also want to thank those who have given Skylar and me their best wishes, and Mrs. Hinkle for her sinfully good dinners." Chuckles rippled through the crowd.

Deloris Hinkle stood from her seat in the fourth row. "Anytime, Matty," she called out, favoring him with a nod and an understanding smile.

Matt sighed. "The last few months have been the most difficult I've ever had to face. You've all helped my son and me to stay strong, and for that I'll be forever grateful. Julie touched a lot of lives, not only as a sixth grade teacher, but as a friend, sister, and aunt," he indicated Skylar, "and as an all-around great human being. Julie always stood for what is right in the world, and fought hard to make sure those in her care, her beloved students, had a wonderful teacher, a friend to talk to, someone who cared."

He was quiet for a moment, gathering his thoughts. A few coughs sounded in the crowd as he removed the microphone from its stand. He stepped away from the podium, mindful of the long electrical cord that was strung across the gym floor.

"Julie went into teaching," he continued, "because she loved children. I didn't think she quite knew what she was getting into by going into middle school." Matt grinned at the round of laughter that garnered. "But, she loved it. The other day I was in her house, watering plants, cleaning, keeping it fresh..." He cleared his throat when his voice broke slightly. *Hold it together, Wilson.* "I noticed in her study upstairs, all the pictures she had on the walls — pictures of her former students. And there were framed letters of thanks from those she has taught over the years. And some small gifts. She kept them all, because each and every one of them was special to her, just like each and every student was special to her."

Many of the young faces in the bleachers were tear-streaked. Memories of the kind, beautiful, and sometimes playful teacher filtered through their minds. Julie's disappearance was heavily felt by all.

Chapter Twenty-one

Julie adjusted her arms, trying to bend them just the tiniest little bit further to make herself more comfortable. She was back down in the pit, darkness and quiet all around her and Pamela. The dark seemed even darker than usual, especially since she hadn't been downstairs in…she wasn't sure how many days.

Pam had been less than welcoming when she was brought in and the new girl taken out. Julie felt bad. It had been a very long time since Pam had escaped from the darkness. Figuring her silence meant Pam was angry, Julie left her to her silent protest. Closing her eyes, she tried to relax. She needed to escape.

❧❧❧❧

Remmy worked Josh's morning shift to try and appease him for her lateness the other day. He was such a woman when it came to holding grudges. Remmy had learned that Sunday mornings in Woodland were dead. Everyone was either at church, still in bed, or — that particular Sunday morning — at Julie's memorial service. She'd been invited, but declined. There was no way she was going to celebrate Julie's life when it wasn't over yet, though she was the only one who believed that; the only one other than Grace Cowan.

Remmy bent over the bullpen counter, resting her chin in the palm of her hand. She automatically turned on the pump for tank number 4, the customer using his credit card to pre-pay at the pump. She turned her thoughts inward, focusing on nothing in particular. Suddenly her vision began to fade, the sounds of birds chirping filling her ears, along with the sound of lapping water, and a gentle breeze wafting over her skin.

❦❦❦❦

The sun was so bright and high in the sky, which was the most beautiful color of blue that Julie had ever seen. She couldn't keep the smile from her face, turning it to the heat of the sun, almost able to see the ball of fire blazing through the thin covering of her eyelids.

Opening them, she saw the familiar figure walking toward her, arms out in invitation. Julie didn't hesitate; she wrapped herself in the strength of her dream friend. "Remmy," she murmured, and the embrace tightened.

"I brought a friend," Remmy said into her neck before gently pulling away.

Julie couldn't make out any features. She wished she could; she wanted to see the face of her savior, but it wasn't to be. Looking past Remmy, Julie's gaze fell upon a figure moving through the trees just beyond the field. She could hear raucous barking, two tiny figures running after the larger one. Her heart began to beat loudly within her breast; her breath caught.

Bursting through the trees was a little boy, no older than eight, grinning as he ran, looking back behind him at the two barking dogs that chased him. Two small dogs that looked nearly identical to one another.

❦❦❦❦

Remmy watched Julie closely, seeing the recognition in the green eyes, the face curling into a loving smile. She gasped, running to the boy who called out for her. She looked on, unable to hide her own smile. She was glad she'd been able to bring some friends with her this time.

✻✻✻✻

Julie gathered the boy in her arms and swung him around, the two dogs barking at her feet, pawing at her as they begged for attention.

✻✻✻✻

"Excuse me? What's my total?"

Nearly gasping as she was pulled back into herself, Remmy blinked several times, looking blankly into the face of the man who stood at the counter.

✻✻✻✻

Julie felt the warmth of the sun leave her body, the coldness of the cement and damp cellar engulfing her again. She blinked in confusion as she took in the familiar surroundings. When she realized where she was, that Skylar, Bonnie, and Clyde were gone, hot, bitter tears stung her eyes.

It was only a dream. Only a fucking dream!

✻✻✻✻

Remmy felt her chest tighten as she looked into the dark eyes that stared at her from a handsome, familiar face. He was the first in a line of three people who waited patiently for her to get to them. She looked down at her hands, shocked to find that she had already scanned the few items that he'd set on the counter — a chocolate milk, a pack of gum, and a bag of diapers.

"Forgot to grab these at the grocery store," he said with a charming smile, indicating the diapers. "What's my total?" he asked again.

Remmy looked from the diapers to his eyes again, and suddenly the air was sucked from her lungs, her skin went cold and prickly. She brought a hand up to her throat, fingers caressing the soft skin there...

Can't breathe! Tight. So very tight. Tightening. Soft skin, cool flesh. Lie still for me. Such beauty...

Dark room, naked light bulb. The deadly teeth of a saw cut through the meat easily. The motion stopped. Something hard, something difficult to cut through...

Carpeting, stained...gray with red. Stained...

Open can of something, stirring, stirring. Heat, smells, dog barking...

Brown hair, brown eyes, dark brown, almost black pubic hair, blonde arm hair, brows darker blonde. Amazing. Beautiful...

Can't breathe! I can't breathe!

Remmy gasped, falling back against the other counter, her hands clutching at her throat, eyes unable to leave him, unable to see the concern in his eyes, the flicker of fear, the flicker of uncertainty and curiosity.

"Get away from me," she whispered, voice barely audible. She reached behind her, desperately scrambling to get out of the bullpen, hand blindly tugging at her open polo shirt bearing the store logo and name. Distantly she heard the sound of ripping material. Even more distant, she felt a hand on her back, words spoken that she couldn't understand. "Get away from me!" she screamed, his dark eyes burning a hole into her very soul. "Get away!"

Quiet murmurs filled the space around Remmy. Slowly she began to discern the individual voices — Grace Cowan, and a stranger. Blue eyes slowly blinked open, then closed at the sight of the intense light placed right over her. Squeezing her eyebrows together, she tried to figure out what she was feeling. She had the worst headache of her life, centralized in a quarter-sized area dead center of her forehead. With a soft groan, she brought a hand up, surprised when she didn't feel some sort of injury.

"Take it easy, Remmy."

Remmy opened her eyes. Grace entered the ring of light above her. She could see the concern on the woman's face. "Where am I, and why am I here?"

"You're in the Emergency Room at Saint Mercy's," Grace said, a warm hand resting on Remmy's shoulder. "What's the last thing you remember?"

"I was at work," Remmy said, concentrating on trying to remember, trying to bring back her day. "I turned on the pumps. Some guy paid outside, with his card..." She knew there was more after that, but just couldn't bring it up. It was almost as though there was a haze or a fog in her brain, sitting right on top of the events that followed. "Shit. I don't know, Grace." Remmy squeezed her eyes shut, bringing her hand up to her forehead. "My head hurts too bad to think straight." She groaned. "Why the hell am I in the ER? Isn't that a little drastic?"

Grace smiled. "You scared the hell out of your customers. They thought you were having a seizure or something. Someone called the paramedics."

"Shit," Remmy said. "Joan is going to have my ass."

"Joan is right outside." Grace left out some of the

choice, colorful comments Joan had made as they waited to see Remmy. Joan told Grace that she was about at the end of her rope. Yes, she understood Remmy had "special issues", as she'd put it, but also stated that it was a business, and anything could have happened while Remmy had her episode, and that they were lucky they hadn't been robbed blind before Joan could get there and get someone to cover.

"Send her in," Remmy said with a long sigh. She dreaded this, especially after the conversation they'd had the other day. "Shit," she said after Grace left her alone in her little cubicle. How the hell was she supposed to explain to Joan what happened when she had no idea herself? The only thing she did know was that she felt exhausted—mentally, emotionally, and physically. "Ugh."

There was a knock on the wall outside of Remmy's curtained-off cubicle. "Remmy?"

"Come on in, Joan."

The curtain was pushed aside and Joan stepped around it. Her face showed concern, affection, and irritation. "How are you?" she asked softly, standing next to the narrow bed. She looked Remmy over, taking in her still body and very pale face. Dark circles underneath Remmy's eyes were stark against the pallor.

"I guess I'm okay. Got quite the migraine right now, but other than that, just peachy keen."

Joan sighed, arms crossing over her chest. "This isn't the time, but we need to talk about the situation, Remmy. Figure something out."

Remmy nodded, turning away. She knew she had disappointed Joan, but couldn't help feeling slightly angry. She had never felt so out of control in all her life, and for someone who had always been self-reliant, never leaning on anyone or anything, this was one of the most difficult things to swallow. She very much felt she was a prisoner alongside Julie. "I know," she said, her voice resigned. "I didn't mean for this to happen, Joan."

"I know that, Remmy." Joan took one of the fluttering hands in both of hers. The skin was cool to the touch, so she chafed it. "Get some rest. We'll talk later."

Remmy nodded, trying to keep her tears at bay. She chewed on her bottom lip to keep it from trembling like a child's. Once she was alone, she took a deep breath, a single, bitter tear blazing a track down her cheek and into her ear, making her shiver.

Grace stood outside of the ER, waiting for Joan. She saw her step back into the waiting room and Grace stood to get her attention. They met halfway across the large space.

"What happened?" Joan asked. She thought the detective looked as haggard as Remmy did.

"I'm not sure. Remmy's not sure, either."

"I'm worried about her. I think she needs to be taken off this case. You guys have put so much damn pressure on her."

Knowing that Joan really didn't know what she was talking about, Grace pushed her anger down, though she couldn't completely keep it out of her voice.

"Mrs. Watson, Remmy came to us with her abilities. We've got three women right now who need her. I don't think I could make Remmy walk away from this any more than she could make herself. She can't control this ability she has. You have to understand that."

"I do understand that, but you have to understand that I have a business that needs to be run. I can't have her freaking out every couple of days, or waltzing in whenever the hell she wants to because she's had some vision!"

Grace crossed her arms over her chest, listening to the rant. She understood it, and racked her brain, trying to think of some way to compromise. They desperately needed Remmy on the case, but she also couldn't allow Remmy to destroy her life while helping them.

"Remmy is a wonderful person and an amazing worker, but I can't have her in the store by herself if she's not going to be reliable. It seems this is getting worse for her." She met dark eyes. "Is it?"

Grace nodded. "I believe it is, yes."

"I don't know what to do. I'm not a heartless bitch, Detective. I'm not going to just fire her. But..."

"Remmy rents a room from you, right?" At Joan's nod, she continued. "I guess she still has to have a place to stay, even if she has no job. What does she pay in rent every month?"

Joan was baffled. "Three hundred. Why?"

Grace reached into the inside pocket of her wrinkled blazer and pulled out her checkbook. She flipped it open to a blank check. Clicking her pen into action, she quickly scrawled out a check for six hundred dollars. Holding it out, she met Joan's gaze, daring her not to take it. "I need her."

Joan took the check, unsure what to think. "You want me to fire her?"

"Do whatever you need to do. Give her some time off, a leave of absence, whatever. It may actually help us speed things up if I've got her full time, with no other distractions."

Joan stared at the check. Was this fair to Remmy? With a sigh, she nodded. "Alright."

Chapter Twenty-two

Julie opened her eyes, blinking away the headache she always woke up with after being brought upstairs. She had no idea what the hell he used, but ugh! She could feel she wasn't alone. Shocking.

Turning her head at the sound of footsteps, Julie saw him stepping out of the bathroom, rubbing his freshly washed hair with a clean, white towel. He smiled when he saw she was awake.

"Good morning, Julie," he said, walking over to the bed, dressed in jeans and bare-chested. He leaned down and placed a kiss on her cheek. "I need you to get showered, and quickly. I've got a treat for you."

His wide smile made Julie flinch. *Now* what?

He unbound her wrists and she immediately drew her arms down to rub some circulation back into them. With a groan, she pulled herself into a sitting position. Her head felt fuzzy and thick, her mouth as dry as the Sahara. She watched as he opened and closed drawers in the tall dresser for a moment, pulling a t-shirt from one, socks from another. Finally she mustered the strength to stand, though she was wobbly. He hurried over to her, catching her around the waist.

"Easy," he said, making sure she was steady before releasing her.

Julie slowly made her way to the bathroom, where steam from his recent shower filled her lungs, making it difficult to breathe for a moment. She went to the toilet, lifted the lid, and sat. Resting her elbows on her thighs, she cradled her head in her hands for a moment, trying to force her fuzzy thoughts into some order. When she glanced up at the bathroom window, she noted with bitter amusement that bars had been applied to the outside.

"Bastard," she murmured.

The warm water felt wonderful on her skin. She was so thirsty, she opened her mouth and welcomed a mouthful inside. Smoothing her greasy hair back from her face, she turned her back to the spray, lowering her head so the water pounded her upper back, which hurt constantly from her arms being always raised over her head. She rolled her head around, moaning softly at the relief.

"Quick. Make it quick," Sergio said from the bathroom doorway before leaving her alone again.

Julie used every bit of willpower she had to not tell him to go fuck himself. Instead, she scrubbed her body, washing away not only the grime, but also his touch. She wondered if she would ever feel clean again, even if she took seven showers a day.

The doctor insisted that Remmy rest, and he had kept her for longer than two hours. Now she was rested out; she just wanted to go home. She made her way through the ER, relieved that the nurses and doctors were too busy to notice. Slipping out into the waiting room, she was equally glad to see that those who had brought her in had left. She thought she remembered Grace coming in while she dozed, and telling her she would be back for her later. No matter. Remmy didn't want to wait, nor did she want to hear a lecture about leaving before she was discharged.

She walked over to the front desk and asked the nurse if she could use the phone. Use granted, she dialed Roman's cell number.

"Hey," she said when he answered. "Can I get a lift from you real quick?" Smiling into the receiver, she thanked him and hung up the phone.

⁂

Julie stepped out of the shower, glad to be clean again, however temporarily. She used the brush she found on the counter and brushed the shaggy strands into some kind of order. She needed a haircut, hair in her eyes and tickling her nose. She wished so badly she could put some clothes on, something, anything. She was surprised that he wasn't waiting for her, but she didn't hear any sound at all coming from the bedroom.

Stepping around the corner, Julie's stomach seized when she realized the bedroom was empty; the door leading to the rest of the house was open. She knew it was too much to hope that he'd had a heart attack and died. Her quick gaze around the room showed a ring of keys casually tossed atop the dresser. She didn't have time to contemplate them, as he was suddenly standing in the doorway, watching her.

Not waiting to be told to lie down so he could cuff her, Julie walked toward the bed. She was surprised when he caught her wrist, which made her flinch, the skin was so raw.

"Come with me," he said.

Sergio was nervous as he led Julie through the bedroom doorway, down the hall and toward the kitchen. She had asked nicely, so he would be nice in return.

Julie watched, wide-eyed as they passed through

to new parts of the house. In the living room, she noticed the deadbolt lock on the inside of the front door, no doubt locked, as well as iron bars on the large picture window. Everything was meticulously kept, though she was surprised to see batches of things lined neatly on shelves.

"You have quite the collections," she said quietly as she was forced to sit in a kitchen chair. She noted the shelves filled with old newspapers, beer cans, and spotlessly clean bottles of many types. She was intrigued by the rows of quarters that were glued to one wall. *What the hell is that about?*

Sergio said nothing. He preferred to think of his things as just that—his things. He placed a sizzling steak onto a plate for himself and half of a steak on a second plate, along with mashed potatoes, peas, and a roll, for her. Setting the plate in front of Julie, he was pleased to see her reaction: her eyes widened and her nostrils flared, as though taking in the wonderful aromas.

Julie couldn't take her eyes off the feast before her. It looked like so much food! Her mouth began to water, which made her angry at herself, almost as if she was betraying herself by wanting anything he offered. He sat across from her at the table made for two and scooted his chair closer. She wasn't bound, and wasn't sure what to make of that fact. She had no idea what to do or say. Would she say something that would anger him, make him tie her up? Rape her again, or even kill her? A thin layer of cold sweat beaded on her forehead.

"Eat," Sergio said, nodding at the place setting that was laid out on a folded napkin next to the plate. He watched with satisfaction as Julie obeyed. He loved to watch her, and allowing her this pleasure was very generous and very out of character for him. But, any means of escape was securely locked up, so she wouldn't be able to wander outside of his protective sights.

⚘⚘⚘⚘

Roman pulled up in front of the main entrance to the ER in record time, his car skidding slightly as he came to a stop. Remmy climbed in, exhausted and mentally drained.

"Where to?" Roman asked as she buckled herself in.

"I guess home," she said, head resting back against the seat. She sighed heavily, glad to be in familiar territory again. She really hated hospitals. As the car began to move, the gentle rocking lulled her to sleep.

⚘⚘⚘⚘

Julie took her time with the steak, though not necessarily to savor its rich flavor, which she had to admit, tasted like a little bit of heaven. She was trying to forestall the after-dinner activities. She had no desire to have that monster touch her; the thought made her skin crawl.

He watched as Julie took each bite slowly, chewing the succulent meat and swallowing, enchanted by every move. "Are you enjoying yourself?" Sergio asked, resting his cheek in the palm of his hand, his dinner long since finished.

Julie nearly choked on her bite of food. "Very good," she said.

"Good. I figure, we'll relax for a while when you finish, then later we'll have dessert." Sergio's heavy brows drew together. "You do like chocolate, don't you?"

Julie took a sip of water before answering. "Did

you get enough for us all?" she asked quietly, trying her best to not look away or let her true feelings show. For a moment she regretted her words; a darkness seemed to fall over his already dark eyes, but then it passed, followed by a smile.

"That would be a nice treat, wouldn't it? I'm sure they'd enjoy it."

Julie smiled. It was difficult, but she managed.

⁂

Silver and shiny. Suffocated light crept in through heavy drapes, bouncing off row upon row of quarters glued to the plaster behind them. Like little round soldiers, they marched across the wall, ending at a calendar, heavily marked in small red writing. Nothing discernible, nothing making sense. The sink, a double stainless steel model, was polished to a shine.

A kitchen. Linoleum tile was old, bubbled up in places, the pattern long since rubbed away by shoe tread and bare feet. The piss-yellow fridge door was covered with alphabet magnets, some forming words, mostly jumbled together to form incoherent sentences — no real rhyme or reason, other than they'd been grouped according to color: red blended into blue, which led to yellow, then green, and finally, orange, with purple as the caboose. An army of plastic letters to perhaps go to war against the quarters, all heads up.

Remmy's eyes opened, a gasp releasing from her throat. She sat up in the seat, looking around, but only seeing the quarters, so shiny.

A table, set for two. Light from a window glinting off a fork raised to a mouth. Steak, juicy and tender. Steak.

Remmy gasped again, her mouth working in reflex

to the taste of the meat in her mouth. She looked around again, this time seeing the scenery whizzing by. She saw they were on the main street of the town, about to turn off onto the road that led to her house.

"Pull over, Roman; give me the keys."

⁂

Wondering if she was to spend the rest of her life that way, Julie lay on her back as his mouth and hands freely roamed over her body. She wanted to buck her hips and knock him to the floor, but that would be insane. She knew retaliation would come quickly, and likely would be deadly. Instead, she lay there, wrists bound to the headboard, eyes focused up toward the window. The blinds were open, so she could see the sky beyond. It looked cold out, the sky gray with heavy clouds, promising snow. At that moment she would have done anything to feel the snow against her, the fresh air.

Sergio took his time, wanting to explore every inch of Julie's flesh. She was so beautiful, her skin pale and soft. His excitement was rising with every touch, every taste of her skin, which mingled with the remnant taste of the steak in his mouth, making him want to eat her alive.

She felt him kiss his way up her stomach, roughly fondling her breasts, his erection scraping along her leg the entire way until finally he looked down into her face. To her surprise, he reached up and unlocked the handcuffs, his hand sliding down her arm before it rested once again on the mattress beneath them.

"I want you to touch me," he said, his voice gravelly with excitation.

❦ ❦ ❦ ❦

"This is crazy, Remmy!" Roman said, stopped at the curb. He was shocked by the look in the eyes of his normally laid-back friend. "Then again, so are you," he muttered, climbing out of the car and jogging around the front, passing Remmy as she did the same. He got into the passenger side as Remmy slammed the driver's side door.

"Buckle up," she said, gunning the engine as she squealed away from the curb and headed toward the highway. Her heart pounded with a need engrained so deeply within her that she couldn't ignore it any more than she could forget to breathe.

❦ ❦ ❦ ❦

He moved between her legs, her hands resting tentatively on his shoulders. Julie continued to stare out at the sky. It wasn't long before he groaned loudly and his movements stopped. She returned her gaze to his, knowing he would expect her to. He grinned, sweat beading his brow. She kept her face expressionless.

"I can't seem to get enough of you," he whispered as he nuzzled her neck. She rolled her eyes, wincing as he pulled out of her. He raised himself up on his arms, looking down between their bodies, liking the look of it. He was insatiable, could feel himself becoming hard again. An idea grew with his smile.

❦ ❦ ❦ ❦

Remmy hit the turn signal that would get them onto the highway. "Call this number." She recited

Grace's phone number for him to dial on his cell. "You tell her exactly where we're going, every turn we take."

Roman nodded, putting the phone to his ear.

❧ ❧ ❧ ❧

Grace sat among the rapt audience at the local community college, the sound of her goddaughter's piano playing filling her ears. The girl was eleven, and already quite the little virtuoso. LaTisha had asked her months ago if she would attend the recital, and there was no way she could tell her no. She could never refuse the girl anything. Grace and LaTisha's mom, Andrea, had been best friends since they were eight years old. She loved Andrea's daughter like she was her own. As much as she was enjoying the music, she kept glancing down at her wristwatch, fidgeting at the need to get back to the office.

"She's really good," Grace's husband whispered in the dark auditorium, their fingers tightly entwined. He was happy to have his wife to himself for a little while.

Grace nodded. "She's great."

The mood in the silent audience was disturbed for a moment when "Achey, Breaky Heart" began to play. It happened to coincide with the pealing of Beethoven's "Moonlight Sonata", and Grace snatched her cell from her inside pocket, glancing at the visual display before flipping the phone open. She ignored her husband's glare as she put the phone to her ear. "Detective Cowan." Grace listened to the impassioned words of the young man on the line. "Okay. Stay with me. Hold on a minute." Grace leaned over and placed a kiss of apology on her husband's cheek then hurried out of the auditorium.

❧❧❧❧

Sergio straddled Julie's hips, careful not to put too much weight on her. He ran his hands over her stomach and chest, spending ample time on her breasts. Finally he slid a couple of pillows beneath her head and scooted himself into position.

"I want you to take me in your mouth," he said, voice trembling. He reached for her hands, placing them around his shaft, eyes closing at the wonderful sensations as she began to stroke him. "Oh, yeah, just like that," he groaned.

❧❧❧❧

Remmy could feel her anger building, a hot wave scorching her brain, but just enough out of reach that she had to concentrate on it, reach for it. As she sped down the highway, she vaguely heard Roman speaking into his phone, giving the name of the road markers they passed. She drove on, her head pounding, a steady beat inside keeping her going, keeping her following the line of anger and fire that stretched out before her.

❧❧❧❧

Grace jumped into her Ford Explorer. Eyes on the road as she pulled out of the parking lot, she reached over to open the glove compartment and pull out the service revolver she kept there. It was loaded. Setting it on the passenger seat, she returned her attention to the phone.

"Okay, Roman. Now where?"

Remmy sped down the highway until suddenly the intense anger began to wane, as though she had left it at the last exit. *No, no, no. No you fucking don't!* She didn't see Roman reach out to grab for anything he could to hold on as she made a u-turn, cars honking at her as she turned around, the small compact car's tires squealing in protest.

"Wait. Now we're headed back south," Roman gasped into the phone. "Jesus! She's gonna kill us."

Julie stared at the penis, so close to her face, her fingers easing around it, stroking it to life. She could feel his weight on her body, his need pulsing in her hand. Closing her eyes, she raised her head from the pillows, opened her mouth and took him inside, just as he directed.

Sergio groaned loud and deep, his hips thrusting weakly as the warmth enveloped him. He brought one hand down to Julie's head, the other holding onto the headboard, where she had been cuffed so many times. "God, yes," he moaned.

Grace swung the Explorer around in a parking lot, trying to visualize what Roman was telling her. His directions were erratic. She plowed down the highway at ridiculous speeds, a swirling red beacon mounted to the roof of the Explorer with magnetic force.

Remmy barely had time to flip her turn signal on before she turned left, taking them off the highway and out of Woodland. She pressed harder on the gas pedal, the car's engine groaning with the exertion of trying to keep up with her demands. She could feel a pulse drawing her down the street, a living, breathing creature that whispered in her ear, pulling her on.

Stopping at a stop sign, Remmy saw she could go left or forward; the right was denied by an Off Limits sign and a field beyond. She chewed on her bottom lip, uncertain. She could hear her heart pounding in her head, the now-familiar pain pulsing dead center in her forehead. A glance to the left made her feel cold. Looking straight ahead, she heard a soft, pleading whisper. She gunned it.

❧❧❧❧

Julie bobbed her head, nearly gagging more than once. His hips were moving nearly non-stop as she sucked him, her hands resting on his hairy thighs. She opened her eyes and looked up along the length of his torso. His Adam's apple moved convulsively as his head arched back, eyes closed and mouth open in rapturous pleasure.

Outside the window, Julie could hear the laughter of a child, one calling out to another.

Skylar grinned at her, his smile melting her heart. He ran toward her, two barking shadows behind him. She felt safe, warm, a presence standing next to her.

Remmy...

She bobbed her head again, taking in the length of him, feeling his engorged flesh against her tongue.

❧❧❧❧

"Wait, wait, no, I was wrong. Don't turn right on Gacey, turn left, turn left!" Roman yelled into the phone, trying to keep up with Remmy's driving. "Then go slight...right! Go slight right onto Ridgeway."

❧❧❧❧

Grace was fighting with the phone, trying to keep it in her hand with no time to attach her Bluetooth earpiece. She sounded the siren as she plowed through a red traffic light then switched it off the moment she was through, the red light spinning. The tires on the Explorer squealed as she took the hard leftt onto Gacey Avenue, gunning the engine.

❧❧❧❧

Julie used her tongue to figure out how far the shaft was into her mouth. She could feel the tip bumping against the roof of her mouth. Looking up at him, she saw his head fall back again. Her hands tightening their grip on his thighs, with every ounce of strength the steak had given her, she bit down, struggled not to gag as her teeth cut through the skin and warm, salty blood filled her mouth.

Sergio's eyes shot open, a scream escaping his lips. He had never felt a pain like the hot fire that engorged his penis, a pain that shot all the way into his stomach. Blackness blurred his vision, shooting red streaks across his closed lids.

Julie used every bit of her strength to shove him off of her, the man rolling onto his side as he clutched his damaged penis. Spitting out the mouthful of blood and flesh, she got her bearings. She shot up from the bed, whimpering in fear as he screamed again. She was just barely able to dodge his arm as it swung blindly for her. She snatched the keys from the dresser and ran.

❧❧❧❧

Roman was startled as Remmy suddenly cried out, her chest heaving with every breath she took. "You okay, Rem?" he asked. She didn't answer, instead taking a left turn at an insane rate of speed. "Left on Fish!" he yelled into the phone.

❧❧❧❧

Julie fought hysteria as she reached the front door, trying desperately to keep herself together long enough to figure out how to get out. She could still hear his screams coming from the bedroom. Trembling hands wrestled with the key ring, and she cried out as she dropped it onto the hardwood floor.

"Fuck." She picked them up, sparing a glance over her shoulder. She heard movement in the bedroom; something slammed. "Fuck, fuck, fuck!"

She tried to insert the first key on the ring; it wouldn't even slide in. She continued down the ring, trying every single key until one fit into the lock.

Sergio was trembling from pain as he slid his jeans up his legs, nearly falling over as he tugged them up over his crotch. Almost instantly, blood seeped through the denim. He staggered over to the dresser and yanked open the top drawer. His .38 gleamed back up at him.

❧❧❧❧

Grace was worried, when she saw the burned rubber as she turned onto Fish Street. Assuming it was from Remmy's ride, she at least knew she was on the right track.

She took a moment to assess the area, one she had never been in. There were lots of trees, almost a woodsy atmosphere. The houses, rustic and hidden by trees and foliage, were further and further apart.

"Right on Rader Boulevard, not Avenue. There's two," Roman said, his voice high-pitched and sounding extremely stressed across the line.

"Got it," Grace said, plowing on.

※ ※ ※ ※

Remmy's thoughts were in a whirlwind, single-minded determination drawing her closer and closer. She was sweating profusely, her hands almost slipping on the steering wheel. She felt as if she might have a heart attack, her heart was beating so fiercely. Fear filled her, almost to an incapacitating level. She brought a hand up to swipe at the sweat that dripped into her eyes.

※ ※ ※ ※

Julie shrieked in victory as the lock clicked open. Leaving the keys in the door, she swung it open, and found herself faced with a glass screen door, which wouldn't open.

"Come on!" she yelled, slamming her fist against it. Then she saw the lock, and quickly switched it over to unlocked. The air was frigid against her naked skin, the blood on her mouth and chin catching the chill and making her face even colder. The street before her was empty, except for the house she could barely see through some dense trees, the children's voices still audible.

Julie didn't even feel the snow as she stepped down onto the porch, her heart racing.

❧ ❧ ❧ ❧

Remmy saw a figure up ahead, a woman, a naked woman, running across one of the yards. Pulling the car to a stop, tires squealing in protest as she swung the driver's side door open, she leapt out and ran forward.

Roman opened his door and stepped out, completely confused. His eyes widened as a man stumbled out onto the porch — one hand holding a gun, the other clutching his blood-soaked crotch.

A shot rang out and the naked woman screamed. She fled toward Remmy and threw herself into the open arms, her fear making her frantic as she clawed for safety.

Another shot rang out and Remmy held Julie close, her eyes glued to the man on the porch. He was firing blindly, apparently in an immense amount of pain. Finally his gaze met Remmy's, and he swung the gun around.

❧ ❧ ❧ ❧

Grace saw Roman duck down behind his open door, and barely had time to wonder why before she heard a shot fired. She threw the cell phone onto the passenger seat and grabbed her gun.

❧ ❧ ❧ ❧

Remmy saw his finger tighten on the trigger and, without thinking, she turned herself, crushing Julie to her. The pain scorched like fire through her back. Not a sound escaped her as her legs crumpled, and she and Julie fell to the snow-covered yard.

❧❧❧❧

Gun leveled in firing position, Grace squeezed off four rounds, each hitting the man squarely in the chest. He jerked under their impact, then fell, the gun flying from his hands to become a shadow in the snow.

❧❧❧❧

The doors of the ER burst open, doctors, nurses and paramedics barking out questions and answers. The woman on the gurney—an oxygen mask taped around her face, skin extremely pale—was jostled during the rush to get her inside. Her bloody shirt was cut open and removed, and her chest was examined before she was turned over. The entry wound was small and deadly; there was no exit wound. She was rushed off for emergency surgery.

Roman sat beside Joan Watson in one of the uncomfortable plastic chairs in the waiting room. Joan was chewing on one of her fingernails, not sure what to feel: guilt at being so hard on Remmy; amazement at what she had managed to do; or fear for the life of the young woman she had grown to care about.

Roman was even paler than the typically fair skin of a true redhead. A uniformed police officer sat across from him, pad balanced on his thigh as he took down the young man's statement. Roman was badly shaken, his hands trembling in his lap. He was grateful when Joan reached over and took one of his hands in her own. She returned his smile, pleased to be of some help to someone.

The doors whooshed open. A stunning breath of cold air mixed with snow was admitted with the frenzied entry of a man on a mission. Matt Wilson sped to the front desk, eyes wild and red from crying. "I'm Matt Wilson. My sister!" he exclaimed to the nurse behind the counter. "Julie Wilson…where is she?"

The nurse didn't even have to check her computer. All of the staff knew about the remarkable events of the past hour. "Sir, she's in with the doctors right now. If you'll take a seat, I promise I'll let you know as soon as we have any news, okay?" She kept her voice kind but firm, aware of the tentative hope in his eyes. He smiled weakly and nodded.

"As soon as I can see her—"

"I'll let you know." She smiled then turned back to her computer, letting him know their conversation was over.

Matt ran a hand through his tousled hair. Filled with adrenaline and energy, he felt like a caged animal. Instead of pacing, he plopped down in one of the chairs and rested his head against the wall, his hands twitching nervously on his spread knees. He ran a hand through his hair again, his nerves getting the best of him as his foot tapped an endless beat on the tile floor.

His grin was huge, though cautious, as he reviewed the life changing phone call.

❧ ❧ ❧ ❧

"Hello?" he said, answering his cell phone, surprised it had rung rather than his house phone. Skylar called for him in the background, the boy anxious to finish their video game marathon.

"Matt, it's Detective Cowan."

"Yeah, Grace. How are you?"
"I'm ecstatic. Are you sitting down?"

❧❧❧❧

It was a damn good thing the kitchen chair had been nearby, or he would have fallen, for sure. He couldn't believe his ears when Grace told him that Julie had been found, alive. He had immediately started to tremble, afraid to believe those precious words. Stupidly, he said, *"But, we had a memorial service for her."* He could still hear the woman's laugh in his ear.

Uncertain about what Julie's condition might be, he didn't want to risk exposing his son to something unpleasant. He had quickly arranged for Skylar to stay with Mrs. Huxby, next door, and then rushed to the hospital.

Unable to sit still, he rose from his chair, only then noticing Joan sitting next to the redheaded kid from the coffeehouse where he and Remmy had met a few times. He saw that Joan had noticed him, as well. She hurried over to him and clasped him in a tight embrace.

"Oh, Matt," Joan said, squeezing tighter. "I'm so happy for you!"

He pressed his face against the neck of a woman who was a veritable stranger to him. "Thank you," he murmured. It felt good for someone else to know, too, and for them to be just as excited as he was. Hell, it felt good to be hugged. They parted, and Matt grinned down at her. "How is she?" he asked, referring to Remmy. Grace hadn't given him any details, just that Remmy had been hurt. He was surprised to see tears well up in Joan's eyes.

"I don't know," she said, a hand moving up to her mouth. "She was shot. They rushed her into surgery."

With a shrug, she sighed. "We're not sure."

"She's a hero, Joan. She really is."

Joan nodded vigorously. "Oh, yes. She is."

"Mr. Wilson?"

Matt turned toward the admitting nurse and she gestured for him to come over. "Let me know how Remmy is." He squeezed Joan's hand then went over to the information desk, his face expectant.

"Your sister's been moved from Emergency to the fourth floor, where she's in with a psychologist. They said she'd be finished in about fifteen minutes, so why don't you go on up. Go to the nurses' station on that floor, and they can direct you from there."

"Thank you so much." He leaned over and gave the blushing nurse a kiss on the cheek. Matt was a blur as he hurried to the bank of elevators. The motor couldn't go fast enough for him as he kept his eyes riveted on the numbers that lit up at every floor. The car stopped on the third floor and he nearly growled at the woman who stepped aboard. Finally they lurched upward again, and the doors slid open on the fourth floor with a cheerful ding.

Matt looked around, trying to locate the nurses' station. When finally he found it, he waited impatiently for the nurse behind the desk to get off the phone. She cradled the receiver and looked at him expectantly.

"I'm Matt Wilson. I'm here to see my sister, Julie Wilson."

"Ah, yes," the plump nurse said, with the same sympathetic smile as the nurse downstairs. "Dr. Corregan is still in with her, but if you go straight down that hall, she's in room 431, on the left."

"Thanks." Matt was off like a shot, looking at each numbered door until he came to the right room. He nearly fell to his knees when he heard Julie's voice just on the other side of the closed door. Bringing a hand up, he cleared his throat before knocking. The talking subsided and the sound of footsteps approached the door. When it opened, a tall brunette stood on the other side, looking very professional and officious in her green skirt suit. She smiled politely then turned back toward the room.

"I'll call you and we'll make an appointment for this week, Julie. Okay?"

"Thanks, Dr. Corregan," a quiet voice replied.

Knowing that his reunion with his sister was only seconds away, Matt let his excitement grow. Dr. Haley Corregan excused herself as she squeezed past him. Matt pushed the door the rest of the way open, not even noticing as it slowly swung shut behind him. The hospital room was dim, the lights turned off except for the reading light on the wall above the head of the narrow bed. The small, extremely thin figure on the bed was resting against the stacked pillows. She wore a hospital gown and booties.

Julie's eyes lifted at hearing someone enter as Dr. Corregan was leaving. She gasped, unable to get off the bed fast enough. Matt caught her in his arms, holding her painfully tightly to his body. She let out a sob, and so did he.

Matt buried his face in her hair, her fingers claw-like as they wrapped around his shoulder. She was so tiny. "Oh God, Julie," he whispered, voice breaking. He heard her sniffle as she clasped him tighter. "I thought I lost you."

Eyes closed, Julie was unable to speak as she absorbed the feel of her brother — his warmth and familiar scent. Finally he pulled back, eyes red-rimmed, face wet with his own tears. His eyes devoured her as he held onto her shoulders. She smiled weakly up at him, pushing his ever-shaggy bangs out of his eyes. He smiled at the familiar gesture — she was always telling him he needed a haircut.

"You're so thin," he said. The thin gown dwarfed her already petite frame. "Are you okay?" he asked, hugging her again before he placed a kiss on top of her head, then helped her climb back onto the bed and tucked her in.

"I'll live," she said, her voice still raw from screaming and crying.

"Yeah, you will." Matt smiled, holding her hand securely in his. "You're so strong." He studied her, not sure whether or not he should ask. He should probably speak to Dr. Corregan first.

"Where's Skylar?"

"He's at home with Mrs. Huxby. I wasn't sure what I'd find," he said, shrugging his shoulders. "He doesn't know yet." He grinned. "Figured you could surprise him when we bring you home."

Chapter Twenty-three

The body on the porch had been bagged and loaded into the ME's van, and Grace and the backup officers entered the house. There was no need to protect the crime scene, Grace just wanted to see what hell Julie had been living in, and if Remmy was right in her other visions.

She was careful not to step in the trail of blood left by the gunman, who they still had not identified. It was curious, his collections of things. She fingered a few, simply glanced at others. She turned down the hall, noting that only one bedroom was being used as a bedroom. The blood spots on the sheet seemed to pool up toward the pillows still stacked against the headboard.

Grace had to smirk to herself—every male present had groaned when they discovered the extent of the man's injuries. The bleeding was profuse. She wondered how long it would have taken him to die if she hadn't shot him. She grimaced when she saw a puddle of blood, already congealing, and some flesh at the center of it.

"Jesus," she muttered, moving out of the bedroom and back toward the living room, bypassing it and heading into what proved to be the kitchen. Dirty dishes were stacked neatly in the sink, though it looked as though they'd been rinsed and were ready to be loaded into the dishwasher.

"What's up with all the magnets?" one of the officers asked. Grace shook her head, clueless.

Continuing on, she found a set of wooden stairs that led down to a basement. She held her breath, gun still in her hand should she need it. Remmy repeatedly told her that Julie and the others were being kept in a space that looked like a basement. The victims hadn't been found upstairs, so if they were there at all, this would likely be the place.

The basement was very dark, the one light bulb at the center of the room doing little to chase away the shadows. Grace felt a little creeped out, like she was down there going after Buffalo Bill from *Silence of the Lambs*. The room they were in didn't seem out of the ordinary: boxes neatly stacked, normal storage. She looked at the two doors off to the left. An officer ducked his head into one.

"Laundry room," he said, leaving the door open.

They all focused on the remaining door. Grace waited patiently for one of the officers to open it then they all stepped inside the second room. It was much like the first, just smaller.

"Fe, fi, fo, fum," an officer muttered, indicating the smaller door at the far end of the room. They chuckled, which helped to break the tension.

Grace felt her stomach tighten, her instincts screaming out at her, though not trying to warn her of danger. She walked over to the door, hand reaching out for the knob. It squeaked slightly as she turned it, the door sticking as it was pushed open. A horrendous stench wafted out to the officers.

"Jesus."

Grace ignored the smell, bringing up her flashlight to reach through the deep darkness.

"There's a light bulb chain right above the door," a woman said from within, startling everyone.

Grace's heart rate picked up as she stepped inside

the room and shone her beam up, looking around for the chain. She reached up and felt the stickiness of a spider web, which she had to shake off, as she was terrified of the eight-legged bastards, then finally grabbed the cool chain. Tugging gently, the room was suddenly awash in dim light.

"Jesus," the officer said again as he stepped inside behind Grace. His eyes were huge as he studied the two women who were chained to the wall. Both women were naked, one extremely thin, the other... "That's Cameron Sanchez!"

"And that's Pam Beecham," Grace whispered, wishing so badly that she could reach out and squeeze Remmy until it hurt. "I cannot fucking believe it. She did it."

❧❧❧❧

The monitors beeped constantly, allowing the surgeon to keep track of the status of his patient's vital signs. The incision on Remmy's back was being retracted by two surgical nurses so he could probe for the bullet. X-rays had shown it was lodged inside the spleen. It took more than two hours of painstaking searching to find it, and then another hour to remove it. The spleen would have to be removed as well.

"Adjust that light over here, Carl," the doctor said, words slightly muffled by his surgical mask. Everyone watched with breath held as, with a clink, the slug was dropped into a stainless steel pan.

❧❧❧❧

Joan had nodded off in the waiting room while watching a re-run of a nighttime drama on the television mounted in the corner. There had been no news on Remmy's condition. It had been a long afternoon, which was swiftly turning to evening.

She was roused by two people racing into the ER—a couple, both looking to be in their late thirties or early forties, the woman near hysterics. They hurried directly to the nurse at the information desk. Joan was unable to hear their conversation, but the couple looked familiar to her. She gasped as she realized she had seen them on TV. They were the parents of the missing girl, Cameron Sanchez.

"What the hell?" she said, sitting up a little straighter. Her gaze was drawn once more to the sliding doors when a large group entered, cameras on shoulders, microphones ready to be thrust into faces. Joan rolled her eyes. "Son-of-a-bitch. Vultures."

The doors to the ER were pushed open and a man in scrubs walked out. He spotted Joan and headed her way. "You're waiting for word on Remmy Foster, right?" he asked.

Joan immediately stood, nodding. "How is she?"

The press got wind of their conversation and soon they were surrounded. "Please!" the doctor said, obviously irritated. "Hospital personnel will give you a full report." The surgeon grabbed Joan's arm and led her back through the ER doors, where the media wasn't allowed. "Vultures," he muttered, not seeing Joan's grin. He led her to an empty part of the hallway and stopped. "The bullet lodged in her spleen, which I had to remove to stop the bleeding. She lost a great deal of blood, but she's doing great. She's in ICU right now. You can go see her."

Joan sighed, long and loud. "Thank you, Doctor."

With a kind smile, he told her how to get to the ICU, then walked down the hall and disappeared through a door.

Joan blew out a breath and headed in the direction he had indicated. Roman had gone home with his family some time ago, promising to return later. Once she saw Remmy, she would call his cell and let him know how she was doing. Doug was out running errands and she wished to God he was home. She needed him.

With every step she took down the long, highly-polished hallway, Joan felt guilt creeping over her. She'd believed Remmy possessed some sort of ability, but to what degree, she honestly hadn't known. There was a hardened, cynical part of her that had wondered—for a moment—if it was all just a show. After all, Remmy was a drifter. Maybe this was the game she played everywhere, leaving when things got too hot. Now, heading toward the nurses' station on the ICU floor, she felt like an asshole. She supposed she was just glad she'd never gotten a chance to have that conversation with Remmy about the job.

The ICU rooms were glassed-in cubicles set up in an octagonal shape around the nurses' station, so patients could be observed at all times. Joan was given directions to Remmy's room. It was dark, the shade drawn on the window and the overhead light turned off. Remmy's pale profile had an eerie green hue from the screens of the machines around her. Her long body was covered by a thin, white blanket. She was laid out on her stomach, her right arm curled up by her face, the left dangling near the edge of the mattress. An I.V. was taped into place on the top of her right hand. Her eyes were closed, the skin around them very bruised.

"Oh, Remmy," Joan whispered, taking the pale left hand in her own. She caressed the back of her hand with her thumb, eyes never leaving Remmy's face. She wished those beautiful blue eyes would open, but they remained closed. Joan's gaze swept over the rest of her body. A thick bandage and wrapping had been applied to her back. The hospital gown Remmy wore was tied loosely for easy access.

A nurse entered, clipboard in hand. She began to write down Remmy's vitals.

"How long will she be in here?" Joan asked, her voice church-quiet.

"Probably just tonight," the nurse said. "The doctor wanted to make sure all her vitals stay within range. She'll probably be moved to a regular room tomorrow." She shrugged. "Be there for a few days."

Joan nodded, smiling her thanks. With one last glance at Remmy, she leaned down and placed a soft kiss on the cool forehead, then left, digging her cell phone out of her purse as she left the ICU.

Chapter Twenty-four

In a remarkable turn of events, psychic Remmy Foster led police to the house behind me, where Sergio Venti had apparently been collecting women. Pamela Beecham, missing for two years, was found handcuffed in a dungeon-like room, as was Cameron Sanchez, who had recently been abducted from her bedroom in the early hours of October 27. Julie Wilson, a teacher here in Woodland, and missing for nearly three months, was the first—"

Matt turned off the television and grabbed his keys. "Skylar!" he called out, heading toward the garage door, Bonnie and Clyde running and barking alongside him. He squatted to pet the dogs, smiling at the fact that their mommy was about to come home. "Come on!" he called again, rolling his eyes. Skylar was worse than any woman when it came to getting him motivated to go anywhere.

Soon enough, the tromping of feet could be heard overhead, the trail easy to follow as they ran down the hall, turned left at the landing, then finally pounded down the staircase.

"I'm ready, Dad!" the boy hollered, continuing his marathon until he reached the garage door and father. He had his Gameboy in hand.

Matt shook his head. The boy never ceased to amuse him. They said their good-byes to the whining dogs, then Matt grabbed the duffle bag he had packed the night before and got Skylar and then himself into the car. Matt navigated the snowy streets with ease, glancing over at Skylar every so often, having to hide the smile that quirked his lips. He hadn't wanted to leave Julie there, at the hospital, but he'd had no choice. When he left, he shared the elevator with Dr. Haley Corregan.

"Be patient with her, Matt," she'd advised. *"Know that no matter what she says or does, it's not personal. This isn't about you, it's about her, and her fear. She will struggle with trust issues. Let her ease back into her life at her own pace. Just be there for her."*

Matt found the psychologist beautiful, but quickly noted the simple gold band on her ring finger. *Well, there goes that thought.*

The hospital parking lot was busy, as usual, but Matt found them a space. He glanced over at Skylar, who was looking around in total confusion.

"This isn't McDonald's," he grumbled, looking over at his dad for an explanation.

"Nope." Matt grinned. "This is better. Come on, Skylar, and leave your Gameboy in the car."

Father and son walked through the halls of Saint Mercy's to the elevators. On the fourth floor, Matt led Skylar to room 431.

"Who are we here to see?" Skylar asked, big eyes scanning the rooms on either side of the hall. He had only been in a hospital once before, and that was when his friend Dillon had broken his leg by falling out of a tree.

"Someone very special," Matt said, stopping in front of Julie's room. He pushed the door open and Skylar followed him inside.

The room was well lit, the blinds over the window open, showing the rooftop of a lower wing of the hospital and the blue sky beyond. Julie sat on the bed, dressed in some scrubs the nurse had brought her that morning.

She was freshly showered—her third since last night—and waiting. She had been told Matt would arrive by ten a.m., and it was seven 'til.

Matt moved to the side, allowing Skylar to walk in front of him. The boy stopped, eyes huge as he took in the apparition before him. Julie's smile grew wider than Matt had seen it since her return. She slid off the bed, bracing herself to absorb the impact of his body as he threw himself at her.

"Skylar," she whispered, holding him close to her. She could feel his tears on her neck.

Matt stood back, watching, never so relieved and happy in all his life. The two people he loved most were back in his life, safe and sound. He would do everything he could to heed Dr. Corregan's advice, and help Julie through this.

Chapter Twenty-five

In her kitchen in Omaha, Nebraska, a woman stood watching the news, almost unable to breathe. Her breakfast long forgotten, her eyes were riveted to the television screen, a hand covering her mouth. She was watching the footage of a woman, dirty, disheveled, and dressed in a man's bathrobe, being led from a house. She was horribly pale and thin. The woman looked up into the sky, a look of profound relief on her face. An officer gently led her to a waiting ambulance. Following close behind the first was a young woman who looked terrified as she was led from the house.

The viewer had long since stopped paying attention to the commentary from the reporter, one name echoing in her head, over and over again. "Remmy," she whispered.

❧❧❧❧

Grace glanced out the window above her kitchen sink, noting the beautiful sky. It would be a nice day. She turned her attention back to the coffee maker, turning the machine on. She was exhausted, even after her first full night's sleep in months. She smiled when her husband came up behind her, hugging her and placing a kiss on her neck.

"It was good to have you still here this morning," he said.

Grace smiled, turning in the circle of his arms.

She allowed herself to be held, relishing the safety and security of the familiarity. They'd been married a long time, but she still loved him very much. She couldn't have asked for a more patient man.

"I'm so proud of you, Grace," he said, looking down into her upraised face.

"Guess it was all worth it, huh?" She pulled away from him to go to the fridge and see what they had for breakfast.

"What's wrong?" Chris asked, sitting on one of the bar stools at the breakfast bar.

Grace sighed. *What indeed?* "I don't know," she said, closing the door of the Sub-Zero and leaning against it. "Guess it's almost like Christmas, you know? You work so hard for it, put so much time and effort into it, then December 26th, it's such a huge letdown. And," she said with a sigh, "I feel I let those women down."

Chris' brow wrinkled in confusion. "Honey, you saved their lives."

"No, Chris, I didn't. Remmy did. Don't get me wrong," she said, holding up a hand to forestall comment. "I don't mean it like that, but I do feel that I should've been able to find that bastard. I really feel like because of me those women had to suffer at the hands of that monster Venti." She felt the anger building, a sense of failure. Turning back to the coffee maker, she had to will herself not to shrug off Chris' touch. Instead, she allowed herself to be held again.

"Let's get away, honey," Chris said, "I mean, I watched you go through college and the Academy, and finally be hired on as a beat cop," he said gently, rubbing her back. "I've watched your frustrations and joys as your career progressed, and baby, I've never known a stronger, more determined woman. But in all that time," he pushed her away just enough to look into her face,

"I've never seen you react so intensely to a case. So, let's go away, do something fun." Grace sighed. "I can't. I've still got work to do." She could tell Chris was annoyed, but he said nothing as he stepped away to make himself a cup of coffee.

❧❧❧❧

Remmy's eyes blinked open, once, twice. The third time, they remained open. She was lying in a most uncomfortable position — head turned to the side, breasts crushed against the mattress beneath her. If her breast discomfort had been the worst of her problems, she would have done a jig. As it was, her entire body hurt, especially the sharp, stabbing pain in her back.

She tried to raise her head but immediately stopped, groaning as she closed her eyes. Had she been hit by a truck? Slowly rolling her head, she saw a chair and a bedside table, which held a pitcher of water and plastic cup. She was also surprised to see a teddy bear sitting there, a big smile on his face. He held a small balloon that read: Get Better Soon!

"Okay," she said, turning her head back the other way. She would feel better if she knew what had happened to her. She realized she was in a semi-private hospital room, the bed nearest the window empty. Her mouth was dry, lips cracking. Her tongue slipped out, sliding over the roughness. She groaned. Not even enough moisture in her mouth to re-wet her lips. She glanced back to the table, eyeing the pitcher of water. She wrapped her fingers around it, but she didn't have the strength to lift it. "Shit."

"Let me help."

Remmy looked up, grateful for the nurse who had walked in. She felt so helpless. "Thanks." She drank slowly, the nurse patiently holding the small plastic pitcher, a straw tucked between Remmy's lips. Once she'd had her fill, Remmy laid her head back on the bed. "I'm in a lot of pain," she said, her voice stronger after the water.

"It's almost time for more meds," the nurse said, her voice soft and understanding. She sat for a moment in the chair next to Remmy's bed. "That was a really amazing thing you did," she said, dark eyes smiling. "I know my family and I will always be grateful to you."

Remmy's brows drew in confusion. "I don't understand."

"Cameron Sanchez is my little sister. You got her away from that sicko. You're really a hero, Remmy. I know Cameron wants to come and thank you herself. I told her to wait until you're a little stronger." The nurse stood. "Is there anything else I can get you?"

Remmy shook her head, exhausted just from their short conversation.

"Okay. I'll be back in about thirty minutes with your pills. Get some rest."

Left alone once more, Remmy's mind tried to recapture the moments before her collapse. She should have asked the nurse the extent of her injuries. She sighed, closing her eyes, doing her best to block out the escalating pain as she tried to relax. Nothing. Absolutely nothing. Her brain was filled with a cold emptiness that was almost frightening. It made her think of a grocery bag — all pushed out to its limits in size, filled with something, or lots of somethings, then suddenly emptied, leaving the bag expanded but with nothing inside. She felt very open, very exposed, but had no idea why.

True to her word, the nurse returned with a paper cup filled with pills. "Let me help you," she said, again bringing the water pitcher to Remmy's mouth, the straw placed between her lips. "It will be hard to swallow them in this position. I'm sorry." She literally had to finger the pills into Remmy's mouth, one at a time. Finally, all the pills were down, and Remmy had drunk her fill of water.

"What happened to me?" she asked, indicating the pain in her back with a slight incline of her head.

The nurse studied her. "You don't remember?" At the shake of Remmy's head, the nurse explained. "You were shot in the back while protecting one of the captives you helped save." She saw the look of confusion on Remmy's face and was startled by it. "Wow. Maybe you should mention to your doctor that your memory seems to have been affected. Perhaps you hit your head."

"Maybe," Remmy said with a weak smile, just wanting to be alone again.

❧❧❧❧

Julie sat in the front seat of Matt's car, huddled in her favorite sweatshirt from Denver University, where she'd gone to college, and the oversized pair of sweatpants he had brought her. The shirt was old and ratty, but beyond comfortable. One hand was extended uncomfortably back between the seats; Skylar had a death grip on it.

Though she hadn't been captive an incredibly long time — just shy of three months, she was told — everything looked so different. It was a different season — gone from hot, sunny skies to the overcast, pregnant clouds above her now, but everything just looked...different. Even houses she'd seen a million times, the same stores and the same people populating the sidewalks, all looked different. The holidays were coming up, and she wondered how many of the people were shopping for Christmas. With easy, carefree smiles on their faces and laughter in the air, no doubt.

As Matt pulled the SUV into his driveway, Julie was filled with conflicting emotions: gratitude beyond anything for being there, seeing the house again; and fear. What would she be expected to do? How would she be expected to act? Would Matt allow her to just crawl within herself? Knowing her brother, probably not.

"Home, sweet home," Matt said, glancing over at Julie. "For now. I think it's probably best if you stay here with us for a little while." He studied her face, looking deep within very dead eyes. "What do you think?"

Julie nodded, giving him a weak smile. "I think I want to lie down."

Bonnie and Clyde just about had mini heart attacks when they recognized Julie. She was overjoyed to see them, too, grabbing them both up in her arms. Tears in her eyes, she allowed them to lick her fears away. She smiled at Matt, silently thanking him for taking care of her babies. He nodded. No words were necessary.

Dogs still in her arms, Julie walked into the house, looking around. Absolutely nothing had changed, though she saw a large board leaning against the wall in the dining room, face to the wall.

"What's that?" she asked, knowing Matt's penchant for a meticulous house with no clutter.

"This is so cool, Aunt Julie!" Skylar gushed, running over to it and turning it over. It was nearly as tall as he was.

"Skylar, maybe this isn't such a good time..." Matt cringed. He had intended to put that away, but had forgotten in the excitement following Julie's rescue.

Julie set her Yorkies on their feet and walked toward Skylar. As she neared, her heart pounded and a wistful smile curled her lips. She saw the smiling faces of every one of her students, all put together in a collage. The caption was: WE WILL ALWAYS MISS YOU, MS. WILSON, THE GREATEST TEACHER IN THE WORLD!

"We had a memorial service," Matt said softly, stepping up behind her. "They gave that to me at the end."

Julie reached out a hand, lightly touching the glossy faces, emotions rising. She felt so confused: happy, relieved, frustrated, and angry. "Everyone thought I was dead," she said, a statement rather than a question.

Even Skylar remained silent, sensing all was not well with her. He'd been told that she had gone away for a very long time, and that he'd probably never see her again.

Matt said nothing, just studied her, unsure what he should say. He wanted to take her in his arms and never let her go, protecting her from everything and anything, just like when they were kids. He knew he couldn't protect her from this—from herself and the specter he had been told would haunt her for a long time. Not for the first time, he damned Sergio Venti's soul to hell.

❧❧❧❧❧

The room was quiet when Grace pushed the heavy door open. She saw Remmy lying on her stomach, eyes closed. She was hooked to a number of machines, each beeping or blinking. It was late on Remmy's second day in the hospital, and the first time Grace had been able to escape from work to come see her. Though Sergio was dead, there was a lot of clearing up to do, as well as trying to see if any other cases could be linked to him. The tires on his van were matched to the tracks found at the site of Roxie Carmichael's body dump, as well as at Cameron Sanchez's house. Proof positive that he had been responsible for both.

Grace laid the flowers she had brought on the side table, gently pushing a teddy bear and balloon aside to make room.

"Gee, Grace, isn't it a little soon in our relationship for flowers?" Remmy murmured, her voice thick from pain medicine.

Grace chuckled, taking a seat next to the narrow bed. "How are you?" she asked, reaching out to take Remmy's hand.

"I think I survived being run over by a tank. Other than that, I'm great. Peachy—"

"—keen," Grace finished with her, a smile on her face. "I'm sorry I didn't get here sooner. We've had quite the mess to unravel, and we had to get Pamela and Cameron back home." She saw the look of confusion on Remmy's face. "What?"

"The nurse mentioned a Cameron yesterday. Who's Pamela?"

Grace's brows drew. "From the house. They were captives with Julie." Still no recognition. "You do remember Julie, don't you?"

"Am I supposed to?"

Grace was extremely concerned as she looked into cloudy blue eyes. She sat back in her chair, wiping her face of expression. "Do you know why you're here?" She indicated the hospital room around them.

"I was shot. In the back." Remmy interrupted Grace's relieved smile. "The nurse told me." Remmy reached for the water on the table next to the flowers, fingertips inching their way toward the pitcher, trying to reach it. Grace helped her, holding the straw to her lips as she drank. "Doc says I can turn onto my back tomorrow. Thank God. This just isn't cuttin' it." She gestured for the water to be put back on the table. "I can't explain it, Grace; it's like this weird feeling in my head. I feel like the harder I try to think, or the harder I try and envision something, the thicker the fog gets." She met concerned brown eyes. "I feel so empty."

Grace sat back in the chair, crossing one leg over the other. "Empty, how?"

"Inside my head, I just feel…I don't know." Remmy sighed at her inability to form coherent thoughts. "I feel used up, somehow. I'm so tired. I know a lot of it is because of my injury, but it's weird," she said again. "I feel soul tired. Does that make sense?"

Grace nodded, feeling quite similar herself. "Yes. It makes perfect sense." She leaned over and placed a soft kiss on the top of Remmy's head. "You get some sleep. I'll come see you again soon." She walked over to the door, stopping with her hand on the handle. "You've two months rent-free, kid. Take advantage of it." With those cryptic words, she was gone.

Left alone again in her room, Remmy sighed. Her neck was about as tired of the position in which she lay as every other part of her body. She would have done anything to be able to roll over onto her back. Hell, even her side would do. "This sucks," she muttered, glancing over at the flowers Grace had brought her. She thought that was really nice and was enjoying their fragrance.

With a heavy sigh of resignation, she laid her head down on the pillow.

Chapter Twenty-six

Julie stood at the window, her arms crossed over her chest, her second shower of the day completed. She hugged herself, forehead resting against the cool glass. The dark night lay beyond, the dim lamp on the dresser across the room reflecting in the mirror-like glass. From the streetlight a few houses down, she could see the snow falling in steady waves. It was quite beautiful.

The night had been nice, she supposed. She knew Matt was walking on eggshells around her, and she hated that. She had sat quietly on the couch, curled up in the corner. Matt sat in the recliner reading the newspaper; Skylar was playing video games. Her dogs hadn't left her side since she'd returned; in fact, they were lying on the bed nearby. Matt had offered to stay with her, but she wanted to give it a go on her own. She felt fine and was determined to not let that bastard win from the grave.

Julie made her way to the bathroom and relieved herself, a hand going to her wrist and gently rubbing it. She could feel the scabbing and slight indentation from the cuffs. Her ankles still stung, too.

Walking back to the bed, Julie realized she was more exhausted than she'd ever been, physically and emotionally spent. Dr. Corregan had given her a prescription for a sleeping pill, but the way she felt right now, she figured she would sleep clear into next week without any artificial assistance.

"Move over, guys," she said. Bonnie glanced up at

her from where her chin rested on her paws, stubby tail wagging. Clyde hopped up, giving Julie a few licks before moving to the other side of his sister as his mommy climbed in. She didn't bother to turn out the lamp; she never wanted to be in a dark room again. Fully clothed in sweats and a t-shirt, she slid between the sheets and wrapped the covers up around her shoulders as she settled on her side. She smiled as her dogs cuddled up in the bend of her legs, Bonnie resting her chin on Julie's calf. Just like the old days, but not in her bedroom at home.

Julie tried to will her mind to relax, but every time she closed her eyes they immediately popped open at the slightest noise, frightened green eyes looking around the bedroom. The door had been kept ajar, and her gaze fell on the dark space beyond. She knew Matt's room was just down the hall to the right, Skylar's to the left. She was perfectly safe. That bastard was dead. He was dead. She took a deep breath, letting it out nice and slow. Adjusting her pillow, she brought her hands up and tucked them under her chin. She sighed in contentment. So happy to have her hands free, she brought them in to her body. She was so happy to be fully clothed and buried underneath several layers of clothing and bedding. She could already feel herself beginning to sweat slightly, but she didn't care—she was covered. With a slight smack of her lips, she closed her eyes.

The hallway was long, slanted light coming in on either side. The source was elusive; doors slammed shut in her face each time she tried to peer inside them. She kept walking, steps cautious, one foot in front of the other. She tried to ball her fists, tried to bring them in close, but couldn't move them.

Panic set in, flooding her body like a wave. She couldn't breathe, couldn't breathe!

Julie cried out, thrashing wildly until there were two thuds on the floor. Green eyes shot open, Julie hyperventilating as she sat up in the bed, fighting with the sheets tangled around her small frame.

"Julie!" Matt hurried into the room, flipping the overhead light on as he sat on the side of the bed. He grabbed Julie's shoulders, shaking her gently, heart racing. "It's me. It's Matt."

Julie's eyes finally began to focus, and she recognized the features of her brother. She broke, allowing herself to be taken into his embrace. The dream images were quickly fading, but the emotions they left behind were still raw.

❧❧❧❧

Remmy cried out as she woke, heart racing as her eyes darted around the room frantically, looking for what had frightened her so badly. She had no recollection of what had chased her into wakefulness, but she was sweating profusely. She brought her hand up and ran it through her hair, pushing it away from her face.

She was desperately thirsty, her medicines drying her mouth out terribly. The last nurse had been kind enough to move the table close enough so she could reach the water herself. She drank greedily, panting between gulps. A look out the window on the far side of the room told her dawn was just around the corner. She was glad. Her doctor told her today she would be turned over and allowed to sit up, the catheter removed. She was grateful. She was convinced that whoever had invented the catheter should be shot.

Shot.

The pain spread through her body like a wave,

starting at the corner of her back and spreading. She gasped, a bolt of pain stabbing her back and reverberating at the base of her skull. She gulped several mouthfuls of air, almost panting. She squeezed her eyes shut, trying to get her breathing, and her pain, under control.

"My God." She breathed, again pushing her hair back from her face. She wanted a shower in the worst way and was tempted to get up against doctor's orders and wash up in the bathroom. For a moment she seriously contemplated that idea, eyeing the distance between the bed and the bathroom. She moved her right leg, then stopped, whimpering as fresh pain shot up her body. "Or not."

Exhausted by her interrupted sleep and the pain medication, Remmy closed her eyes, intending to doze. She awoke six hours later to a soft nudging from one of the nurses.

"Mornin', Rob," she muttered, voice thick with sleep.

"Rise and shine, Remmy." He smiled at her, checking her vital signs. "You've got a busy morning today. Are you ready to turn over?"

"Does a bear shit in the woods?"

Rob chuckled. "Wouldn't know. I'm going to get your bandages changed after the doctor comes in to take a look, then we'll get your catheter out and get you up and moving. Sound good?"

"Sounds like Heaven."

Rob patted her on the shoulder then left, soon to return with everything he would need, and her doctor. After the doctor proclaimed that Remmy was healing well, he left two nurses to take care of her, cleaning and changing her bandages, then the three of them got her turned around until she was seated, a groan of mingled pain and relief escaping her throat.

"You okay?" Rob asked, watching Remmy's face carefully for any signs of the usual pain. She nodded, chewing on her bottom lip in concentration as she allowed the pain to settle. "Okay. I'll go grab your breakfast and meds."

Left alone, Remmy was able to view her room in its entirety. She had never been so glad to sit in her entire life. She slowly—oh so slowly—reached beside the bed and grabbed the pitcher, which was nearly out of water, and sucked down the remainder. Her smile stretched across her face as her breakfast tray was brought in and set on her side table, which was rolled over to the bed and positioned above her lap.

"I almost forgot, Remmy, someone's here to see you. I told her to wait until you finished eating and we can get you showered and feeling a little more human. Is that alright?"

Remmy nodded, mouth too full of French toast to respond verbally.

"Cool. I'll be back in a few. Enjoy your breakfast."

❧❧❧❧

Julie stepped out of the shower, intentionally turning her back toward the mirror as she quickly dried herself then tugged on her clothing — flannel pants and a sweatshirt, sized too large to define any sort of form beneath. That was one of the great things about having a brother: everything he owned was large. For the briefest of moments it made her smile, thinking back to when were children. They had come in from a long afternoon of playing in the snow, and were tired and cold. Matt went downstairs to the dryer, grabbing his own sweats and sweatshirt from the freshly dried warmth, only to have a little blonde blur steal them from his hands. He chased her upstairs, nearly running headlong into the slammed bathroom door. For years after that, whenever his clothes had gone missing, he would look through Julie's drawers, always finding them.

Julie ran a comb through her hair, shaggy and in her face. She hadn't decided if she wanted to get it cut or just let it grow. Part of her wanted to cut it all off in retaliation. She shook that childish thought away and opened the bathroom door, nearly tripping over Skylar, who had camped out on the floor, back against the wall and stockinged feet against the opposite wall. She couldn't believe how much he'd grown even in the three months she had been gone.

"Well, excuse me, little man," she said, stopping herself with a hand on either side of the open bathroom door. "I don't think you were put on this earth to be a roadblock."

Skylar looked up with big, almost sad, eyes. "Remember when I was little and you used to call me speed bump?" he asked, almost as though he was trying to make sure she was really his beloved aunt.

Julie sensed something was up, so she knelt down beside him, running gentle fingers through his disheveled hair. "You are my little speed bump," she said softly, smiling at him. "Always."

Overwhelmed with a surge of love, he threw himself into her arms, nearly knocking her backwards into the bathroom. "I love you, Aunt Julie," he whispered.

"I love you, too, Skylar." After a moment she pulled away, brushing a thumb over freckled cheeks, wiping away his tears. "Don't ever forget that, okay?" At Skylar's nod, she turned him around and sent him scampering back to his bedroom to make his bed with a playful swat to the Spider-Man pajama-clad butt.

Julie padded down the stairs, following the smell

of bacon frying and coffee brewing. She stopped mid-step, hand on the banister, and closed her eyes, inhaling the fragrance that brought a million and one memories back from her childhood and her life before... Before. She walked through the entryway of the house toward the kitchen where Matt was standing in front of the stove, the radio tuned to a country station on the corner of the counter. Oblivious to the amused eyes watching him, he swung his hips as he sang along with Brad Paisley.

The jingling tags of Bonnie chasing Clyde as they slid around the corner into the room finally alerted him that he wasn't alone. Matt turned, immediately becoming an adorable shade of pink when he saw Julie leaning against the butcher block island, doing her damnedest not to laugh.

"Mornin'," he said, turning back to the bacon, flipping over the sizzling strips. He easily shook off the embarrassment, remembering the night before instead. Turning back to her, he set the spatula down on a folded paper towel and reached out to gather her in a hug. When she flinched away, he dropped his arms and smiled.

Don't take anything she says or does personally... It's not about you, it's about her.

"How are you today?"

Julie hugged herself tightly, worried she'd hurt him. She hadn't intended for him to see her shrink from his touch, but she couldn't bring herself to apologize. "Alright, I guess." She gave him a weak smile, nodding toward the stove. "Smells good."

"Thanks," Matt said, eager to get onto a safe subject. "I figured, throw some toast in the toaster, plenty of butter, just like you like it, then some eggs—"

"No eggs," Julie said, her eyes immediately filling

with fear, the sting of emotion making her eyelids flutter.

Matt was confused. "Alright," he said slowly. "No eggs. I thought you loved eggs. I was gonna fry them, just how you—"

"No eggs, Matt."

"Okay. Um…" He turned back to the carton on the counter, wondering what he would make for the main breakfast course.

Julie felt her heart pound, but then she felt guilty. She could see the confusion on his face and knew he was just trying to do a good thing for her. "Why don't I whip up some pancakes?" she said, her enthusiasm patently forced.

"You don't have to, Jules. I can do that."

"No." She smiled at him; this time it was almost genuine. "You keep watch over the bacon and potatoes; you've got them all cubed up and spiced over there. I'll make pancakes."

The three of them sat at the kitchen table, Skylar digging into the pancakes as if he'd never eaten them before, pouring on more maple syrup with every bite. Julie grimaced in disgust, feeling her mouth fill with cavities as she watched. She listened as Matt and Skylar chatted with each other, Skylar filling them in about his new friend at school and his teacher this year. Their conversation and camaraderie were nice, familiar, but somehow Julie felt as if she was watching an episode on television. She couldn't shake the feeling of disjointedness, like she didn't belong there, didn't have anything to add. She turned to her breakfast, trying to brush away her sadness as easily as she brushed her bangs from her eyes.

Chapter Twenty-seven

Dressed in a fresh gown with fresh dressings on her injuries and surgical incisions, Remmy was wheeled back to her room. She felt glorious. Well, that might have been too strong of a word, but she felt better for sure. She had bathed; an old biddy of a nurse had helped her. She mused that it would have been a much nicer experience if Cameron's sister had assisted her.

Her stomach full and her body clean, Remmy allowed herself to be settled on the bed, sitting with her back against a cloud of pillows behind her. She was ready for her visitor. She told the nurse as much, and he went to fetch her.

Remmy was left with her thoughts. The nightmare that had woken her, which she still couldn't remember, left her troubled and feeling mildly frightened. What made it worse was that she was frightened of something she had no knowledge of. When Grace had come to visit her the night before, the detective had seemed startled and concerned that Remmy didn't remember the women she named: Pamela and Julie. Neither name rang a bell, though she felt as if they should. The names, and any link to them, were sucked into the void that was the emptiness in her mind. Her troubled thoughts were interrupted by the opening of her door.

A woman poked her head inside. She wore her long dark hair pulled back in a French braid. Her eyes were nearly as dark as her hair. Seeing Remmy propped up on the bed, she pushed the door open, stepped inside, and let the door slowly slide closed behind her.

Remmy studied her, dark eyebrows drawn, but they slowly rose as her mouth fell open. Standing before her was a ghost of her lost and misspent youth. She tried to push herself up, but stopped as pain scorched through her.

"Stay put. Don't hurt yourself." The visitor walked over to the bed and stared down at Remmy, eyes full of mischief. Without a word, the cousins embraced, Monica holding Remmy's head against her chest as strong arms encircled her waist. They said nothing, just as they'd never had to say anything in their disjointed past.

Finally Remmy pulled back and looked into the face of her beloved Monica. As her cousin sat in the chair next to the bed, Remmy grasped her hand, refusing to relinquish physical contact. "Where did you come from? Where did you go? Jesus, I thought you were dead."

Monica smiled, soft wisps of dark hair framing her pretty face. "I nearly was. Picked myself up out of a gutter one day. The money I'd made the night before had been stolen, and I decided I was going to die. Just up ahead I saw a small church and staggered inside." She squeezed Remmy's hands. "I've been looking for you for years, Rem. I had no idea where you'd gone."

Remmy smiled. *Hot damn! I've got family again.* "I've been everywhere. Nowhere. Ended up here." Her brow wrinkled. "How did you know I was here?"

"Saw it on the news. You're quite the hero. It's everywhere — how you led the police to those women." Monica smiled, pride glowing in her eyes. "I guess you found a use for your visions, huh?"

Remmy studied her, slowly shaking her head. Her

voice was a whisper. "I don't remember, Mon. People keep telling me that, but I have no clue what they're talking about. I'm a little scared."

Monica studied their joined hands for a moment before she met troubled blue eyes. She had always wished she'd gotten Remmy's eyes from their grandfather, too. "Rem, you're so important to me, and we're all each other has as far as family goes. I don't want to lose you again. I've got a small house in Omaha. I came here with the intention of taking you back home with me."

The words made Remmy happy, eager to be with her cousin, but then something else crept in. Something...something missing. She thought back over her life in Woodland, brief though it was, and tried to figure out what it was that was telling her to stay. She thought about her small apartment, which was nice but certainly expendable. She thought about her job, which was also nice, but she'd had a million of those. Yes, she'd made friends, but none that could compare to Monica… her family…her best friend.

Monica studied Remmy's face intently, hoping she'd say yes. At Remmy's nod, Monica grinned, hugging her to her again.

❧❧❧❧

Grace was making notes on her research for her latest case, a hit and run that had left a ten year old girl dead in the gutter. She was pushing her reading glasses up on her nose when she was interrupted by a tap on her shoulder. She glanced up and smiled at seeing Joan Watson standing there. Joan fell into the chair next to Grace's desk.

"Hi. Sorry to interrupt you at work, but an officer showed me where you were."

"No problem, Joan. How's it going?" Grace removed her glasses, setting them aside as she leaned back in her office chair.

"Oh, fine. I'm a little bummed, though," she said, digging into her purse and producing a small, folded piece of paper. She set it on the edge of Grace's desk. "I've lost my favorite employee. And tenant."

Grace took the paper and unfolded it. It was the check for six hundred dollars she'd given Joan just over a week ago. She raised questioning eyes.

"Remmy's gone, Grace. Knowing she was due to be released, I went to see her this morning. I had planned to take her home. The room was empty, the bed freshly made. The nurse said Remmy was released this morning, and left with her cousin. She left this, though." Joan handed Grace a folded piece of paper.

"Cousin?" Grace repeated, taking the paper. She hadn't been aware Remmy had any family. It was irrelevant now. She released a heavy sigh. "Oh. And she left the area?" Grace unfolded the page to find a couple words jotted down in ink.

Thanks for everything. Best of luck.
R.

"I guess. The cousin was from the Midwest somewhere, the nurse said. I guess she'd been here for the past few days." She shook her head. "I wish...I don't know. I guess I wish things could've been different, that she would have stayed and returned to the life she'd made here. She had a job, a place to live, friends."

Grace refolded the note and pocketed it, then smiled. "But consider her life here, Joan," she said softly. "She was tortured with visions of Sergio Venti, and forced to live the horrors that Julie, Pam, Roxie, and

Cameron did." Grace sipped her coffee. "To be honest, I just hope she can find some peace."

Joan sighed, knowing Grace was right. "I feel we all let her down, somehow," she said, her voice soft. "Maybe we should've been there for her more." She laughed nervously. "Hell, I'm palming off my own guilt. Maybe I should've been there more for her."

Grace patted Joan's knee. "Don't beat yourself up, Joan. Remmy is one of the strongest people I've ever met. She'll be okay."

"Yeah, but I'll miss her." Joan sighed. "I think a lot of folks will."

Chapter Twenty-eight

Julie walked around the room, looking at everything, fingers grazing her things. The house smelled stuffy. She knew Matt had come over when he could to air things out, but he had his own home and son to take care of. Distantly she heard Bonnie and Clyde running through the house, also happy to be home. She walked into every room, forever grateful that the abduction hadn't happened here. She knew there was no way she could have stepped foot back inside if it had. The mere thought of going back to the school made her stomach churn.

She had been seeing Dr. Corregan every day for three and a half weeks, and the good doctor felt it was time for Julie to start expanding her borders, edging outside of Matt's house. Matt had gone back to work at the beginning of the previous week, which terrified her, as she had to start getting herself back and forth to see Dr. Corregan, but at the same time, it had filled her with a sense of accomplishment. She had even offered to take care of Skylar occasionally during the past week. Earlier in this day, Julie had asked to use the car to visit her own house.

She walked over to the French doors that led into the backyard, where she had spent so much time over the summer, planting flowers and a small garden. The yard wasn't huge, but it was large enough for her and her dogs, and she'd had a barbecue or two on the small cement patio.

Taking a deep breath, Julie grasped the ends of the two heavy curtains in her fists and pulled them apart. She half-expected to see that bastard standing on the other side, but he wasn't there. She had expressed her fears to Dr. Corregan that part of her couldn't reconcile with the fact that Sergio was dead. Her therapist had suggested maybe she should visit his grave, prove to herself that he was, in fact, dead and could never hurt her again. She was considering it but wasn't ready. Not yet.

She unlocked the French doors and stepped through, drawing her winter jacket tighter around herself. Her legs immediately felt tight and stiff in her jeans as the frigid November air swirled around them. Thanksgiving was the following day and a part of her dreaded it. She wasn't looking forward to being with a group of people. With Matt and Skylar her only family—and vice/versa for them—they always had Thanksgiving dinner with friends, one year at Matt's house, the next at hers, and then the next at someone else's. Matt had offered to have a small celebration with just the three of them, but she knew how much Matt and Skylar enjoyed the festivities, so she insisted they keep to tradition. That was important for her, as well. She couldn't hide forever.

She walked over to her patio furniture, grateful that Matt had covered it in plastic in her absence. Brushing off the newly fallen snow, she felt a small smile tug at the corner of her mouth. Next summer maybe she would be ready for another barbecue.

Back inside, Julie went through all the rooms, feeling her smile get bigger with every one. She wanted to try spending time there, just her and her dogs, and maybe Skylar sometimes, too.

The nightmarish images had continued, just as Dr. Corregan said they would. After the first night, Matt gave her the option of staying with him or Skylar. Julie had tried a second night on her own, but her nocturnal world had been rocked with garish images and fear. The next night she had curled up with Skylar, whose warmth and youthful innocence had provided her with quiet strength.

She had felt strange since her return, not only drained emotionally and physically, but also feeling something was...missing. She couldn't quite put a finger on it, but felt it clearly. She hadn't wanted to think much about it, as it forced herself to go back there, back to Hell. She wasn't ready.

Sadness washed over her as she called her dogs to her, getting ready to drive back to Matt's. She felt she had left a part of herself back at that house, that Sergio had taken something from her that she could never get back. The sadness turned into a burning anger, bright enough that her hands curled into fists at her sides.

"You won't win, you son of a bitch," she muttered, her anger, though hot and quick, leaving her just as fast as it had flared. She took a deep breath and left her house.

❧❧❧❧

Remmy sipped her coffee; Monica made the best around. She stood at the sliding glass door in the kitchen, looking out at the white wonderland, ignoring the sounds of laughter and conversation behind her. She supposed she had a lot to be thankful for, but she just wasn't in the mood to share. Instead, she stayed inside her own head, the taste of wonderful food still on her tongue. She'd been with Monica in her Omaha home for nearly a month, and was loving the familiarity that came with reuniting with her best friend. Monica was becoming her hero—the way she'd managed to pick herself up out of the gutter, literally—and had a productive life and a beautiful home.

If she had been asked five years ago where Monica would end up, or what her home would look like, it would not have been the small, homey, country-style house that came to mind. In some ways, it wasn't Monica at all, but in others, it made Remmy feel more at home than she'd felt in a long, long time. Their closeness had picked up right where it left off, without the drugs, this time. Hell, in their own ways, they had both become respectable.

"Hey."

Remmy turned to find Monica standing just behind her, a plate in each hand, both with a generous piece of pumpkin pie topped with whipped cream. "Oh, for me?" Remmy grinned.

"Yes, it is. You always loved it." Monica handed over one of the plates then snagged two plastic forks from her back pocket. "I remember you once told me that you could live off the stuff. That…and pizza."

Remmy chuckled. "Good thing I don't. I'd die of clogged arteries by age thirty."

"That you would." The cousins ate in silence, watching the snow fall. Monica studied her profile. "Something's wrong," she said after a while.

Remmy said nothing for long moments, then turned to Monica. She knew damn well that Monica could read her like a book; it was futile to lie. She thought it was ironic that it took Monica's vocalized observation to make the problem click into place. "I feel lost, Monica," she said, her voice quiet.

"What do you mean?" Monica set her plate down on a kitchen counter. One leaning against the sink and the other against the fridge, Monica waited for her to expound on her statement.

"I don't know. It's hard to explain." Remmy sighed, running her hands through her hair. "I don't know. It's like, for the past few weeks, since I got shot, I just feel like something is wrong. Something is...missing."

"What is it?"

"Mon, if I knew that, I wouldn't be confused." They both chuckled at the absurdity of Monica's question. "It's just there. I want to cry. It's almost like I've lost something I need, and I don't know what it is. I feel like if I found that one thing," she held up a single finger to emphasize her point, "life would be great."

"What do you want to do? Maybe you should talk to someone, Rem. I know my minister would be more than willing to listen."

Remmy smiled, reaching across the small space and squeezing her arm. "Thanks. I think I need to get through this on my own. I'll figure it out." She shrugged. "Who knows? Maybe I'm just missing my spleen."

❧ ❧ ❧ ❧

Julie lay in her bed with Bonnie and Clyde snuggled up on either side of her. She stared up at the ceiling, studying the shadows the moon painted across it. The day had been a success, for the most part. The usual participants had arrived to celebrate Thanksgiving, many bringing food to add to the feast Matt and Julie had prepared. Julie had seen many of them since she'd returned, but others had kept their distance, giving her time and space to recover. Though grateful for their consideration, she had to admit she had been happy to see so many familiar faces.

No one commented on the fact that, most of the time, Julie either kept to herself or stayed with the children. Their youth and laughter were a balm to her badly damaged soul. Throughout the day she kept turning around, expecting to see someone she felt should have been with her, someone she couldn't put a face to or a finger on, but who should have been there. It was a strange feeling.

It felt good to be warm, fully clothed, and stuffed. She was a fortunate woman. She'd been thinking a lot about Pamela Beecham. Part of her wanted to speak with her, as Pam was the only person who could truly understand what she was feeling. She wondered how she was doing, how she was handling her return to her family. Cameron had only been in the pit for a very short time, lucky for her. She was young, and Julie had no doubt she would bounce back. She just hoped that she, herself, would. She was tired of not feeling like herself, and wondered if she ever would again. She knew she was forever changed, but she was waiting for the core of who she was to begin to seep back into her daily life.

There were things about the new Julie that she didn't like. Her patience, for instance, was at an all time low. She had snapped at Skylar a few times over things that she never would have in the past. She had apologized later, once finding him with tears in his eyes, which broke her heart. Maybe she needed to move back into her own place. By herself, she couldn't hurt anyone else.

Julie's thoughts were interrupted by a soft knock on her closed bedroom door. "Come in," she called, not wanting to disturb the dogs by getting up to open it. The door squeaked open—she refused to allow Matt to oil it, so she could always hear if someone entered—and Matt popped his head in.

"Hey," he said softly. "Were you sleeping?"

Julie shook her head. "No. Come on in."

Matt softly closed the door behind him so their voices wouldn't wake Skylar. He nodded toward the end of the bed, wanting to know that he could sit without making Julie jumpy. At her nod, he made himself comfortable. "It was fun today," he said, a lopsided grin on his face. "Even when my boss accidentally dropped his teeth into the mashed potatoes."

They both had a good laugh at that, and Bonnie glared up at her mommy for interrupting her sleep. "Yes, that was one of the funniest things I've seen in a very long time."

Matt sobered. "How did you feel today? Other than being quiet, you seemed like you were okay."

"It was alright. It was good to see some of those people again. I'm really glad Grace stopped by, too. She seems like a nice woman."

"Damn good detective, too," Matt said. "She was so dogged, Jules, she just wouldn't quit. Great gal." Matt was silent for a moment, then, "Julie, will you ever tell me what happened to you? I mean, I'm not pushing you…I want you to feel comfortable…but, will you?"

Julie nearly melted, her brother seeming like a little boy again. She smiled, slipping an arm out of her cocoon and reaching for his hand. He grasped it tightly. "I will. Someday. To be honest with you, Matty, I don't want to upset you. Trust me. It will."

Matt nodded. "I'm sure. But I want to be able to understand. Like the thing with the eggs… You love eggs."

"Not anymore." Julie studied the top of Clyde's head for a moment, loving the way the thin hairs stood up like he was a little Rocker dog. When she spoke again, her voice was very quiet. "When he brought me upstairs, he always fed me omelets." She stared past Matt, back into a memory that was burned into her brain. "Cheese and ham."

Matt swallowed down his emotions at the dead look in Julie's normally vibrant green eyes. "How often?"

Fear and anger swelling inside her, she shook her head. "I can't, I'm sorry. I don't want to talk."

Matt hid his disappointment. He wanted to understand, but knew better than to push. He squeezed her hand. "Okay. Get some rest."

Julie watched as he stood up and went to the door. When his hand reached for the doorknob, she called, "Matt?" He turned to look at her. "Happy Thanksgiving. I have a lot to be thankful for."

Matt smiled. "Me, too. Goodnight, Jules."

"Night, Matty."

Chapter Twenty-nine

Walking along Maple Street, Remmy admired the storefronts. It was her day off from the laundromat on Sixth, where she was working as general help. If someone needed quarters and the machine was broken, she was your girl; if the dryer stopped working or overheated due to lint buildup, she was your girl; if someone was dropping off laundry to be washed by the employees at Gil's Fluff & Fold, she was your girl. She enjoyed the work, nice and laid back, and she was able to wear jeans. She enjoyed tinkering, so fixing the machines was satisfying too.

It was a gorgeous day for January—blue skies and no snow in the forecast, a mild forty-six degrees. Bundled up, she walked along, absently sidestepping a kid on a bike as her eyes fixed on the simple white letters on a store window: BRENDEN—SPIRITUAL HEALER AND GUIDE

Underneath the large letters was a list of the services that Brenden could provide for the customer, including palm reading, magic stones, and mapping of past lives.

Curious, Remmy pushed through into the shop, the tinkling of gentle chimes announcing her presence. The store was long and narrow. Shoulder high shelving units offered a variety of books on spirituality, past lives, astro-projection, dream interpretation, and astrology, among others. Candles of every shape, size, and color were gathered in an open glass case; handwritten signs beneath each explained what it was used for. The store was filled with the scent of an earthy incense, which Remmy thought was wonderful, if a little too intense for the space. She stopped and stared at a large cloth poster—the face of a man, a round glow seeming to emanate from dead center in his forehead.

THE LIFE'S THIRD EYE, it read in black lettering across the top.

"Wonderful work, isn't it?"

Remmy jumped. She hadn't heard him come up beside her. A man, short in stature and frail of frame, stood beside her, a smirk on his boyish face. His short, light brown hair fell into one brown eye. "A friend of mine made that for me."

Remmy nodded in acknowledgement, realizing that the man pictured on the cloth was the man standing beside her.

"I'm Brenden." He held out his hand and shook hers briefly.

His gaze was intense as he studied her, and it made Remmy extremely uncomfortable. She flinched when he reached up and gently tapped the center of her forehead. A strange sensation flowed through her body at the contact, almost as though she had received an electrical shock. She backed away one step. "You have the sight, don't you?" he said softly, his words a statement.

"I don't know what you mean," she said, unable to shake his dark gaze.

Brenden smiled. "How can I help you today? Are you in need of a Tarot reading? Or perhaps a deck of Angel cards instead? Maybe a charm or magic stones."

"Oh, uh, no. I was just looking around." She'd been in spiritual shops many times before, always drawn by that which many people did not understand. "This is nice," she said lamely. In truth, the shop felt very different. It felt as though she was being watched. She knew it had nothing to do with security cameras. There was a buzz in the air, a feeling as if the shop itself was a sentient being.

"You look lost," Brenden said, once again appearing stealthily at her side.

Remmy wondered if his observation was as simple as it sounded. "Do you have any pendulums?" She didn't really want one, but she had no response to his observation. It was likely that her own misgivings and uncertainties were hearing things in Brenden's voice that weren't actually there. Looking at him, she had the strangest sensation that he had all the answers. If only she knew the questions.

"Of course." He led her through the maze of aisles and displays to the cash register, which sat on a glass case filled with a variety of pendulums. There were large ones, small ones, some made of stone, and others made of semi-precious jewels. "Do you have much experience with pendulums?" he asked, all business.

"I used to have one."

"What happened to it?" Brenden asked, unlocking the cabinet door on his side of the case and reaching inside. He brought out the large display case and rested it on top of the glass countertop. The pendulums were laid out, chains pinned to the felt.

"I don't know," Remmy said with a sheepish grin. "One move too many, is my guess."

He nodded. "You're a restless soul. A wanderer." Remmy said nothing, only barely holding his gaze. Brenden smiled again, indicating the pendulums at his fingertips. "Well, since you've had one before, you know that not all pendulums speak to you. The spirit inside it must feel you, and you it, or it won't work."

Remmy had heard that before. She glanced at him

with questioning eyes. At his nod, she gently unpinned a teardrop pendulum made of onyx. It was heavy in her hand, the chain made of thin silver. She studied the pendulum, seeing if she could feel the heat from the stone as she had with her old one.

"I don't think that's the right one for you," Brenden said, plucking the onyx from her hand. She would have been irritated if she hadn't agreed with his assessment. "Try this one."

The pendulum was a single heavy piece of jade shaped into a smooth cone nearly three inches long. A small jade button fastened at the top of the chain served as the grip. She held it in her palm, closing her eyes as she tried to feel the pendulum, allowing it to speak to her. She could feel the subtle heat pouring into her palm, almost as though the jade were aflame from the inside. Taking the grip between thumb and index finger, she let the pendulum slip from her hand, its weight pulling the chain taut as she held it aloft, her palm no more than an inch below the point of the cone.

Brenden watched waiting for the pendulum to stop spinning.

Remmy wanted to see how the pendulum reacted, so asked it to show her "yes". After a moment, the pendulum shook slightly, as though unsure which way to move. The heat began to swell once more in Remmy's palm, the jade slowly circling clockwise.

"Stop," Remmy murmured. The pendulum came to an almost instant stop. "Show me 'no'." Again the stone seemed somewhat unsure, then began to circle counter clockwise.

"It seems like a good match," Brenden said. "The stone responds to you well."

Remmy nodded, watching the hypnotic movement

as the pendulum circled in a swift, strong movement. "Stop," she said, the stone immediately complying. "How much?" she asked, glancing up at the small man.

"Pendulums are seventy-five."

"Oh." Bummed, as she would have liked to have had a pendulum again, Remmy handed the jade back. "That's a little steep for me. I'm sorry. But thanks for your help." She turned.

"Remmy?" he said, stopping her dead in her tracks. "For you, twenty. This would be good for you." He held the pendulum out to her in invitation.

Shaken, Remmy scrutinized him. "Do I know you?"

Brenden met her gaze, cupping the stone in his hand, the chain dangling from between his fingers. "We all know each other. The Sight doesn't lie."

Truly disturbed, Remmy backed away from Brenden, her back stopping abruptly against the front door, which sent the chimes tinkling again. "I gotta go," she muttered, pushing out into the sunny day.

ᘓᘓᘓᘓ

"Skylar, I need you to bring in the rest of the dogs' stuff," Julie called out from her kitchen, where she was unpacking groceries. She had been thoroughly shocked when the community had given her a check for twenty thousand dollars for Christmas, monies collected through donations from Woodland's citizens and local businesses. Moved to tears, she had accepted the money. She was going to have to use a portion of it to catch up on her house payments. While she'd been captive, the bank had been working with Matt, as there was no way he could afford two mortgages. Now that she had returned, their generosity had come to an end.

Tonight would be the first night she was going to stay at her own house, and Skylar had happily volunteered to stay with her. They had a video game marathon planned for later—nearly six months in the making—with giant bowls of popcorn to munch. Julie smiled, listening to her dogs tear around the house as they chased each other, their quiet growls audible every once in a while.

Skylar ran back into the house, the dogs' bed and toys in hand, immediately heading toward the living room where he knew they belonged. Bonnie and Clyde tore out of the kitchen and nearly knocked Skylar over in their excitement to get into their bed. The boy giggled as he plopped down onto his butt and accepted the Yorkie bath.

For a short while, Julie felt normal again. She laughed and cried out as Skylar kicked her butt with the Wii system he had brought over. She was exhausted from their intense tennis match, then giggling like a schoolgirl as they boxed. She couldn't believe they had actually worked up a sweat.

"Uncle! I give!" she called out, plopping down on the couch. With a cry of victory, Skylar jumped at her, ultimately landing with his head in her lap and torturing her with quick pokes in the stomach. "You little shit," she growled, laughing wildly as she tried to avoid his fingers while getting in her own licks. Pooped and hungry, boy and woman headed off toward the kitchen to make dinner.

⁂

The blue sky above shimmered with the bright sun. A few lazy clouds floated by, their shadows painted across the wild flowers, erasing the sun's reflection on the calm waters of the nearby water for just a moment.

Julie felt the softness of her dress flowing around her legs, a sense of peace and happiness filling her. She turned in a slow circle, eyes scanning the seemingly endless field where the fourth side faded into dark woods and the waters of a small stream gurgled to her left. Knowing she was waiting for someone, she started toward the water. She would go to the coolness of the stream and wait.

Bending down, she dipped her fingers in the water, finding it strange that she didn't feel the cool wetness she expected, but rather hot air, which nearly burned her fingertips. Suddenly she felt a trickle of fear dripping lazily down her spine. She rose to her feet, squeezing her eyes shut as she dreaded turning around. Her heart was pounding, and she felt faint. Opening her eyes she saw a shadow on the bank of the stream, right next to, and slightly behind, her own.

❧❧❧❧❧

"Remmy!" Julie shot up, nearly knocking Clyde to the floor. She didn't notice. Her heart pounded, and a thin sheen of sweat covered her body. Wide green eyes took in the darkened room. She felt a presence and turned. Skylar was standing next to the bed.

"Are you okay, Aunt Julie?" Fear made his voice tremble. "You were making funny noises."

Julie took several deep breaths, her hand trembling as she ran it through her hair, pushing it off her forehead. "Yeah," she said, "Just a bad dream." She calmed as he wrapped his arms around her neck.

"I'm sorry you're so upset, Aunt Julie," Skylar said into her neck.

She hugged him tightly then kissed his forehead. "I'm sorry I woke you up, baby. Go back to sleep, okay?"

He studied her with eyes far more mature than they should have been. He'd been through a lot.

"Are you sure you're gonna be okay?"

"I'm sure." She watched him reluctantly leave her alone, listening until she heard him climb into the bed that was reserved for only him, then she blew out a breath. Two pairs of large brown eyes looked up at her. "Sorry, guys," she said, gathering her two little dogs to her and closing her eyes, reveling in the comfort they gave her.

Unable and unwilling to go back to sleep, Julie went down to the kitchen and made herself some coffee. Ironically, that had been one of the most difficult things to deal with during her captivity — no coffee. She had no idea just how addicting it actually was until she started getting caffeine headaches. They had passed quickly, but she had missed the taste, as well as what it did for her.

Sitting at one of the breakfast barstools and sipping her coffee, she tried to direct her mind back to the nightmare, needing to discern what it was about. She had always been a fan of dreams, feeling that it was the soul speaking of desires, fears, or needs that the conscious mind wasn't ready to admit or was too busy to consider. She knew the nightmare had to do with Sergio, and the fear that she felt would forever be her companion. The details of the dream were fading fast, leaving Julie with only the sense of unease it had aroused.

Chapter Thirty

Matt drained his coffee, and Roman walked over and grabbed his mug to refill it. "How are you?" Matt asked. He was grateful to the young man who had helped Remmy find Julie and the others.

"I'm great, Matt. How is Julie doing?"

"Good, good. Day by day, you know?"

Roman nodded, set the freshly filled cup on the table, then walked away to wait on other customers.

Matt looked around the coffeehouse with mild interest, overhearing snippets of conversation: "...telling you, it's wrong; ...thought it was time we actually went out; ...time does the movie start." After another ten minutes, the door opened and a customer was blown in on the cold January wind. Matt raised his hand to get Grace Cowan's attention.

She wove her way through the busy shop, removed her heavy overcoat and hung it on the back of the chair across from him, and sat down. "Sorry I'm late," she said.

"No problem. Glad you could meet me on such short notice."

"Anytime, Matt, you know that." Grace waved at Roman, and the young man quickly made his way over and took her order. In less than five minutes, he had returned with a muffin and a cup of hot chai tea. As she stirred in some cinnamon and honey, Grace looked up at Matt Wilson, her dark eyes expectant.

"Julie moved back into her own house." He sipped

from his cup. "Skylar stayed with her about a week ago. He said she woke up from another nightmare, and he told me about something that she said that rattles me, Grace."

"What did she say?" Grace asked, biting into her muffin.

"Remmy."

She stopped chewing.

At Grace's silence, Matt continued. "How would Julie know that name? I've never mentioned her. I didn't want to bring back anything that might upset her. And Julie refused to watch any news coverage of the story."

"Her therapist?"

Matt shook his head. "I asked her. Dr. Corregan said she's never discussed the details of the case with Julie." He took another drink of his coffee. "Do you think we should tell her about Remmy? By the way, have you heard from Remmy at all?"

Grace shook her head, swallowed a bit of muffin, then sipped her tea. "I haven't heard anything from her. Aside from the nurse saying that Remmy was heading to the Midwest somewhere, I know nothing."

"Then do you think we should say something to Julie?"

Grace sighed and sat back in her chair. She had felt all along that Julie should be told about Remmy. She also was curious as to whether Julie had ever felt the connection that Remmy had. "I'll talk to her," she said, leaving no room for argument. She and Remmy had worked closely together to solve Julie's case, and she felt the need to share all she knew with Julie. Remmy deserved that recognition.

❧❧❧❧

When the doorbell chimed, Bonnie and Clyde ran to the door, their butts moving from side to side as their stubby tails wagged in anticipation of meeting a new friend. Julie nudged them aside and looked out onto the porch through the peephole. Grace was right on time. She pulled the door open and said, "Welcome to my home, Detective Cowan."

"Thank you, Julie. And please, call me Grace." Grace stepped across the threshold, looking around the modest, yet wonderfully maintained home. "This is really nice."

"Thank you," Julie said, pride evident in her voice. "Come on into the kitchen; I have coffee ready."

Grace followed Julie, who was showing physical improvement every time she saw her. Her clothing no longer hung on her as it had over Thanksgiving. Though still thin, Julie had put on some weight. Grace accepted the mug of coffee, and she and Julie sat at the round kitchen table.

"How have you been?" Grace asked.

Julie nodded, her hands cupping her own mug. "I've been okay. I love Matt dearly, but it's really good to be home."

"I bet." Grace laughed. "I would've throttled my brother long before now." They both laughed, then settled in. "Listen, speaking of your brother, he told me something the other day, and I felt it was really important to talk to you about it."

"Alright." Julie set her coffee cup down and pushed it away.

"First off, what, if anything, do you recall about your rescue?"

Julie sighed. "I know you were there. I know the bastard was shot and killed. I remember someone else being there, but I have no clue who it was. That's pretty much it. The rest is a blur."

"Matt told me that you were woken up by a nightmare one night when Skylar was staying with you. Your cries woke him." Grace saw the recollection and embarrassment in Julie's usually clear green eyes. "You said a name."

"Remmy. I said it once before, too, when I was there, in the pit."

"Do you know who Remmy is?"

Julie shook her head and grabbed her coffee cup, more for something to do with her hands than because she was actually thirsty. Her eyes took on a faraway look. She hadn't told anyone what she was going to tell Grace.

"When I was at that son-of-a-bitch's house I would have these dreams. At first they started out like actual dreams, at night. But then, somewhere along the way, they turned into daydreams. I don't know." She shrugged and shook her head. "It seemed like…when things were at their worst, I would find myself in the field."

"Field?" Grace listened intently, her mind spinning as she tried to put the puzzle together.

"Yeah. A field. It was always beautiful there, the skies clear and bright. A happy place. One time, even Skylar and my dogs showed up." She chuckled; it sounded silly, even to her own ears. "That was only once, but in that dream, as well as all the others, there was someone there with me, walking with me, holding me…" Julie's eyebrows drew together in thought as she struggled to remember details about the blurry figure who always accompanied her, giving her strength and comfort. "I don't know. The night Skylar heard me… dreaming, I was back in that field, waiting for my dream friend." She met Grace's gaze. "She never showed."

"So, this guardian in your dreams, was her name

Remmy?"

Julie thought for a moment, resting her chin in the palm of her hand. Finally she nodded. "I think so. I don't know that I'd swear to it, but I think so, yes."

"Okay." Grace took a long drink from her coffee then set the mug aside. "I'm going to tell you a story. You're going to think I've lost my mind, but I swear it's the truth."

Julie was intrigued. "Alright. Let me get us some more coffee first so we can settle in." She got up and refilled Grace's cup, topping off her own as well. Resuming her seat, she waited.

"Not long after you disappeared, a young woman came to the police station and spoke with my partner. She claimed that she had information on your disappearance, and that there was more than one woman missing. Unfortunately my partner didn't take her as seriously as he should have, but she didn't give up. She claimed to have what she called 'visions', and dreams."

Julie listened in disbelief as Grace continued with her story, telling her that the woman was able to pick up on all the weird collections Sergio had, as well as realizing that she had actually come face to face with the abductor at her job at the convenience store and gas station. Julie felt sick when she found out the young woman had even picked up on Roxie's murder.

Julie was quiet for a long time, absorbing all that she'd been told, calmly sipping her coffee. At last, Julie met Grace's patient gaze. "What's her name?" she whispered.

Grace's gaze was unwavering. "Remmy."

Chapter Thirty-one

Remmy glanced up at the storefront window, chewing aggressively on a piece of strawberry Bubble Yum. She shoved her hands into her pockets, bouncing on the balls of her feet to stay warm. It was a frigid February day, but she was trying to muster her courage to go inside. Her first visit into Brenden's shop more than a month earlier had disturbed her deeply. She couldn't get her exchange with the shop owner out of her mind. The solid wooden wall blocking her memory was beginning to weaken, and though she feared what was on the other side, she instinctively knew Brenden could help.

The tinkling above the door announced her entrance, and she was immediately soothed by the soft African music playing in the background, as well as the scent of incense—soft and musky. The few customers looking around the store made Remmy fidgety; her fingers played with the loose change in her pants pocket. She saw Brenden speaking with a young man, a teenager apparently interested in buying a deck of Tarot cards. Brenden was explaining the differences between two decks that were resting on the glass counter. She saw his dark eyes dart over to her then return to the customer.

Remmy was perusing a section of charms when she was approached by a beautiful black woman in traditional African dress. Her skin was flawless, eyes, large and chocolate brown. When she smiled, her teeth were straight and very white against her dark skin.

"Hello," she said. "Can I help you?"

"Oh, uh, no. I'm waiting for Brenden. I see he's busy, so I think I'll go." Remmy gave the tall woman a weak smile then turned to bolt.

"Remmy, is it?"

Remmy froze. She turned slowly and took in the gentle warmth in the woman's eyes. "How do you know my name?"

"Brenden told me. He's been expecting your return."

The woman stayed rooted a few feet away from Remmy. Brenden joined her, placing a kiss on the dark woman's cheek then turning to Remmy with a smile.

"I'm so glad you returned," he said, his voice as soft as she remembered it.

Remmy felt trapped, even though the door was only five feet behind her. The couple studied her, Brenden very much looking through her. "How do you know my name? And don't feed me the bull you did last time."

Brenden smiled fondly as he approached her. "Would you join me? I'd like to speak with you, explain some things."

Remmy warily eyed him and the woman. "Alright," she said at length.

"Wonderful." He turned to the beautiful woman behind him. "Fayola, please watch the front.

"Of course." She turned to Remmy. "Pleased to meet you, Remmy. We shall talk later."

Brenden rested a hand on Remmy's lower back to get her moving in the direction he wished her to go. They walked toward the back of the long store where Brenden held a curtain aside, allowing Remmy to enter the small room ahead of him. She noted the mural of the night sky painted on the ceiling, twilight painted on one wall, dawn on another. There was a small square table at the center of the room. A well-worn deck of Tarot cards lay in the center of the wooden tabletop.

"Are you going to tell my fortune?" she asked as she sat, nodding at the deck.

"No need. You wear your soul on your sleeve," Brenden said with a friendly smile. "Can I get you some green tea?" He indicated an industrial sized pot plugged into the wall behind his chair.

"Uh, sure." Remmy watched as he busied himself. Soon she had a steaming cup of tea sitting before her.

"I'm glad you returned, Remmy," Brenden said, setting his cup on the table. "I hoped you would."

"The lady out there said you were expecting me."

"My wife, Fayola. Yes, I was. Still," he shrugged, "we don't always get what we want. Right?" At Remmy's nod, he smiled and sipped his tea. "So, tell me about you. How long have you known you had The Sight?"

Remmy was tempted to tell Brenden to go to hell and get up and walk out. She grabbed onto the edge of the table, forcing herself to stay seated. Dark eyes followed the movement, a slight smirk lifting the corner of Brenden's lip. She took a drink of tea, her hand trembling. If Brenden was what he claimed to be, it would be the first time she'd ever met anyone else with "The Sight". The tea was surprisingly good, but still she set the cup down and concentrated on the man waiting expectantly across from her. "I've had visions ever since I can remember. When I was young, they started out small. I'd know what song was coming on the radio next. I knew my dog was going to get a drink of water, that kind of thing."

"Ah, yes," Brenden said with a nod. "I remember those days."

"As I got older, it would happen far more often.

It started turning more sinister, too. Some guy would walk by me on the street, and suddenly I felt the pain of the leg he broke when he was fifteen, you know?" At Brenden's nod, she continued. "It began to filter into every part of my life. I really think everyone thought I was nuts. God, I've been fired from so many jobs because of this." Remmy stared past Brenden, back into a past that was troubling and often painful. "Yep, everyone thought I was nuts."

"And what do you think? Do you think you're crazy?"

Remmy was silent for a long time, contemplating his question. Her mother had admitted her to a mental hospital when she was fourteen. She had run away. That was the last time she'd seen the woman. "I don't know. Right now I'm not fully myself. I…" She abruptly took a sip from her tea. "I can't remember."

Brenden misunderstood what she was saying. "Can't remember what?"

She met his steady gaze. "I can't remember the last five months of last year. I arrived in a small town off the interstate, Woodland, I know that much. I know I had a job, and even an apartment. I remember the people I knew — Roman, Detective Grace Cowan, even Matt Wilson. But I don't know why I know them. Just that I… do. I woke up in a hospital, shot in the back and missing my spleen. I was told how I came to be shot, but I have no recollection of it."

Brenden was intrigued. "What were you told?"

"That I led the cops to rescue some women from a madman who was a rapist and a murderer. That supposedly I had a connection to one of the captives." She began to feel uncomfortable under Brenden's intense scrutiny. His dark eyes studied every inch of her face, seemingly memorizing her features. He finally settled on her eyes.

"You're so troubled," he said at last, his voice a whisper. He sipped his tea. "You have a very strong, very powerful soul, Remmy. Your Sight is amazing. What is your connection?"

"My connection?"

"Yes. What draws you in to your target? For instance, with Fayola she seems to be attracted to immense disappointment, failures, that kind of thing. She can sense it and tap into it."

Remmy leaned forward in her chair, her interest piqued as she was beginning to recognize that maybe she had found a kindred spirit. "What about you?"

"For me it's a little different. My gift is reading the souls of those like us. I can read you, I can read Fayola. I can always spot someone with The Sight. I spotted you, didn't I?"

Remmy nodded. Meeting a kindred spirit made her feel immeasurably better, yet Brenden's knowledge of her was also truly disturbing. "Okay, so what's in my soul now?"

"You're lost, deeply troubled. Don't block things out, Remmy. You were given a gift, allow that gift to work for you. Your mind is very much like a boarded up room right now, but there is also a sledgehammer leaning against the barricade, just waiting for you to use it."

"I don't know how to break through, and I'm scared to death of what I might find if I tried. What would I find on the other side?"

"Your Destiny," he said, not batting an eye. "Don't allow the emotional pain of others deter you." Brenden smiled, a very knowing smile. "Trust me, Remmy. You really want to get to that other side."

❧ ❧ ❧ ❧

Julie ran her fingers across the smooth surface of a desk under one of the windows. She stopped, turning her back to the desk and looking out over the small apartment. Joan Watson stood in the open doorway, casually leaning against the doorframe.

"How long did she live here?" Julie asked, eyes grazing the bed — only a bare mattress and headboard.

"Not long. A couple of months. I've got all her things packed up in the basement."

"Why did you keep them?"

Joan shrugged. "In case she ever decided to come back for them, I guess. Same reason I haven't rented the place out."

"But it's February," Julie said with a small smile.

Joan chuckled. "I know. I really liked the kid. She was a good egg." *Plus, I feel guilty as hell.*

"She worked at your store, right?" At Joan's nod, Julie sighed. "Tell me about her. What was she like?"

"Very sweet. A bit quirky, but now I understand a lot of that had to do with her...visions. Beautiful young woman. The most gorgeous eyes I've ever seen." She smiled at her memories. "Very ballsy." She chuckled, thinking of her first meeting with Remmy, when she applied for a job. She told Julie about it.

"Wait," Julie said, holding up her hand as she tried to grasp onto something floating in her mind. "What day was that?" When Joan told her the date, Julie's mind reeled back to that day: Skylar's game. "What does Remmy look like?"

"Tall, dark hair, bright blue eyes, a bit thin."

"Oh my God!" Julie's eyes widened as her hand covered her mouth. She met Joan's surprised look. "I gave her a ride into town that day. That was her." She looked down at her hands; they were trembling. She thought back to that day, to the short drive into town and how odd she had thought her passenger. Remmy had seemed to disappear for a few moments, returning to her surroundings with a look of terror in her eyes as she looked at Julie. *Be careful, okay?* Those words echoed in Julie's mind. "She knew," she whispered. "She knew even then."

"She put so much effort into trying to find you, Julie. I remember the first time she had a vision in front of me. My husband and I thought she was having a seizure or something. Scared the hell out of me." Each of them was lost in her own thoughts for a moment before Joan spoke again. "You know, once Remmy was in the hospital, she didn't remember any of this." She gestured around the room and then at the two of them. "She doesn't remember you, or Sergio Venti, none of it. I kind of wonder if it was her mind's way of saving her sanity while her body healed."

"She saved my life, didn't she?" Julie said softly. She had heard reports that Remmy had taken the bullet meant for her, but she couldn't recall the exact events all that well. The shock and excitement from that day had caused one big blur.

"That she did. Took a bullet in the back. Lost her spleen."

"I owe her so much, Joan. I really hope I can thank her someday."

"I'm sure you'll get the chance, Julie."

<hr>

Remmy was on her knees, pieces of the coin changer machine on the tile around her. The laundry was closed, so she had the place to herself. She had music from the musical *Aspects of Love* playing, Michael Ball singing about just how much love could change everything. She hummed along, suddenly on a Broadway musical kick for no particular reason. Last month it had been Tori Amos, even though she'd never been a huge fan.

As she listened to the musical's characters of Alex and Rose arguing—Alex's Uncle George was coming between them—Remmy continued to tinker. She was amazed by just how much she loved fixing the equipment, and by how good she was at it. The coin changing machine was an ancient piece of junk that the laundromat owner, Sid, had bought from a closing arcade twenty years earlier. It had probably already been twenty years old at that time. She pulled the machine apart at least twice a week, un-jamming the worn tumblers inside.

She held the penlight between her teeth as she pulled apart the final panel, which covered the jam. When it was free, she set the light aside and reached up into the channel with the screwdriver, poking until she felt the resistance she'd been feeling for.

"There you are," she said, grunting as she removed the screwdriver and then unscrewed the plate that covered the fourth side of the channel. The Phillips screws gave way easily, allowing her to remove the long, thin piece of metal. Remmy nearly lost her lunch when she saw what the problem was. "Oh Jesus."

With an expression of disgust, Remmy used the screwdriver to push out the decomposing roach parts, the bug apparently having gotten itself stuck inside the machine where it perished.

The spider scurried out through the long, jagged crack, the barest hint of daylight coming in through it. An empty pair of shackles rested on the dirt floor, the chain snaked around one metal bracelet.

Drip, drip, drip...

A dog whined, scratching at the door. On the stovetop was a pan, something simmering inside. Water turned on, pipes protested.

Shower turned off, a towel snatched from the towel bar next to the sliding doors.

Drip, drip, drip...

A naked woman lay on the bed, arms above her head, legs together, stretched out, crossed at the ankles — looked like Jesus. A blonde head. The head turned and the eyes opened. Intense green eyes stared, lifeless. The pale lips opened—

"Remmy..."

Remmy gasped, startled enough to throw the machine part to the ground where it clattered against the bubbling linoleum. Her heart was pounding, her breathing uneven, in danger of hyperventilation. She scooted across the floor until her back came into contact with a washing machine. Running a trembling hand through her hair to push it off her face, she tried to catch her breath.

"My God," she whispered, gulping in a lungful of air. She looked around for her bottle of Dr Pepper, finally spotting it on top of one of the dryers. She scrambled to her feet and, in two huge leaps, had it in hand. She chugged like a woman dying of thirst, eyes closing against the pain dead center in her forehead. Familiar pain.

Setting the bottle of soda back on the metal lid, she took several deep breaths. She visualized the face in her mind's eye—blonde hair and green eyes. Suddenly the lifeless eyes were transformed; they blinked. A small smile curled the lips as the face slowly lost its pallor. The face was beautiful, the eyes alive and with a bit of a twinkle.

"Thank you."

Remmy looked around, startled by the words that seemed to echo inside the laundromat. She realized they were coming from the woman in her thoughts. Suddenly image after image crashed into her consciousness:

Sitting in the passenger seat of a small car. "Be careful, okay?"

Sunlight coming in between iron bars on a window.

Dark eyes closed in ecstasy, along with the sounds of loud grunting.

Blood, the taste of it along with flesh.

Driving like a lunatic, tunnel vision as she careened around a corner onto a new street.

A naked woman running out of a house, screaming. The feel of her cold flesh against Remmy's warm hands. Soft skin.

A sense of absolute terror.

The loud sound of a gunshot, a sharp sting in her back. The feel of the cold snow underneath her cheek.

With startling clarity, Remmy had the entire picture. She consciously remembered the cold day in November, leading Grace through an obstacle course to find Julie, to save her. She remembered the naked woman running from the house, running straight to her, clinging to her, clawing at her. She remembered thinking that she would do anything to save Julie, anything to protect her, even put herself in the line of fire. She remembered the day she thought Julie had been killed, but in fact it had been Roxie. The relief that had flooded through her when she found out Julie was alive; their embrace in the field. Relief.

"Julie," she whispered, eyes closing with a soft sigh and smile.

Chapter Thirty-two

Julie pushed the grocery cart along an aisle, a third of the way finished with picking up her monthly groceries. She stopped in front of the spices, picking up oregano and chili powder. Setting the containers in the basket, she smiled at the two figures walking toward her, the woman pushing a half-full grocery cart.

"Bob," Julie said warmly, stepping into the warm embrace of her former boss. He gave her a fatherly squeeze then released her. She accepted a second hug from Bob's wife. "It's good to see you too, Charlene."

"It's good luck that I ran into you here, Julie. I was actually going to give you a call tomorrow."

"Oh?"

"I want you to come back. I've got a position opening up for seventh grade, and I'd love nothing more than for you to fill it starting in August." Julie's fear and panic were apparent on her face, and the principal raised his hands to forestall any protest. "Take some time to think about it. It's only the beginning of March, so you don't have to make a decision right away. Okay?" He gave her a gentle smile.

"Okay. I'll think about it."

"Excellent. It was great seeing you again." Bob gently squeezed her shoulder as he and his wife passed by.

Julie watched them go, her heart beating wildly in her throat. Could she possibly go back to that building, see that parking lot again? She drove past one day, hoping to pull into a space and sit it out, let her nerves and fears melt away. She hadn't even been able to turn in the driveway.

"I don't know if I can do this," she said with a heavy sigh.

❧❧❧❧

After dinner was eaten and the dishes cleaned up, Julie sat on the couch watching the evening news, her dogs resting on either side of her. She absently ran her fingers through the thin hair atop the dogs' heads. She wasn't listening to the news anchor; her thoughts were drifting back to running into Bob Greene at the store, and his offer. She wanted to go back to work; she missed the kids terribly, missed feeling whole. She wanted her life back.

A phone call to Matt to get his opinion hadn't been helpful. He reluctantly admitted that he felt she wasn't ready. Wasn't ready for what? To stand alone all day in a classroom with her students? To interact with her peers? To step outside her house? She felt she would be able to do all of those things, if only she could take the first step and pull into that parking lot.

❧❧❧❧

The trees whispered to each other as a soft breeze blew through them; the breeze also rippled the water in the stream. The landscape seemed so clear, so vivid. Julie walked to the edge of the water, feeling the soft material of her dress brushing against her calves. The dress pooled around her as she knelt down and reached out. She dipped her fingers into the water, smiling at its coolness as the water lapped at her skin.

Julie remained still, looking out over the water, trying to see what lay beyond, but she couldn't. It was almost as though the boundaries of the world ended there, just at the edge of the stream. Fear clutched at her heart, making her want to cry out. Blood raced through her body, crashing into her stomach. She felt the heat of her unwanted companion against her back, as hot as the sun's rays upon bare skin.

Standing, she squeezed her eyes shut, her mouth gone dry. She was afraid to turn around, afraid to face him, though he didn't move. His shadow stood tall, legs spread in aggression. Julie began to tremble, a small whimper escaping her lips.

Julie thrashed, her legs scissoring beneath the sheets. Her fingers grabbed convulsively at the pillow like a pulse. "No. Please, no..."

The shadow moved closer. She tried to breathe, but the breath was stolen from her lungs by her all-consuming fear.

A soft touch on her shoulder—

Julie cried out in surprise, Bonnie raising her head from Julie's hip at the sound.

The hand didn't belong to him; his shadow's hand hadn't moved. Turning her tear-streaked face, she saw kind blue eyes staring back at her. Emitting a sigh of relief, Julie allowed herself to be engulfed in a tight, safe embrace, her fingers digging claw-like into Remmy's shirt, holding her close. She no longer felt the shadow behind her, no longer felt the fear. She rested her head on the strong shoulder, holding on tighter.

Julie rested on her side, her legs relaxing into a more comfortable position, a deep sigh released as she settled into a deep, restful sleep.

Chapter Thirty-three

Hey, Monica?" Remmy called as she entered the kitchen and tossed her jacket across the back of a chair. She could hear her cousin working in her art studio in the back. Together they had renovated the former garage into a painting studio. Remmy strode to the back door and pulled it open so Monica could hear her calling.

"Be right there!" Monica called back. "I sure am glad that spring is on the way, I've had more than enough of this damn winter. It's been harsh, even for Nebraska," Monica said, entering the kitchen, and heading to the bathroom.

Remmy was making coffee, her stomach in a turmoil about how Monica was going to react to her news. She could hear the water running and knew Monica was washing up. Remmy poured her cousin a cup of coffee and fixed it just how she liked it, and sat expectant for her return.

"How was your day?" Monica asked, picking up the mug and raising it to her lips. "Ohhh, perfect. Thank you."

"It was good. Spent some time with Brenden and Fayola after work."

"Oh yeah? How did that go?"

"Went well." Remmy was quiet for a moment, sipping from her coffee, trying to decide on the best way to approach a difficult announcement. "Mon, you know I love you, and I'm so glad you found me."

Monica studied her, glancing down at the fidgeting of her hands around the mug, and the way she wouldn't meet Monica's eyes. "Remmy? Rem, look at me." Remmy slowly looked up, blue eyes brimming. "Honey, what's wrong?"

She reached out and clasped Remmy's hand, and Remmy appreciated the touch. Finally she laid it on the line. "I have to leave. I need to go back."

Remmy winced as she could easily see the disappointment and pain in Monica's eyes. Even so, she gave Remmy a brave smile and asked, "Why? What is there for you, honey?"

Remmy shook her head. "I don't know, Mon. I just feel drawn there. It's like something's calling to me. Who knows?" She shrugged. "It may be because now that I remember everything, I need to make sure everything's okay. I don't know."

"When will you leave?"

"I'm thinking I'll head out next weekend. I talked to Sid today, gave him notice."

Monica nodded and was silent for a long time. Finally, she cleared her throat and spoke. "Don't lose touch again, okay?" Monica said, voice husky with emotion.

"Okay."

❧❧❧❧

A week later, Remmy rested her forehead against the cool glass, tugging the collar of her jacket up a little higher. She hated how cold Greyhound buses were. She watched the scenery whiz by. The snow had melted in most areas, and some frosted grass and barren dirt patches could be seen from time to time. She adjusted her headset to fit more comfortably, the music of John

Lennon calming her as her heart raced.

Remmy drew her legs up until only the toes of her boots were hanging off the front of her seat, arms wrapped around her shins. John Lennon's "#9 Dream" playing in her ears, her fingers began to tap against her denim-clad legs. Before she left Omaha, she'd considered calling Joan to see if it was possible to get her job back, but she changed her mind. She had always been able to find some kind of job at the drop of a hat, so if it didn't work out with the store, she'd find something else.

Forehead nearly numb, Remmy raised her head and looked around, taking note of several passengers near her. She was able to watch unobserved, so decided to put some of Fayola's lessons into practice. Surrounded by so many people, it was inevitable that she would pick up on something from one or more of them. They couldn't hide their souls from her.

Sitting across the narrow aisle from her was a woman, probably no older than thirty. Her shaggy, short brown hair had lighter highlights, which needed to be touched up. Her gaze was fixed on a laptop computer set up on her lap, her fingers typing at ridiculous speeds. Tapping continuously, the woman looked over at Remmy, dark eyes smiling politely before returning to her task. Apparently feeling somewhat nervous at the scrutiny, the woman reached out and placed her left hand atop the backpack that sat in the empty seat next to her.

Amused, not getting anything from the woman anyway, Remmy shifted her gaze elsewhere. She turned her attention to the man sitting in front of the typing woman. He sat in the seat on the aisle, his profile clearly visible to seeking blue eyes. She remembered seeing him get on the bus at the previous stop. He reminded her of a farmer. The weather beaten skin was tan from many seasons outside. His baseball cap was worn and just as weathered as he was. A short-sleeved button-up shirt was tucked into blue jeans, with work boots completing the outfit.

Movement caught her attention and Remmy's gaze dropped to the large, thick hand that was tapping lightly on his thigh. She watched it for a moment before looking back up at his profile. He glanced at her over his shoulder, smiling with a curt nod, then turned around to face front. Remmy gasped.

The room was empty, a few pieces of trash littering the carpets that still showed imprints from the furniture that had been there just the previous night. Head in his hands, he sat alone on a small, wooden cabinet that had been left in the middle of the room. Hot tears streamed between his fingers...

Feeling the man's loss and confusion, Remmy sent a sympathetic glance his way. More images began to come.

Yelling...fighting...crying...broken shards of a glass tossed into the trashcan...

Remmy closed her eyes, breathing deeply, forcing the images down. Strong iron bars of her mind slid into place with an audible clang, keeping the impressions at bay. Opening her eyes, she returned her gaze to the man, trying to see if she was getting something from him, anything. Nothing. The trick had been successful. Remmy grinned, resting her head back against the glass.

❧❧❧❧

Julie clenched the steering wheel, blowing out a loud breath. She was parked across the street from the school, eyes glued to the parking lot, which was filled with cars of faculty. Her eyes were drawn again and again to the two parking spaces that were forever burned into her memory — one for her white Miata, the other for the blue van with the plumbing logo on the side. Now a deep red Suburban and a small blue Toyota were parked in those spaces, but in her mind's eye, she was still there, struggling to get away from him.

She took a deep breath against the remembered feel of the large hand wrapping over her mouth and nose. Her chest heaved as she sucked in air.

Hands shaking, Julie started the car and drove toward the driveway into the parking lot. As she drew closer and was just about to pull in, fear consumed her and she gunned the engine, nearly hitting the chain link fence surrounding the parking lot as she peeled out.

"Fuck!" she yelled, pounding the steering wheel. "Goddamn you, Venti!" Ignoring the strange looks from her fellow drivers, she headed toward home. She stopped at a stop sign, waiting as a Greyhound bus pulled through, the large bus groaning as it turned toward the depot.

With a long sigh, Julie took her turn at the four-way stop, disheartened.

❧ ❧ ❧ ❧

Wide awake, Remmy was more than ready for her long trip to be over. The bus pulled into the small parking lot outside of Drew's Drug, which was lit up in orange neon. A young woman stood outside the store waiting, the large bag at her feet speaking volumes.

The air brakes whooshed in the late afternoon, then the driver took his time with paperwork before he rose from his seat and climbed down the three short stairs to step out into the day. Remmy stretched as best as she could in the confines of her seat, groaning at the stiffness in her legs and butt. She was in desperate need of a hot shower and a good meal.

Gathering up her duffel bag, she scooted toward the aisle, taking her place in the queue of passengers lining up to disembark at their final destination or just step off the bus to stretch their legs. Finally it was her turn to step off the bus. Remmy held her bag in front of her like a shield so she wouldn't bang anyone in the back of the head with it, slinging it to her back in the wide open space of the parking lot.

Back in the small town of Woodland, Remmy looked around, trying to get her bearings. It was a mild March day, the sky blue, fluffy white clouds floating around. She set her bag down, shrugged her jacket off and shoved it inside the duffel before slinging the bag up on her shoulder and heading out of the parking lot.

This time around, Remmy had ready cash, so she made her way to the Days Inn on Fremont Avenue rather than the rat trap she had stayed in the first time. She considered going to Joan's place, but in truth, felt guilty about how she had left, with just a note. At the time she hadn't thought anyone would much care if she left. In retrospect, she wondered if perhaps that had been a poor way to handle it. Securing herself a room, she showered, allowing the warmth to seep into her muscles and bones, a low groan escaping at the wonderful feeling of being clean. Once she was dressed, she grabbed her wallet and slid the black leather into the leg of her cargo pants, then shoved the big green bag underneath the bed. She was anxious to explore some of the town that had been home for a short time, though her stay there had been longer than any other before she went home with Monica. *Monica.*

"Crap."

Remmy stepped out onto the street, digging her

cell phone out of her pocket. Flipping it open, she dialed Monica's number. A quick conversation let Monica know Remmy was safe and sound, and would call her again later.

✥ ✥ ✥ ✥

Grace was pissed at her partner as she typed up her report. Brian had taken crappy notes, leaving her with the task of playing Columbo just to translate what had happened.

"Incompetent idiot," she muttered, bringing the page up to get a closer look at the particular word in question. Thinking perhaps it said "eloquent" instead of "elephant", she hit the delete key on the computer keyboard and typed in the new word. "Damned incompetent idiot."

"Hey, Cowan," one of the other detectives called from the hallway. She glanced up, glaring at being interrupted when she was almost finished. "You got someone here to see you."

"Damned incompetent town," she muttered, shoving her chair back and tossing her glasses to the desk. The hot day was making her irritable, despite the below zero setting on the air conditioning and she rolled the sleeves of her button up dress shirt as she walked down the hall. In the lobby, she looked around for someone who appeared to be waiting for someone. She stopped in her tracks, shocked to see Remmy, very relaxed, sitting in one of the prite plastic chairs.

"I'll be damned," she murmured, walking over to the young woman who apparently heard her voice because she glanced her way. Remmy grinned from ear to ear as she met Grace halfway, their embrace tight with emotion. When they parted, Grace held on to Remmy's arms, looking her over like a mother hen. "You look fantastic," she said, smiling warmly.

"Thanks. I feel fantastic."

"What brings you back? Everyone thought maybe you were just a figment of our collective imaginations, or something. Come on." Grace led Remmy through the inner workings of the police department, finally seating her in a chair next to her desk with a cup of bad coffee in front of her.

"I needed some time away, some time to heal physically. And mentally." She met coffee-colored eyes. "How is Julie?"

Grace was surprised but very pleased to hear that name from Remmy's lips. "She's doing well, from what I understand. I go to see her from time to time. I know her brother and nephew keep her busy. Word has it she may be teaching this coming fall, but I don't know."

"I'm really glad to hear it." Remmy knew she hadn't answered Grace's initial question of why she had returned; she had no intention of answering it. She wasn't sure herself. When she thought about it, even after hours of contemplation during the long bus ride, she still came up empty. "How about Pam and Cameron? Everyone make it okay? No one injured with the gunfire?"

"No, ma'am." Grace shook her head. "You and Venti were the only ones hurt, physically, anyway. Pam went to Texas to stay with her son, and Cameron moved in with her folks. Went back to college part-time, I hear." She stared at the young woman. "I was really worried about you, Remmy. To be honest, I'm not sure who suffered more last fall—the captives, or you."

"None of that matters, Grace. It's over."

"Yes, it is. My marriage thanks you for bringing the case to an end, too."

Remmy laughed, catching the attention of a few officers nearby. "Well, listen, I've got a few stops to make before the sun goes down and I get to crash for the night. Sleeping on a bus for two nights doesn't cut it."

"Okay." Grace walked Remmy to the lobby and gave her another hug. "You stay in touch, okay?" She handed Remmy one of her cards, her cell number jotted on the back with a pen borrowed from the desk sergeant. After giving Grace her promise and a final hug, Remmy left.

જી. જી. ૐ. ૐ

Julie was still upset with herself for her failure, thinking it ridiculous that she couldn't even pull into the damn parking lot. Distracted, she pulled the small white car up next to the gas pump then cut the engine. Reaching over to grab her purse from where it had fallen to the passenger floor, she didn't see the young woman jogging across the parking lot, hurrying to avoid having a Jeep Cherokee run her over. Extracting her wallet with a victorious cry, Julie stepped out of the car then cursed softly when she realized she had pulled the wrong side of the car up to the pump; the gas cap was on the other side.

"This has not been my day," she muttered, starting the Miata up and pulling away to turn around.

જી. જી. ૐ. ૐ

Remmy hesitated as she entered the store, a tightening in her chest as she felt something, a strange something. It felt as if there was a tether connected to her chest, pulling, tugging. Closing her eyes, she envisioned the prison bars once again, using them to sever the tether. She grinned, loving her new skill.

Looking down the few aisles of her old stomping grounds, she smiled at the memories of all the crazy displays she had constructed during her tenure at the store. She was pleased to see the Coke display, her last, was still being used. Grabbing a bottle of peach Propel from the cooler, she headed toward the bullpen. She found Mabel behind the counter.

"Well, hello there, stranger," the clerk said, ringing up the water. "How you been?"

"Alright, and yourself?"

Remmy handed over a couple of dollars. Mabel put the money in the register, then leaned on the counter.

"Okay. Been busy around here lately. Josh quit, and the new guy Joan hired is a real idiot, so…"

Remmy nodded in understanding. "Is Joan here?"

"Yep. In her office." Mabel hitched a thumb toward the back of the store. "You know the way."

"Thanks."

Remmy twisted the cap off of her water and took a long drink before replacing the blue top and heading down the hallway, past the men's and women's restroom to the partially closed door of Joan's office. Raising a hand, she rapped her knuckles on the door a couple of times.

"'S open," the distracted voice said from inside.

Taking a deep breath, Remmy pushed the door open the rest of the way. Joan was typing away on her computer. Remmy remembered that her chicken pecking took forever to type just one email. "One of these days you'll actually learn how to type," she said, leaning against the open door.

Joan looked up, mouth slightly open in surprise. She quickly composed herself. "The wayward daughter returns, I see."

"Hi, Joan," Remmy said softly, feeling shy and

guilty. "May I?" She indicated the chair in front of the desk. At Joan's nod, she took a seat, setting her water on the floor. "I owe you an apology."

"For...?" Joan rested her elbows on the desk and settled her chin on her clasped hands.

"Running out on you the way I did — the job and the apartment. I'm really sorry. I just needed to get away. If you need me to pay—"

"You don't owe me anything, Rem. Including an apology. If anything, I owe you one. I should've been more understanding and sympathetic to what you were going through. I'm sorry."

Remmy blinked several times, fighting tears. She took a deep breath and cleared her throat. "I guess we agree to disagree and move on, yeah?"

Joan smiled. "Sounds like a plan." She leaned back in her chair, arms resting on those of the desk chair, hands dangling off the ends. "How long are you back in town? A visit?"

Remmy shook her head. "No. I don't think so. My cousin was kinda upset with me, but I felt the need to come back to Woodland."

Joan was surprised and didn't try to hide it. "Really?"

"Yes, really. You don't uh..." She cleared her throat again. "You don't happen to know of any jobs in the area, do you?"

Joan studied her for a very long time, a slight smirk lifting the corner of her mouth. "Yeah, I do." She pushed out of the chair and went straight to the coat hooks on the wall beyond her office doors, where aprons hung in wait for employees. Stepping back into the office, she tossed an apron at Remmy, who caught it. "Last chance. Next time I just nail you to the wall."

Remmy grinned, rubbing the rough material

between her fingers. "Thanks, Joan."

"You staying at that roach-infested place again?"

"No. Got a room at Days Inn."

Joan's eyebrows rose. "Well, aren't we just the shit?" She loved the sight of Remmy's genuine smile. She hadn't seen that for a long time, not since early on in the case. "If you truly plan to stay, the apartment is still open. If you want it, that is, if Her Majesty wouldn't prefer the continental breakfast of the Days Inn."

Remmy was stunned. "You haven't rented it out?"

Joan studied her for another moment, tempted to lie and say it just recently became vacant. Instead, she shook her head. "No."

Looking down at the apron in her hands, feeling like she was home again, Remmy glanced up at her. "You've got a deal."

Chapter Thirty-four

Julie unraveled the hose, screwed the spray nozzle on the end, and turned on the water. The plastic coverings on her patio furniture were littered with winter debris, so she had moved the set out onto the grass, which was still winter-yellow. She squeezed the trigger, sending a powerful jet of water spraying over the furniture. Bonnie and Clyde hightailed it when they felt the mist from halfway across the small yard.

March was quickly coming to a close, the temperatures rising and the last of the snows nearly melted away. Not much for summer heat, Julie usually loved the snow better, but this year she relished the thought of the imminent warmth. She was ready for the cold to go away, hoping her memories and fears would melt away in the bright sun. It seemed to be working because over the past couple of weeks, she had felt much better. She felt more safe and contented than she had since the whole nightmare began. Perhaps she was finally healing, finding the balance in her life that she needed to become whole again. As whole as possible.

Finished with the patio furniture, she turned the hose onto the patio itself, spraying off the dead leaves that had gotten caught under the snow, and the dirt that had been washed up with them. She also saw a few Bonnie and Clyde poops that hadn't been picked up before the storms hit. Releasing the handle and dropping the hose, she grabbed the pooper scooper and began to collect them, a surge of anger and resentment rushing through her at having missed an entire season. She had missed fall entirely. She hadn't been able to enjoy the first fire of the season, hadn't been able to hand out candy to the trick-or-treaters in the neighborhood or decorate her home for the holidays. Julie still couldn't ignore the urge to take at least two showers a day; only while standing in that stall, soap rubbing over her skin, did she feel clean. The moment she stepped out onto the mat, she felt like immediate grime attached itself to her skin, and also to her soul. Would that ever be clean again?

Finished with the backyard, Julie went inside, hearing the distant hum of the washing machine, accompanied by the intermittent thump of the heavy curtains she was washing. The living room looked almost naked with only blinds on the windows. She was getting bored staying at home, so three days ago she had started all-out spring cleaning and revamping of her home. The gallon cans of paint she had picked up from the hardware store still sat just inside the door to the garage, new paint trays and brushes next to them.

Julie hurried up the stairs to her bedroom, where she eyed the empty space. She had taken the bed apart that morning, moving the pieces to one of the spare bedrooms before going outside to clean off the patio furniture and patio.

She walked into her bathroom. Taking out the CD player/radio that she used to listen to while getting ready for school in the mornings, she set it up in the corner of the modest-sized room, hitting PLAY. The Doors' "Riders On the Storm" began to play, the rain and storm effects beginning the song. Roll of blue painter's tape in hand, she began to tape off the windows and wood trim.

It was easy to get lost in the music and her task, head bobbing when she wasn't singing along. Typically she wasn't one for the music of the late Sixties, early Seventies — the music a little before her time and generation — but there had always been something about The Doors and Janis Joplin that had reached inside and touched her in a way that very few other bands could. Maybe it was the tragedy of their short lives, or maybe it was just kick ass music. Either way, she allowed herself to enjoy her solitude, rolling on about a four foot wide section of new paint before stepping back, roller in hand. She cocked her head to the side in contemplation, chewing on her lower lip. The color, a deep mocha, was darker when wet, she knew, but she tried to imagine the color it would dry to, and whether it was the color she intended. The woodwork would be white to provide contrast for the brown. The room was large enough to accommodate such a rich color.

It felt wonderful to be making so many changes in her house. It almost felt like they were the physical manifestation of the changes within her soul — shedding the old, and bringing to light a fresh canvas.

❧ ❧ ❧ ❧

Remmy was humming the chorus of The Doors' great, "Light My Fire", fingers tapping along the sides of her legs. She was enjoying the warm day, perfect weather for jeans and a t-shirt, though a light jacket would be needed later as temperatures cooled.

Exploring several of the neighborhoods of Woodland — to reacquaint herself with the town, and to find out where Julie lived — Remmy noted the older houses: some in desperate need of repair, others beautiful representations of an era lost. She was using what she had started calling her J-dar to try and tap into this Julie woman. She had been back in town for two weeks, getting settled in her job and her apartment. She was so grateful that Joan had kept her things stored safely in her basement. Remmy hadn't realized just what kind of friends she'd made there the last time. She had even reconnected with Roman, though he told her she was never allowed to drive his car again.

Feeling happy and carefree, Remmy smiled. She stopped at the street corner and closed her eyes as she looped her arm around the stop sign planted in the grassy corner formed by the meeting of adjoining sidewalks. She sent out her feelings, allowing them to ride the air in search of a location. It was far more difficult now to pick up on Julie, which was good in so many ways. That meant her emotions were not overwrought; she was calm.

As Remmy stood on the corner, she suddenly had a quick vision of a splash of brown color and lyrics from another classic Doors song. The music was tinny, almost as though coming from an old transistor radio. Remmy turned toward her right, concentrating on the lyrics. The music began to come into sharper focus. She strode down the sidewalk, the smell of fresh paint suddenly invading her senses. The volume of the music increased, now coming in stereo surround sound, almost like a soundtrack to her quest.

As Remmy listened to the words of "Hello, I Love You", her heart began to pound.

❧ ❧ ❧ ❧

Julie walked over to the small player, cranked the volume then danced back over to her paint tray, singing along with Jim Morrison. She tilted the paint can until more rich brown poured into the plastic tray. Running her roller back and forth through the thick paint, she then returned to the third of four walls that were getting the mocha treatment.

She couldn't keep her hips still as the music filled the space, head bobbing in time with the beat. She grinned widely as "Love Her Madly" began.

※ ※ ※ ※ ※

The words to "Hello, I Love You" ended and the words to "Love Her Madly" began. Remmy knew she must appear crazy, bobbing in time with the music in her head, hand tapping against her leg. She looked at the houses on either side of the quiet street. *Well maintained.* The yards were starting to recover from the harsh winter. She chuckled as she passed one house that had a smattering of garden gnomes placed strategically — hiding behind trees, peeking out from underneath bushes. *Amusing.*

Breath catching in her throat, Remmy stopped at a small two-story, the paneling a light blue, windows and doors trimmed in a darker shade of the same color palette. The meticulous yard looked as though it was well-loved. What caught her eye, though, was a white Miata parked in the driveway.

※ ※ ※ ※ ※

Julie stood back, admiring her handiwork. Her shoulders already hurt, and she had barely begun the transformation in her house. It didn't matter; it would be worth it.

Suddenly a smile spread across her face; her breath caught. A feeling of exhilaration filled her, and she felt like crying because she was so happy. She chuckled, feeling ridiculous. "Jesus, what's wrong with me?" She thought she dimly heard the sound of the doorbell, but then realized it was simply the music.

Shaking the grin off her face, she walked back over to the paint tray, rolling the paint roller to recoat it then starting on the fourth wall. She glanced over her shoulder at the first wall. It was still tacky, but beginning to dry. She realized it was going to need a second coat. "Damn," she muttered, turning back to her task. "Should've primed it first."

⁂

Hands shoved into the front pockets of her jeans, Remmy stood on the front porch, rocking nervously on her heels. When there was no answer to her ring, she took a step back on the small front porch, nearly falling off backwards. She looked up at the house, knowing in her heart that Julie was just on the other side of those walls.

Chewing on her lower lip, Remmy tried to decide what to do. She felt shy and somewhat embarrassed about just showing up like this. Suddenly, the music in her head stopped.

⁂

Julie stopped, listening again. *That had to have been the doorbell.* Setting the roller in the paint tray, she hurried over to the CD player and hit the stop button. The sudden silence was thunderous. She grabbed an old towel that she had tossed in the center of the room, using it to wipe away the excess paint on her hands. The last thing she wanted was to have a trail of mocha through the whole house.

⁂

Feeling really stupid, Remmy decided it would be best just to leave well enough alone. She stepped off the porch and down the few stairs that led to the sidewalk. She missed the music in her head. At least it had given her something to listen to while she walked. Hands back in her pockets, she left.

⁂

Julie nearly tripped over Bonnie in her haste to get to the door. She felt an urgency that she couldn't explain as she fumbled with the locks, finally pulling the door open. There was no one there. For a split second, fear fingered its way down her spine, but then it froze when she saw someone on the sidewalk, walking away from her house.

Pushing the screen door open and hurrying down the stairs, Julie called out, "Hey!"

Remmy turned to see Julie standing just below her porch, looking right at her. Her stomach lurched and her breath caught as a wave of nervousness crashed over her.

Julie's heart was beating wildly as she watched the figure turn around, breath catching with realization. "My God," she whispered, taking a step forward before stopping in uncertainty.

⁂

Taking a deep breath, Remmy took two steps toward Julie before stopping. She could see such confusion in the green eyes and wondered whether perhaps her coming was a mistake. Did Julie know who she was? If she did, would it bring back memories that she would rather forget? Her hesitation was moot when Julie jetted across the space between them and stopped right in front of her.

❧❧❧❧

Julie's heart was beating almost painfully in her chest. She was unable to take her eyes off Remmy's face, her gratitude shining in her green eyes. Remmy looked as though she might be about to bolt at any moment. Not wanting to chance that, Julie hurried over to her and looked deeply into the calm, kind blue eyes. She had no doubt that this was her dream savior. This was the woman who had brought her peace and calm, who had gotten her through the most harrowing experience of her life. This was the woman who saved her life.

With a small cry, Julie wrapped her arms around Remmy's neck, feeling the embrace returned, strong and warm, as they pressed together. Julie wanted to say in words what she'd been feeling for months, but her mind wouldn't work; nothing would come out. She seemed to be running on instinct as she clutched Remmy to her, unable to move or think or speak. They just...were.

❧❧❧❧

Remmy's soul seemed to mend as she held Julie. She had never felt so complete. After long minutes, Remmy felt the slight body against hers begin to tremble, and then a wetness fell against her neck. She drew away gently, just enough to look into Julie's tear-streaked face. She brushed away some of the tears. "It's okay," she whispered in understanding.

Julie looked away, feeling stupid. "I'm sorry," she

said after a moment of trying to get her emotions under control. She felt raw. Never had she been so completely overwhelmed by pure emotion. She felt out of herself, like only her soul existed.

"Don't apologize unless you've done something wrong." Two fingers under Julie's chin lifted brilliant green eyes up to look into Remmy's own. She smiled gently. "And you haven't."

Julie smiled then, big and bright, and filled with gratitude. She hugged Remmy again, and the taller woman gently rocked her, calming her with just her presence. A strength radiated from Remmy like a warmth from within which called out to Julie, assuring her it was alright to lean on it, touch it, and allow it to warm her from the inside out.

Several minutes later, Julie pulled away from Remmy and noticed that she had gotten paint on her t-shirt. "I'm so sorry!"

"See? Now your apology is appropriate."

Julie burst into laughter, feeling more free and light than she had...ever. Sobering, she looked into Remmy's beautiful face. "Thank you, Remmy. I've wanted to tell you that for a long, long time. You saved me."

Understanding the multiple layers of meaning in those words, Remmy simply nodded. "You're welcome." She studied Julie. "I'm going to guess either you're painting or have been playing in a vat of chocolate."

Julie brought her hand up to her face in confusion. She felt the dried paint on her face. "Painting," she said. Clearing her throat, she stepped back. "Would you like to come in? Have a cup of coffee or lemonade, something? Anything." She hated herself for the almost desperate tone in her voice, but she couldn't let this woman walk away, not yet. She needed to understand so much of what had happened…and how.

Remmy was suddenly nervous again. She glanced over at the house, then back at Julie, who was looking at her expectantly. She nodded.

As Remmy followed Julie through the front door, she was greeted by two of the cutest dogs she'd ever seen. She remembered them from the pictures Matt had shown her. "Which one is Bonnie and which one is Clyde?" she asked, missing the shocked expression on Julie's face as she bent down and attempted to pet the squirming Yorkies.

"The lighter one is Bonnie, then, of course, Clyde is the one who resembles Chewbacca with a haircut."

"They're adorable." Remmy laughed, trying to dodge doggie kisses, the two each trying to outdo the other at getting the most licks in. Finally she was able to get to her feet, both dogs still pawing at her ankles and shins to get her attention. She carefully stepped over them and followed Julie to the kitchen.

The house seemed to confirm everything she had heard about Julie: comfortable, well-kept, and well-loved. The kitchen was no different—lovingly decorated with simple furniture. She sat at the spotless round oak table, watching as Julie moved efficiently around the largish kitchen.

"Is coffee okay?" Julie asked, holding up a bag of specialty coffee. At Remmy's nod, she began to fill the maker. "I'm sorry you had to see things in such a mess. I was starting spring cleaning, then got the crazy idea to repaint."

"So I saw." Remmy chuckled, not minding about her t-shirt in the least. Hell, it added character to the green color of the shirt, and it made a memory.

Julie smiled sheepishly but said nothing as she grabbed the container of cream from the fridge and a canister of sugar, setting them on the table with two spoons and mugs. "Are you hungry?"

Remmy shook her head, her big lunch with Roman still heavy in her stomach. "Thank you, though. Please," she said, noting Julie's nervous fidgeting as she leaned against the counter, "sit down. I won't bite."

Julie did as asked, sitting across from Remmy. She didn't know why she was so nervous, but she was. She felt as though Remmy could look inside her soul and read all, and it made her nervous, though not afraid. In fact, Remmy's presence seemed to take her fear away, which amazed her. She smiled inwardly. *If Remmy could bottle that, she'd be a millionaire.* "When did you come back into town?"

"A couple of weeks ago." Remmy grabbed the sugar dispenser and began to play with it, her own nerves in evidence. "I wanted to come see you, but I was too afraid, I guess."

"Afraid?" Julie was shocked. Looking into the warm, calm depths of the ocean of Remmy's eyes, she would never have guessed anything could frighten her.

"Yes. I didn't want to stir up memories that were better forgotten. I thought that maybe you had managed to forget, or at least deal with them."

"Remmy," Julie's voice was soft, "I'll never forget. But yes, I've learned ways to deal. I hope." Remmy matched her small smile. "I'm so glad you came. I've been wanting to thank you for what you did. And not just for me. I know Pam and Cameron have been hoping to talk to you, too. Especially Pam. She spent two years of her life in that hell."

Remmy nodded, her focus returning to the sugar dispenser, watching the sunlight from the French doors gleam off the chrome top. It had been wiped clean, no fingerprints or residual sugar granules. "I'm glad everyone got out okay." Sad eyes met Julie's gaze and then turned away. "I'm so sorry I didn't get there in time to save Roxie."

Julie was shocked by the haunted look in Remmy's eyes. She moved to the chair next to her and placed a warm hand on her back. "Hey." Suddenly it hit her just how much of herself Remmy had lost. The captives weren't the only ones who had suffered. She turned her chair so she was facing Remmy then slowly pulled Remmy toward her. Remmy resisted at first, but then allowed herself to be held.

Mortified that her emotions were getting the best of her, Remmy tried to pull away but Julie held her tight. To make things even worse, she felt tears stinging her eyes. *No, no, no!* With Julie's whispered words and soothing arms around her, Remmy let it all go. She cried, not even trying to stop the tears. She cried for Roxie, she cried for Pam, and she cried for Julie. She knew of the horrors they experienced, as surely as if she'd lived through them right alongside them. She even cried for herself a little. She allowed herself to soak in the comfort Julie offered. She felt it tug at her heart, at her soul, at the very core of who she was. She had never experienced anything like it, not even in Monica's arms.

❧❧❧❧

After long moments, Julie felt the tears slow then stop, but still she held Remmy, rocking her gently. She could feel just how much Remmy needed to be comforted, and wondered what it had been like for her. What had she experienced? Grace and Joan had both told her about Remmy's visions, but what all did they entail? Was it like watching a horror movie unfold?

Somehow Julie felt it was more than that. She could sense Remmy's deep pain, and realized she recognized herself in the taller woman. She saw her own fears and pain reflected back at her through Remmy's eyes. She knew deep in her heart that Remmy had given more than just her time to save her; she had given a part of her soul.

Chapter Thirty-five

Remmy awoke feeling rested and alive. She'd had a deep, undisturbed sleep—not one dream, not once waking with visions of the lives of others. *God, how wonderful!* She sat up in her bed and stretched her arms high above her head, her yawn large and loud. The sun was piercing the closed blinds, throwing patterns of light on the hardwood floor.

Glancing over at her small kitchenette, she realized she was starving. Throwing her blankets aside, she yelped at the cold wood beneath her bare feet. She tugged on her slippers, then scampered to the bathroom to do her business. Immediately after, she drew open the blinds then opened the windows behind them, allowing the cool, spring morning breeze to air out the apartment. It filled her with a sense of rejuvenation. She felt like she had swallowed the Fountain of Youth while she slept; she couldn't keep the grin from her face.

She went to the fridge and was about to pop it open when there was a soft knock on her apartment door.

"Remmy?" Doug called from the hall. "You awake?"

She padded over to it, unlocked and opened the door. "Hey, Doug. What's up?"

Startled by her huge grin, he smiled himself, pretending to peek inside. "Remmy," he whispered, "did you get laid last night?"

Remmy burst into laughter, shaking her head. "I

wish."

"Well, if you want breakfast, Joan just made a huge stack of waffles."

Remmy glanced from Doug to her tiny fridge; she'd been planning on a banana and a bowl of Total Raisin Bran. She didn't have to think twice. She nodded with a wider grin and followed Doug down the staircase. She hopped off the last stair and down onto the main floor with a child's enthusiasm and vigor. The wonderful smells assailed her nose, and she groaned in appreciation.

Joan had the table set for three, which made Remmy smile. Immediately after she moved in again, Joan and Doug had made her feel like part of the family, as if she'd never left. It meant a great deal to her. She wordlessly filled three glasses with orange juice and helped Joan bring the food to the table.

Without discussion, the three sat down and began to dig into the hearty breakfast.

Eventually Remmy said conversationally, "I met Julie yesterday."

Joan looked up from her coffee. "Did she come into the store?"

Remmy shook her head. "Nope. I used my J-dar."

Doug choked on his juice. "Your what?"

"My J-dar," Remmy repeated. "Zeroed in, found her house."

"God, that's creepy," Joan muttered, setting her coffee aside and finishing off a sausage. "How did it go?"

"Fine. She seems like a really special person."

Joan nodded. She hadn't told Remmy that Julie came searching for her, or at least for information about her. "I've spoken with her a few times. Very nice."

Remmy nodded. *Very nice, indeed.* She had left not long after her little breakdown, which had been incredibly embarrassing. She hadn't wanted to leave, but felt it was only right. She had searched for Julie to... to what? To make sure she was okay? Certainly not to cry on her shoulder. She wanted to go back, but had no reason to. None that made sense, anyway.

"Oh, Remmy, I've been meaning to tell you— Mabel is going on a trip with her boyfriend; she'll be gone for a few days. Can you cover for her?"

"Absolutely," Remmy said without thought, then glared at Joan. "It's not like I've got too many hours or anything."

Joan smirked. "Hey, honey, you leave the party, you get what's left over."

Remmy rolled her eyes.

❧❧❧

Julie chuckled at the mess that was her nephew. She knew that Matt would kick her butt when he saw Skylar. The nine-year-old had come over for the weekend to help her paint. He had helped, alright. He was more colorful than any rainbow, certainly more colorful than her walls. She made him go scrub all the paint off his skin and out of his hair before she took him for the promised ice cream.

❧❧❧

Remmy took a step back, head cocked to the side as she tried to decide how to proceed with the display. They had about two hundred cases of Miller Genuine Draft and no room for them in the back room or in the coolers, so she was being creative, to Joan's chagrin. She had already created the legs and feet of her intended robot, held sturdy by various hard materials she had scavenged — pieces of Plexiglas and wood — to help stabilize everything.

All morning she'd been feeling the buzz of her emotions reaching out, searching. She was starting to see her mind like an antennae: always reaching out to seek a signal from someone, picking up on random channels without her permission. Suddenly her mind would be filled with scenes she didn't want to see, things she didn't want to feel. When Fayola taught her how to clamp down on it, she'd given the greatest gift. The beautiful dark woman told her that her own visions had nearly ruined her life, certainly running it, just as Remmy's had. In the past weeks Remmy had known more peace than she had in her entire life, now that she had learned how to block the signals. Now she was able to choose when she wished to "tune in".

She closed her eyes and the buzzing came back. It wasn't an audible buzz, more like a sensation, like her body beginning to vibrate, as though a wave of energy was trying to find a way around the prison bars she visualized to hold back the searching probe and all the information it gathered. It was strong today, and she was becoming exhausted.

The bells above the door jangled and the excited chatter of a young boy filled the store, along with the quiet hushing sounds of his companion. Remmy shot up, turning to face the store, eyes searching for the owner.

Over near the slushy machine, she saw the back of a blonde head. Swallowing nervously and running her hand through her hair, she moved the cases of beer out of the way and headed over to the bullpen, trying to keep her eyes off the two. She smiled at the debate Julie and Skylar on what size he would get, Julie finally settling on a medium, which he had to share with her.

After five very long minutes, Julie and Skylar

approached the counter, Julie digging through her purse. Wallet in hand, she looked up, eyes widening in surprise when she saw Remmy behind the counter. "Hi," she said.

"Hi. Find everything alright?" She nodded at the slushy that Skylar held against his chest, red straw never once leaving his mouth.

Julie glanced down at him. She brushed the straw from his lips.

"Skylar," she said, "we haven't paid for that yet."

Remmy was amused. "Is that it for you?"

"Yeah. That'll do it." Julie plucked a couple of singles from her wallet. Her heart was racing, fingers shaking slightly as she handed over the bills. She met the gentle blue eyes, and smiled. "How are you?" she asked, thinking of Remmy's emotional meltdown the last time they'd met.

Remmy smiled and shrugged. "I'm good. And yourself?"

"Just fine. Skylar here helped me paint this weekend," she said, mussing the boy's hair. He glared up at her as he sucked on the straw.

Remmy rested her forearms on the counter and leaned down. "Are you a good helper?" Skylar nodded vigorously, not releasing his straw. Remmy chuckled.

"He apparently preferred to paint himself and me more than the walls," Julie said, capturing Remmy's attention again.

"Like nephew, like aunt," Remmy teased, an eyebrow raised as she stood to her full height. She grinned at the slight blush on Julie's face.

"I said I was sorry about your shirt," Julie said, smiling at the loud burst of laughter from Remmy—a decidedly wonderful sound.

"Well, were you able to finish the mighty project

of repainting?" Remmy asked, smirking at the twinkle in Julie's eyes.

"Not even close." Julie said, thinking of the third bedroom, kitchen, and living room. Between her and Skylar, they'd managed to finish one bedroom, all three bathrooms, and the hallway upstairs.

"If you need help, I uh..." Remmy's eyes looked everywhere but at Julie. "I could help." The silence that ensued made her finally look at Julie, who was smiling at her.

"Don't offer something like that unless you mean it."

"I mean it," Remmy said indignantly.

Julie studied her for a moment, then nodded. "Okay. I'll let you help, then."

Chapter Thirty-six

Julie wiped her hands on her old cut-offs before reaching to open the multitude of locks she had installed on the front door. Their counterparts could be found on every door that led inside her home. She wondered whether this was a good idea—she didn't even know Remmy Foster, yet she was bringing her into her home to help her paint. She was extremely grateful for what Remmy had done for her—saved her life—but she still needed to be careful.

Unfortunately, the very events that had brought the two women together had made Julie beyond paranoid about any- and everyone who entered her personal space. Last night while she had been lying in bed, knowing that Remmy was coming over, she wondered how Remmy knew where she'd been. Maybe she was in cahoots with Sergio Venti, and no one had realized it. Was Remmy trying to worm her way into Julie's life simply to finish the job Sergio hadn't?

Julie rolled her eyes. Any of her concerns could possibly be true, but she knew she was being ridiculous. She opened the door and found Remmy standing on the other side, just as she knew she would. The ever-present backpack was slung over one shoulder, the eyes, gentle and clear, darted nervously toward Julie's face, and then away.

Julie smiled. "Hi."

"Hello." Remmy remained on the porch, her heart pounding at being face to face with Julie again.

"Are you sure you want to subject yourself to this?" Julie asked, giving Remmy, and herself, a chance to back out gracefully. She had never had such a reaction —feeling so close, feeling such a draw—to any one person in her life, and it frightened her. It was almost as though Remmy had some sort of spell over her that made her nearly breathless every time she saw her. It made her feel small and vulnerable, yet so filled with strength and calm at the same time.

"I'm sure." Remmy looked past Julie, who still blocked the doorway. "But, unless you intend to give me a roller with a majorly extended handle, I can't do much from out here."

Julie frowned at her own rudeness. "I'm sorry." She stepped aside, allowing Remmy to pass. Looking back into the beautiful spring day, Julie took one final breath and closed and locked the door with finality.

When she turned around, she saw Remmy standing in the center of the room, backpack still in place, waiting for instruction. "You can put that on the couch if you want," she said, pointing. Remmy did as she was directed, then stood with her hands in the back pockets of her cargo pants.

Looking intently at Remmy, Julie noted the clear, beautiful face. The eyes, which had caught her attention from the start, were watching her. It wasn't just the unusually blue color of the irises, but the depth of Remmy's eyes that was astonishing and somewhat disconcerting. They seemed to be the eyes of a woman who was three hundred years old rather than twenty-something. They looked at her with so much gentleness and seemingly endless understanding, Julie felt as if she might cry, or beg to be saved and protected from all the unknowns of the world.

Realizing she was staring, Julie looked away, but

not before noting the slender form, a bit of flat stomach visible where Remmy's shirt had ridden up. "Well," Julie said at length, purposefully breaking the curious tension in the air by clapping her hands together, "we've got a lot of work to do today. Well," she clarified with a sheepish grin, "I've got a lot of work to do today. You're not captive here, Remmy." She froze, realizing what she'd said.

A lopsided grin on her lips, Remmy walked over and placed a gentle hand on her shoulder. "I'm here for the duration, Julie," she said. "Let's git 'er done."

Julie smiled. "Let's git 'er done."

With George Michael's "Freedom 90" blasting through the speakers in the CD player that sat on the hall carpet, Julie and Remmy went to work painting the second spare bedroom. Not much conversation passed between them, each fully concentrating on her task, as well as her own thoughts.

It took all of Remmy's self-control to not stop painting and console Julie. Though she did her best to turn off her mind, she could still feel the slight unease radiating off her. She wasn't certain of the cause, but had formed some idea. Perhaps Julie thought it strange that Remmy would come seek her out after months of no contact. Or, perhaps Julie thought she was a freak, her abilities creepy. Or, perhaps Julie was just unsettled by her being there. Maybe she shouldn't have offered to help. She knew what a warm, loving person Julie was, and maybe she hadn't had the heart to reject her offer. Or maybe she needed the help, but felt uncomfortable with a veritable stranger helping her. A furrow formed in her forehead as the possibilities flitted through her brain.

She really wanted to send out her probe, enter Julie's mind to see what she was feeling, where her distress was coming from, but she'd promised herself she wouldn't do that. It would be an invasion of privacy.

ᘏᘏᘏᘏ

Feeling a strange...sadness, Julie glanced over her shoulder. She didn't feel like it was coming from her, but from Remmy, who was working diligently on the other side of the room. As she continued to paint, Julie studied her. Remmy's shoulder's seemed slumped, almost as if she were dejected.

Suddenly Julie's roller was sailing across a surface that was very smooth. She turned and looked, crying out in anger and shock when she realized she'd just painted over the window. "Shit!"

Remmy turned. Seeing the now very yellow window, she hurried over. Julie had dropped her roller into their paint tray and was scrubbing away at the window, making more of a smeared mess than progress.

"Hey," Remmy said, gently touching Julie's hand. "Calm, grasshoppa. I think you're about to break your window."

Julie wanted to be annoyed, but then she saw the amusement in Remmy's eyes and realized she was being anal. It was glass, for crying out loud. She grinned. "Don't paint the windows," she muttered.

Remmy nodded sagely. "So glad you told me. That one over there," she pointed to one near where she'd been working, "was calling to me."

Julie burst into laughter, playfully shoving Remmy away and returning to her mess. Feeling the tension flow out of Julie like water into a stream, Remmy picked up her roller. She even allowed herself to get into the music, now "Faith". *How ironic,* she thought.

Chapter Thirty-seven

Pamela Beecham hadn't been to Beaumont County since before she had been snatched almost three years earlier. In the time she'd been gone— two years, three months, fourteen days—her house had been sold; everyone thought she was dead. That was fine with her. She had no desire to return to the place where that bastard had set foot. After her rescue, her son had come up from Texas where he had decided to stay after graduating college. After all, he had a wife, a local girl, and nothing to return home for anyhow.

At first their reunion was everything Pam could have hoped for. She and Patrick cried together, clung to each other, and she was invited to go back to Austin with him and Christy. Without a second thought, she accepted. Her relationship with him had been so spotty over the years, it meant more to her than she could ever express to Patrick, that he cared.

Unfortunately, even tragedy hadn't taken Patrick's father out of him; the arguing and the hair-trigger temper were fully intact. After nearly six months with him and the girl he had married, Pam was more than ready to set out on her own. She packed the car she had bought with money she'd earned working for a dentist in Austin, and started back home. At least there she had friends, and a former boss willing to give her old job back. She missed going out with the girls, and the men, and looked forward to having a cold beer with Shelly and Ellen.

Pam drove with her window rolled down, allowing the wind to rush in and whip her hair every which way. She didn't mind; she was alive. She had also heard that the psychic who saved her had returned to the area and was staying in Woodland. She was glad; she really wanted a chance to talk to the woman. Pam had always been interested in the spiritual. She'd read books by Sylvia Browne and watched John Edward on TV. She wondered what Remmy Foster had to say about the whole episode. Was the Venti case her first? Or was she one of those psychics who helped the cops all the time? Pam had seen those on TV, too.

Pam pulled the coffee cup from the console's holder then sipped, enjoying the taste. McDonald's always did have the best coffee. She'd been a coffee addict before Sergio happened. That was one of the things she missed most while she was held captive. Patrick had forced her to go to therapy, which she supposed had helped, but she was still torn over how she felt about Sergio. She had been around him nearly every day for more than two years. He kept her fed and mostly warm, but, it was because of him that he'd had to keep her fed and warm.

She grinned, remembering how she'd felt when she found out exactly how that feisty little blonde had escaped. She couldn't believe Julie had bitten his cock. What guts! Pam, herself, had had the opportunity to do that. He always waited a while before he allowed one of the women to perform a blow job on him. She was surprised he let Julie do it after only having her for a few months. He must have really thought he could trust her.

"Dumb ass," she muttered, pushing her arm out the window and allowing the wind to move it as it would—flowing up and down, up and down. She glanced in the side mirror, noting the sunglasses she had bought on her way out of town. Her hair was cut short again, the way she liked it. That kept it out of her eyes. Her mother had made her keep her hair long when she was younger. Just after she got married the first time, she chopped it off, keeping it short ever since. She lost a lot of weight while she was with Sergio; she was actually grateful for that. She had managed to keep it off, too. Over all, she looked pretty good. Another thing she was grateful for was that her time with him had gotten her off cigarettes. She'd been trying to quit for ten years and hadn't been able to. Though she craved a cigarette now and then, she had no desire to go back to that. *Nasty habit.*

During the intervening five months, Pam had wanted to get on the phone with Julie Wilson and thank her for what she'd done, but she didn't. The mere thought of speaking with her fellow captive brought back a myriad of memories and thoughts that she really didn't want to relive. She had forced herself to let it go, to forget about it, but now was the time to start thinking about it again, to say a simple thank you. She owed Remmy Foster her thanks, too.

Chapter Thirty-eight

S o, you actually knew I was in danger that first day?" Julie asked, leaning back against the arm of her couch, bare feet curled up under her. She took a long drink from her bottle of water. Remmy, who sat on the arm chair adjacent to the couch, nodded.

"Yes."

Julie glanced out the window for a moment as she absorbed that. "Guess I should've listened, huh?" she said quietly, attempting a joke that failed miserably.

"It wasn't your fault, Julie," Remmy said, draining her third water bottle of the day. They had finished the second bedroom and the kitchen. The only reason they stopped before painting the living room was because all the furniture needed to be moved out. "I truly believe he would've gotten you no matter what." She looked deep into green eyes, making sure she had Julie's full attention. "He was watching you."

"How do you know that? Do you realize how creepy crazy that sounds? How can you sit there and tell me what this guy was doing long before you ever met me?"

Remmy shrugged. "Just know." She tapped the empty water bottle against her paint-stained pant leg. "One night I had a dream. It scared the hell out of me. It was actually a few nights before I started toward Woodland." She stared off into the distance. "I saw his kitchen, all the weird crap he had in there." She met Julie's gaze again, eyebrows drawn. "You saw his kitchen, didn't you?"

Julie nodded with a small shiver. "The last day," she whispered. Her stomach was in knots, going back there, but somehow talking about it with Remmy sitting a few feet from her made it far less scary. By remembering without the accompanying fear, she almost felt like she was standing up to Sergio.

"What was in it? I was never in the house." Remmy grinned. "I was too busy getting shot."

Julie chuckled at the disarming smile tossed her way. "Yeah, about that—"

"I'd do it again," Remmy said quickly, cutting her off. "Any day of the week and twice on Sunday."

Julie studied her, shocked. "Why me?" she finally asked. "Why were you in my head? Why not Pam's, Cameron's, Roxie's? Hell, Sergio's, for that matter. Why me?"

Remmy shook her head. "I don't know. I met some friends while I was in Omaha, people who understood me, understood my...ability. They explained it to me in a way that made sense. Basically, my soul is highly sensitive, almost like an antennae trying to pick up radio signals, but these radio signals are the emotions of others: high emotions, deep emotions—distress, guilt, pain, whatever. It always used to be previous emotions. You know, the guy who accidentally ran over his daughter's dog seven years ago, and never forgave himself for telling his kid that Rover ran away. That kind of thing. But with you..." She shook her head and shrugged. "I was picking up on you and everything you were feeling. It was powerful." She smiled, trying to inject a little lightness into a situation that still bothered her. "You've got quite the ticker, Julie."

Julie's smile was small as she played with the water bottle. So many questions plagued her, and she decided that now was the time to get them all out. "I had these dreams," she said softly, feeling shy about the admissions she was about to make. "While I was there." She couldn't bring herself to look at Remmy, and therefore missed the slight intake of breath from her companion.

Remmy never knew whether or not she was reaching Julie with her dreams. She'd hoped, prayed even, that she was able to offer some kind of comfort, and that the visions she was seeing in her own dreams weren't simply that — dreams. "What about them?" she asked, when it seemed Julie wasn't going to continue.

Julie took a drink, more for something to do than because she actually wanted it. Eventually she continued. "I always found myself in a field. Well, at first, anyway, and then there was a lake or stream, something like that. Not a huge body of water, but water all the same. And trees," she said, her voice growing softer with each memory of her dream paradise. "There was always someone with me, holding me, standing beside me. I could never see the person, just knew they were there to help me, to take it all away." She swallowed reflexively then glanced over at her silent companion, a question in her eyes.

When she spoke, Remmy's voice was very soft and filled with emotion. "I wanted to give you a safe place to hide, Julie. Wanted you to know you weren't alone."

Julie's eyes filled with tears, which she tried to hold back but couldn't. "It was you," she murmured.

Remmy was pulled to her feet, and her arms were filled with Julie, who clung to her. She cupped the back of Julie's head that rested on her shoulder.

Chapter Thirty-nine

Remmy stood off in the corner of the yard, a can of Dr Pepper in her hand, the two dogs at her feet chewing on the small bones she'd brought them. She glanced up at the gathered revelers, all talking and laughing with each other. She had come to not like large crowds, had never been one for idle chit chat with strangers, so she felt thoroughly uncomfortable. When had she gotten so shy? She remembered a time when she and Monica would walk into a bar or club, and she would own the place. But then, that likely was easier to do when she was higher than a kite or drunk on her ass. She was neither.

She was quite surprised when Matt Wilson came to the store and invited her to Julie's barbecue. He said all she needed to bring were herself and a hearty appetite. So, there she sat, entertaining the dogs. That was a lie—they were entertaining her, keeping her from feeling like a total outsider. She glanced up periodically, eyes always finding Julie, who held a bottle of beer lazily between two fingers, listening intently to what an older, plump man was saying. Remmy smiled at Julie's boisterous laughter.

"Hey."

Remmy was startled by the voice that suddenly sounded by her side. Grace grinned down at her, a handsome man by her side. Remmy realized they had come in through the back fence, which was just behind her lawn chair.

"Hey!" she said, relief washing through her at seeing a familiar face. She stood and accepted Grace's hug. "What are you doing here?"

"Thought we'd crash," Grace said, her voice dry. She grinned when Remmy rolled her eyes. "Rem, this is my husband, Chris. Chris, Remmy the Wonder Girl."

"It's a pleasure to meet you, Remmy. I've heard so much about you." He took Remmy's hand and shook it firmly.

"You, too, Chris. Sorry I kept Grace away so much."

Chris' laugh was full and rich. "Not a problem." He turned to Grace. "I like this girl. She has my priorities straight." He headed toward the patio. Grace's eyes turned serious and she lagged behind.

"I need to talk to you later, Remmy," she said, then hurried to catch up with Chris.

Remmy raised her pop can in acknowledgement then sat back in her chair. Bonnie and Clyde had taken off in search of attention from the new arrivals.

"Thanks, guys," she muttered, crossing an ankle over her knee. She looked around the yard, which was already turning a deep, healthy green. Flowers had been planted, fresh dark soil indicating their presence. She noted the hose wrapped and hung on a hook mounted on the six foot privacy fence at the back of the yard. She also noted, with a smile, the new shed she had helped Julie put up two weeks ago. It had been a long, arduous task, but a rewarding one.

"Hey, Miss Anti-Social." Julie walked over to Remmy and squatted down next to her. She picked up one of the bones the dogs had left, holding it up with a raised eyebrow. Remmy grinned sheepishly. "So, I wasn't so thrilled that my big brother got to you first before I could invite you. After all, I'm the one throwing this little shindig." She grinned. "Why don't you come over and join us? I know a lot of people really want to talk to you."

Remmy nodded. They were a part of the reason she was being "Miss Anti-Social". "I'm just observing."

"I see. Well, would you like to chew on a hotdog or a hamburger while you 'observe'?"

"Hotdog."

"With…?"

"Uh, bun?"

Julie rolled her eyes as she pushed to her feet. "You can put your own condiments on it," she said, swatting Remmy on the arm.

Remmy watched her easily mix with the throng of guests. She hadn't spent a great deal of time with Julie, really only while she helped with the painting and then the shed. Julie insisted she wasn't just using Remmy for her muscle. In truth, Remmy wouldn't have minded in the least.

After a few moments, Julie returned, a paper plate containing two hotdogs balanced on one hand, small bottles of ketchup and mustard clutched in the other. She handed the plate to Remmy and set the two condiments in the thick grass near the legs of her chair. "Okay, what else can I get you? Another soda?" She indicated the can in Remmy's hand. "Chips? Fruit salad?"

Remmy grinned, shaking her head at Julie's solicitous offers. "No, thank you. You don't have to wait on me, Julie."

"I know, but I want you to feel comfortable. I hate seeing you sitting over here all by yourself." Julie sat in the grass in front of Remmy's chair. Legs stretched out and crossed at the ankles, she leaned back on her hands.

"I'm always by myself, Julie. It's nothing new."

Remmy picked up the ketchup, applying a generous amount to both hotdogs then adding a wee stream of mustard.

Julie studied her, head slightly cocked to the side. "Why are you such a loner? Just naturally your personality?"

Remmy chewed, thinking about the question before swallowing the food down with a drink of her pop. She shrugged. "Always have been. Guess it comes from moving around so much. After my cousin and I went our separate ways years back, it was just me." She met Julie's gaze. "Guess I just got used to it."

"A rolling stone gathers no moss, Rem."

Remmy smiled, liking the shortened version of her name on Julie's lips. "Hmm. And the static deer shall grow stagnant."

Julie's brows drew. "What?"

Remmy chuckled. "No clue. My mom used to say that when I was a kid."

"Are you close with your mom?" Julie accepted half of the second hotdog that Remmy offered her.

"Nope. I haven't seen her since I was a teenager." Remmy swallowed the last of her lunch, washing it down with the remainder of her Dr Pepper.

"Really? Why?"

Remmy was saved from going into the whole story when Grace stepped up beside Julie, causing the petite blonde to have to look way up into the dark face.

"Hey, guys," Grace said, squatting next to Julie. Remmy gave her a small wave; Julie smiled in greeting. Grace looked from one to the other. "You know, I have to say, it's a wonderful sight to see the two of you together, in person." Her smile was big and genuine.

Julie returned the smile, reaching over and taking Remmy's hand, squeezing it gently. "It's been wonderful to get to know Remmy in person, and not just in a dream." She looked over at Remmy, and they shared a private smile.

Grace watched them, their bond apparent even to her cynical self. Seeing how Remmy was with the flesh and blood Julie, she wondered how torturous it must have been for her during the most trying times of the case—thinking Julie was dead, then finally the rescue. She cleared her throat, remembering why she had intruded in the first place. "Remmy, there's someone here who would like the chance to talk to you."

❧❧❧❧

Pam was chatting with a man to whom she hadn't been introduced, still, she thought he was pretty interesting. She was holding the paper plate that now held only a few crumbs of chips, and a pickle she hadn't wanted.

"I don't know," the man was saying. "I think the dental industry has gone downhill. Hell, my dentist steps in for about three seconds to tell me that his assistant will be taking care of me, then, poof." he gestured for effect, "he's gone."

Pam chuckled. "Yeah, then he gets to take home six figures while we fight over squat." Pam was interrupted by a touch on her shoulder. She turned to see Detective Cowan standing next to her, a young woman at her side.

"Pam, I'd like to introduce you to Remmy Foster. Remmy, this is Pam Beecham." Grace stood between the women, a hand on each one's shoulder.

Looking into the blue eyes of the beautiful young woman standing not three feet away from her, Pam's life-hardened eyes softened. Without a word, she took Remmy into her arms and held her tightly for a long moment before releasing her. A smile softened Pam's haggard features. "Honey, this is one of the greatest introductions I've ever had," she said. "I owe you my life, and I thank you, from the bottom of my heart."

Not sure what to say, Remmy nodded. She had no connection with this woman, though she was one of the captives she had seen through Julie's eyes. "You're welcome, Pamela. I'm glad we got you out of there in one piece." *Unlike Roxie.*

❧❧❧❧

As the barbecue wound down, Remmy sat alone on the front porch of the house, a bottle of water between her feet. She rested her chin on her clasped hands, lost in thought.

Julie sat on the stoop next to her friend. Grace had taken Remmy into the house, where they stayed for about an hour. When they came out again, Remmy's eyes were stormy, her brow knit in deep concentration. Grace and her husband had stayed for a short time then left with a tight hug for Julie and a shoulder squeeze for Remmy. "Hey."

Remmy almost missed the soft voice next to her. She glanced over. "Sorry." She cleared her throat, centering her attention on Julie. "Did you need help cleaning up?"

Julie bumped Remmy's shoulder lightly. "No. You do know that your sole purpose is not to help me out around here, right?" Remmy tipped her bottle of water and took a long swallow. "What's wrong, Remmy?" Julie could feel worry coming off her in waves. Remmy was concerned, perhaps even scared.

Remmy sat silently for a moment. Did she want to talk about it with Julie? Glancing over at her, she saw just how much Julie wanted to be there for her. Turning away, she said, "Grace asked me to help her with another case."

Julie's heart was gripped by ice cold fingers, the breath nearly knocked out of her. "Do you think you can do it?"

Remmy sighed heavily, shoulders slumping. "I don't know. I told Grace to get me the crime scene photos and I'd see if I can connect."

"What crime?"

Remmy shook her head. "I don't know. I asked her not to tell me." She smiled ruefully. "Don't want any preconceived ideas."

"Remmy?" Julie reached out and gently brushed strands of dark hair away from Remmy's face, tucking them behind her ear. After a moment blue eyes met her own. So often when she'd been around Remmy, she had seen the haunted look in them, as though just looking at Julie made Remmy want to cry. Those times made Remmy's already ancient eyes seem positively ageless. "Can you do this?" she whispered.

"I don't know. I mean, I connected with you, but—"

"I don't mean your abilities, Remmy. You're so wonderfully sensitive, there's no doubt you can do this. But, can *you* do this?"

Remmy sighed, leaning back on her hands, the cool cement of the porch under her palms. "Guess we'll find out, huh?"

Chapter Forty

Remmy sat on her bed, legs tucked under her. She opened the manila envelope Grace had dropped off at the store. Inside were eight by ten glossies of the crime scene Grace wanted help with. She took a deep breath and laid the six pictures out across her comforter.

The first picture was of a kitchen, dishes stacked in a strainer to dry next to the sink, a frying pan on the stove top, a dishtowel hung over the handle of the oven door. A glass on the counter held the remnants of what looked to be juice of some sort. A child's highchair was tucked into the corner near the back door.

Remmy's gaze moved down to the tile floor in front of the almond-colored fridge. There was blood, two puddles, as though someone had been lying there bleeding.

The next picture showed a close up of a phone hanging on the wall, the light blue chord twisted. Next to the phone was a wooden frame with slanted shelves, probably for holding phone messages or notes. What caught Remmy's eye was the blood spatter. From the pattern, it was obvious someone had been hit, and hit hard.

The third picture brought a hand to Remmy's mouth as she swallowed her nausea. It was akin to the first picture, but the body had not yet been removed. The victim lay on her stomach, head turned to the side. Her eyes were open, wide with fear. Blood stained her shirt to the point where portions of the floral pattern disappeared beneath the crimson. Her feet were bare, jeans also stained with blood. Her hands were up by her face, the fingernails of her right hand chipped and torn. This woman had fought for her life.

Taking several deep breaths, Remmy set the pictures aside. She glanced over at the chair in the corner of her apartment, wishing that Julie was sitting in it. After several more breaths, Remmy turned back to the pictures. So far nothing had touched her, nothing had called out to her. She had never before attempted to get any sensations from photographs, and wasn't sure whether she would be able to. It was like she wasn't able to send herself out, as there was nothing to reach back.

Blowing out a loud breath, she put the three pictures back into the envelope, grateful to get them out of her sight and out of her hands, which felt dirty. She rubbed her fingers together, grimacing. They felt wet and sticky. She glanced at them, wondering whether Grace had spilled coffee or something on the photos before sliding them into the envelope. Nothing. She brought her fingers to her nose, closing her eyes as she inhaled. She gasped, eyes flying open. She looked at her fingers again, the coppery stench of blood fresh in her nostrils.

Large hands, fingers spread, a small cut on the pad of the thumb. The glint of a ring on the pinky, large and bulky. Stained with blood. In the distance, the crying of a child.

Remmy gasped, grabbing onto the comforter underneath her to steady herself. She heard something crumple and looked. Tucked into her right hand was a fourth photograph. Taking several deep breaths, she flattened the paper out, smoothing its image. At the center of the photo was an empty playpen, a child's toy lying on the carpet just beyond.

Chapter Forty-one

Julie preceded Remmy into yet another store, hoping that maybe this would be the one. She glanced back at her shopping companion, chuckling at the bored look on her face. "Oh, come on," she said, tugging playfully at Remmy's sleeve. "This isn't that bad, Remmy. Jeez. You act as though we've been at this for a week."

Remmy met her gaze, a dark eyebrow rising. "We have."

"Okay, so we have. But what can I do? If I'm going to start teaching this fall, I have to have clothes." She noted Remmy's doubtful look. "What?"

"Uh, Julie?" Remmy said, dutifully following her past racks of clothing.

"Yes, Remmy?" Julie said, holding up a blouse for inspection.

"Don't you have clothes from last school year?"

Unable to meet her gaze for a moment, Julie slowly hung up the shirt. Finally she met amused blue eyes, which quickly lost their mirth at the seriousness of Julie's expression. "A lot of my clothes don't fit me anymore. I've lost a lot of weight since last year, Remmy," she said softly. "I just can't seem to put it back on."

Remmy's eyes softened immediately. "I'm sorry," she whispered, glancing away. She felt warm fingers bring her face back until she met Julie's gaze again. Julie's smile nearly broke her heart. Why couldn't she have prevented all of this? What good were her abilities if she couldn't stop bad things from happening? Especially since she had seen Julie's danger.

"Remmy?" The fingers underneath Remmy's chin slid up to cup her cheek. "I'm not entirely sure what's going through your mind, but I know it has something to do with Sergio Venti. Am I right?" Remmy's downcast eyes told her all she needed to know. "I'm okay. Alright? I'm here, and you're here, and everything's okay." Remmy nodded, doing her damndest to give Julie a smile.

"Come on. Help me find something to wear on my first day. Okay?" Julie gave Remmy a winning smile. "Whatever you pick, I'll wear." She immediately wanted to take back that rash promise, but knew she couldn't. She could only pray that Remmy had good taste.

A little while later, Julie's trunk was filled with bags and packages, and they were driving through Woodland, a comfortable silence filling the car. Remmy was amused to be sitting in the passenger seat, thinking back to the last time: just entering Woodland, unsure what the future held for her, unsure whether she would even stay in the town. Not half an hour after getting out of the Miata, she'd had a job and a place to live at the Maple Tree.

"So, are you excited to be starting classes in August?" she asked, focusing on the present. Julie was quiet so long Remmy wondered whether she had heard the question. Finally Julie blew out a breath but didn't look at her.

"Yes and no."

"Why 'no'?"

Julie looked over at Remmy sheepishly. "I still haven't been to the school. I can't—"

"Can't what?"

"I can't even pull into the parking lot. I haven't been able to go into the school."

Remmy was aware that was where Julie had been abducted. "Have you tried?"

Julie nodded. "A couple of times. Shit, I park across the street and can't even turn into the lot." She sighed, disappointed in herself. She felt a warm hand on her leg. She looked down at it then followed the arm until she was looking at Remmy's eyes, hidden behind her sunglasses. The hand squeezed lightly.

"Let's go," Remmy said.

"Oh no, Remmy. No, I can't." Julie felt panic fluttering in her stomach, sweat beading between her breasts, and her palms were sticky on the steering wheel. The hand squeezed again.

"Let's go."

⁂

Julie felt sick to her stomach as the car idled across the street from the school — her usual parking spot when she tried to convince herself she could do this. Remmy's presence next to her almost gave her the courage. Almost.

Studying Julie's profile, Remmy said nothing. She sensed how scared Julie was. She wanted to be able to take that away, but knew she couldn't. This was a demon Julie had to face, but she would be with her every step of the way. "Are you ready?" she said quietly, resting her hand on the back of Julie's seat.

Julie blew out a loud breath, nodding. "I can do this." She turned and looked at Remmy with pleading eyes. "Can't I?"

Remmy smiled, shoving her sunglasses to the top of her head. She knew Julie needed to see her eyes, needed to be able to read the confidence there. "Yes. You can."

"Okay." Julie pulled away from the curb, looking in each direction about five times.

"There's no one coming, Julie," Remmy said, amused at the stall tactic.

Julie grinned. She knew she couldn't put one over on Remmy. She pulled the small car onto the street, the entrance to the empty parking lot not twenty yards away. Her heart was racing as her lunch threatened to make an encore appearance. She calmed at the feel of Remmy's hand on her leg, rubbing up and down as though calming a skittish colt.

"You can do this," Remmy said, her eyes never leaving Julie's face.

As the sports car reached the driveway, Julie's foot slammed down on the brake, almost throwing Remmy into the windshield. "Sorry," she whispered through the sting of fear.

"Don't sweat it," Remmy said, getting readjusted in her seat. "You can do this, Julie. You can."

Julie released the pressure on the brake and the car lurched forward. To a passerby, it might have looked as if Julie was getting a driving lesson as the car hiccupped its way through the final ten yards. Julie signaled her turn into the lot.

Remmy felt the heat rolling off of Julie in waves, her fear obviously nearly all-consuming. She wondered for a moment if maybe they should abort. But, to her surprise, Julie pulled the car into the parking lot and eased the car to a stop diagonally across two spots. Glancing at her, Remmy realized it was because Julie had her eyes closed.

"Julie?" she said. No response. "Julie, honey?" Green eyes opened, focusing solely on her. Remmy smiled. "You did it."

Julie looked around her, noting they were just three spaces away from where she'd parked that day. She let out a long, slow breath, her heart still pounding but calming ever so slightly as she felt Remmy's hand still resting on her leg. She reached down and covered it with her own. "I did it," she whispered, eyes returning to Remmy's.

Remmy pulled her hand out from under Julie's and pulled Julie into her arms. It wasn't long before the tears came with the embrace. "I've got you," she whispered. "I'll never let anything bad happen to you again. I swear."

Chapter Forty-two

Grace sipped her coffee. Remmy was late, but that was okay—Remmy had said she might be. Grace had considered having their meeting at the police station, but decided it was best to be in an environment that was more comfortable and quiet, rather than one that was so chaotic. The coffeehouse seemed a good place to meet. It was purely a bonus that they had the best muffins in town.

Having skipped lunch, she was on her second by the time Remmy walked through the door, some of the scattered patrons bidding her hello. "Do you know them?" Grace asked, amused, nodding toward the older couple with a smattering of birdwatching magazines spread out over their table.

Remmy shook her head as she pulled out a chair. "Not a clue."

"I think you've become a legend, my friend."

Remmy glared up at her then both cracked a smile. "Somehow I don't think so. I imagine they've seen me at the store."

Grace shook her head, waving the young waitress over. "That's a negative, captain. They don't embrace new folk here just 'cause you happen to sell them gas and lottery tickets."

Embarrassed, Remmy looked away. "Stop," she said with a dramatic wave of her hand, making her friend laugh. The young waitress who came to the table was accompanied by an older man who Remmy recognized as the owner.

"Remmy, you tell Michelle what you want and it's on the house," he said.

"Oh, uh, that's not necessary—"

"Sure it is. Our very own hometown hero!"

"What about me, Ron?" Grace asked, affecting a wounded look.

"You want a refill, Grace?" he asked, completely missing the intent of the question.

Grace glanced at Remmy—*so not fair*—then handed her cup over. Remmy gave her order to Michelle, and the girl came back with a mocha breve and half of an apple pie. Remmy's eyes lit up, and she grinned at Grace's glare.

"Alright, I'm assuming you've had time to look at the pictures?" Grace said, getting right to the point of their meeting.

Remmy didn't say anything for a moment then glanced up at Grace. "The baby's still alive, Grace," she said softly. "Though I really don't have any sense of how much longer."

Grace sighed, running a hand over the tension knot at the back of her neck. In most cases, children were dead within hours of being taken. She had figured the baby was long dead, just like his mother. "The killer did a good job of covering his tracks. I think he used gloves. Not a fingerprint anywhere."

Remmy's brows furrowed. Again she could see the bloody hands. Shaking her head, she sipped from her drink. "I don't think so, Grace. Or at least he messed up somewhere. There is a fingerprint in that house, I know it—"

The ring glinted in the light, blood splattered on it. Large ring. Hefty ring. Look at the stone, look at the stone...

Remmy shook herself from the vision. "He wears a ring. I've seen it twice now. A big ring..." Remmy looked around at the other patrons. She was trying to find something—anything—that reminded her of what she saw, the fingers of her right hand wiggling of their own accord as she felt the weight of the ring on her finger. Finally she spotted a young man sitting at a table by himself, working on homework. "Like that!" She rose from her seat and headed over to him, Grace following.

"Jerry," Grace said as the teen looked up at them with questioning eyes. "Can I see your ring for a sec?"

"Uh, sure, Detective Cowan." He grunted as he tugged at his high school ring, the silver finally sliding from his finger. He handed it to Grace and she handed it to Remmy, who studied it intently.

"A class ring, yeah," she said, no longer seeing the details of Jerry's ring, but those of the vision in her mind.

"What's going on?" Jerry asked, watching Remmy.

"Working on a case," Grace murmured, not wanting to break Remmy's concentration.

"It's gold." Remmy turned the ring around and around in her fingers, but every time she tried to turn the face of the ring to her mind's eye, it blurred. She shook her head, mildly frustrated, handing the ring back to Jerry. "I don't know. But it's like that, except it's gold."

"You feel this ring is important, don't you?" Grace said, as they returned to their table.

Remmy nodded. "It keeps coming back to me." She grabbed the fork Michelle had dropped off with the pie and dug in, moaning at the exquisite explosion of tastes. "Have you found the murder weapon yet?"

Grace shook her head. "Nope. Our victim, Linda Hartman, died of blunt force trauma, but we're not sure what was used to beat her. Nothing was missing. There was a perfectly clean hammer in the garage. No pieces of wood were lying around. Very neat, tidy residence, actually." Grace watched Remmy. "How do you know the baby's still alive?"

Remmy met her dark gaze. "'Cause he's crying in my head."

⁂

Julie chuckled as Bonnie nearly ran into the wall as she shook herself completely dry after the bath and toweling she'd received. Her brother followed, sniffing some water droplets that had splattered the wall in the hallway.

"You guys are nuts," she said lovingly, heading past them and down the stairs to get all three of them some dinner.

It was a beautiful night in April; most of her windows were standing wide open, as they had been for a good part of the day. She would probably be closing them soon, however, as the night was starting to cool down. Once in a while she caught the scent of rain on the incoming breeze. That put a smile on her face. She loved rain, always had. Once upon a time, rain had eased her body into a wonderful state, making her skin tingle as she craved to be touched. In short, rain made her horny as hell.

Somehow she doubted that would be the case anymore. She had no desire to ever be touched like that again. Other than friendly shows of affection, her body had become something that she held sacred, and she couldn't imagine allowing anyone to touch her intimately again. The temple her mother used to talk about, that was what Julie's body had become to her.

She had not even allowed her own fingers to wander. *Never again.*

In all honesty, she wondered whether denying herself sexual touch was actually the loss someone else might perceive it to be. She'd had sexual partners over the years, and she definitely felt desire and need, but more often than not, she was left wanting and unsatisfied. She could count on one hand the times her boyfriends had brought her to climax. Typically she just took care of it herself after they left.

Julie pushed the thoughts from her mind. It was a subject that no longer mattered in her world. She filled the dogs' bowl then set about looking in cabinets and the fridge to see what she had to make for herself.

꧁꧂

"Seems like you and Julie have begun a true friendship," Grace said, sipping her bottle of water, coffeed out.

Remmy nodded, shoving the nearly empty pan of pie away. She hadn't eaten all day and the dessert really hit the spot. "She's wonderful. I don't think I've ever made such a close friend in such a short time." She shrugged. "I really enjoy the time I spend with her, even if it is usually helping her out with something."

Grace grinned. "You've become her handyman."

"Something like that. I love it, though."

Grace had watched them together, and it always brought a smile to her face, not just because of the happy ending of Julie's ordeal, but because it was more than obvious the two had a real connection, a bond like she rarely observed between two people. "Do you still sense her like you did before?"

Remmy nodded, sipping from her third breve.

She knew she would be up all night, probably with a stomachache from the strong brew. "I won't allow myself visions, though. It's not right. It would be like invading her personal space, you know?"

Grace nodded.

❧❧❧❧

With the pasta already beginning to boil, Julie vacillated between the jars of marinara and Alfredo sauces. She chewed her lip in indecision, finally reaching for the marinara. Alfredo was rich, and she wasn't sure her stomach could handle it.

She set the jar of Prego down and was reaching for a rubber spatula from the holder on the counter when she heard a knock at the door. Dark blonde eyebrows drawing, she turned the burner heat down and went to the front door. Bonnie and Clyde beat her there, their tails wagging in anticipation.

Julie looked through the window and saw a dark car parked in her driveway. She groaned when she saw Ray Lambert standing on her front porch, blinking rapidly at the sudden illumination of the porch light. After undoing the locks, Julie pulled the door open, leaving the glass screen door closed between them.

"Hey." He held up a hand in greeting.

"What are you doing here, Ray?"

"I came to see you, see how you're doing. My daughter told me about everything that happened."

"That was months ago. Why are you here now?"

"Julie, can I come in, please? It's starting to rain, and I'm not too keen about having a discussion with you through a glass door."

Against her better judgment, Julie flipped the lock and turned away from the door. Ray pulled the screen door open and followed her inside. "I think it's going to be a pretty bad storm tonight," he said, glancing outside over his shoulder. The night sky was starting to light up as lightning raced across the sky.

Julie stopped in the middle of the living room and turned to face him, wrapping her arms around herself.

Ray stepped to within a few feet of her. "So, how are you?" he asked, apparently genuine concern in his voice.

"I'm fine. Doing well, actually." Her heart was pounding and she wasn't sure why. She felt sweat beginning to gather under her arms and between her breasts.

"Good. That's really great to hear. I'm sorry I didn't come by before but I've been working on a new plant in Florida for the past six months so—"

"That's good. Sounds exciting." Julie tried to sound interested, but she could think of nothing beyond wanting him to leave. She hadn't forgotten about the problems she'd been having with Ray just before she was abducted. Nor had she forgotten that their relationship was very much over. She had no desire to see him in any capacity, not even on a friendly basis.

"So, what happened to you? Some guy snatched you or what?" Ray asked, walking over to the couch and sitting down.

Julie swallowed her anger. "I don't want to talk about it, Ray. You can read about it in back issues of the newspaper, I'm sure."

"Why? Why can't you just tell me? I'm really curious."

"And I'm really talked out. Please leave."

❧❧❧❧

Remmy wanted to get home before the storm started, but she and Grace had stayed talking too long. "Crap," she muttered, as she stood at the door to the coffeehouse watching the heavens open up.

"I'll give you a lift home, Remmy." Grace tugged her jacket into place as they stepped out onto the sidewalk.

"Thanks. I appreciate it." They were walking toward the green Ford Explorer when suddenly she slowed, fear creeping up her spine and lodging itself in her throat. She could barely swallow over the lump.

Grace noticed the look on her face, the pale skin and wide eyes. "Remmy, you okay? A vision?"

Remmy shook her head. "No. Julie."

❧❧❧❧

"Ray, I really want you to go. I'm not comfortable with you being here."

"Why not?" Ray got to his feet and moved around the room in agitation. "Why didn't you ever return any of my phone calls? Why the hell did you end our relationship without even so much as a 'fuck you, Ray'?"

This was the Ray she was afraid of, the Ray he had turned into at some point in their relationship. Her heart pounding, Julie tried to keep her breathing even. "I can't take this. Please just go."

❧❧❧❧

Ray followed her as she backed away from him. "See? You need me, Julie. You're afraid of your own shadow without me here." His gaze traveled over the sleek torso, taking in Julie's heaving breasts and sliding down to her legs. The last time he had seen her, she hadn't looked this good. He grasped her arms, rubbing the soft skin. Looking into her face, he was shocked to see terrified green eyes staring back at him. "Why are you afraid of me? Baby, I love you, remember?"

Julie wanted to scream, she was screaming in her head, but no sound would escape her clenched throat. Almost faint from the lack of breath, all she could do was shake her head, tears streaming down her cheeks.

Ray stepped closer, to wrap his arms around her. Suddenly he was grabbed by the shoulder and spun around. A fist made solid contact with his cheek and he went down, the carpet burning his palms as he reached out to break his fall. Stunned, he looked up to see a tall woman glaring down at him with blue eyes filled with fire, her hands still balled up in fists.

"Jesus Christ!" he yelled, anger filling him. He was about to get to his feet when another woman stopped him with a hand pressed against his shoulder. He met the stern gaze of Grace Cowan. "What the hell are you doing here, Detective?" he asked, bringing a hand to his cheek to check for blood.

"Get a clue and stay away from her, Ray," Grace said, glancing over at Remmy and Julie.

Remmy turned to Julie, who was looking at her, past her, through her. She looked terrified, as though she were about to bolt. She hugged herself, her already petite frame seeming to nearly disappear within itself.

"Hey," Remmy said softly, stepping into Julie's line of sight. "Julie? Honey? It's me. It's Remmy."

Though the words were muffled, as if spoken through cotton, still Remmy's voice penetrated the fear. Julie tore her gaze from the past, Sergio's face fading into the darkest recesses of her mind, concerned blue eyes filling her gaze. Realization broke through, and Julie dissolved.

Remmy caught the sobbing woman, holding Julie as she glared over at Ray who now stood near the door, talking to Grace.

"I didn't know she'd freak out like that," Ray muttered, grudgingly realizing he had really scared Julie. "But that bitch still didn't need to hit me." He met Remmy's glare.

"Ray, just leave, okay? There's nothing here for you. Go home," Grace said. She reached for the front door and pulled it open. With one last glance at Julie, Ray stomped out. Grace turned back to the women, almost feeling as if she was intruding as Remmy held Julie, whispering words that were not for Grace's ears. Deciding Julie was fine where she was, Grace left, quietly shutting the door behind her.

The world ceased to exist for Remmy as she held Julie, their bodies flush, one hand holding her close while the other gently combed through thick blonde hair. She felt Julie's tears stop, a soft sigh brushing against her neck as arms snaked around her waist.

Julie's eyes slipped closed, the steady beat of Remmy's heart beneath her ear calming her like nothing else she had ever known. All but forgetting the extreme stress of moments ago, she allowed herself to get lost in the warmth that enveloped her, her mind clearing of fear and discomfort.

Remmy's heart began to pound, and she suddenly worried that Julie would be able to hear it. She reluctantly pulled away and smiled down into questioning green eyes. "Are you okay?" she asked, trying to ignore the heat engulfing her body, a reaction which stunned her and left her feeling weak and ashamed.

Julie nodded, running her hands over her face. Her skin felt hot. "I'll be right back," she said, going into the kitchen. She wet a paper towel and placed it on her face to cool herself off. She heard Remmy enter the kitchen. "I forgot I was making dinner before Ray showed up," she said, a small smile on her lips when Remmy's gaze settled on the pan on the stove. "Can't say I'm real hungry anymore."

"You should eat, Julie. You can't let any of this rule you."

Julie knew Remmy was right. "Have you eaten? Will you join me?"

Patting her stomach, Remmy shook her head. "God, no. I filled up on apple pie."

Julie glanced at Remmy. "Will you stay? Maybe have a Coke with me or something?"

Remmy didn't have to be asked twice. "Of course."

As Julie finished preparing her dinner, chatting about her day and about new outfits she had bought, Remmy's thoughts were on what had happened a few moments earlier.

She was no stranger to the passion of a woman, but never, ever had she thought of Julie in that way. But tonight, standing there holding her, she had wanted nothing more than to lift Julie's face and kiss her. She had been passionate about Julie, but until a few moments ago, hadn't recognized it as anything sexual. She was protective of Julie, she liked Julie, and she felt a strong connection to her, a closeness.

"Hey."

Remmy was startled by the soft voice and the even softer fingers that gently ran through her hair. She looked up to find Julie standing next to her.

"Are you okay?" Julie asked, luxuriating in the thick softness of Remmy's dark hair, allowing her fingers to play.

Remmy's eyes closed, her head resting against Julie's side. "Yeah. I'm really tired," Remmy said, which was at least the partial truth.

"Long day?" At Remmy's nod, Julie leaned down and placed a soft kiss on the top of her head. "You wanna stay here tonight? I've got the bed set up in the second bedroom."

Remmy grinned. "I know. I moved it in there for you."

Julie chuckled. "Yes, you did, and I believe I thanked you with a fine steak dinner."

Remmy's eyes closed as the fingers continued to comb through her hair. It felt wonderful. "I think your spaghetti is boiling over," she murmured, nearly asleep.

"Oh crap!" Julie hurried over to the stove, turned the heat down, and blew on the boiling froth. Deciding the noodles were tender enough, she strained the boiling water into the sink, then heated up sauce from the jar of Prego on the counter. Within moments Julie joined Remmy at the table and began to eat her dinner. As Julie ate, she wondered about Remmy just showing up like that. How could she have known? She hesitantly met Remmy's gaze and forced herself to ask. "How did you know?"

Remmy ran her hands through her hair, shivering at the memory of Julie's fingers having been there moments before. "I felt it," she said. "I knew you were afraid."

Julie nodded, not able to meet Remmy's eyes. She didn't understand Remmy's gift, but tonight she had seen it firsthand. There was no other way for her to have known that Julie was frightened. Grace's presence with Remmy helped to seal the deal. What on earth was behind Remmy's gift, anyway? It didn't matter. "I'm glad you came, Remmy. Thank you."

"Any time."

Chapter Forty-three

Remmy blinked a few times as she woke to surroundings that were not her room. The hissing of TV snow filled the room, the black and white patterns throwing strange shadows on the walls and floor around her. Feeling a weight against her, she looked down. She was stretched out on the couch, her head resting against two stacked throw pillows. The weight she felt was Julie using her as a pillow, Julie's body squeezed between Remmy and the back of the couch. Julie's head rested on Remmy's chest, an arm thrown across Remmy's stomach.

After Julie had eaten, the two of them settled in to watch TV. Remmy knew she was tired, exhausted, actually, from working a double shift to cover for the new guy, who hadn't shown up. Also, the mental gymnastics she had been putting into Grace's new case had caught up to her. She had obviously fallen asleep while watching TV.

Remmy knew she should probably get up and go to her own bed or she would have one hell of a cramp in her back in the morning. Her body was already protesting her current position. Instead, she laid her head down on the pillow, grabbed the remote control from the coffee table, and turned off the TV. She observed the woman who was sleeping against her. Julie's body was relaxed and warm. Remmy lightly ran her fingers through soft blonde hair. Julie sighed and shifted her position, but didn't wake. Remmy smiled at the soft snore as Julie fell back into a deep sleep, her fingers gripping a handful of Remmy's shirt.

She placed a soft kiss on Julie's forehead, then her fingers traced across soft skin, outlined dark blonde eyebrows, relaxed in sleep, down the slope of Julie's nose, then quickly retreating from the slightly parted lips.

Utterly loathe to move, Remmy desperately had to pee. She slowly slid out from underneath Julie, trying not to wake her. There was a small grunt of protest, but then Julie nestled back into a deep slumber.

Remmy hurried to the bathroom, sighing heavily in relief as her need was met. She ran her hands through her hair and tried to shake herself into wakefulness. Glancing at the display on her cell phone, she saw that it was after two in the morning. She could hear the rain still coming down, though not as fiercely as it had earlier. The idea of trudging home in the rain didn't appeal to her, but she didn't want to be any trouble. She decided that the best solution would be to get Julie to her bed, then she would crash on the couch.

Julie was exactly as she had left her, and Remmy was charmed. She crouched in front of the couch, studying her. She was truly beautiful. Remmy knew she needed to detour her mind from the direction it was heading; there was no future there.

Remmy had never had a girlfriend, never stayed anywhere long enough to allow messy emotions to develop. She'd had a fling or two that had lasted longer than one night, but even those had happened a very long time ago. She hadn't been with a woman in over a year. The closeness she and Julie shared was a new experience for her, something she hadn't felt even with Monica. She felt so safe with Julie, accepted and cared for. So many different things clicked into place when they were together. And when she touched Julie…

Remmy sighed heavily, her heart saddened for a moment at knowing that as wonderful as her time with Julie was, friendship was all they would ever have. That was probably enough. She herself never stuck around long, she chided herself, so what did it matter?

Julie had become the most important person in her life, and Remmy wanted to protect her from anything that would put a frown on that beautiful face; she wanted to eradicate anything that would cause terror such as Julie felt tonight. When she thought about Ray, Remmy felt the anger still simmering just under the surface. What the hell had he been thinking, attacking her like that? The man obviously didn't give a shit about Julie.

Later, when they'd been sitting quietly on the couch watching TV, Julie told Remmy about her relationship with Ray, how unhealthy it had been. He had tried to control and possess her, much like he'd been trying to do when Remmy and Grace arrived. The sadness and confusion in Julie's eyes nearly broke Remmy's heart. Her heart did break when Julie told her she planned to just live for herself, her brother and nephew, and her career, as soon as she got it back on track. She had no desire to allow another man into her life, and certainly not into her heart or her bed. Remmy thought it was tragic that someone as young and beautiful as Julie, who had so much to offer, was going to lock that part of herself up and throw away the key.

Green eyes blinked open. Julie looked at Remmy, trying to focus tired eyes. Finally she sighed, turning onto her back and stretching. "Why are you sitting there watching me?" Julie asked, pushing up onto her elbows.

"I was contemplating whether I wanted to wake you or not. You looked so comfortable. And…I don't know…your little snores were just too cute."

Julie's eyes opened wide. "I do not snore."

Remmy shrugged, a smirk curling her lips. "I beg to differ. You drool, too," she lied, tugging at her t-shirt collar. "You might've farted a time or two, too." Her eyes wide, Julie's mouth opened but nothing came out. Remmy couldn't keep up the charade. She burst out laughing. "I'm teasing. Come on. Let's get you to bed so I can crash on the couch."

Julie sat up, running her hands through her hair to get it out of her face. She glared at Remmy and swatted at her playfully as she stood. "Snoring, drooling, farting," she muttered. "I don't think so." She grabbed Remmy's hand and yanked her toward the stairs. "And I don't think you're sleeping on the couch. That's ridiculous when I've got a whole bed upstairs for you."

"Oh, Julie, that's not necessary. I don't want to make a mess for you; I can sleep anywhere—"

Julie stopped suddenly, causing Remmy to nearly run into her. Julie turned and looked up into Remmy's eyes through the darkness in the upstairs hallway. "Stop," she said softly. "You don't make messes for me, and even if you did, you're always welcome here. My house is your house." A soft smile played around her lips. "After all, you did help me remodel it."

Remmy smiled. "Okay."

"Good. Get some sleep." Julie cupped Remmy's cheek for a moment before heading to her own bedroom, the dogs trotting along behind.

ᘓ ᘓ ᘔ ᘔ

The dishwasher roared to life, the smell of freshly scrubbed floors…Pine Sol. The dishrag was in her hand as she finished wiping down the counters. Good thing lunch is finished. Taylor will be asleep soon. Maybe I can catch Oprah. She reached for her juice, intending to finish it. Thirsty.

A crack. Break. Something falling to the floor. She turned and looked, surprised, unsure. Questions flared in her mind. Why was he *there?*

Remmy gasped, her pillow falling to the floor with a thud as she sat bolt upright. "She knew him!" she yelled, chest heaving, breath rattling painfully. Her eyes were wide, unseeing, as she could still feel the frightened familiarity in her dream. Her vision. She glanced over at the floor where her pants lay in a heap. She carried a rattle that Grace had taken from the crime scene; it gave Remmy a material link to the victim.

The bedroom door pushed open and a sleep-tousled Julie hurried to the bed. "Are you okay?" she asked.

Remmy's heart raced, fear still flaring in her eyes. "She knew him," she said again, looking up at Julie.

"Who, Remmy?" Julie sat on the edge of the bed and took both of Remmy's trembling hands in her own.

"She did. She knew her killer. I gotta call Grace. I gotta tell her—"

"Shh. Remmy, sweetie, shh." Julie pushed dark hair away from hollow eyes. "You need sleep."

Remmy shook her head, trying to summon some saliva in her dry mouth. "No. I gotta tell Grace. She knew him."

"Remmy? Remmy, honey, look at me. Focus on me." Julie waited until blue eyes were trained on her, clear and awake. "Honey, telling Grace in the middle of the night isn't going to make any difference in the case. The poor woman is dead already, honey. She's not going anywhere."

Remmy blew out a breath, long and shaky. She

could still feel the woman's fear, and it scared her. Julie picked up her pillow and placed it back on the bed, then Remmy was being pushed back onto the soft mattress. She tried to shake off the hand that rested on her chest.

"Shh," Julie cooed, lying beside her. "Come here, Remmy." Julie's hand squirmed under Remmy's shoulders. After several deep breaths, Remmy finally moved into her arms and rested her head against Julie's shoulder. Julie lay there, wide awake, able to feel the fear rolling off Remmy like heat. She buried her hand in long hair and placed a kiss on Remmy's forehead. "You're trembling," she whispered.

"She was so afraid, Julie," Remmy whispered, eyes staring blankly at the wall, still seeing the kitchen, so neat and clean. "She knew him."

"Who was he?"

Remmy shook her head. "I don't know."

Julie was quiet for a moment, a myriad of questions swarming through her mind. She was recalling memories of her own case, along with the few facts she knew about this one. "Did you see it, or did you just feel it?"

"Both." Remmy shifted her head, finding the softness of Julie's breast, feeling its fullness under her cheek. Julie's arms tightened around her.

"So, this is almost like a delayed reaction? I mean, this woman was murdered, so you're experiencing what happened in the past."

"That's usually how it works." She raised her head, resting it in the palm of her hand as she glanced past Julie and out the window that was above the headboard. "Except with you."

Julie studied Remmy's face, noting the way the moonlight shone in her eyes, making the color almost transparent. She repressed the urge to reach up and trace the proud jaw, set and hard at the moment. She wished there was something she could do to ease her tension.

"Why was it different with me?" she asked softly, meeting Remmy's gaze as she looked down at her.

Remmy shrugged. "I really don't know. With you, it was so strange. There was one time… When you were in the basement, I guess it was. You were looking over at Pam."

"How do you know?"

Remmy's smile was sad. "Because I could see her, too, through your eyes. That was when I told Grace that there were more than just you there. She started to do a little investigating and digging in the nearby counties. She found out about Pam's and Roxie's cases." She chuckled ruefully. "I really think she thought I was completely nuts."

"How many nights did you wake up from the dreams, when I was…there?" Julie asked, her voice a whisper. She wasn't sure whether she even wanted to know the answer. She could see the haunted look returning to Remmy's eyes, and it made her sad. She wondered how much of herself Remmy lost every time she had a vision.

Remmy heard the question, but didn't answer for a moment. She gazed down at Julie, memorizing her face and the look of unshielded concern and affection in her eyes. She didn't want Julie to know the truth, to know that she had nearly lost her mind during those very dark months. Unexpectedly, she smiled. "A few."

Julie knew Remmy was holding out on her, but didn't press. Her adrenaline was draining away, leaving her exhausted. "Come here," she said, bringing Remmy's head back down to lie against her. "Get some sleep, Remmy." She placed a kiss on top of the dark head. "Let me watch over you tonight."

Chapter Forty-four

Grace was getting frustrated, Remmy could tell by the way that she kept watching carefully for any change in her expression, a twitch of an eye, anything. Finally Remmy sighed and pushed the photo array book away. "I don't think he's in here, Grace," she said, leaning back in her chair.

Grace sighed in frustration "We haven't gone through all of them, Rem. There are still about three pages of pic—"

"He's not in here." Remmy tapped the page with her finger. She looked into dark eyes. "I'm telling you, he's not."

"How do you know, damnit?" Grace pushed away from the table and snatched her cup, heading over to the coffeemaker to pour herself another. It was her sixth cup since eight that morning, just two hours ago. *So much for trying to curb my caffeine intake.*

"How do you know the sky is blue? How do you know you're drinking liquid mud?" Remmy indicated the cup in Grace's hand.

Grace looked down into her cup then met angry blue eyes. "I just know," she said with a knowing sigh.

"Bingo."

Grace sighed again, walking back over to the table. The book of mugshots still lay face-open on the table. She slammed it closed with finality. "You said she knew this guy. How do you know? Did she say his name?"

"Nope." Remmy perched on the edge of the table,

grabbing Grace's mug from her hand and sniffing before taking a drink. "Jesus, that's gross," she said, handing it back.

"Yeah, well, it keeps me awake. There's a Coke machine in the hall, or a drinking fountain near the bathrooms."

"Nah, that's okay. I need to get back to work. Besides, I'm having dinner over at Julie's tonight." Grace studied her for a long moment, to the point that it made Remmy uncomfortable. "What?" Remmy asked, feeling like a bug under a microscope.

Grace shook her head, a knowing smile on her lips. "Nothing. Okay, so tell me how you know she knew this guy."

"He came into the house. Was the door locked?" At the shake of Grace's head, she continued. "I could tell she was afraid, but more curious about why he was there. Oh, and last night, while I was re-stocking the maxi pads, something else came to me. If you can find the murder weapon, I really think it will lead you right to this guy."

"And any ideas about what we're looking for in said weapon?"

Remmy grinned, pushing away from the table. "Now that, Grace, is why you're paid the big bucks to be Dick Tracy, and I'm the lowly convenience store clerk." She grabbed her wallet and phone from the table. "I gotta go. See you later."

"She's gonna be the death of me," Grace muttered, taking a seat back at her desk. This case was driving her mad.

Yvonne and Clive Bailey had been married for six years, happily so, as far as their investigation could determine. Clive's alibi had checked out; it was watertight. He'd been at work at the post office that entire day, seen by no less than fifty people during the hours the murder and abduction had taken place. They had no serious debt, no problems, and no enemies. A well-liked couple, Yvonne was twenty-eight and Clive, thirty-four. Their son, Tyler, twenty-two months old, was deeply loved by both parents.

Grace and Brian had thought that the crime was random, though the missing baby had cast doubt on that theory, and now Remmy was telling her that Yvonne knew her killer. That just blew the "random" theory right out of the water. She knew better than to doubt what Remmy said. They were back to square one.

Exhaling a loud breath, she tossed her reading glasses onto her desk and rubbed at her eyes. It would be anther late night.

Chapter Forty-five

I think you're lying," Julie said, her tone matter-of-fact. Not bothering to turn around to see Remmy's expression, she finished watering her backyard flowers. It was May. Summer was almost upon them, but the heat hadn't been turned up full-blast yet, so it was enjoyable to be spending a beautiful day outside.

Julie was dressed in a tank top and shorts. Her legs were already a lovely bronze color from working tirelessly in the yard. It showed. The grass was pristine, the flowers coming up beautifully. There were two reasons for the gorgeous yard and tanned flesh. The first was that Julie was trying to enjoy her time at home before she had to start working again; the second was that she was trying to keep herself from pulling her hair out from boredom. She was a worker; staying at home wasn't her bag.

Remmy stopped weeding the flowerbeds along the back fence and turned to face her. "You think I'm lying?"

"Yes. I don't believe for a minute that you have a tattoo of Woody Woodpecker on...well, on your body."

Remmy smirked. "You mean on the inside of my thigh?"

"The inside of your thigh is on your body, smart ass." Eyebrows drawing behind her sunglasses, Julie glanced at her. Remmy was stretching her long, lean body to reach a weed that was tucked back near the fence. Her breath caught for a moment; the image reminded her of a graceful panther or tiger.

"Why don't you believe it?" Remmy asked in mid-stretch. She glanced over at Julie, surprised when she hurriedly looked away. Sitting back on her haunches, Remmy rested her hands on her thighs, bare knees covered with dirt and small scratches from crawling around on her knees in search of weeds.

"Because. Who in their right mind would get a damn tattoo on the inside of their thigh?" Julie released the trigger on the hose nozzle and the water stream stopped. She faced Remmy. "That would hurt like crazy."

"I'm sure it would've, if I'd been sober." Remmy grinned, pushing to her feet and wiping her hands on the long legs of her cargo shorts. She began to saunter toward Julie, hips swaying exaggeratedly, making Julie laugh. As she walked, she began to unbutton her shorts.

Not sure what Remmy was doing, Julie backed away. "Uh, Remmy..."

"Nah, I'll show you." Remmy was within three feet of Julie, slowly pulling the zipper down on her fly.

Julie felt a flush rise up her neck, and a wave of heat rushed through her. Suddenly extremely uncomfortable, she did the only thing she could think of.

"Ah! Julie!" Tugging her shorts up as she ran, Remmy dashed away from the ice cold stream of water that hit her squarely in the stomach.

❧❧❧❧

Sitting at Julie's kitchen table and having some lunch, Remmy had a bath towel wrapped around her waist while her shorts tumbled in the dryer. "So, when do you go in and get your classroom, ready?" Remmy asked.

"Usually not 'til about a week before classes start." Julie popped a chip into her mouth.

Remmy nodded, sipping her iced tea. "I bet your boss is happy you're coming back. I bet the kids are too."

"Hell, I'm happy to be going back. God, this has driven me crazy, staying home like this. Talk about cabin fever." Finished, she pushed her plate away, sighing with contentment.

"Well, I'm sure you'll go in there and kick ass, Julie. You've got the parking lot knocked out, anyway." Remmy's grin was met with a sheepish look. "What?"

"I still can't get out of the car," Julie said, her voice little girl shy. She had driven to the parking lot twice since she had gone with Remmy, and both times she'd been able to pull in. The second time, she even parked in the exact spot where her car had been parked when she'd been grabbed. But when she tried to open her door and step out, she began to shake and then cry.

"Why not?" Remmy asked, shoving her own plate away, sandwich forgotten.

"It's stupid, Remmy. It's really not worth talking about," Julie said, waving the subject away. "Conversation closed."

"Okay," Remmy said. She could bide her time.

⁂

The ice cream was heaven on Julie's tongue, especially since they'd been hit with the summer heat earlier in the day while doing yardwork. The cool, early evening breeze played with the tendrils of hair that had fallen out of her ponytail. She hadn't had it long in nearly ten years, so she had decided not to cut her hair after all. Probably not wise, though, to grow it out right before summer. Either way, she enjoyed having more styling options to work with. It was nice. Remmy seemed to really like it.

Remmy stretched her legs out, the cool grass tickling her bare calves, making the backs of her knees itch. She rested back on one hand, the other holding her chocolate cone. She smiled as Julie — sitting cross-legged next to her — dug into her sundae with child-like excitement. She glanced out over the park. The sun should be up for a couple more hours.

"When we were kids, Matt and I used to ride our bikes to a little ice cream stand that was about a mile from our house. I used to get bubblegum ice cream," Julie said between bites of ice cream and gooey hot fudge.

"Bubblegum ice cream? That sounds disgusting." Remmy licked around her cone until she had a very fine tip at the top, which fell over into a curl.

"Oh, no. It was so good. It was basically vanilla ice cream, but it had these tiny little square pieces of gum inside, about the size of a Chiclet. Made the ice cream taste bubblegummy, too. I used to shove the pieces of bubblegum into my cheek." She laughed at the memory. "It would be bulging by time I was done."

Remmy smiled at the visualization of chipmunk Julie. She took a bite of her ice cream and allowed it to melt on her tongue as she mused. "What were you like as a kid?"

"Evil." Julie grinned, her eyes twinkling mischievously. "I used to get in all sorts of trouble and then I'd let Matty take the fall for me." She laughed at the memory.

Remmy studied her, happy to see Julie excited and bright, her eyes so filled with life. It was intoxicating. "Do you ever wish you'd had more siblings?"

Julie thought about it for a moment, licking fudge from the corner of her mouth. "No. I don't think so," she finally said, meeting Remmy's gaze. "I think that just the two of us got into enough trouble as it was. Any more of us and world beware! What about you? I know you had Monica, but do you wish you had more family?"

"Sometimes," Remmy said honestly. "I have no idea what it's like to have parents. I sometimes wish I did."

"The holidays?"

Remmy shrugged. "I've never celebrated Christmas with anyone other than Monica, and this past year was the first time I've celebrated it in...wow, maybe seven years or so."

"Now that's a crime. I wish you'd been in Woodland this past year, Rem. You could've joined us." Julie met Remmy's smile. "This year," she said emphatically, pointing her plastic spoon at Remmy.

"Yep. This year."

❧❧❧❧❧

"I absolutely love driving this car." Remmy said, shifting the little Miata into another gear as it purred over the streets of Woodland.

Julie chuckled. "This little car is the only thing I've ever truly spoiled myself with."

"Why white?"

Julie shrugged. "I love white. It's pure, it's natural, and a sign of good things to come."

"Yeah, but red," Remmy said, her voice low and dramatic. "Now that's a color."

"Well, that may be, but how many friggin' red sports cars do you see on the streets? Too many," Julie said, waving away the idea. She looked around and realized Remmy's destination. "Why are you going to the school?" she asked, her voice trembling.

"Who said I'm going to the school?" Remmy asked

innocently.

"Could be the School Zone sign we just passed."

Remmy grinned as she pulled into the parking lot. "Which one?" she asked, gesturing to the spaces. Julie pointed and Remmy eased the little car into the space where it had been parked the previous August. She cut the engine.

Julie looked out over the lot, the setting sun radiating an intense golden red to the end of the day. "Why are we here?" she said quietly.

Remmy turned the key to Accessory and turned on the radio. The Drifters' "Under the Boardwalk" was playing. "Perfect." Remmy opened her car door and stepped out into the beautiful night.

Julie's heart pounded. "Remmy! Get back in here!"

Remmy ignored her, moving to the wonderful classic. Her lips moving as she sang along with the words, she backed up far enough so she could see Julie in the low slung car.

"Remmy, please," Julie choked out, fighting back tears. She watched Remmy dance her way to the front of the car, the headlights shining double spotlights on her for just a moment as she made her way to the driver's side door, pulled it open, and reached inside. Julie snatched her hand back, out of Remmy's reach.

Remmy sang along with the Drifters, reaching in and getting a firm grip on Julie's hand, tugging gently.

Julie took a deep breath and allowed herself to be pulled from the car. She was trembling as Remmy placed a hand on her waist, the other clasping Julie's shaking hand.

Remmy danced Julie along with her as she moved in front of the car, knowing that the van had been parked two spots to the left of Julie's Miata. They reached the open passenger door and the music filled the night. She pulled Julie close, expertly gliding across the parking spaces, still singing.

Julie finally looked up and met her gaze, a ghost of a smile finding its way to her lips. She was safe, she knew, especially in Remmy's arms. She allowed herself to hear the song, allowed her body to move with Remmy's. Her eyes squeezed shut as they danced in the space where the van had been parked.

"Just dance with me," Remmy whispered in her ear.

Julie took a deep breath, her hand sliding out of Remmy's, both arms snaking up around her neck. She felt Remmy's hands on her waist as the music drew to a close.

No longer singing, Remmy was intent on the feel of Julie's body against her own, the smell of her hair and skin, the music and the feel of the breeze as it washed over them. It was magical. She met Julie's gaze and couldn't look away.

Julie felt herself becoming lost in the blue eyes that bored so intently into her own. She could see a storm swirling in their oceanic depths. Her heart began to pound again; this time, fear had nothing to do with it. Before she could formulate a reaction, Remmy was leaning toward her.

Remmy's eyes closed at the feel of Julie's lips, so very soft against her own. She stopped moving, allowing the new sensations to fill her. She felt the tiniest amount of give in Julie's lips, almost imperceptibly moving with hers.

A streak of emotions sliced through Julie: surprise, confusion, fear. Gasping, she pushed away, staring up at Remmy with eyes wide. Flustered and deeply hurt, Julie let her hands fall away from Remmy's neck. "Why did you do that?" she whispered, backing toward the car.

Stung by the rejection, Remmy rubbed the back of her neck, feeling foolish. "I..." She had wanted to kiss Julie, plain and simple. But it wasn't that simple. Not for Julie.

"I think I need to get home," Julie said. She was desperate to be alone, to get away from Remmy. Her heart was pounding and her lips tingled.

"Okay." Remmy shoved her hands into the pockets of her cargo shorts and backed away from the car.

"Get in, Remmy. I'll drop you off at your apartment," Julie said, unable to meet Remmy's eyes.

"No. I'm going to walk. Nice night and all."

Julie watched as Remmy turned and hurried across the parking lot, disappearing into the deepening shadows. Forgetting that she was standing on the very spot, in the very position she'd been in the night Sergio had taken her, Julie continued to stare at the spot where Remmy had vanished into the night.

Chapter Forty-six

The town was quiet, the only sounds being those of the insects and the few animals that were out. Remmy sat on Overlook Hill, aptly titled, as all of Woodland could be seen from the wooded area which ended in a steep rock ledge. That was where Remmy sat, legs dangling over the side, a bottle of Corona in hand. The town was breathtaking at night, all the lights flickering on as the sun fell, an orange glow just barely visible at the horizon. She had already seen the sky go from baby blue to steel blue, explode with fingers of pink, orange and red, and finally settle to navy. Soon it would be black.

She had gone up to Overlook Hill every night after work for the past two weeks, starting with the night she had left Julie standing alone in the parking lot of the middle school. Off in the distance, she heard a coyote calling out, a melancholy, solitary sound, as was the lonely train whistle somewhere south of town. She hated the cry of trains at night. It sounded like a ship lost at sea.

Remmy tipped her bottle and the cool liquid slid down her throat; she swallowed with a contented sigh. She wasn't a drinker anymore, but she'd treated herself to a beer and it was a welcome relief. She had been taking longer shifts at the store since Joan had fired the new guy. Last week alone she'd put in nearly fifty hours. Fine by her. It helped her to not think.

The sun was fully gone now, leaving the night

cool. Remmy shivered, and decided it was time to go home. She pushed up, dusted off the seat of her shorts, and loped around to where Overlook Hill sloped down to the outskirts of the town below, the bottle of beer swinging gently between two of her fingers. She kept a watchful eye on her surroundings.

Remmy had to admit that since she'd been involved with the Venti case, and now Grace's current case, she had stopped taking people's basic goodness for granted. She had hitchhiked hundreds of times, stayed with strangers, and partied with guys she'd known for fifteen minutes. Now she realized just how lucky she had been. She'd had her share of trouble, had people try and take advantage of her, but overall, she had never found herself in any sort of dire situation. Never again would she casually put herself in that kind of danger. She had seen the face of the devil in Sergio Venti.

Her mind clear while she had watched the sunset, Remmy now roamed the streets of Woodland, her thoughts filled with images of Julie smiling at her, then backing away from her in anger and fear. The look in her eyes had haunted Remmy for two weeks. She had tried her best to not think about it. Sometimes she was successful, but as night fell, she was always inundated with memories, thoughts, and guilt.

She hadn't tried to get hold of Julie, hadn't stopped by her house, hadn't called her. That was the hardest thing she'd ever had to do — stay away. She had hurt Julie that night, betraying a trust that had been built over the months they had spent time together. Julie had been abused by Sergio Venti, and then Remmy had kissed her. Had she been any better than that monster? She hoped that Julie knew somewhere deep inside that Remmy's kiss was born from love and an enjoyment of their time together — nothing more, nothing darker.

Off to the right were the fairgrounds, a lot of noise and movement. Remmy stopped at a break in the stone wall that enclosed them, fingers latched into the chainlink gate. The rides were being assembled, large lights hooked up to generators so the men could see what they were doing. They called to each other, yelling out instructions as the Ferris Wheel went up. Posters and flyers had been circulating for weeks, the excitement in Woodland growing over the fair, which would be in their town for a month.

With a heavy sigh, Remmy turned away, tossing her half full bottle of beer into a trash can as she passed it. She needed sleep.

Chapter Forty-seven

Brian Wong stared at Grace, doubt clearly etched on his face. He glanced over the crime scene photos again, then tossed them onto her desk. "I don't buy it. We've found nothing to indicate that Yvonne knew this guy. Or girl," he quickly added.

"Brian, I trust Remmy's instincts. Okay?"

"I see. So, because this psychic said the victim knew her killer, and he wears some sort of gaudy ring, we should be looking for some long lost buddy who wears a class ring?" He threw himself into the chair next to Grace's desk.

"Brian, you're such an ass." Grace stacked the photos neatly and slid them back into the manila envelope.

"I just don't think this entire investigation should be based on what Remmy Foster says."

Grace smirked. "I hardly think this entire investigation is based on what Remmy Foster says. She's given us some good leads." Grace brought up the file on the Bailey couple, skimming through the details until she came across the baby's information. Twenty-two months old. Almost two years old. "Brian," she said, voice rough. Brian removed his hand from his eyes, looking at her questioningly. "How old was your kid when she started talking? I mean really talking."

"I don't know. Maybe fifteen months. Eighteen." He shrugged. "Why?"

Grace turned in her chair, leaning forward so her

elbows rested on her thighs and looking at him over the rims of her glasses. "Was she able to talk by twenty-two months?"

"Oh, yeah. Jesus, she was a little gibbermouth by then—" Brian cut off the fond memories of his daughter at that age. He saw recognition of his own epiphany on Grace's face. "The baby would've talked," he said.

Grace nodded. "Yep. You can't threaten a two year-old to make him keep his mouth shut." Grace threw her pencil onto the desk and sat back in her chair. "Yvonne knew her killer, Brian, and so did Tyler."

Brian looked away, not wanting to admit that maybe Remmy was right. Again.

❧❧❧❧

"Thank you, Mrs. Albright. Have a wonderful day." Remmy smiled at the older woman who was exiting, her weekly lottery tickets in hand. Remmy was about to do some cleaning but saw Skylar Wilson scurrying across the parking lot toward the store. The bell above the door jingled and the boy ran up to the counter, a big grin on his face.

"Hey, little man," she said in greeting. He gave her an excited wave, which made her smile. Matt must not be angry with her; he'd sent his son in to pay. "How's it goin', Skylar?"

"Good. My dad let me come in to pay for his gas." He carefully set two twenties on the counter.

"I see that." Remmy took the money then leaned down so she was closer to his height. "Tell you what. Go grab you a can of something, and it's on me. 'Kay?"

The boy's eyes widened in pleasure. He nodded then ran to the coolers. Remmy wondered if he ever walked anywhere. Within moments, he was back, setting a can of Sprite on the counter. Remmy dug a dollar out of her pocket and rang the pop up with the gas.

"Are you going to the fair with us tonight?" Skylar asked.

"Oh, uh…who — you and your dad?"

Skylar nodded. "And Aunt Julie."

Remmy's heart hurt at the mere mention of her name. "Well…" Remmy thought quickly. Skylar obviously had no idea there was anything wrong, and she didn't want to be the bearer of bad news. "I'm kinda stuck working tonight, Skylar. You know, someone's gotta work since you won't get a job."

Skylar giggled, showing the space for his missing front teeth. "I'm too young!" he said.

Remmy rolled her eyes. "Whatever, Skylar." She winked at him, handing him his can of soda and the change for his father. "You guys have fun tonight, okay?" She leaned down again. "Take a spin in the Ferris Wheel with your aunt for me, okay?"

Skylar's eyes brightened, excited to be given a mission. "Bye, Remmy," he called, running out the door.

"God, I wish I had half that kid's energy," Joan said, stepping up to the counter.

"No joke."

"So, why aren't you going to the fair with them? You know damn well you're off in two hours." Joan raised her clipboard. She had spent the entire afternoon working on the inventory in the back. Now she began to finger through the candy displays near the register, marking down how many bars of each type of candy were left.

Remmy sighed, watching as Matt's truck drove off into the warm afternoon. "It's a long story, Joan."

Joan eyed her, eyebrows raised. "Good thing you've still got two hours left on your shift then, isn't it?"

Remmy studied her boss, friend, and landlady. She wasn't sure she wanted to talk about what had happened with Julie. It was private.

"Remmy?" Joan's voice was soft, all hint of teasing gone. "Honey, what is it? You look like you're about to cry."

Remmy blinked her emotion away. "It's nothing, Joan. Julie and I got into a...fight." There was no way in hell she would tell Joan what actually happened. She couldn't stand the embarrassment, or the look of disapproval she was sure she would see on Joan's face. "I've been lying low." She forced a smile. "That's all. I'll get over it."

"Well, it happens. Hell, it happens between Doug and I on a weekly basis." She smiled sympathetically. "If you ever want to talk, Rem, I'm here. Okay?"

Remmy nodded her gratitude. "Thanks, Joan."

≈≈≈≈≈

Remmy's hand wiggled into the hip pocket of her jeans and grasped the small rattle. She drew it out, not looking at it as she walked home. Her fingers moved across the smooth plastic, some places still slightly tacky from sticky little fingers touching it, a young mother not having had the chance to clean it off. Remmy concentrated on those areas, knowing that Tyler had touched the rattle there. His presence was still with it.

She could readily hear the cry of Tyler Bailey, a comforting sound as it echoed in her mind. As long as she could hear him, he was still alive. Her eyes combed the streets, meeting the gaze of everyone she passed, many nodding a greeting or wishing her a nice evening. She politely spoke with a couple who actually stopped and wanted to chat, her mind always on the cry she was hearing.

On her own street, Joan and Doug's house stood proud down the block. She stopped on the corner, turning in a small circle, listening, thumb absently rubbing across the toy. She could hear cooing, garbled words that made little sense, except in the language of babies. But just below that, always the crying. She couldn't get a hit on the direction of the crying. No matter where she looked, or which way she turned, it was steady.

With a sigh of frustration, she headed to the back stairs which led up to her apartment.

❧❧❧❧

Julie smoothed her hands over the front of her summer dress, turning this way and that, looking at herself in the free-standing mirror in the corner of her bedroom. As she moved, the flowing skirt of the dress brushed against her bare legs. It reminded her of the dress she had always been wearing in the field, when Remmy was there. She studied her reflection. The halter straps of the dress left her shoulders bare; the neckline dipped, but not very low. It was a nice dress, very cute, and she had to admit, she looked good in it.

She sighed. Remmy. It had been the two longest weeks of her life. She hadn't known it was possible to miss someone so much. She desperately missed Remmy's company. Even if Remmy was just sitting on the couch, chilling as she watched some TV, not a word spoken between them, the house somehow seemed warmer, happier.

That night in the school parking lot wasn't something Julie allowed herself to think about in detail, and she hadn't said anything to anyone else about it. She could still see the hurt in Remmy's eyes, the confusion. The sadness. When her mind started rewinding to the kiss, Julie shook her head. She couldn't go there.

Her gaze wandered to her hair, trying to decide what to do with it. She thought about putting it into a French braid, but changed her mind. Remmy liked it down. "God!" she cried, covering her face with her hands. Remmy wasn't even going to be there! She missed her, damnit. She really, really missed her. Compromising, she kept her hair down but tied in a braid that ran down the side of her head. Slipping into sandals, she was ready to go. Matt and Skylar would be picking her up at any minute. "Maybe I should call Remmy. Invite her," she whispered.

Julie heard the front door open. It was undoubtedly Matt using his key, as the doors were always kept locked. The sound of Skylar's feet pounded up the stairs and he called out, "Aunt Julie!"

Julie smiled at his obvious excitement, warmth filling her at the thought of spending time with her favorite pint-sized man. He burst into her bedroom and she caught him up in her arms, tickling him mercilessly as he squealed. She knew her days of doing that were numbered, as he was growing fast and would soon be too strong for her.

"I saw Remmy today," he said, proudly escorting his beloved aunt down the stairs.

"Oh, yeah?" Julie tried to sound casual, but her stomach immediately twisted into knots at the mere mention of the name.

Completely unaware of her distress, Skylar jumped down the final two stairs and landed hard on the ground level. "She said she couldn't come with us tonight 'cause she has to work."

Julie felt a sting of disappointment, but hid it well.

"Well," she said, ruffling the boy's hair, "somebody's gotta work, right?"

Skylar glanced up at her, perplexed. "That's what she said," he muttered. The sight of the two frisking dogs was enough to make Skylar forget about how weird adults were.

"You ready?" Matt asked.

"Yep. Let me feed the trouble twins, and we can head out."

⚘ ⚘ ⚘ ⚘

The early evening was beautiful, with just enough of a breeze to make the temperature pleasant. The fairgrounds were already filled with laughter and voices calling out, separated parties finding each other in the maze of rides and food and game booths.

Matt paid the admission fee for the three of them, shelling out another ten bucks a person for an armband which would allow the wearer unlimited rides on the amusements. Julie wasn't big on rides, especially at a fair-type situation. Her gaze ran up the Zipper, each individual car seating four, then independently spinning head over heels. She knew that the rides were constantly being taken down and put up, and it made her wonder just how safe they were.

"Are we ready?" Matt asked, wrapping Skylar's bracelet around his thin wrist.

Big eyes took in the fun. "Yeah! Let's get some cotton candy!"

Julie was happy to be with the two most important men in her life. She loved watching Skylar's excitement, and yet, something was missing. She felt the void as an ache in her heart. *Remmy is missing.* She would have made the night complete. A soft smile brushed her lips as she imagined Skylar and Remmy bantering back and forth, as they always did. She could imagine Remmy grabbing Skylar unawares and tossing him over her shoulder, bouncing him, like she always did. Skylar would squeal in surprised delight. Like he always did.

"Hey, Jules, you okay?" Matt asked, handing her a cone of pink cotton candy.

She took it absently, nodding with a forced smile. "I'm fine."

❧ ❧ ❧ ❧

Her hair still wet from her shower, Remmy tugged on a pair of cargo shorts and a tank top. She felt better after a long day at work, and was mostly successful at keeping Julie out of her mind since she had gotten home. She grabbed her brush from the small dresser next to her bed and began to brush out the long strands, wincing as she raked through a couple of tangles. The sun was just barely visible above the houses and treetops.

Her brush strokes slowed as she witnessed the beauty just outside her window. She almost wished she were back up on Overlook Hill to watch the sunset. With a contented sigh, she opened her window, allowing the evening breeze to air out her apartment and cool her shower-heated skin.

All afternoon she'd been contemplating the information she had gotten from Skylar, and trying to decide what to do. She could easily go to the fair. If she saw Julie there, it would be just an accidental encounter. Or she could stay away, just as she had been doing. Julie was such a part of her that their being apart made her feel empty inside. It took all of her willpower to not reach out to Julie with her senses. She wanted to meet her by their lake, walk through their field of flowers.

She'd had to shut her mind down to Julie, deny her emotions and her need.

The sun eased into the darkness of twilight and Remmy turned away, finishing her brushing. She tossed the brush on her bed, deciding what to do with her night. Who was she kidding? She knew exactly where she wanted to be, needed to be.

By the time Remmy got to the fairgrounds and paid for her ticket, night was fully upon them. The crowds were dense, and excitement was all around. Scents from concessions filled in the air, and distant calypso music pulsed with a Caribbean beat. She wove through the throngs of people, grateful to get to the concourse, which was a little less crowded.

All along the outside rim of the grounds were booths for food or games, cheap prizes touted by barkers trying to get someone to waste a dollar on a dart game to win a bear or stuffed monkey. Remmy had no interest in the games. Her hands shoved into her pockets, she wandered, taking in the brightly colored lights and loud music that came and went as she passed a food tent blaring country music.

Remmy passed a game where a tall thermometer-type structure assessed the strength of its participant with a sledgehammer and a padded target. She laughed outright at the insults the game controller yelled at the man who barely got the block halfway up to the bell at the top. She laughed even harder when a large burly woman took the sledge from the man and with one stroke sent the wooden block surging to the bell, which dinged loudly in the night. The man walked away, embarrassed.

Remmy's gaze searched everywhere, looking into every face. She finally allowed her mind to reach out, seeking. She turned to her left and moved in that direction.

❧❧❧❧

Julie was finishing the steak on a stick she was having for dinner, studiously avoiding any contemplation of what insects had likely landed on her food before she got to it. But, it was all part of the experience. She had allowed herself to be pulled onto at least a half dozen rides already, and was shocked that her stomach was still able to handle the greasy food. Surprisingly, she was having a good time. She couldn't help but surreptitiously look at everyone they passed, peeking into the shadows, wondering if maybe...

❧❧❧❧

Remmy placed her hand on one of the beams supporting the Ferris Wheel and peered through to the other side of the concourse, all the rides lined up dead center. Her heart begin to race; her stomach roiled.

She walked underneath the flashing lights of one of the rides toward where the twinkle of color bounced off of golden hair. Still on the other side of the Ferris Wheel, Remmy kept pace, her view of Julie blocked every few feet by the thin bars that braced the huge wheel. Julie was walking with Matt, Skylar between them, one of their hands in each of his, swinging to and fro. She watched as Julie's dress flared out slightly behind her, the breeze picking it up. The material molded itself to the front of her body.

❧❧❧❧

Julie looked around, her heart pounding. She

knew she was being watched, but it didn't frighten her — she would never be frightened by blue eyes on her. She tried to peel away the layers of the sea of people around her, to find the one face she so wanted to see, but it eluded her.

જાજાજા

Remmy could tell that Julie was looking for something, or was it someone? Could she feel that she was being watched? Could she hear the thudding of Remmy's heart? Could she feel how sorry Remmy was?

Moving beyond the Ferris Wheel, Remmy was very suddenly left with nothing to hide behind. She stood there feeling vulnerable as Julie, Skylar, and Matt came to the bend in the concourse where they would be walking directly toward her. She held her breath, eyes locked on Julie, noting the simple braid. She wondered if she should run, hide out in the open. She would quickly be swallowed up by the throngs around her. In only a moment, she could disappear.

જાજાજા

Julie's breathing was rapid and shallow. She knew Remmy was near; she could feel her. She let go of Skylar's hand to spin in a small circle, looking. She rose up onto her tiptoes, trying to see over the heads of those around her. All she could see was more people.

"Julie?" Matt asked, glancing behind them to try and see what Julie was looking for.

She ignored him.

જાજાજા

Remmy stopped, struck as her breath caught and chills ran down her spine.

Dirt. A growing mound. The dark sky above, a hand waving aimlessly. The face looking down, baseball cap on backwards. Something in his hands. Dirt. Cold, heavy. Dirt. Digging. The sound of digging. Dirt. It was cold. It was heavy.

Baby crying.

Remmy gasped, her hand trembling as she dug the rattle out of her pocket, holding it so tightly she could hear the plastic creak under the pressure. She couldn't breathe, shivering.

"No," she whispered. "No, no!"

❧❧❧❧

Julie hurried to the curve of the concourse, stopping so abruptly that a teenager behind her ran into her, then cursed as he hurried around her. Her eyes were fixated on Remmy. Remmy was standing there, looking at her, but not. She was looking through her.

"Remmy?" she said, taking a step toward her. She was torn between happiness at seeing her, and concern at the look of terror that was whitewashing her features.

Julie was nearly knocked down as a large group of laughing fairgoers rounded the corner and swarmed around her. She fought her way out of their group, roughly pushing one boy aside. When she reached the Ferris Wheel, Remmy was gone.

❧❧❧❧

Remmy nearly got herself hit by a car as she ran across the street and into the darkness. Her lungs were burning, but she didn't care. The rattle in her hand felt hot to the touch; it scorched her skin. Still she held on, fingers nearly crushing it.

Inside her head was a symphony of children's laughter and nearly unintelligible words, and always the underlying crying. It was about to drive her crazy. She could hear nothing of the night sounds around her. The birds disappeared, as did the traffic on the busier streets and the laughter and catcalls of the group of teenagers she passed on the sidewalk as she ran toward the outlying woods of Woodland.

She kept getting more images of the dirt, feeling its cold, grainy texture against her face. She tried to brush the feel and image away. She ran on, grateful when the moon appeared from behind the heavy clouds that had been threatening rain, showing the way.

The town proper ended where the woods began. She had never been in this area, but she couldn't allow her fear to make her falter. The crying was a constant now, no more laughter, no more garbled speech.

Remmy slowed, her breathing labored, hair stuck to her sweaty forehead. She stopped, hands resting on her thighs as she sucked in large gulps of air. She looked around her, trying to figure out where she was. Something caught her eye, something in the brush, glinting in the moonlight. A beacon.

Pushing her way deep into the foliage, Remmy ignored the cuts and scrapes on her hands and bare legs as she pushed through to the object. Stepping on the thorny bush at its stem to keep it out of her way, she bent down. Fingers, pushing away some dirt, came into contact with something cold and hard. Taking it between her fingers, she stood and held it up to the moonlight.

The red stone glinted almost magically, awing the eye. She could feel the smooth surface of the underside of the thick band, either side of the large stone rough from inscriptions she couldn't read. She wished she had a flashlight. She set the ring down in a clearing just beyond the foliage in which it had been lying. She swallowed down her rising emotions.

Using the bright moonlight from above, Remmy surveyed the area, kicking at things with the toe of her shoe. When she felt her foot sink down, she crouched to look at the area. Dirt. Darker than the rest around it, and devoid of any of the leaves or debris that littered the forest floor around her.

Remmy searched for something to dig with. She noticed for the first time that she was alone. The crying had stopped. Setting the rattle down next to the ring, Remmy grabbed a small branch that lay on the ground. Taking a deep breath, she gripped the wood with both hands and began to dig, light passes, each one going a little deeper. A tear slid down her cheek as the end of the branch came into contact with something. Something that was very soft.

Chapter Forty-eight

Remmy sat on the bumper of the Coroner's van, unable to watch as the tiny body was taken from the ground. She felt sick. Her tears pushed at the backs of her eyes like tiny pinpricks, but she couldn't seem to allow them to fall. She turned as someone squeezed her shoulder.

"How are you?" Grace asked.

Remmy's eyes were red-rimmed; she struggled to control her emotions. "How was I so wrong?" she asked, voice nearly a whisper. "He was supposed to be alive." She stared out into the night, the night which had been turned into day by the cruiser lights and flashlight beams that painted the area.

"Grace?" one of the officers called. "It's starting to rain. We're not going to get anything else tonight."

Grace nodded her understanding. "Okay, Tom. Get everything wrapped up." Grace turned back to Remmy. "The ME's gonna have to get in here, Remmy," she said, knocking on the side of the van. "Why don't you let me take you home?"

Remmy shook her head. "I'd rather walk." She pushed to her feet and strong arms wrapped around her. Remmy tolerated a brief hug before pulling away. She held out her hand, the small rattle lying in the center of her palm.

Grace took the baby's toy with a heavy sigh. "I'll need to talk to you tomorrow, okay?"

Remmy nodded, then turned and walked away.

Grace watched her go, with half a mind to send a patrol car to follow her at a discreet distance. She was worried about her.

Hands buried in the pockets of her shorts, Remmy trudged to the street. She was cold and wet, the rain falling harder. It was refreshing on her overheated face. She felt as if she'd been at the crime site forever. It actually had been quite a long time. More than three hours earlier, after she had uncovered the baby wrapped in a plastic garbage bag, she had pulled out her cell phone and called Grace. The first officers arrived in less than ten minutes, and Remmy had been there answering questions ever since. She hadn't been able to leave the infant, like a dog waiting by his dead master, ever faithful.

Remmy felt as if she had let down Tyler Bailey, Clive Bailey, Yvonne Bailey, and Grace. She had let herself down, too.

As the rain beat down, Remmy began to shiver. She glanced up as the sky opened up, cracked open by brilliant lightning and booms of thunder. It was a frightening experience. At any moment, the power of Zeus could hurtle down and end her life with one touch. Maybe that would be for the best. She felt lost and alone. Her heart was empty and cold, her emotions raw. She wanted to cry, wanted to get it out, but the tears still refused to come.

⁂

Julie felt restless. Something was bothering her, deeply, but she had no idea what it was. She had convinced herself to stay in bed because she was tired. Her eyes burned, begging her to sleep. Part of that had come from all the cigarette smoke in the food tent at the fair. She was allergic, and it always gave her a headache and made her eyes turn red. The lightning and thunder didn't help matters. Bonnie jumped with every clap of thunder, which was keeping Julie awake.

With a heavy sigh, Julie turned on her side to look out the window and watch the raindrops pelt the windows. She wished it weren't raining; the cool breeze of the night would undoubtedly help her get to sleep.

Clyde's head popped up, his little ears perking as he stared at Julie's bedroom doorway. Bonnie followed suit. Instantly they were tearing off into the darkness, barking.

Julie felt uneasy; she hated it when her dogs behaved like they were hearing something she couldn't hear. It was usually nothing, but it always scared the shit out of her. Deciding that any distraction from her insomnia was a good thing, she slid her legs over the side of the bed. Pulling on a pair of shorts to go with the tank top in which she slept, she was puzzled by the intensity of her dogs' barking. The doorbell sounded, and she reflexively glanced at her bedside clock. It was after midnight.

She padded through the house to the front door, wary as she called, "Who is it?" and flicked on the porch light.

"Remmy!" the voice called from the other side.

Instantly worried, Julie quickly unlocked the door and pulled it open. Remmy stood on the stoop, beyond drenched, in the same clothing she'd been wearing at the fair. "Oh god, Remmy," Julie whispered, quickly pushing the screen door open and pulling Remmy inside. "You're soaked!"

Remmy stood dripping on the tile in the entryway, her head hanging and shoulders sagging. She was icy cold, but that didn't even register. She raised her eyes to meet Julie's, and the floodgates opened. "He was dead all along," she murmured.

"Oh, Remmy." Julie pulled Remmy to her, holding her as she cried, whispering words of love and compassion. Remmy clung to her, her grasp almost painfully tight.

Even as her heart broke, Remmy's soul mended. Julie's warmth was enfolding her, and the words were assuring her that everything would be okay. She grieved for the Baileys, and for the last two weeks without Julie.

She raised her head from Julie's shoulder and wiped at her eyes and face. "I'm really sorry, Julie," she said, voice hoarse with emotion and tears.

"Oh, honey, don't you dare apologize—"

"No," she said, shaking her head. "I'm sorry. For what happened."

Julie looked up into the haunted eyes, and suddenly she wanted nothing more than to go to bed and hold Remmy against her. She wanted to run her fingers through the soft hair and tell her that everything was fine, and it would all be okay.

"Remmy," she said softly, "come with me." She locked the front door and turned off the lights, took Remmy's hand and led her up the stairs.

Remmy followed without a word, a bit worried that Julie hadn't responded to her apology. They ended up in Julie's bedroom, where Julie stopped in the center of the room. She turned Remmy around to face her, grabbed the hem of Remmy's shirt, which was glued to her body, and tugged it off. She tossed the shirt to the floor then crouched, quickly untying Remmy's shoes. Remmy placed a hand on Julie's shoulder as she stepped out of one, then held the foot up as Julie removed a sock. The other shoe and sock followed.

Julie rose to her feet, meeting Remmy's eyes briefly before she turned her attention to the shorts, unbuttoning and unzipping them, allowing them to fall to the floor. She noted with amusement that Remmy did indeed have a tattoo on the inside of her thigh, though she couldn't see much of it the way she was standing. Remmy stepped out of the shorts, leaving her in only her bra and underwear. Julie firmly directed her eyes away from the sleek body to gather the wet clothing on the floor.

"Leave your bra and underwear on the toilet lid in the bathroom before you step into the shower, Remmy. I'll throw them in the washer with everything else." Remmy's soaking wet clothing in her arms, Julie left the room.

Remmy's heart pounded in her ears. She felt exposed and vulnerable, and it wasn't just because she was standing in Julie's bedroom nearly naked. She still didn't know how things stood between her and Julie. From the floor below, she heard a washing machine rumble to life, so she scampered off to the en suite bathroom, stripping out of the rest of her clothing as Julie had directed.

A long groan escaped her throat as she stepped under the hot spray. Eyes closed, she raised her face to the water. Her nipples had hardened to the point of pain from the cold rain, Julie's presence, and the hot water. She hoped that Julie hadn't noticed her body's reaction as the wet clothing was removed.

Why did she do that? she wondered, wiping the water from her eyes. She decided that it was likely because Julie was trying to get her out of her soaked clothing quickly. Remmy knew that she was probably shivering too hard to get her clothes off for herself. Still, she wished Julie had just let her shiver. Now she would endlessly feel the sensation of Julie's hands on her body. As innocent as the contact had been, it would torment her forever.

༄ ༄ ༄ ༄

Having tossed the last two articles of Remmy's clothing inside the washer, Julie closed the lid. She closed her eyes and rested her hands on the top of the machine, sharply exhaling breath that she'd been holding practically since she'd removed Remmy's shirt. Remmy's appearance on her doorstep had roused a spate of conflicting emotions that she wasn't sure what to do with. First and foremost, she'd wanted to help Remmy, to be there for her. She was beginning to get some sense of the strain that Remmy's gift put on her mind and spirit.

Leading Remmy up to her bedroom and getting her out of her soaked clothing was a very natural course of action. Julie had not even stopped to think about what she was doing, until now.

That day at the school, when Remmy had coaxed her out of the car, Julie had felt free, as if she could do anything. She felt strong and capable, primarily because Remmy was at her side telling her it was okay, not in so many words but with a look, a smile, a touch of her hand. And then Remmy kissed her.

Julie rested her back against the vibrating washer, crossing her arms over her chest. She'd been drawn to Remmy since the very first time Remmy had brought them to their field. She could feel Remmy's strength, and the calm in her eyes set Julie at ease no matter what else might be happening. She felt compelled to be with Remmy, laugh with her, talk with her, or enjoy the comfortable silence that they so often shared. Much like herself, Remmy was quiet and didn't need exciting scenes to stimulate her senses. Julie also had to admit that she loved to cuddle with Remmy. The night they had fallen asleep on the couch while watching TV, Julie remembered nestling into Remmy's embrace, resting her head on Remmy's shoulder. It had been the best night's sleep she'd had since her captivity.

And then, the kiss.

Julie had been avoiding thinking about that kiss for two weeks, her stubborn nature refusing to analyze it, or even talk with Remmy about it. Julie needed an explanation. Not necessarily because the kiss was an awful sin, or anything as crazy as that, but she needed to know where it came from, needed to understand Remmy's thinking. Was it just something that happened in the joy of the moment? Maybe Remmy was feeling the need to get closer? Or was it something deeper?

Julie had never once given a thought to dating a woman. During her teaching career, she'd had colleagues who were lesbians. She had no problem with it at all, but it had never been something she had considered in relation to her own life. Although she had never found that her relationships with the men in her life were mind-blowing experiences—she was still single—it never occurred to her to try another option. As she mulled it over even now, she couldn't say that such a thing was a possibility.

Then she pictured those blue eyes. She thought about just how easy it was to allow herself to be enfolded in Remmy's arms, held safe and warm. How easy it was to talk to her, to hold her, just to be with her.

And then she kissed her.

Julie sighed, pushed away from the washing machine, and turned out the light as she went upstairs. The shower had long since stopped.

The overhead light was still on in the bedroom when Julie entered the room. Remmy, hair still damp and falling down her back, huddled in the armchair in the corner of the room, dressed in the clothes Julie had set out for her—Matt's sweats and t-shirt. She seemed to still be chilled. Julie crouched down in front of her, reaching up to brush away a few wet strands of dark hair.

"Are you okay?" Julie's voice was as gentle as her touch.

Remmy nodded, but didn't look up. She wasn't okay, and Julie knew it. With a tug of Julie's hand, Remmy was pulled to her feet and led over to the bed. Julie pulled down the covers and gestured for Remmy to climb in, which she did.

Julie made sure Remmy was settled, then turned off the light and climbed in with her. "Come here," she whispered, pulling Remmy over to her. Within moments, both of Julie's arms were wrapped tightly around the strong shoulders, and Remmy's head rested on Julie's chest. "Tell me what happened," she said, tracing lazy patterns on Remmy's back, feeling her body relax against her.

Remmy tried to order her thoughts. Her heart was still racing slightly, and she knew she needed to get her mind off of Julie's touch; she had already gotten herself into trouble by following her desire. Finally, she cleared her throat.

"The case I was working on for Grace. The baby was missing, and I swore he was alive. I kept hearing his crying in my mind. I just knew he had to be alive." She sighed heavily. "I misjudged my own signals. It was all in the past. He was dead and buried over in the north woods the entire time."

Julie petted Remmy's hair. She could feel Remmy's pain and profound disappointment in herself. "Oh, sweetie," she whispered. "You realized something tonight, didn't you? At the fairgrounds?"

Remmy nodded, glad Julie couldn't see her. At least Julie didn't know that she had been stalked. "It hit me like a ton of bricks." She sighed again, adjusting her head to a more comfortable position, her cheek resting against Julie's breast. She tried to ignore the softness, and Julie's wonderful scent. The slight pucker of Julie's nipple. She cleared her mind, returning to their conversation. "I feel like I really let them down — Tyler, his father, and Grace."

Julie cupped Remmy's face between her hands, tilting her head up until the blue eyes met her own. "Don't you dare say that." Anger hardened her voice. "Don't you dare say that," she repeated emphatically. "You have a gift, Remmy, and don't you ever forget that." She stared deeply into Remmy's eyes, seemingly looking into her very soul. "I know I never will."

Remmy closed her eyes at the soft kiss she received, so quick she didn't have time to respond to it before her head was again resting on Julie's breast, but long enough for her to be surprised.

Julie squeezed her eyes shut, mentally kicking herself for the kiss. How hypocritical was that? She hadn't spoken to Remmy for two weeks because she had kissed her, and yet here Julie had returned the favor. They needed to talk.

"These have been a very difficult two weeks, Rem," she said, voice soft.

Remmy nodded, clueless as to what to say. She had already apologized, but she didn't know whether that was what Julie wanted. In fact, she was confused as hell about what Julie wanted.

Julie picked her next words carefully. "I wasn't sure what to do after you kissed me that night. It frightened me on a couple of different levels, I guess. Can I ask you something?"

Remmy lifted her head and rested it in her palm. "Of course."

"When you kissed me, well..." Julie's brow scrunched as she considered exactly what it was she was trying to ask. "Why did you do it?"

Crap. Remmy knew the question was coming but hadn't decided how much she should admit. She owed Julie the truth, but she wasn't entirely sure of the truth herself. "We were having such a good time that day. The ice cream, playing in the backyard..." She smiled at the memory of that practically perfect day. "I don't know. The music, the dancing, the way the moonlight shone in your eyes." She studied those same eyes, which were gazing at her. "I felt close to you. It just happened."

Julie realized that the answer just raised more questions. "Have you done that before?"

"What?"

Julie frowned. "Felt close to other women?"

Blushing, Remmy looked away. Julie's laughter brought her head back around, a feigned glare on her face. "Yes," she finally said.

Julie's laughter stopped. Wondering was a very different thing from actually knowing. "Often?"

"Julie, I'm not going to discuss that with you." Remmy rolled onto her side, immediately feeling Julie's warmth along her back as a hand gently plucked at her arm.

"Why so shy?" Julie rested her chin on Remmy's shoulder, bewildered by her own persistence. *Why am I pressing the issue? I got her answer; let it go and go to sleep.*

"Because! I don't feel comfortable talking about my sex life."

"With me?" Julie teased.

Remmy was annoyed by the amusement she heard in Julie's voice. "With anyone."

"Have you had girlfriends in the past? Somehow I don't think you have one now." Julie had to move away as Remmy shifted onto her back.

"I've never actually had a girlfriend, only casual encounters."

"Why not? Why no girlfriends? You don't date guys, do you?" Julie rested her head against her fist, very interested in what Remmy would say.

Remmy sighed. It was obvious Julie wasn't going to let it go. "No, I don't date men, and I haven't had a girlfriend because I never stayed in one place long enough." She met Julie's gaze before quickly looking away. "I guess I just had no interest in giving that much of myself to anyone."

Julie studied Remmy, wondering whether their shared kiss — albeit an extremely brief kiss — had just been another of those moments for Remmy. Had it meant anything more than simply wanting to be close?

"Well," she said softly, brushing Remmy's cheek with the backs of her fingers, "let's get some sleep."

Chapter Forty-nine

Julie was awakened by loud breathing and the bed vibrating beneath her. She was lying on her side, her back to Remmy. Glancing over her shoulder, she saw Remmy was curled up in a fetal position, shivering violently. Julie rolled Remmy over and found that she was flushed and sweating.

"Oh, sweetie," she murmured. She wasn't entirely surprised, considering how cold and drenched Remmy had been when she had arrived in the night. She had no idea how long Remmy had spent out in the cold rain before ending up on her doorstep. Judging by how soaked her clothes were, Julie knew it had been quite some time.

Pushing the blankets aside, Julie got out of bed and quickly unfolded the blanket that was at the end of the bed. She spread it over Remmy and placed her cool palm on the sweaty forehead. "You're burning up, Remmy," she whispered, eyebrows drawn in concern. She hurried downstairs, let the dogs out to pee, then started a pot of hot tea. The day was gorgeous, the grass and flowers insanely green after the rains they had been getting.

Hot water whistled in the teakettle on the stove. Julie quickly poured some water into a large mug containing a teabag and then saturated the concoction with honey; she knew how sweet Remmy liked everything. She took some flu medicine from the medicine cabinet in the downstairs bathroom, then went back up to her bedroom.

❧ ❧ ❧ ❧

Remmy was just beginning to come around; her head pounded and her body shook with aches and chills. She groaned, covering her face with her hands. She felt like shit and she had a long shift at the store today.

"Hey," Julie said, entering the room with her remedies.

Remmy peeked at her from between her spread fingers. "I need to get going," she croaked, throat burning. "I got work."

"Not today, you don't." Julie set the tea on the side table, along with the bottle of medicine. "You're going to sleep today, Rem. You managed to catch the flu last night."

"Shit." Remmy groaned again. "I hate being sick. I need to call Joan—"

"Already done." Julie helped Remmy to sit up, piled both pillows behind her then gently nudged her back against them. "Here. Drink this, and I want you to take some medicine." Remmy dutifully took the small plastic cup filled with purple liquid that tasted like motor oil. Julie chuckled at the face Remmy made as she drank it down.

"Drink." She handed over the steaming tea. "Careful, it's hot."

Remmy closed her eyes as the honey-scented steam wafted up and warmed her face. She sipped carefully, sighing at the sweetness on her tongue that replaced the medicinal taste of the Nyquil.

Julie perched on the edge of the bed. "How long were you out in the storm last night?"

"A while." Remmy relaxed against the pillows,

cupping the mug between her palms. "I walked around for a long time after I left the site. I was trying to decide what to do."

"What do you mean?"

Remmy glanced briefly at Julie before finding an interest in the wall opposite the bed. "I really needed you, but I wasn't sure I'd be welcome here."

Julie's heart ached. She gently extracted the teacup and set it on the bedside table, ignoring confused eyes as she gathered Remmy into her arms and cradled the dark head against her breast. "Don't ever feel that way," she chided. "Remmy, you're always welcome in my home. I don't care what has happened between us that might possibly make you feel otherwise."

She closed her eyes and let herself wallow in the wonderful feeling of being so close to Remmy. Whenever they touched one another, she felt so much that was wrong, suddenly become right. "I'm glad you needed me." She stroked Remmy's hair, enjoying the feel of the silky strands between her fingers. "I need you, too," she whispered.

❧ ❧ ❧ ❧

When the doorbell chimed, Julie looked up from the newspaper she had spread out over the surface of the kitchen table. Setting her coffee cup aside, she pushed back from the table and went to the door. A glance out the window told her it was Joan on the porch.

"Hi." She stepped back from the open door and allowed Joan, and the heavy crockpot she was carrying, to enter. Joan was directed toward the kitchen, where she set her pot on the counter and plugged it into an electrical outlet.

"I brought some homemade chicken noodle soup,"

Joan said, somewhat out of breath. "How is she?"

"Sleeping." Julie lifted the lid on the pot and peeked inside. Fragrant steam wafted up. "That smells wonderful. Remmy has frequently mentioned that you're quite the cook."

Joan was pleased. "It's been nice to have someone around who actually appreciates it. My husband Doug…" She waved the thought away, "You know how men are."

Julie chuckled. "Yes, I do."

They stood in silence for a moment as Joan gathered her courage to broach a potentially volatile topic. Julie eventually broke the silence by offering Joan something to drink, which she gratefully accepted. Taking the iced tea with a smile, Joan stared into the clear depths and cleared her throat.

"Julie, Remmy has become very dear to me. I mean, hell, if I had kids, I'd want a daughter just like her." She met steady, calm green eyes. "I feel very protective of her."

Julie leaned against the counter. Arms crossed over her chest were the only indication that Joan's words had created some tension. With no idea what Joan was leading up to, she held her tongue and listened.

Joan sipped from her tea, buying some time to think. She was usually an outspoken woman, but she felt somewhat tongue-tied around Julie. She knew it was because of how much Julie meant to Remmy, and she truly didn't want to piss off either of them.

"Over the past couple of weeks, Rem has been really upset, and I found out yesterday it was because of some argument or something between the two of you." Setting the tea on the counter behind her, she held Julie's gaze, able to see the churning inside. "I think you're a great gal. I don't know you as well as Remmy does, obviously, but from what I know, you're good people.

I just..." She sighed, floundering with how to express what she wanted to say.

"Joan," Julie said, "Remmy and I did have a misunderstanding a couple of weeks ago, and I needed to figure some things out. I care deeply for Remmy, and I would never do anything to intentionally hurt her. She knows that, and now you do, too." She felt her throat constrict as her emotions rose. She suddenly felt the loneliness of the past two weeks flow over her, and the sting of the fear that she had lost Remmy for good. "We had a long talk last night and worked things out. Honestly, you don't need to worry."

"I meant no offense by intruding, Julie. It's just that, well, I've never seen her like that before. Hell, I think if it weren't for that damn pride of hers, she would've broken down right there in the store."

Julie blinked rapidly to hold back her tears. She would die before wanting Remmy to cry over something she had done. She studied her shoes for a moment, getting her emotions under control. "Did Remmy tell you what happened?"

Joan watched her intently, the wheels in her brain turning. "No. She wouldn't say."

"Listen, Joan, I'm glad Remmy has someone like you who cares about her," she nodded at the crock pot on her counter, "and I think you're good people, too. But, what happened is between Remmy and me. As I said, we've talked some things out. I never meant to hurt her, as in all relationships, it happens."

Joan recognized the polite "mind your own business" in Julie's words, but she also caught what was between the lines. *Relationship?* Her eyes opened wide. So much more made sense now. Clearing her throat, Joan pushed off the counter and took a sip from her tea. "Do you mind if I go up and say hi?"

"Not at all. She's in my room, upstairs at the end of the hall." Julie turned back to her newspaper.

Joan headed toward the stairs, mind racing. She'd had no idea. Whatever floats your boat, but she'd had absolutely no idea. She found Julie's bedroom easily enough, and sure as the day, Remmy was lying on her side, some of the covers apparently kicked aside in her fretful sleep.

Sitting on the edge of the mattress, Joan reached out a hand and checked Remmy's forehead. It was warm, but not hot. She brushed dark locks away from the pale face, withdrawing her hand when blue eyes blinked open.

"Hey," Remmy croaked. "What are you doing here?"

"I brought you some soup," Joan said. "Came to see how you were doing."

"I'm alive. Feel like absolute shit, but I'm alive."

"Yeah? Well, you look like shit. Does that help?"

Remmy grimaced, turning onto her back and pushing herself into a sitting position against the headboard. Joan tucked the covers back around Remmy's waist. "Do I need to bring you some clothes?" she asked, noting the too-large t-shirt, one shoulder canting slightly off her shoulder.

"I don't know. Not sure how long I'll be staying here. I feel like I'm busting in on Julie's day. She shouldn't have to play nursemaid to me."

"No, but I imagine a game of doctor might be acceptable, huh?"

Remmy was thunderstruck by the unexpected words. Unreadable eyes met her gaze. "What?"

Joan opted for being direct, feeling far more comfortable doing so with Remmy than with Julie. "Are you two in a relationship, Remmy? Like, a relationship?"

Remmy was stunned, blinking several times while her brain caught up with Joan's question. Surely her fever wasn't making her hear things. "Why did you ask that?" The gears were turning in her mind. "Did Julie tell you we were?"

Joan shook her head. "No."

"Then why did you ask?" Remmy reached for the glass of water on the bedside table. Joan picked it up and handed it to her. Remmy drank deeply, the trembling of her hand making the glass chatter lightly against her teeth.

"Listen, Remmy, I just wanted to make sure you're okay. I know how upset you were yesterday, and you've been out of it for a couple weeks, working ridiculous hours—"

"I kissed her, Joan."

Remmy's blurted admission took a moment to penetrate Joan's brain, but when it did, she stopped speaking and just stared. "You what?"

Flushed with embarrassment, Remmy couldn't believe she'd actually said it; it had just kind of fallen out of her mouth. She looked up at Joan. "It just sort of happened. I guess I scared the hell out of her." Remmy ran a hand through her hair, which felt sticky from her feverish sweating. She grimaced at the texture and returned her hand to her lap.

"She said you guys talked it out," Joan said. "What now?"

Remmy shrugged. "I don't know. Guess I won't do that again." She averted her eyes as she confessed, "I love her, Joan. She's the most important thing in my life." When she finally looked into Joan's eyes, she saw only concern and caring. "She's my best friend. Guess I'll just continue hanging around, being her handyman." Her smile was rueful.

⚜ ⚜ ⚜ ⚜

Julie quickly brought a hand up to stop the bowl from rattling on the tray. As close as she was to the bedroom door, she knew Remmy couldn't help but hear it, even in her current condition. Julie flushed with emotion at Remmy's quiet words, engulfed by a wave of guilt at the despair in Remmy's voice.

Chapter Fifty

Julie sat in the armchair in the corner of her bedroom with only the moonlight coming in through the windows for light. Curled up, hands dangling off the arms of the chair, she studied Remmy's sleeping form. Her charge had slept off and on all day, with Julie loading her up with medicines to help her sleep off the effects of her nasty case of the flu. Remmy had eaten some of the wonderful soup Joan had brought, then had gone right back to sleep.

Julie's thoughts returned to the conversation she had accidentally overheard earlier that day. She wasn't sure what to think about Remmy telling Joan about the kiss. Part of her wanted to be angry with Remmy. That truly wasn't anyone else's business. But then, she wasn't ashamed of what had happened, and she knew Remmy had a right to confide in whomever she wished.

"She loves me," Julie whispered, astonished by Remmy's admission. She loved Remmy, too. After all, Remmy had saved her life. She'd been a good friend. The bitter "handyman" comment had stung. Was that all Remmy thought she meant to her—cheap labor?

Julie glanced off toward the window, the night beyond so beautiful, aglow with the full moon. She was confused. She felt as though she'd been numb for the past few months since Remmy had come into her life, existing but not living. She had enjoyed their time together, had so much fun with Remmy, but hadn't allowed herself to analyze her feelings. Perhaps that was a side effect of her captivity, perhaps it was just plain cowardice. Either way, that kiss two weeks ago had broken the dam and brought on a firestorm of thoughts and feelings, all of which were hitting her at once.

Julie's hungry gaze devoured Remmy's form and face. Words couldn't adequately express how much she had missed Remmy in those two weeks, or just how empty she had felt. It was as if a piece of herself was missing when Remmy was absent from her life. She wanted to fight the feelings, wanted to fight her need for Remmy. She realized that it would be a losing battle.

Uncurling herself, Julie padded over to the bed and pulled the sheet back just enough to slip underneath. She lay on her back, not touching Remmy but looking at her, an up close and personal study. Remmy was pale, and she looked exhausted, dark circles under her eyes. She also looked thin.

"You definitely need some TLC," Julie murmured. She turned onto her side with her back to Remmy, only waiting a moment before she shifted her body backward. Remmy grabbed onto her, wrapping herself around Julie, a protective arm laid across her waist.

With a deep, contented sigh, Julie closed her eyes.

Chapter Fifty-one

As she left the school building, Julie had to stop herself from running across the parking lot. She knew it was a childish inclination, but quite strong all the same. She managed to maintain a steady, even pace while returning to her car about halfway down the last row. Classes would be finished in a couple of weeks then summer break would begin, but for now the lot was full of cars when she'd arrived to meet with Bob in person, rather than on the phone.

Though she wouldn't be teaching her favorite grade, she was glad to have a job again. She would make the most of working with the seventh graders. She visited her classroom and reviewed the roster of her prospective students.

As she unlocked her car door, Julie surreptitiously glanced around to make sure she was alone. Pulling her car door open, she tossed her purse inside then slid behind the wheel, quickly closing and locking her door. She blew out a long breath as she dropped her head back against the seat. She'd done it. Baby steps. Someday she might even be able to go back to living without fear. Someday.

Julie gathered the mail from the box on her way into the house, flipping through the various pieces as she tossed her keys onto the coffee table along with her purse. "Remmy?" she called out, separating the junk from bills. *The only good thing about email and spam is that snail mail junk is less prolific,* she mused absently, tossing the circulars and solicitations into the trash. "Remmy?" There was still no answer, and for a minute she was afraid that her guest had left.

Glancing out the French doors, Julie spotted Remmy outside in the backyard, dressed in the laundered tank top and shorts she'd been wearing the night she showed up on Julie's doorstep. She was aggressively picking weeds, which had sprung up at an alarming rate after the rains. She was on her hands and knees, tossing the offending vegetation behind her onto a large pile in the rocks. Bonnie and Clyde pranced around the back lawn, playing.

As Julie watched, the craziest sensation washed over her. It felt so natural, so right: coming home, expecting to see Remmy there, finding her tending to their yard.

"Whoa." Julie stepped back as though she'd been punched. She felt lightheaded, overwhelmed. It was at that moment Remmy glanced up, her eyes meeting Julie's stunned gaze.

Remmy stood, brushed off her knees, and walked to the house. "Hi," she said, pulling open one of the French doors.

"Hi," Julie echoed, taking a deep breath. "What are you doing out of bed? And why the hell are you playing lawn boy?"

Remmy wiped her hands on the legs of her shorts, glancing back at the yard behind her. She shrugged, turning back to Julie. "I got sick of being sick, and I knew the weeds would be pretty bad after the rain. Man, they were," she said, indicating the small piles all along the flower beds.

Feeling a strong desire for a hug, Julie stepped forward and wrapped her arms around Remmy's neck, holding her close.

After a startled moment, Remmy returned the hug, allowing herself to absorb and feel. "What's this for?" she said against Julie's hair.

"I missed you so much." Julie buried her face against Remmy's neck. She could smell her sweat, the earthy smell that was her skin and the late May breeze.

Remmy's world shifted on its axis. "I missed you, too," she whispered, her hand gently cupping the back of Julie's head and pressing it against her.

Julie tightened her grasp. "I don't think I could stand it if you stayed away from me again."

Remmy shook her head. "Never again."

After a long moment, Julie drew back and looked up into Remmy's face. She smiled at the smudges of dirt on her cheek and just under her nose. She gently wiped at it. "Why aren't you in bed? You need to rest, Remmy."

"I know, but I hate being cooped up."

Remmy's whining tone brought a smile to Julie's face. "Okay. You can stay up, but at least get out of the sun." She grabbed one of Remmy's hands. "Come on. I'll make you some lunch."

❧❧❧❧

After washing up, Remmy padded into the kitchen where she found Julie making her a Dagwood sandwich, with layers of meat, cheese, lettuce, and tomato.

"Julie, just a thought, but it's only one meal."

Julie grinned, continuing with her creation. "Yes, it is. And you need every bite of it." She carried the sandwich and a bag of chips over to the table. "Now sit and eat."

Remmy eyed the sandwich, trying to figure out the best angle of attack. A large glass of iced tea was placed in front of her as Julie sat down across from her with a much smaller sandwich. "Why is your sandwich for a normal-sized person, while mine is for Jabba the Hutt?"

Julie grinned, picking up one half of sandwich. "Because you need to put on some weight. You're too thin, Remmy."

Remmy rolled her eyes, but began to eat. She still didn't have a hearty appetite, but ate as much as she could without irritating her touchy stomach.

Julie sat in thoughtful silence as she chewed her lunch and followed it down with iced tea. Eventually, she glanced up at Remmy. "How much do you pay Joan in rent?"

Surprised by the question, Remmy set her sandwich down and wiped her fingers on a napkin. "Why?"

Julie shrugged. She had asked the question before she'd thought things through. "Just curious."

"Three hundred a month." *What's going on in that pretty head of yours?*

"Do you like it there?" Julie took another bite of her sandwich.

Remmy shrugged with a nod. "Sure. I guess so. I like Joan and Doug a lot, but I do have to admit that sometimes it really sucks to be living under my boss' roof." She grinned. "It makes it really hard to play hooky from work."

Julie chuckled. "I imagine it does."

Chapter Fifty-two

Matt followed Julie around the house, anger and confusion clear in his raised voice. "What the hell do you think you're doing, Jules?" he said, watching as she brought another load of personal things downstairs from the spare bedroom that she'd been steadily emptying since he'd arrived fifteen minutes earlier.

"I'm removing decorations," she said unnecessarily, the bundle of stacked pictures in her arms indicative of that.

"You know damn well what I mean. What are you thinking? Do you really even know this woman?" He grabbed her shoulder to get her to focus on him. "Julie, I know you're grateful to Remmy, hell, we all are, but Jesus! Why are you letting her move in here?"

Julie knew he was genuinely concerned for her but her mind was made up. "Matt, I'm not letting her do anything, I asked her." She was off again, mounting the stairs, Matt not far behind.

"But why? She's got a place over at her boss' house. She has her own apartment, Julie. Isn't it enough that she's here all the damn time?"

Julie stopped short, just outside of the bedroom that would be Remmy's. Matt almost ran her over. She turned and faced him, her own anger rising. "What is your problem with her being here, Matthew?"

Matt knew he had no right to say anything, but he felt something was off. "I like Remmy, she's a nice woman, but Julie, this is extreme, don't you think?" He gestured at the room. "Are you two going to be the 'happy roommates of Woodland'? Jesus, you guys will be the laughingstock of the damn town!"

Julie was stunned. "Tell me you're not saying that I should just turn my back on the best friend I've ever had because the people of this town might not understand how close Remmy and I are becoming. Please tell me you're not that shallow, Matt, and please tell me that's not the way you're teaching your son to think."

Matt rubbed the back of his heated neck as he tried to think of a different tack. "Listen, she's done a lot for you, Julie. No one will dispute that. I just think it's a lot to move her in with you," he said, voice cajoling.

"I feel so safe with her, Matty. It's like, when she's around, nothing can hurt me and I can do anything. She's helped me recover from so much of what happened. Hell, she got me to go to the school all by myself." She tapped her chest. "I haven't been able to do that since the day it happened last August. We're in June, now."

"All of that's great, it really is. But are you going to have to have her as a security blanket for the rest of your life? Give yourself a little bit of credit for your healing. You're a strong woman. Somehow I don't think you need to have Remmy around as your good luck charm."

Julie turned her back on him and went into the room to give it a final once over. She knew Matt was right; she needed to stop depending so much on Remmy for emotional support. Hands on her hips, she took in the stripped down room: nothing remaining but the bed, dresser, and two night stands. She imagined Remmy's things on the walls, on the furniture surfaces, and a slow smile spread across her lips. Shaking her head, she turned back to face Matt.

"It's not like that. Not totally like that, anyway.

I love having her in my life. I love having her close to me. And, you're right—she is here all the time. I like it that way. So does she."

Matt ran a hand through his hair. "What do I tell Skylar? You know he's going to ask."

Julie's receding anger was replaced by hurt. "What is that supposed to mean?"

"Damnit, I'm not trying to piss you off, Julie, but jeez! This is incredibly sudden. I don't understand where any of this is coming from."

"We're best friends, Matt! What is so fucking hard to understand about that?" Julie knew she was getting defensive, but Matt was throwing questions at her—spoken and unspoken—that she knew she didn't have the answers for, and didn't really want to sort out. It just...was.

Matt stared at her in shock. He had pushed too far. "Alright, you're a grown woman, responsible and all that. If this makes you happy, then I guess, good for you. But I still want to know what the hell I'm supposed to tell my son when he spends the night with you, or the weekend, or the week — now that school's almost out — and suddenly here's this other person living with Aunt Julie. He's nine goddamn years old, Julie. How is he supposed to understand this?"

Julie cocked her head to the side and studied her brother. He refused to meet her gaze, hands and body language speaking volumes. "You're not asking for Skylar. You're right—he is nine. You're asking this for you, but you don't have the balls to just spit it out. What's on your mind, bro?" she said, voice dripping with sarcasm.

Matt turned angry eyes on her. "Fine. Are you two fucking?"

Julie's breath caught and she stumbled back a step,

a nervous hand fluttering to her chest. "That's none of your business, Matt," she said, her voice quietly hurt. "But, no. We're not."

Matt felt his anger drain from his face, replaced by the knowledge that he was an asshole. "I'm sorry. I think I'd better go."

"Yes. I think that's a very good idea." Julie listened as he stomped down the stairs and then slammed the front door behind him. She heard his car start then drive away. She took a deep breath and looked around the room, taking in the bare walls and furniture, a blank canvas. She played with the thin gold chain at her throat. "What am I doing?"

Chapter Fifty-three

Remmy stood back, hands on her hips, head tilted to the side. She thought the picture was straight, but wasn't positive. "What do you think?"

Julie studied it. "I think it is." Chewing on her lip, she walked over to the picture and shifted it slightly to the left.

"Uh, no," Remmy said, taking the edges and tilting it further right.

"No, it needs to go left."

"No. Now's it's dipping." When Julie tried to slap Remmy's hands away, Remmy grabbed her wrists. "Woman! I'm gonna beat you!" Remmy teased.

Julie's eyes widened in shock. It wasn't long before she burst into laughter, Remmy doing the same. "I'd really like to see you try, Wonder Girl."

Remmy's eyebrow shot up. "Tempt me and I might."

Julie raised an eyebrow of her own, silently challenging Remmy to start something. The battle of wills lasted only a few moments before Julie broke into laughter again. "Come on. Let's go watch TV."

After Julie sauntered out of the room, Remmy glanced back at the picture. After one last look to make sure Julie was truly gone, she tilted the frame slightly to the left.

"No, I actually wanted to go into journalism in college," Julie said. She and Remmy were seated at opposite ends of the couch. Remmy's longer legs were curled up under her, Julie's stretched out, crossed at the ankles.

"So, how did you end up in teaching, then?" Remmy asked, letting one leg slide along the edge of the couch, next to Julie's. She wasn't entirely surprised when Julie took her foot in her lap and began to gently massage it.

Julie shrugged, her fingers absently working at Remmy's heel. "I don't know. During my junior year I worked at a newspaper, shadowing a journalist for a while." Her nose scrunched up in distaste at the memory. "Her name was Doris Regal. Real bitch. I remember going out on stories with her. I'd watch her with whomever she was interviewing, and god, she was just so damn aggressive. Downright rude, sometimes. I thought: if this is what being a journalist is like, no thank you. I changed my major from Communications to Social Sciences."

Remmy wrinkled her nose. "I hate science of any kind."

Julie playfully swatted her foot. "Goof. What about you? College?"

Remmy smirked. "Now, Julie, that would require me to stay in one place and commit to something." She was surprised to see Julie's eyes suddenly become shadowed. "Julie?" she said softly. "What's the matter?"

Julie spared a glance into curious blue eyes. "Do you intend to stay here, Remmy? To stay in Woodland?"

Their eyes met, and Remmy couldn't look away. *There's nowhere in the world I'd rather be.* "Yes." She swallowed, deciding to add, "I can't imagine being anywhere else."

Julie studied her for a moment then tugged on her foot. "Lie down." When Remmy complied, she crawled down toward Remmy until she was sandwiched between her and the back of the couch. She rested her head on Remmy's shoulder, an arm casually flopped over the taut stomach. Gentle fingers ran through her hair, lightly tugging it out of its ponytail.

The strands slipped through Remmy's fingers like silk. "You have the softest hair."

Julie smiled, relishing the feel of Remmy's warmth and calmed by the strong heartbeat beneath her. She toyed with the neckline of Remmy's tank top, fingers grazing the tanned skin of her upper chest. "You know, after what Sergio did to me, I never thought I'd want to be touched again," she whispered, unable to meet Remmy's eyes. "When I got back, I stayed with Matt and Skylar for a couple of months. I couldn't stand the thought of being alone." She went silent, gathering her thoughts.

"Anyway, Matt and I had always been affectionate with each other. Our entire family was. But afterwards… I would flinch whenever Matt came near me. He was really good about it, but still… It took all the courage I could muster to be as normal with Skylar as I could. He's so young. I knew there was no way he could possibly understand if suddenly Aunt Julie didn't want his hugs anymore."

Remmy listened, her fingers never stopping their stroking. She sighed when Julie cuddled even closer, wrapping an arm almost possessively around her middle.

"That first day you showed up on my doorstep, it was like I couldn't hug you enough. My dream savior had come to life," she said softly.

"I'm just a person, Julie," Remmy said, fingertips trailing softly along Julie's arm. "Nothing more, nothing less."

"Not to me." Julie raised her head and looked into Remmy's face. "You're my hero."

A burning heat radiated off of Remmy's body; she hoped Julie couldn't feel it. Her heart was pounding as she looked into the trusting eyes, so close to her own. She needed to defuse the seriousness. "That may be, but I refuse to wear tights. Maybe a cape, but definitely not tights."

Julie felt the tug of the invisible thread that drew her to Remmy time after time. Her gaze flitted over each feature of Remmy's face, landing on full lips, still curved in a smile. "Has anyone ever told you that you're beautiful?" she whispered, surprised that she'd spoken the words out loud.

Remmy shook her head. "No one whose opinion I cared about."

"Well, I hope you care what I think, and I think you're gorgeous." Julie grinned at the blush that swept up Remmy's neck and stained her cheeks. Graciously letting her off the hook, she changed the subject. "Tell me about some of your other jobs over the years."

Remmy chewed on her bottom lip. She was acutely aware of Julie's eyes on her, and of the feel of one of Julie's breasts pressed against her side. "Well, I worked as a maintenance worker off and on—public schools, office buildings, things like that. Um, oh! One of my more interesting jobs was as a bartender at a strip joint."

"Really?" Julie raised a honey-colored eyebrow at the mischievous grin on Remmy's face. "Did you ever—" She faltered. It was really none of her business. "Never mind."

"No. Finish. Did I ever, what?"

Green eyes reluctantly lifted to meet Remmy's. "Any of the women...the strippers..."

Remmy cared too much about Julie to lie to her. Head down, she nodded. "A couple."

Julie forced a smile. "I guess that must have been exciting, huh?" She was surprised that she felt...jealous.

"It had its moments, yes, but," she shrugged, "that was a long time ago."

This time the grin was genuine. "A long time ago? You're all of what, twenty-three, maybe twenty-four?"

"I'm twenty-five, thank you very much. And, yes, it was a lifetime ago."

Julie screamed when Remmy attacked her extremely ticklish sides. She struggled, slapping at the ruthless fingers, finally grabbing one of the hands and pinning it to Remmy's body. That left only the assault of one torturous hand. With a loud grunt, she managed to restrain both hands, bringing them up above Remmy's head, while holding both wrists. Her maneuvering resulted in her lying on top of Remmy, breast to breast, their faces mere inches apart, and both gasping for breath from their playful exertions.

Julie's gaze strayed to Remmy's lips. She felt herself leaning in, but Remmy's words stopped her short.

"Oh, kinky, Julie." There was teasing in Remmy's voice. "You into handcuffs, too?"

Julie froze. With a small whimper, she pushed up and off the couch in recoil, her arms wrapping around herself protectively.

Remmy leapt up off of the couch, wanting to cry at the terror in Julie's eyes. "Oh, god, Julie, I'm so sorry!" she said, keeping her distance. "It was a joke, I wasn't thinking. I'm so sorry."

Julie nodded. She knew it had been a jest, but it had tapped into a deep well of fear and memories that she thought she had closed the lid on. Apparently she hadn't. She tried to control her trembling as she ran a shaky hand through her hair.

Remmy stood stock still a few feet away, eyes focused intently on Julie. "Is there something I can do? What do you want me to do, Julie?" She kept her voice soft and soothing. "Do you want me to leave for a while? I can go upstairs and leave you be—"

"No," Julie said, shaking her head. "No. Please don't leave."

Remmy let out a long, slow breath. "Okay. Um…" She glanced back at the couch, then at Julie. "Why don't we just sit and watch some TV? Maybe a movie? Pop some popcorn? Or, I could just shut the hell up and let you do whatever you want to do."

Julie mustered a tenuous smile at Remmy's attempted humor. "Go ahead and watch some TV or whatever. I need to feed the dogs."

It was an hour and a half too early to feed Bonnie and Clyde, so the excuse was patently lame, but Julie disappeared into the kitchen, appreciating the comforting sounds of the TV in the living room. She leaned against the kitchen counter, taking deep breaths to calm her racing heart. She hated the cold prickle of fear that trickled down her spine. She hadn't felt it for months, not since Remmy had arrived. She was surprised that the off-the-cuff comment had hit her so hard.

Julie cradled one wrist in her other hand. She could still feel the hard, cold metal of the bracelets around her tender flesh, causing painful bruises that never got a chance to heal throughout her captivity. For months after returning home, her wrists ached and were tender to the touch. The doctors at the hospital said that the bone was deeply bruised. Even now, as she rubbed the skin, she could feel the sting, realizing that it likely was only in her head.

She glanced toward the living room, able to hear the murmur of the TV, knowing full well that Remmy was sitting there beating herself up, probably not hearing a word of the program or seeing one image. She wasn't angry, or hurt, or any other unwarranted emotion. She knew in her heart of hearts that Remmy would never do anything to hurt her in any way. Maybe that was why she was so quick to trust Remmy. In every way. She was able to touch her without thought, and be touched by her without thought.

Julie turned and stared out into the dark night beyond the windows, which had turned into mirrors. She could see her own silhouette, though no specific features. She could also see Remmy's silhouette as she approached. Julie ducked her head, feeling foolish as warm hands came to rest on her shoulders.

"I'm really sorry, Julie," Remmy said, her voice soft and tinged with emotion. "I would never scare you like that on purpose."

"I know. It was me, totally me." She exhaled sharply, still staring out the window. "I shouldn't let him get to me like that anymore. The bastard is dead. He can't hurt me. My brain knows that."

Remmy felt Julie's frustration, and it broke her heart. She took a chance and stepped closer. Her arms snaked around the slender waist and clasped together over Julie's stomach. She smiled in relief when Julie leaned back against her and placed trembling hands over those that held her in a strong, comforting embrace.

Julie rested her head against Remmy's shoulder, all her fears melting away. "Why do I feel so safe with you?" she whispered, closing her eyes at the feel of their fingers entwining.

Remmy dropped a light kiss on the golden crown and then rested her cheek against the soft tresses. "Maybe because I've been in your mind, reading your thoughts."

Julie chuckled. "No, I think it's more that you've been in my soul." She turned in the circle of Remmy's arms and looked up at her. "I feel you there, you know," she said softly.

Remmy looked into Julie's eyes, so open to her but deeply shadowed after her scare. She brushed her fingertips across a soft cheek, fighting the urge to kiss the inviting lips. She had made a vow that she would never do that again, not to herself or to Julie.

Julie's hands ran up over Remmy's arms, following the line of her shoulders until her hands rested there, one stroking the rich, dark hair at the nape of Remmy's neck. Unable to look away, she searched Remmy's eyes. Within their June sky depths, she saw emotion and caring, and struggle. She could tell that Remmy was exercising great restraint, and she knew why. She felt the pull, too. She respected Remmy for keeping her word, though a large part of her wished that she wouldn't.

She had never been so drawn to anyone in her life. What she felt like doing at that moment—kissing Remmy—wasn't a matter of a sexual desire. She needed to feel close to Remmy, needed to connect with her. Before she knew what she was doing, she took a handful of the dark hair in an insistent fist and pulled Remmy down to her.

Remmy resisted for a moment, but then allowed herself to be tugged down until her lips were mere inches from Julie's. She looked into the green eyes, wanting to make sure Julie knew what she was doing. Pleading eyes met hers, and Remmy gave in that final distance, her eyes sliding closed as she felt the softness press against her. She wrapped her arms around Julie's waist, pulling her closer until their bodies molded together.

Julie felt as if she was surrounded in a warm

cocoon where nothing could hurt her, nothing could touch her. It was as though she had never been kissed before that moment. Remmy's gentle caresses calmed her, and a soft hand came to rest against Julie's face, brushing the soft skin there.

❧❧❧❧

Sensing that her tongue would be an unwelcome intrusion, Remmy used only her lips. This wasn't about anything as base as a seduction. Remmy understood that this kiss was Julie reaching out to her, a connection that was deeper than a hug or empty words. It was primitive, but honest.

Julie drew away slowly, at peace yet completely overwhelmed. Her entire body felt energized, like someone had reached inside and lighted her from within. She brushed her fingers lightly over Remmy's lips before returning her head to the strong shoulder.

Remmy rubbed soothing circles on Julie's back. Eventually she stepped away, giving Julie some space. "How about that movie now?" she asked softly.

Her smile sheepish, Julie nodded. "Except, I really do need to feed my dogs now."

❧❧❧❧

Julie lay in bed, staring up at the ceiling. She wasn't sure how long she had lain awake; all noise from Remmy's room had long since ceased. The bedside clock read ten past one, yet sleep was still elusive.

Dressed only in her tank top and panties, she was still warm, the night air stagnant and hot. Julie kicked the covers off, earning a glare from a sleepy Clyde. "Sorry, buddy," she whispered. Her mind kept returning to the kiss they had shared. She could feel Remmy's hands on her, so gentle as they touched her as if she were a fragile, priceless vase of fine crystal. She had never been touched that way, never been made to feel so cherished. And the kiss. It had been quite basic, a simple touching of the lips, softness sampling softness. Wonderful.

Julie's fingers lightly touched her own lips, feeling the tingle of Remmy's kiss. That simple contact had erased every fear she'd had, every image of Sergio Venti and his damned handcuffs. How was that possible? How was it possible that with only one touch from Remmy—a caress, a hug, or a kiss—Julie was immune to all that could harm her, able to bask in the safe harbor that was Remmy Foster.

❧ ❧ ❧ ❧

Remmy's body was on fire, and she couldn't, for the life of her, find a comfortable position in which to sleep. Every window was open, the ceiling fan above, swirling and rocking. It didn't matter. The outside temperature wasn't the problem.

With a soft groan, she returned to her back, resting her palm on a flat stomach. "Fuck," she whispered with a heavy sigh. She would do anything for Julie, but that kiss had nearly killed her. Not necessarily the act itself, though that had been bad enough, but having to control her response, keep it at a level that was safe for Julie. Had she followed her own desires, she would have picked Julie up, set her on the countertop, and stood between her spread legs to show her what kissing a woman was all about.

Maybe moving in with Julie hadn't been such a good idea after all. She remembered the day Julie suggested it. Remmy had immediately said "yes" to the enticing prospect of spending so much more time with Julie, being able to watch over her and protect her... there had been no other choice. But now things were coming up that she hadn't counted on, things she was not sure she would be able to control.

Remmy often wondered if Julie could hear her heart pounding whenever they were together. Could she see through the carefully controlled expressions? Did it ever slip? No doubt. Julie seemed to be able to sense nearly as much about Remmy as Remmy sensed of Julie, just perhaps not in as visual a way. She had never experienced such a connection, and sometimes it scared her.

The thing that probably most scared Remmy was that never in her life had she known a home, a place where she truly wanted to be. With Julie—in her presence, in her house, in her life—she felt roots that had grown sturdy and solid in only a few short months; nothing would budge them. If Julie were to leave Woodland tomorrow, Remmy would follow. She felt complete with her, she felt a sense of self that she had never known before. That scared her too.

Remmy sighed and turned over onto her stomach, spreading her legs, finding cool spots on the mattress. She determinedly closed her eyes. She was exhausted, and she had to work in the morning.

Chapter Fifty-four

Remmy cursed under her breath, catching several cans of canned chili before the entire case scattered across the floor. Once she was certain that she had the carton stabilized, she hurried after the cans that had rolled away as far as the dairy cooler. Quickly collecting the runaway cans, she hurried back to her display.

"You are the oddest person I've ever known," Roman said, standing back, watching the slow creation of this week's display.

Surprised by the sudden voice, Remmy glanced up at him and smiled. "Hey, man, how are you?"

He grinned, eyes twinkling. "Doing okay. Just laughing my ass off here as you chase cans of chili."

"Laugh it up, asshole." This only made Roman laugh harder. Remmy grinned as she walked over and gave him a heartfelt hug. She knew Roman wasn't sure what to make of her and their adventures the previous fall. Though a good guy and a good friend, he'd pretty much kept his distance since she had returned to town. Remmy took no offense. Over the years she had learned how to let relationships roll off her back. "Need to pay for something?"

"Yeah. Got gas on pump three."

Roman followed her to the bullpen, the half-door squeaking as it swung shut behind Remmy. She typed in her employee code and rang up the gas.

"Anything else?"

"Nope. On my way to work. I get all the crap I want to eat or drink while I'm there."

"Yeah, no kidding. Save me a lemon muffin, will ya? I'll pick it up after work and take it home to Julie."

His wallet half open, Roman stopped and glanced up at her. "You guys shacking up?" he asked, voice level but filled with surprise.

Remmy silently cursed, taking the money he offered. "Not like that, Roman. I just got tired of living with my boss so Julie offered me a room." Because of the wonderful kiss from three days ago, she couldn't look him in the eye, instead pretending to be concentrating on getting his receipt.

"How long have you been there?" He accepted his change, tucking the bills into his wallet and pocketing the coins.

Remmy shrugged. "Couple of weeks."

Roman took his receipt. "Well, I'll see you around." With a final smile, he left the store and trotted over to his car.

"Did you know that people are idiots?" Joan called out, the back door to the store slamming behind her as she walked down the back hall. She tossed her purse and keys into her office, then proceeded into the store.

"Yes, I've been aware of that for a very long time," Remmy said, leaning against the counter, arms crossed over her chest. "What happened that finally brought you to this realization?"

"Smart ass." Joan leaned on the counter. "The damn drivers in this town, I swear to god. Idiots, every single one of them."

Remmy grinned, amused at Joan's short temper and lack of patience with just about everything. "That's typically what happens when you share the road with mere mortals, Joan, unlike your godly self."

Joan stared at her for a moment, then broke into laughter. "Smart ass," she said again, reaching out to take a playful swipe at Remmy. She studied Remmy thoughtfully. "You're in a good mood today."

"I'm always in a good mood, Joan, it's part of my charm. Every room I bless with my presence glows with the golden hue of my tarnished halo."

Joan cracked up. "You are so full of shit today. Did you get laid or something?" A powerful blush lit up Remmy's cheeks at the innocent jibe. Joan's eyes narrowing, she leaned forward conspiratorially. "Julie?" she whispered.

Remmy cringed at the pure joy in Joan's eyes. Pure joy, and what she knew would be Joan's gossip later. "No, Joan, I didn't get laid, and if I had, it certainly wouldn't have been Julie."

"But something did happen," Joan said.

Remmy was irritated. She didn't want to share the beautiful thing that happened between her and Julie. She knew Joan wouldn't understand it, would only see it at its basest level. Remmy met her gaze dead on. "No, Joan. Nothing happened." She was a good liar. "I'm just happy. Isn't that enough?"

"I apologize, Remmy. Truly. I'll leave it alone."

"Thank you."

"How's business?" Joan asked, reaching across to check the gas log that they kept next to the register. It was nearly half full already. "Busy morning?"

"Fairly. But I had time to figure out what to do with all that chili." Remmy grinned, eyes mischievous. "Been working on it for a while."

Joan rolled her eyes. "Lord save us." Setting the log down, she turned and headed back to her office, leaving Remmy to her own devices.

Julie hummed as she worked in the kitchen, her hair twisted back off her neck into a loose bun to help beat the heat. She had done laundry and cleaned house. The yard work would be tackled as soon as she had eaten lunch. As she assembled bread and cheese, she found herself glancing from time to time at her neckline, making sure the baby doll tank wasn't dipping too low. "How the hell did I become puritanical?" she muttered, finishing the creation of her sandwich.

It was the first time since her ordeal that she'd worn anything so revealing. It wasn't in poor taste, but it certainly showed more skin than her usual t-shirts. Sergio had made her fearful and ashamed of her own nakedness, and that was something she resented. She'd managed to get her bathing down to one or two showers a day, but still felt painfully shy about revealing anything more than what showed with long shorts and a t-shirt. That morning she'd decided it was time to try and overcome that.

She sat down at the table, looking out the window to make sure the sprinklers she had set near the flowers were, in fact, watering them and not half the neighborhood. Satisfied, she started on her meal, thoughts wandering from flowers and water bills. It had been three days since she'd kissed Remmy. Three days and two nights. The day after the kiss, there'd been a new closeness between them, a bond that was stronger than before the kiss.

Julie glanced at the counter where she'd been standing as Remmy held her, their lips exploring. The kiss wasn't passionate, but it hadn't been entirely chaste, either. She could still feel the softness of Remmy's mouth, the gentleness in her touch. It had been wonderful beyond anything Julie had ever experienced. And yet, over the past couple of days she had kept her distance from Remmy, no longer sure what was appropriate. The line in the sand seemed to be shifting and disappearing, leaving her confused.

Julie had seen Remmy look at her when she thought she was unobserved. Her eyes spoke volumes of words that Julie thought Remmy might never say. The blue depths burned with love and caring, and a deep desire that scared Julie.

The thing that surprised Julie the most in the strange situation was that even though she had only known Remmy for a scant few months, she felt as though she'd known her for her whole life. Even more surprising, and definitely frightening, was the realization that Julie had no idea how she had lived the first twenty-nine years of her life without Remmy.

"That's crazy," she muttered, finishing her lunch and sliding the dishes into the dishwasher.

❧❧❧❧❧

Remmy nearly flew up the stairs to the front porch, hot from her walk home, but damn glad to finally be home. It had been a long day, and her back hurt from being on her feet all day. Why couldn't she have Joan's job — sitting back in the office all day with a fan blowing directly on her. No standing, no pain in the ass customers. "Guess that's why she gets the big bucks," she muttered, pulling the screen door open and using her keys to unlock the front door.

The house was quiet and smelled of Pine Sol and air deodorizer. Remmy had never known anyone who was as clean as Julie. It amazed her. When Skylar was over for the weekend, or even just the night, the house was trashed with his toys, food wrappers, video games and controllers. Julie didn't blink an eye, though she did make him clean up after himself. Within an hour of his leaving, the house was in perfect condition again.

"Honey, I'm home!" Remmy called out, jogging up the stairs to her room to change clothes. More than once she'd tried to talk Joan into letting them wear shorts at the store, but she steadfastly refused.

"How was your day, dear?" Julie said from Remmy's open doorway, a stack of folded laundry in her hands and a lopsided grin on her face.

"Oh, it was just peachy," Remmy joked back. "How were the Beav and Wally today?"

Julie laughed, handing Remmy her laundry, accepting the "thanks" and quick peck on the lips in greeting. Neither reacted; it seemed a natural thing to do.

"Well, I'll have a martini waiting for you downstairs, darling," Julie bantered, waving as she left the bedroom.

Remmy put her clothing away, pleasantly surprised that Julie had washed hers, too. After changing into mesh shorts and a tank top, she padded downstairs, tennis shoes and socks in hand. She wasn't surprised to find Julie out back, Bonnie and Clyde involved in a heated tug-of-war with the rope Remmy had bought them a month ago. Remmy sat on one of the patio chairs and slipped her socks and shoes on, her eyes on Julie.

Julie was wearing a shorter pair of shorts than Remmy had ever seen on her, and a top that exposed her smooth shoulders and arms and the soft play of muscle underneath as she prepared the grill for their dinner. Something was different. Dark eyebrows drew together as Remmy tried to figure out what it was. The smooth, graceful movements, the controlled awareness

Julie had of her body…it was a new sort of confidence. She seemed to stand a bit straighter, seeming almost at peace within herself.

"Why are you watching me?" Julie asked, her back still to Remmy.

Jeez, eyes in the back of her head. Embarrassed at being caught, Remmy's eyes darted out to the yard. She ignored the question, assuming it was rhetorical. She pushed up from the chair and joined Julie at the grill. "Can I help?"

"Yeah, you can. In the fridge, second shelf, there's a plate with the hamburger patties already made. Grab 'em and bring 'em out here, please."

"Will do."

Within moments Remmy returned, the plate in her hands. She set it on the small wooden side rack connected to the barbeque, then stepped back and leaned against the house. In the relaxed setting, she decided to broach something that had been bothering her. "There's something I want to talk to you about, Julie."

"Okay," Julie said absently, placing the patties on the heated grill. She closed the lid and gave Remmy her full attention.

"I tried before, but you blew me off. This time, I really want you to listen."

"Alright." Nervous, Julie bought some time by walking over to one of the patio chairs and sitting. Remmy followed. "What's up?"

"Rent. No, don't turn away from me," Remmy placed her hand over Julie's, preventing her escape. "Julie, I'm not going to let you let me live here without helping out financially. I don't care whether it's paying for the space, or food, or utilities, or whatever."

"Remmy," Julie said, entwining their fingers, "I

can afford this house just fine on my own. And, I'll be back with the school district in a couple of months—"

"It's not about money, Julie," Remmy said insistently. "It's about me not pulling my weight. I've always been self-sufficient, so I'm not comfortable with this Sugar Mamma thing." She smiled at Julie's laughter, but the smile quickly slid from Remmy's face. "I'm serious."

"How about this: you need a car. Set the money aside for that. I hate the fact that you have to walk all over this damn town, and I've told you more than once that you're welcome to use my car until I go back to work."

"I am not leaving you stranded."

"As noble as that may be, the offer still stands. Take this time, Rem. Save up and get yourself a car. I'm really okay with that. I mean," she shrugged, "you help out around the house, a lot, and…" She echoed Remmy's own words to Joan. "You could be the handyman."

Remmy saw the hurt in Julie's eyes. "You heard that?"

Julie nodded. "I did, but that doesn't matter."

Remmy frantically tried to think back to that conversation, trying to remember what else Julie might have overheard. Julie re-focused her attention with a squeeze of her hand.

"I understand your pride, honestly, I'm the same way. So, let's find a compromise if we can."

"You let me pay half the mortgage, half the food, and half the utilities," Remmy said with a grin.

Julie chuckled. "That's a compromise? Uhhh, no. I'm serious about the car. We're in the middle of summer right now, but I think you saw last year how ugly the winters can be. I can't stand the thought of you tromping through the friggin' snow."

"Alright. Fair enough. So, what's your suggestion?"

"You save your money for a car or for pretty things for me." Julie's eyes twinkled with mischief. "Okay, so I'm kidding. How about I take care of the mortgage and utilities, and of course my own car, and you take care of food. Okay? Except," she held up a finger, "I'll take care of my dogs' needs, of course."

Remmy could see the wisdom in Julie's word; she knew she needed a car. She hadn't owned one in a lot of years because she'd never been anywhere long enough to bother. It was a hell of a lot cheaper to hitch or ride the rails than to worry about gas money when she traveled. Finally she met Julie's eyes. "Once I get a car, then we re-negotiate. That's the only way this is going to fly."

"Deal." Julie held out her hand to seal the deal with a handshake. It was enveloped in Remmy's firm grip. "Good." She smiled sweetly. "You can start contributing by turning over the burgers."

Chapter Fifty-five

This is really good, Grace," Julie said, savoring the dinner she had prepared for them.

"For sure," Remmy said, "Who knew you could do more than bug the shit out of me."

Chris and Julie laughed as Grace threw a roll at Remmy's grinning face. She caught it easily.

Grace chuckled. "I figured it was about time we met under more civilized conditions rather than just at a crime scene." She enjoyed Julie and Remmy's company. She also found observing them one of the most amusing and entertaining things she had seen in a while. From the raised eyebrow she received from her husband, Grace could tell she wasn't the only one who saw the heat between the two. She glanced back at Remmy, meeting her gaze with questioning eyes. Blue eyes looked away.

⚜ ⚜ ⚜ ⚜

Julie tossed her keys on the kitchen table, tired but content after an evening of fun with Grace and Chris. She had been surprised when she'd also been invited to dinner.

Remmy pushed the button just inside the garage door, sending the big door closed with a mechanical whir. She closed and locked the inside door and went into the kitchen to join Julie, who was getting the pitcher of iced tea from the fridge.

"What were you and Grace talking about all hush hush?" Julie asked, pouring two glasses of tea and handing one to Remmy.

Remmy took hers with a quiet "thanks". Grace had taken her aside to tell her what had happened with the Bailey case. "Aren't you Little Miss Nosey."

Julie could judge Remmy's mood by her tone. "I see. It must have been pretty serious business if you won't tell me."

Remmy mirrored Julie's position, leaning against the counter, arms crossed over her chest. "Maybe we were planning your demise."

"Oh yeah?" Julie raised an eyebrow. "Is it gonna hurt?"

Remmy's grin was evil. She stalked over to Julie, who moved to put the butcher block island between them. "Why do you think I would make it hurt?" Remmy said, eyes never leaving her prey, four feet of cooking space separating them, both hunched, ready to bolt or give chase at any moment.

"Well, I don't know," Julie said, eyes twinkling. "Maybe because the look in your eyes is a little too mischievous for my liking..."

Remmy's grin widened. "Mischievous, huh?"

"Oh, yeah." Julie moved, never taking her eyes off Remmy, slowly trying to move around so she could bolt into the living room. Her glance toward freedom gave her plan away.

"What, you don't like my company here in the kitchen?" Remmy grinned, slowly prowling around the island, carefully gauging Julie's reactions. Julie's eyes hadn't yet lost their spark, her body tensed with their game.

"Well, I don't know," Julie said, voice entirely too sweet. She saw her chance and bolted, squealing as she heard Remmy give chase. Julie pounded up the stairs, ignoring Bonnie and Clyde who barked wildly.

Remmy was hot on Julie's trail, reaching for her, only to have Julie squeal again as she managed to elude her grasp. They ran along the upstairs hall toward the master bedroom. Julie disappeared inside, trying to close the door on Remmy, but Remmy's size advantage burst it open. She plowed into Julie, and both of them stumbled backwards onto Julie's bed.

Julie tried to wriggle away from Remmy, who held her lightly. Both of them knew that she could get away in a second if she wanted to. She realized she didn't want to.

Her chest heaving with exertion, Remmy trapped Julie's wrists along either side of her head. Julie's breathing was also heavy, her gaze fixed on Remmy. Slowly she pulled her hands free and brought them to rest on Remmy's waist. Her heart was pounding, her mouth dry. She ran a quick tongue over her lips, Remmy's gaze drawn to the movement.

Slowly Remmy lowered her upper body until she was resting on her forearms, her breasts just barely grazing Julie's. The casual grip on her waist tightened, urging her down. Stomachs pressed together, she could feel the heat of Julie's skin through the thin layers of their shirts.

Julie felt the heat from the body above her; it matched hers. Her gaze strayed to Remmy's lips. She wanted to bring the dark head to her lips, but didn't know how.

The doorbell rang, shattering the moment. Remmy pushed off from the bed, running trembling hands through her hair as she left the room and went down the stairs, giving Julie a chance to get herself together.

"How are you?" Matt asked when Remmy

answered the door, doing his best to be friendly.

"I'm great. Come on in." Remmy held the door open as Matt and Skylar entered the house. Moments later Julie hurried down the stairs, her hair pulled into a ponytail, eyes calm and welcoming.

"Hey, guys." She gave Skylar a big hug, but didn't hug Matt.

"Hey, Jules. Sorry to drop in on you like this, but I was wondering if you'd mind if Skylar stayed the night. Me and the guys are going out to play pool, and Mrs. Huxby couldn't watch him."

"Of course I don't mind." She smiled down at Skylar, both relieved and irritated at Matt's just dropping by and putting her on unanticipated babysitting duty. Skylar grinned back at her before brushing past her and heading for the TV to hook up his video game system. Remmy went into the kitchen, leaving the siblings alone.

"Thanks for doing this," Matt said, shifting his weight uncomfortably.

"No problem. I love Skylar, you know that."

Matt glanced toward the kitchen. "Listen, I'm really sorry about the other week. That was wrong of me."

"Yeah, Matt, it was. In fact, you were a complete asshole." Julie's voice was low, but filled with anger. "Personally, I think you owe Remmy an apology."

Matt's brow wrinkled. "What? Why? I didn't say anything to her, Julie. I don't owe her shit."

"Fine. Well, you do owe me the right to live my life as I see fit. How's that?"

Matt sighed. "Fine. I still…" Matt shoved his hands into the back pockets of his jeans. "Just be sure, Jules, okay?"

Julie held his gaze, hers unwavering. She felt Matt's warning was a blanket caution, not knowing just how close to the truth he was, not ten minutes before. "Have fun playing pool," she said, voice soft. "Don't drive if you're drinking."

Matt nodded with a tight smile. "Okay." He gave her a quick one-armed hug, then left.

Chapter Fifty-six

*T*he sky was a crystal clear blue, the breeze cool, the water shimmering. Julie closed her eyes, inhaling the wonderful fragrances around her. A small smile touched her lips when she felt someone behind her. Nothing to fear this time. No one would hurt her.

Warm hands rested on her hips; the warmth of a strong body pressed up against her back. She fell against it with a contented sigh. The hands moved around until the fingers had splayed out over her stomach. Soft lips brushed her earlobe, and Julie's head tilted to give the lips better access.

The body behind her pressed closer, the sound of the nearby water nearly forgotten, her breathing becoming rapid. The hands slowly moved up over her stomach and came to rest just below her breasts. The material of her dress was so thin, the hands burned her. Her back arched of its own accord, desperately wanting those hands on her. Her breasts were full, nipples hard. Waiting, wanting...

Soft lips moved away from her ear, making their way to the side of her neck, leaving a hot, wet trail. Julie moaned, one hand reaching back, tangling in the long hair she knew she would find. The other hand reached down, covering the left hand just below her breast, urging the hand to cup her, which it did.

"Oh, Remmy." She gasped as the hand gently squeezed her, testing the size and weight of her breast. Her nipple was taken between two fingers, tugged gently, sending warmth throughout her body and ending between *her legs. "Oh, god," she whispered, her fingers tightening on the dark hair, her head now resting back against a strong shoulder, a hot mouth sucking on her neck.*

A pulsing aching low in her belly, Julie was growing wetter. The body behind hers pressed tighter against her and Julie thrust her ass back into it, desperately needing to feel her. With a whimper, she turned, needing to seek her mouth...

Julie shot up, panting, heart pounding, her body aching. She was wet, heated. Flopping back against the pillow, she shoved the sheet away from her body, her panties and tank top sticking to her skin.

❧❧❧❧

Remmy jerked twice, crying out softly, leaving the field as her body convulsed around her fingers. Eyes blinked several times before she saw the warm night around her, the cliffs of Overlook Hill beneath her.

"Holy shit," she whispered, withdrawing her fingers from her shorts and wiping them on the grass. That was intense, and incredibly wrong. Covering her face with her hands, she groaned.

❧❧❧❧

Julie tugged on a pair of shorts and padded out of her bedroom, the sweat on her body drying, leaving her skin feeling tight and unpleasant. She didn't bother turning on any lights as she walked through to the hallway. She glanced at Remmy's bedroom door, which—to her surprise—was not only open, but open on an empty room. The bed was unmade, but the pillows were fluffy with no tell-tale sign of a head lying there recently.

Suddenly Julie felt angry. She had a very good idea where her erotic "dream" came from. "Damn it, Remmy." She returned to her bedroom and slammed the door shut behind her. She felt angry, violated, though not in the same way as she had with Sergio. She was confused.

Stepping into the bathroom, Julie flipped on the light and looked at her face in the mirror above the sink. Her eyes were wide, the pupils still dilated from her intense arousal; her nipples were also hard. She still throbbed, which was a new sensation. She hadn't felt even remotely sexually stimulated before the attack, and since the attack, she hadn't touched herself, hadn't even much looked at herself.

Now she closed the bathroom door, which was silly, she knew, but she did it all the same. Closed inside the small room, she looked at her reflection again, her gaze traveling to her breasts, then back up to her face. With one fluid movement, her tank top was removed, leaving her standing there in a pair of shorts. She studied the smooth skin of her shoulders and upper chest, tan from hours outside in the yard. Her breasts were very pale, the tips dark rose and extremely sensitive. She cupped one of them, the tanned hand a strong contrast to the creamy white of her chest. Her breasts weren't large, but they weren't small, either. Past boyfriends had said she was well proportioned. She supposed she was. She hadn't really given it a thought in a long time.

Julie cupped both breasts, gasping as she ran her thumbs over erect nipples, her hands falling from her chest at the thrill that brought to her. It was an alien feeling. Technically she hadn't had sex in over a year. She would never consider anything that happened with Sergio as anything but rape. Nothing he did felt good. Everything he did left her feeling ashamed and dirty. She wanted to get past that; she wanted to be whole again.

Pushing her shorts down, her gaze rested on the light blue panties, cut high on the waist and low on the leg. They might be called granny panties. They clung to her narrow hips, her legs slender but muscular. It was a nice body. Last summer she had worked for hours on her physique, running long miles through the neighborhood and lifting free weights. She hadn't done either of those things in a long time. Perhaps she should start again.

Julie met her eyes briefly in the mirror before taking a deep breath and pushing her panties down. She stepped out of them and the shorts, then kicked them aside. She turned to the mirror on the back of the bathroom door to take in her entire body. The hair between her thighs was dark blonde, the same color as her eyebrows, and at the moment it was quite bushy. She'd had no reason to care for it, and in fact, had been almost nun-like while showering or bathing. She shaved her legs and armpits, but that was it. She didn't like spending too much time looking at herself or giving herself any special attention. It was not like anyone else saw it anyway, not like she would let anyone else see it.

Now she brought a hand down, feeling the wiry hair still damp from her erotic dream. She didn't venture beyond the hair, just simply touched it, almost as though reacquainting herself with the fact that she was a woman. That had not been taken from her.

She grabbed the tiny pair of manicure scissors from the medicine cabinet and hiked one foot up on the closed lid of the toilet. She trimmed carefully and methodically, feeling a bit of a sexual rush. It made her feel almost...sexy. Once she had the patch shaped, she grabbed her can of shaving cream, squirted a generous amount in her palm, and spread the fragrant cream along the delicate flesh of the insides of her thighs and around her pubic line. It felt wonderful — the attention to something that she had thought dormant. Permanently dormant.

With razor in hand and stroking carefully, she began to rid herself of the cold apathy toward her sexuality, moving toward her sensuality. Each stroke of the razor indicative of the new woman she had become, was becoming, Julie slowly shaped a new future for herself.

Long moments later, Julie cleaned off the remnants of the darkness of the last ten months, the warm wash cloth feeling wonderful on her skin, leaving her beautiful and feeling clean for the first time since the previous November. It was a wonderful feeling, a liberating feeling.

Nude, Julie walked into her bedroom, lights still off, and opened her underwear drawer. She dug toward the back, where all her old panties were, the panties she had worn before Sergio. She found a pair of black satin, bikini-cut panties and slid them on, moaning softly at the wonderful feel against her freshly shaven skin. She felt beautiful. Though still not ready to go out and conquer the world, she felt closer to herself than she had in a long while.

Heading back into the bathroom, she cleaned up the clippings. Taking her tank top in hand, she tried to decide whether or not to put it back on. Not quite ready to give up covering, she slid the shirt over her head and returned to her bed. Sleep came swiftly.

❧ ❧ ❧ ❧

Remmy felt like a complete asshole as she snuck back into the house. Her bedroom door clicked closed and she turned to the room, only lit by the moonlight streaming in through the window over the bed. Quickly undressing, she threw her clothing to the floor and climbed under the sheet.

She hadn't intended to enter their field and seduce Julie's dream alter ego. She had been so worked up over the past several days, each day seeming to be filled with more touching, more teasing. It had left her frustrated and in need of release. She'd even considered heading over to a bar in another county, maybe finding some woman and fucking her brains out, just to get Julie out of her head.

Not only could she not bring herself to do that, she knew the chances of her finding someone in these backwoods towns were slim to none. She'd considered touching herself and getting it over with, but with Julie's bedroom right next door, for some reason she felt it was better to get some fresh air. So, unable to sleep, with her body on fire, she had pulled herself out of bed.

The desire for fresh air led to Overlook Hill, which led to Remmy being alone, which inevitably led to thoughts of Julie, which led right back to her sexual frustration. Before she knew it, her hand was in her shorts and she was walking through the field toward the beautiful woman standing by their lake.

"Damn," she whispered in the darkness, still able to smell her own desire on her fingertips. What would she do if Julie remembered? What if she figured it out? "Damn, damn." She hated herself for not being able to keep herself under control when it came to Julie. Sometimes she felt that moving into Julie's house was one of the stupidest things she'd ever done.

What was she going to do? Julie was her friend, her best friend, and she loved her. Remmy's dark eyebrows drew together as she stared up at the ceiling fan, watching the blades lazily turn. She loved Julie;

that was no secret, no big deal. As close as she felt to her, as bonded as they were, she felt like she had loved Julie since the day she'd been given a ride in the white Miata. But now, living with her, she realized that her day wasn't complete without seeing one of Julie's special smiles, seemingly saved just for her. She hurt when Julie wasn't with her, missing her badly while she was at the convenience store.

Remmy had known love: love for Monica; love for her mother, at least until she was fourteen; but this was different. This was a love that was so deep it made her soul ache because she couldn't find the words to express to Julie just how important she was in her life. Just how much she felt her, in her heart and in her soul. When Julie was sad, she felt sad. If Julie was happy, Remmy was overjoyed. She needed Julie like she needed her next breath.

"Shit." She rolled over onto her side and stared at the bedside clock. It was nearly three-thirty in the morning. "What am I going to do?"

Chapter Fifty-seven

When Julie woke up in the morning, Remmy was gone. She knew that Remmy had come home from her midnight foray because her bedroom door was pulled closed, as per usual, and there was a juice glass in the dishwasher, along with a small plate from Remmy's morning toast.

As the day wore on, she had to work harder to keep her growing anger in check. Her irritation sprang not only from what Remmy had done last night, but also from her apparent avoidance of a face-to-face, which really pissed Julie off. She was an upfront kind of person, always facing her own bad decisions or judgments, and she expected the same from the people around her. Remmy hadn't lived up to that expectation, and so Julie stayed angry.

⚜ ⚜ ⚜ ⚜

Julie managed to keep herself busy around the house, all the while looking forward to the end of summer so she would no longer have to be a full time homebody. She loved her home, loved making it comfortable and attractive, but she was sick and tired of being there all of the time. At one point, she jumped in her car, loaded Bonnie and Clyde, and went to the park. The dogs ran and romped and played together, while Julie enjoyed the time out of the house and just sitting in the sun. She was tempted to run by the store and chew Remmy a new one, but decided that wasn't an appropriate thing to do to someone at their job; it could wait. She hoped Remmy would come home after work. If she avoided an encounter one more time, Julie was going to skin her alive. They obviously needed to talk.

⁂

Remmy took Joan up on her offer to stay late to help take inventory, but she knew it was only buying her an extra hour before she had to go home and face the music. She felt that Julie knew about the dream seduction, and she felt — even more strongly — that Julie was not happy.

The walk home went far too quickly for Remmy's liking, but finally she couldn't put it off any longer. She took a deep breath and braced for the worst, then opened the screen door, unlocked the front door, and pushed inside. The house smelled of bleach. *Shit.* Julie had been doing some deep cleaning; not a good sign.

Remmy went upstairs to her bedroom and changed into her shorts, then went to the bathroom, brushed out her hair, and finally went downstairs. She found Julie sitting at the kitchen table, reading the newspaper.

"Hey," she greeted tentatively as she poured herself an iced tea and topped off Julie's glass.

Julie didn't answer, her focus fixed on the paper. She had read the same paragraph four times since she'd heard the front door open. Remmy leaned against the kitchen counter, sipping her tea as she kept her eyes on the bowed head. "How was your day?"

Julie took a deep breath, looking up and meeting timid blue eyes. "How was my day?" she asked, slamming the newspaper on the table. "My day was peachy." She shoved her chair back, legs skidding on the kitchen tile.

"But, as peachy as it was, I must say it was pretty damn boring compared to my night." When Remmy looked away, Julie knew it was because she felt guilty. *Bingo.* "I guess your night was pretty darn exciting, too, wasn't it?"

"Julie, listen—"

"No!" Julie held up her hand, cutting off anything Remmy might have to say. Now that she'd begun, had Remmy in front of her, Julie's anger boiled over. "Our lake is supposed to be somewhere I can go to feel safe. It's a place where I can be protected and have all the darkness taken away. It's not a personal playground for you, Remmy. It's our place, our special place, not your seduction scene." She was surprised to feel tears trickling down her cheek. She swallowed, trying to calm herself, unable to look at Remmy. When she continued, her voice had softened. "You violated something very sacred. It really hurts."

Remmy harnessed her own emotions before speaking. "I can't say that I'm sorry, because somehow 'sorry' just doesn't seem enough. I never meant for that to happen, Julie, I swear."

"Then why did it?"

"Because I want you so goddamn bad! But there is nothing in this world that could make me hurt you or scare you or push you away from me. I don't know what you want. I'm so damn confused... My thoughts just got away from me. Our lake is always how I connected with you, always how I reached you, and I guess I was so desperate to reach out to you, it just kind of happened." Running out of words, Remmy waited for the worst.

Julie felt Remmy's anguish. And she'd admitted what she had done and didn't try to excuse it. Her anger draining from her, Julie still needed time to think, time away from Remmy. She grabbed up the newspaper and her tea. "Look, I'm going to, uh...I need some time."

Remmy watched Julie go out into the backyard and curl up in one of the patio chairs, the newspaper lying forgotten on the table next to her. With a heavy sigh, Remmy grabbed her own tea and went upstairs to her bedroom.

❧ ❧ ❧ ❧

Julie had always been amazed by sunsets. Despite how many she had seen, each time she saw a new one, she was dumbstruck all over again. She watched as the brilliant pinks painted the undersides of the clouds, enjoyed the almost perfect silence as the colors spread across the sky, tinting everything around her with the brilliance.

The newspaper still lay on the table next to her, folded neatly, her glass of tea now just a few pea-sized bits of ice floating in water. Her legs were pulled up, heels tucked into the seat cushion beneath her, arms wrapped around her shins. She rested her chin on her knees, watching as the colors began to lose their brilliance as twilight slowly swallowed the day.

She felt lonely. That was an unusual feeling for her. She so often lived her life in her own head, contemplating herself and the world around her, she rarely, if ever, felt lonely. Now, sitting on her back patio, the silence around her, she felt lonelier than she ever had in her life. The good part, and the bad part, was that she knew why she was feeling so low. Her heart was no longer her own, and her own company no longer made her complete or content. She was connected to another, and that other person wasn't with her. She felt as though Remmy had cut her off somehow, as though the innate communication between them had been turned off or tuned to another station, leaving her swaddled in a heavy silence.

Julie knew it was up to her to fix things between them, though she wasn't at all sure how it could be done. Deciding she had been by herself long enough, she stood, scooped up her glass and the newspaper, and went inside. Waiting until Bonnie and Clyde ran inside, she locked the French doors.

Glass in the dishwasher, newspaper on the counter, Julie shut off the downstairs lights and made her way to the second floor. Remmy's bedroom door was closed, which didn't surprise her in the least. She didn't stop to listen to see whether Remmy was still awake. She moved on to her own bedroom, hand poised to flick on the light.

❧❧❧❧

Remmy sat with her back against the headboard, legs stretched out on the bed, bare feet crossed at the ankles. The TV was on, but she wasn't watching the program. She'd been staring off into space; she had no idea for how long. It wasn't until she heard a soft knock on her door that she realized night had fallen, the soft glow from the television providing the only light in the room.

"Come in," she called nervously, waiting as the door opened and Julie stepped inside. Their gazes met for a moment before Julie's eyes dropped as she made her way over to the bed. Remmy scooted over, making room if Julie wanted to sit down.

"What are you watching?" Julie asked.

With not a clue as to what was on, Remmy glanced over at the TV. Her smile was sheepish. "I have no idea."

Julie understood. She sat on the edge of the bed.

She could see that Remmy was just as conflicted as she was, the typically calm eyes filled with regret and pain. Julie took a deep breath, as if to say something, but she realized that she had no idea what to say. In that moment it seemed there was only one thing to do. She leaned over and placed a soft kiss on Remmy's lips, then drew back just enough to see the startled look on her face. She leaned in again, pressed her lips against Remmy's again, this time lingering, basking in the feel of her soul opening, offering a door for Remmy to walk through.

꙳ ꙳ ꙳ ꙳

Setting her surprise aside, Remmy felt the emptiness she'd been feeling all day begin to disappear. She felt Julie's lips open to her, inviting her inside, an invitation she quickly accepted. She heard a soft sigh as Julie's tongue brushed against her own, one of Julie's hands coming up to rest on her shoulder.

As the kiss deepened, Julie scooted further onto the bed. The hand that had rested on the side of her face curved around to the back of her neck, gently pressing her mouth more firmly against Remmy's, the gentle exploration within igniting a fire deep inside of her. She wanted more.

Remmy felt herself pressed down to the mattress. Her body slid down into a reclining position, and she adjusted the pillow beneath her head as Julie moved on top of her, their bodies flush, lips never parting. Remmy stroked Julie's back, tracing random patterns on the thin cotton of her shirt, the skin beneath warm and pliant. As the kiss continued, Remmy was well aware that she had an unimaginable responsibility — rebuilding Julie's comfort and enjoyment with intimacy after her experience with a world of physical pain and sexual torture and abuse.

❧ ❧ ❧ ❧

Julie felt tentative hands caress from her back to her hips, a fingertip just barely brushing the skin of her lower back where her shirt had ridden up. She broke the kiss, panting. As she stared down into Remmy's flushed face, Julie reached back to grasp Remmy's hand and place it under the hem of her shirt.

"Touch me, Remmy. Please, touch me," she whispered. After a brief hesitation, both of Remmy's hands slid up underneath Julie's t-shirt and ran all along the smooth, strong back. Julie's head fell forward to rest against the strong shoulder beneath her, her mind racing. She knew she should feel panicked, she should feel wicked shame, but she didn't. She felt the love Remmy had for her, and the gentleness in her touch. Remmy had replaced so many horrid memories with brand new wonderful ones, and Julie wanted this to be no different. She wanted the memory of her body being touched to be that of Remmy making love to her. She needed to shed that shell, hard and prickly, created by Sergio Venti.

Suddenly Julie pulled away, sat up, and straddled Remmy's hips. She grabbed the hem of her shirt in both hands and tugged it over her head. The shirt flew off into the eerie shadows created by the light of the television.

Remmy's eyes feasted on Julie's perfect breasts, the smooth skin of her stomach, the delicate structure of her shoulders and collar bones. "I have never seen anything so beautiful," she whispered.

Her hands moved up Julie's sides, tactile bliss, until they cupped the pert breasts. Julie's eyes slid closed and her head fell back. Her nipples were instantly hard against rough palms. Remmy's mouth found Julie's as surprisingly strong arms wrapped around Remmy's neck and drew her closer. This kiss took on a new aspect; it was hotter, deeper, and filled with so much need.

Julie needed to feel Remmy's skin against her own, so she broke away from the kiss and tugged at the hem of Remmy's shirt, swiftly pulling it over Remmy's head and immediately finding Remmy's mouth again. She moaned as their naked breasts pressed together. "God, this feels incredible," she murmured against Remmy's lips.

Remmy moved away from her mouth, finding Julie's neck, suckling and kissing, much as she'd done at their lake. One of her hands moved up between them, cupping Julie's breast, rolling the rigid nipple against her palm before taking it between two of her fingers.

Julie gasped, a hand moving up to cup the back of Remmy's dark head as the avid mouth kissed and licked a trail down across one collar bone, ending with a nipple in her mouth. "Oh, Jesus," Julie whispered.

Remmy gently pushed Julie back until she lay down, her head at the end of the bed. She hovered above her, looking into her eyes, waiting for assurance that this position was okay.

Julie reached for her, pulling her down on top of her. "Make me forget," she whispered, cupping Remmy's face, pressing it down to her breasts. Eyes closed, head turned to the side, Julie felt herself open up even more as Remmy took that first step inside of her, joining with her. It was so beautiful, it was almost painful. She could feel Remmy inside her skin.

Remmy stroked Julie's hip, curving her hand along the underside of one of her thighs and gently bending one of Julie's legs at the knee, the other leg instinctually doing the same, Remmy's body fitting snugly between. She knew, as well she knew her own name, that she was home as she tasted Julie's skin, heard her soft gasps and cries. She felt her own heart pounding in Julie's chest.

Julie felt her shorts being unbuttoned, and then slid down her legs. She opened her eyes, watching as Remmy knelt between her spread legs, lifting her hips as Remmy removed her panties. This was the ultimate test—lying there in all her nakedness. Her ability to give that gift to someone was something that Sergio had taken from her. She watched Remmy's eyes carefully, reading her expression.

Meeting the troubled eyes, Remmy leaned up and cupped Julie's face. "I love you, Julie," she said softly, leaning down and placing a soft kiss on full lips.

The dam broke and the tears began. Remmy laid herself down between Julie's legs again, resting on her forearms as she cupped Julie's face. Soft kisses rained down upon Julie's lips, her cheeks, her forehead, and moist eyes. "Why are you crying?" Remmy whispered against Julie's lips.

Julie's hands buried themselves in Remmy's hair. "I thought I'd never be able to do this again, never be able to give myself to someone and not feel ashamed."

Though Julie's whisper was barely audible, Remmy heard it. But even more, she felt it in the depths of her soul.

"Julie, he used your body, but he never reached your heart, never touched your soul." She kissed Julie softly. "Your heart, your soul, those are the gifts, the rest is just the wrapping. The wrapping may be the most beautiful thing I've ever seen, but your soul," another kiss, "that's the most beautiful thing in the world. No one can take that away, no one can touch that."

"No one but you." Julie drew Remmy down for a long, deep kiss that left them both panting. "Make love to me, Remmy."

Remmy removed the rest of her own clothing, then settled her body atop Julie's, her mouth exploring across Julie's upper chest, hand massaging Julie's hip, fingernails trailing along her sides, making Julie shiver. She began to kiss her way down, taking in each breast, one at a time, sucking hard nipples. She felt Julie's fingers in her hair, pushing her deeper. Julie's moan was long and languid as Remmy's body slid even lower, her intent clear.

Julie was lost in a haze, her soul opening up in response to Remmy's touch. She felt long hair tickling across her stomach, then on the inside of her thighs, hot breath moving across her recently shaven pubic area. Her fingers massaged Remmy's scalp as soft lips kissed a trail from her pubic bone over and down to the apex of her thighs. When a wet tongue trailed through her folds, Julie cried out, her hips lifting off the bed.

Remmy had never wanted so badly to make love to someone with her mouth as she did in that moment. Each sound Julie made, each lifting of her hips, brought Remmy's own pleasure to new heights. She could feel her own sex pulsing in time with her raging heartbeat.

Opening Julie to her, Remmy ran her tongue from the entrance to the clit, then back down. She wrapped her arms around Julie's thighs, anticipating that Julie might actually buck her off the bed. As she heard her name whimpered from Julie's lips, Remmy made her way back up to suckle the clit, her tongue batting across it before letting it go, giving it several licks before moving her attention back down Julie's seam, her tongue finding the entrance. She gently toyed with it, unsure what Julie would do, or if she'd allow her to enter her. She felt Julie's hips stop moving.

Julie had been violated so deeply, she wasn't sure she would ever again want to be entered. She was on the verge of objecting, when Remmy's mouth moved away from her opening.

"It's okay, baby," Remmy whispered, kissing Julie's mons then returning to her clit.

Julie felt a hand reach up and find one of her own, their entwined fingers resting on Julie's stomach as she began to lose herself again, Remmy's tongue doing amazing things to her. She felt the slow burn beginning, a storm that threatened to break with each stroke of Remmy's tongue.

Remmy could feel that Julie was close, her panting nearly constant, small whimpers escaping her throat. She latched onto her clit, suckling it and giving it firm strokes with her tongue.

"Oh, god!" Julie's body exploded with a pleasure that she had never experienced, her fingers holding painfully tightly to Remmy's hand and hair, holding Remmy in place. Her body consumed with release, Julie couldn't breathe for a moment. In that instant, she felt as if she was released not only from her sexual need, but from the pain and hurt, the suffering, the fear and loss. She was letting it all go, making room as Remmy stepped inside her soul, their connection complete.

Remmy kissed her way back up Julie's body, aftershocks still racking Julie. She found her mouth, and suddenly her body was pulled tightly against Julie's, her kiss hungry and all-consuming. Her own need had reached a place of near desperation. Remmy fit her hips between Julie's thighs again and pressed down. Groaning at the contact, Julie reached down to Remmy's ass and pulled their hips closer together. Remmy planted her hands on either side of Julie's shoulders and ground herself against Julie, their stomachs slapping together as she thrust against her. Eyes squeezed shut, Remmy threw her head back, crying out loud and long as she came, pressing into Julie's wetness.

Julie's arms twined around Remmy's shoulders; her legs wrapped around Remmy's waist, pulling Remmy as tightly to her as she could. Once again, she felt as though she were wrapped up in a warm cocoon, wrapped in all that was Remmy.

"Oh, baby," Remmy whimpered, burying her face against Julie's neck.

"I know," Julie whispered, holding her tight. "I know."

☙ ☙ ☙ ☙

The intense rays of the morning sun roused Remmy from her deep, dreamless sleep. She was lying on her stomach in the middle of the bed, naked, a sheet barely covering her from the hips down. Lifting her head, she blinked a few times, wondering why her body was so sore. With jolting clarity, it hit her.

Turning onto her back and sitting up, Remmy looked around the small room. Her clothing had been folded and placed on top of the dresser. The door was closed, the TV turned off. She ran a hand through her hair, pushing it away from her face. For just a moment she felt out of sorts and slightly worried. Julie's voice carried in from the open window, followed by one of the dogs barking. It sounded like Clyde.

Remmy hurriedly dressed and padded downstairs. As she passed Julie's room, she noted that the bed was still made, exactly how it had been the night before. Obviously Julie had stayed with her the entire night. *A good sign*, she figured. *I hope.*

One of the French doors was open, allowing the early morning breeze to cool the house before the heat of the day struck. She smelled fresh coffee, but wanted to see Julie.

Julie was curled up in one of the patio chairs, dressed only in an oversized shirt, a cup of coffee cupped between her palms. A serene smile on her lips, she stared off toward the horizon. It was such a beautiful picture, Remmy didn't want to disturb her. She needn't have worried; Julie knew she was there.

"Hi," Julie said, setting aside her coffee cup and uncurling herself. She padded over to Remmy, the cement cold on her bare feet. Seeing the uncertainty in guarded blue eyes, she smiled at Remmy and slid her arms around Remmy's waist, resting her head against her shoulder. Strong arms immediately wrapped around her protectively. She turned her face to Remmy's neck, inhaling her scent.

"Why'd you get up?" Remmy asked, lightly nuzzling Julie's hair.

"I needed to watch the sun rise," Julie said, turning her head to stare out at the yard, the sun smoothly rising for the new day. "I feel reborn, and I wanted to share that with the birth of a new day."

"I missed you this morning."

Julie hummed happily. "I'm here."

Remmy stroked long, blonde hair as she also stared out at the day in front of them, wondering what it would bring. Last night had been such an amazing experience, and today she was virtually bursting with love for Julie. Underneath the new-found happiness was a niggling worry.

"What is it?" Julie asked, placing a soft kiss on Remmy's neck before stepping away far enough to look at Remmy, who gave her a brave smile.

"Nothing."

Julie raised an eyebrow. "Don't lie..."

"I was just thinking about your previous preference." Remmy brushed a few wind-blown locks out of Julie's face.

"Previous preference?" Julie said, brow wrinkled in confusion.

"Yeah, card carrying penis bearers."

Chuckling at Remmy's choice of words, Julie dropped her hands from Remmy's shoulders. "I was thinking about that this morning, too." She hugged herself with a sigh, watching as the dogs chased each other. *Do those two ever stay still?*

Remmy walked over to the steps that led into the house and perched on the top one, elbows balanced on her spread knees. She hoped Life wouldn't be so cruel as to bring Julie into her life just to take her away on such a tedious technicality.

"You know, Remmy, I've never given any thought to sexuality. Never thought about any of it, just went with the flow. I've never looked at a woman with particular interest, and honestly," she glanced at Remmy over her shoulder, "never really thought about a man, either. They just were the ones who asked me out, I guess." Her smile was tentative. She turned to face Remmy. The rays of the morning sun shining into those blue eyes made them glow; the burnished red highlights in her hair formed a burning halo around her head. "I don't see why we have the issue of sexuality. I see it as the meeting of two souls, intertwined irrevocably."

"Society won't see it that way, Julie," Remmy said, silently berating herself for introducing logic into the discussion.

"I know," Julie said, turning back toward the new day. "But," she said, again facing Remmy, "if I have you,

I can face anything."

"You'll always have me."

Remmy pushed to her feet and went over to Julie, raising her chin with two fingers. Julie fell into the promising kiss, allowing her mouth to open, inviting Remmy inside. Julie felt herself melting against the solid body, her fingers finding Remmy's hair and lodging themselves there.

"Can I have you for breakfast?" Remmy whispered against Julie's lips, her hands gliding down her back, finding the hem of the long t-shirt.

Julie whimpered when Remmy's hands found her bare butt and squeezed gently. "Breakfast is served," Julie murmured, pressing herself against Remmy.

❧ ❧ ❧ ❧

An hour later, Remmy was spooning Julie on the couch. Their clothing was scattered around the living room, which was as far as they had gotten. Remmy ran her hand along Julie's naked thigh, and up and over her hip, just to feel the softness of her skin.

"They think they might know who killed Yvonne and Tyler Bailey," Remmy said, nuzzling her face against the nape of Julie's neck, bringing her hand to rest on Julie's stomach to pull them even closer together.

"The ring?" Julie asked, running her fingertips in lazy patterns on Remmy's forearm.

"Yeah. It was a college ring. Belongs to a guy named Dennis Collins, who has disappeared." She laid a trail of soft kisses along Julie's shoulder, finally resting her chin there. "Apparently he used to work for Yvonne's husband, Clive. There's some evidence that he and Yvonne may have been having an affair."

"Oh, no," Julie whispered, lacing her fingers with

Remmy's and bringing their joined hands to her mouth to kiss Remmy's palm.

"I think he lost the ring while he was digging Tyler's grave."

"Is that what Grace was talking to you about at their house?"

"Yeah." Remmy sighed. "I have a decision to make, Julie."

Hearing the heaviness in the voice, Julie rolled onto her back and looked up at Remmy. "About what?"

"Grace wants to continue to use me, to have me help them with cases like yours and the Bailey's, cases with no leads."

Julie studied Remmy's face; there were dark shadows in her eyes. She reached up and caressed her cheek. Remmy's eyes closed at the gentle touches. "And what do you want?" Blue eyes slowly opened, looking off into a distance where Julie could not join her.

Though wrong about Tyler's death, Remmy knew that she'd helped the police by finding his grave. His body might never have been found otherwise; Collins might be getting away with two counts of murder. She gazed down at Julie's patient face; her fingers brushed absently against dark blonde brows.

Remmy felt again the intense heartbreak she'd felt when she thought it was Julie who died at Sergio's hand. She thought of the scars on her own back from the bullet wound. She would go through it all again tomorrow, if it was for Julie. She thought about three women returning to their homes, a mad man stopped.

"What's going through your mind?" Julie took Remmy's hand, kissed it, and tucked it against her chest.

"I'm thinking that it drains me — emotionally, physically. But I'm also thinking that there's no way I can't do it. I was given this ability for a reason, and I think it would be utterly selfish, and wasteful, not to use it."

Julie smiled, curling her hand around the back of Remmy's neck, pulling her down. "I love you," she whispered, bringing Remmy's lips to her own.

Remmy moved on top of her, gently insinuating a thigh between Julie's legs, which opened for her. They both sighed into the kiss, hips pressing together in a slow, lazy thrust. They continued to kiss in a leisurely, exploratory way. Their lust was sated; this was about a deep need to connect. There was no destination in mind, only the pleasure of the slow journey.

Julie's hands ran down Remmy's back, fingernails grazing across her buttocks, making Remmy flex in response. The kiss broke, both beginning to breathe hard as the pleasure built. Remmy refused to increase the speed of her hips, bringing them both to a slow, but intense climax. Julie cried out as she held Remmy to her.

Gasping for breath, Remmy started to move away but Julie held her. "No, stay." Remmy rested her head on Julie's chest, humming happily as her hair was stroked. "Interesting little interlude." Julie chuckled, and Remmy smiled. "What did you tell Grace?"

"I told her to give me some time to think about it."

"You'll make the right choice, Rem. I'm sure of it."

Chapter Fifty-eight

"A re you sure this is okay?" Remmy asked as they finished putting clean sheets on the bed in her former bedroom, which was now a guestroom.

Julie put a knee on the mattress as she reached across to rest a hand on Remmy's. "Yes. As I've told you about a dozen times this morning, it's very okay. Your cousin is always welcome here, Remmy. Okay?"

Remmy reluctantly met Julie's gaze, chewing on her lower lip as she nodded. "And you're sure you don't want me to stay in one of the guest bedrooms instead of in our...your..."

With a frustrated growl, Julie grabbed Remmy by the front of the shirt, pulling her onto the bed, then straddling her hips, effectively pinning Remmy to the bed. She planted her hands on the mattress to either side of Remmy's head. "What's your deal?" Julie asked, tilting her head enough that her hair fell to one side. "Why so insecure today?"

Remmy felt stupid beneath the intent gaze that pinned her to the spot. She knew she couldn't lie. Before she had a chance to respond, Julie sat up, her lips opening in realization.

"Wait," Julie said, "you're not embarrassed about us, are you? Do you not want Monica to see us together?" Julie squealed as she suddenly found their positions reversed, Remmy looking down at her, blue eyes twinkling.

"Now who's being insecure?" she asked, a lopsided

grin quirking her lips. "I could never be embarrassed or ashamed of you, or of what we share. At the same time, this is very new for you, Julie. We can be every bit the couple inside the safety of the walls of our house, but to the world..."

Julie looked up into Remmy's face. Though her eyes shone with amusement, Julie knew she had a valid point. She had yet to tell Matt about the turn of events, which he had predicted. If she were being entirely honest with herself, and with Remmy, she was scared to death to walk outside those walls, but ultimately she knew she couldn't be unfair to Remmy, couldn't be unfair to what they had. She loved Remmy with all her heart and would let nothing come between them.

She cupped Remmy's cheek. "I love you, Remmy. I want your cousin here, and I want her to see how happy you are. I want her to see us."

Remmy smiled, placing a soft kiss on even softer lips, but sobered quickly. "I have an idea, though I have no idea what you'll think of it."

"Read my mind," Julie teased, grinning as Remmy rolled her eyes.

"Uh, no, thanks. I think you'd have my head for that one."

"Probably. Okay, what's your idea?" Julie twirled a stray strand of dark hair around her finger.

"What if, while Monica is here, we have a barbecue? You know, invite those that we're close to — Matt and Skylar, Grace and Chris, Joan—"

"Get it over with in one fell swoop?" Julie said, finishing Remmy's thought. At Remmy's nod, Julie sighed, glancing out the window. She knew she had to, but her stomach roiled at the thought. She felt Remmy's eyes on her, knew she was waiting for an answer. Meeting blue eyes again, Julie nodded. "Okay," she said softly.

The look of absolute joy she received was worth the risk of alienating the people she loved.

❧❧❧❧

Monica looked around inside the tiny sports car, her eyes finally coming to rest on Remmy's profile as she easily maneuvered through traffic, driving them back to the small town of Woodland.

"You look fantastic, Remmy," she said.

Remmy grinned over at her, only daring to take her eyes off the road for a second. Julie would have her ass if she let anything happen to the Miata. "Thanks. You, too. I bet you're glad to get away for a few days, huh?"

"Oh, yeah. It'll be so nice to disappear in your little town." She glanced at the scenery around them, appreciating all the trees and green, green grass. "So, you said you had some things to talk to me about." She returned her gaze to Remmy's profile. "What's up? And where the heck did you get this cute little car?"

"It's Julie's."

"Julie? Julie who? You didn't mention you were seeing anyone."

"Well, I am." Remmy grinned. "Julie, as in Julie Wilson. She's the reason I came back to Woodland, Monica."

Monica looked utterly confused. "You're talking about the woman who was kidnapped, right?"

"The very one."

Twin eyebrows rose. "You saved her life, and now you're driving her car around?"

"Mon, I don't just rent a room from her. Yes, that's how it started, but she and I connect in a way that I can't explain to you. She's a part of me, and I'm a part of her. We love each other very much."

"So, you're in love?"

Remmy nodded, grinning at the wheels she could hear turning in Monica's head. Monica knew her history better than anyone. "Very much."

"Holy crap."

⁂

Remmy made another pass with the mower, finishing the last two strips of the lawn. From time to time, she glanced over at the back patio, watching as Monica and Julie got everything ready for the barbecue, which would start in a couple of hours. She had admittedly been nervous about Monica and Julie meeting, unsure of what her cousin would think. The worry had been unnecessary.

Two days ago, when Remmy and Monica had arrived at the house from the airport, Monica had accepted the tour Remmy offered, then they had settled in the kitchen where Julie had dinner ready for them. At first the conversation was somewhat stilted, neither Monica nor Julie sure what to do or say. But soon enough the ice had broken, and it was immediately obvious that each woman had found a kindred spirit.

When Remmy wasn't the chosen target for both Julie and Monica, who quickly ganged up on her, she simply sat back and watched, delighted that the two most important people in her life were becoming friends.

That night, as Remmy lay spooned around Julie in bed, Julie had thanked her for bringing Monica into their lives.

"Hey!" Julie yelled above the motor of the lawn mower. "Chop, chop! Quit your daydreaming!"

Remmy glared playfully then continued with her

chore.

⁂

"It's far too gorgeous out here," Grace said, resting on one of the loungers that had been set out. Sitting in matching comfort, Remmy grinned.

"That it is. I'm sorry Chris couldn't come today, Grace."

Grace waved a hand dismissively. "Don't worry about it. He was pissed he had to work, but you know what?" She glanced over, but her eyes couldn't see through the sunglasses that Remmy wore. "I can't tell you how many times he went to events — games with his friends, whatnot — while I worked." She grinned up at the hot, late June sky. "I think turnabout's fair play."

Remmy chuckled. "Indeed it is." She glanced over at the patio, sensing Julie's presence. Sure enough, Julie stood with a glass of iced tea in her hand, seeming to be in a deep conversation with Monica. Remmy grinned in utter contentment.

⁂

"I'm thinking that I might try and get back to sixth grade next year, maybe," Julie said, chewing her bottom lip in thought. "I don't know. I've never taught seventh before, so who knows?" She shrugged with a grin. "I may like it better."

"Julie." Matt stepped up next to the women and gave Monica an apologetic smile. "Can I steal you for a minute?"

Julie groaned internally. *Here we go.* "I'll be back in a few, Monica. Go eat some more. Lord knows I made enough hamburgers."

Julie followed him into the kitchen. From the window there, they could see the small party. Julie's gaze landed on Remmy and Grace, chatting and lying around like fat cats in their loungers. "What's up?" she asked finally, keeping her voice as chipper as possible.

"So, were you planning on coming clean with me? About you and Remmy?" he asked, keeping his voice even.

"Come clean? Matt," Julie said, annoyed. "I don't owe you anything, okay? I'm happy. Isn't that enough for you?"

Matt leaned against the counter, arms crossed over his chest. "How did it happen?"

Julie shrugged. She mirrored his position against the butcher block island. "I don't really know, to be honest. It just felt so…right."

Matt eyed her. "To…"

Julie reached across to place her hand on his forearm. "To love her, Matt. It's the most natural, right thing I've ever done. I didn't realize it, but I've been looking for her my whole life."

"I really don't get it, Jules." Matt sighed, placing his much larger hand over hers. "Yes, it means a lot to me that you're happy. In truth, I've never seen you this happy." Finally he was able to meet her gaze, a boyish grin spreading. "I guess it's better than having you be with Ray Lambert."

Julie rolled her eyes. "Gee, thanks. Somehow I think seeing me 'shack up' as you called it, with a lamp post would be better than me being with Ray Lambert."

Matt chuckled, crossing the short distance between them until he stood directly in front of her. He took her in a warm hug, resting his chin on her head. "I love you, Jules. I'm really glad she makes you happy."

Julie closed her eyes, her head resting against his

broad chest. "She does," she murmured, arms wrapped around his back. "Now we need to find you someone to make you just as happy."

Matt grinned. "I don't know, her cousin's kinda cute." He jerked when she pinched his side, but just held her closer.

Chapter Fifty-nine

Remmy lay on her back, hands behind her head. She tried to keep her eyes off the woman sleeping next to her, but was having a hell of a time. They had agreed they would behave while Monica stayed with them, her bedroom being right next door and all. Monica would be leaving the following morning. Julie would drop her off at the airport before going to school to start organizing her things, all of which had been packed up and stored after her disappearance the year before. Julie was lying on her side, her back toward Remmy.

With an internal growl, Remmy returned to contemplating the ceiling.

"I can't sleep, either," Julie murmured, never changing her position.

Remmy glanced at her, surprised to hear the soft words. She turned to her side, scooting over until she was pressed against Julie's naked back. "Why can't you sleep?" she asked, maneuvering herself closer until her crotch nicely cupped Julie's butt.

"Because my body won't obey," she said with a sigh.

Remmy's hand, which had rested on Julie's hip, moved up along her side, squeezing underneath Julie's arm until she cupped one of the breasts.

Julie sighed, relaxing into the touch. "You are so not helping, Remmy," she said, wriggling back against the lean body even as she protested.

"No, but I could help."

Julie smiled, running her hand up and over Remmy's hip. "I'm sure you could. But, wasn't it you who recommended we not act like, oh, what were your words, 'horny fourteen-year old boys', while Monica is here?" She smiled at the low chuckle against the back of her neck. The sound made her shiver.

"I never said that," Remmy said, her hand fondling the breast, the nipple already hard against her palm.

"You most certainly did." Julie had to suppress the moan that threatened to escape. She knew she would never win this battle, but it would be fun to try.

"I must've been out of my mind or half asleep or something," Remmy said, her lips finding the back of Julie's neck. She smiled at the soft whimper and slight jerk of Julie's hips. She pressed forward, already wet and very aroused.

"We really shouldn't, Remmy," Julie whispered, though her protest didn't even sound believable to her own ears.

"I haven't been able to touch you in two nights," Remmy whispered against Julie's ear, swiping at the lobe, "three days..."

Julie gasped as her nipple was taken between two very nimble fingers, sensation shooting to her lower belly. She couldn't respond, her body stirring wide awake, and very responsive. Finally she turned over until she was facing Remmy. "We have to be really quiet," she whispered against searching lips.

"Very quiet," Remmy agreed, bridging the scant distance between them and kissing Julie deeply, pressing Julie onto her back in the process.

Julie moaned into Remmy's mouth, her legs spreading to make room for the body that settled on top of her. She couldn't get enough of the feel of Remmy's skin against her own. Sometimes she wondered how she had lived without it. "Oh, yes," she whispered as fingers and lips ran a fiery trail across her skin until finally her breast was consumed by a hot, demanding mouth.

Remmy was lost in the bliss of Julie's gorgeous body, one hand cupping the other breast as she feasted on the first. She felt Julie's hips thrusting against her, copious wetness painting Remmy's stomach. She groaned at the feel; her fingers itched to explore.

Julie gasped, back arching and legs falling further apart as gentle fingers slid through her wetness. She closed her eyes, concentrating on the feelings Remmy was stirring within her. She felt Remmy pressing against her, her wetness slick on Julie's thigh. Her hand ran over Remmy's back, her intention to reach around to Remmy's mound, but she stopped as Remmy's questing fingers found an extremely hard clit. She soaked up the pleasure at the insistent pressure. She wanted more. She wanted to complete the healing.

When Julie's hand moved down between their bodies and grasped Remmy's, she stopped kissing the lovely neck, worried that she'd done something displeasing. She lifted her head and met Julie's eyes, which held only love and intense desire. As she held Julie's gaze, insistent fingers guided her hand. Remmy raised a questioning eyebrow and received a passionate kiss in answer.

Julie groaned deep in her throat as Remmy entered her, her hips rising to meet her fingers. She was nervous, her stomach queasy, but she reminded herself that this was Remmy, loving her.

Fully inside, Remmy kissed Julie then pulled back to rest on her elbow, using her free hand to brush blonde hair away from Julie's face and stroking the skin there to encourage and comfort. When Julie showed no signs of discomfort or distaste, Remmy began to move, fingers slowly sliding in and out. She watched as green eyes slid closed, a wrinkle of concentration forming on Julie's brow. Awed by the gift she was being given, Remmy couldn't look away.

❧ ❧ ❧ ❧

Soft lips brushed across her face and lips, and Julie could smell Remmy's skin. *Remmy.* It was Remmy who was inside her, claiming her. Her orgasm started low, building and gaining speed and heat.

Julie's body convulsed, hot wetness soaking Remmy's fingers. Julie did her best to keep quiet, and Remmy helped, swallowing her cries with her own mouth.

Julie calmed gradually, her body twitching with aftershocks. She closed her thighs to keep Remmy inside her as she wrapped her in grateful arms and kissed her deeply. "I love you," she whispered again and again.

When at length her hand was released, Remmy took Julie into her arms and cuddled her. Her own body was on fire, but it was far more important to hold Julie, to let her know how much she was cherished.

Chapter Sixty

Remmy broke down a box, tossed the flattened cardboard to the polished tile, then took her utility knife from her back pocket and sliced through the tape of yet another box. The shelves were pretty damn empty, and Remmy was irritated. She was going to have to have a chat with Joan about the other employees and how much they didn't do. The only reason she wasn't ready to commit murder was because the store was pretty slow. It was the middle of a Monday afternoon; everyone in the bustling little town was at work. Other than having to stop now and then to take care of a gasoline customer, she'd been able to work pretty much undisturbed.

Hearing the bell above the door jingle, Remmy glanced over the shelving units, installed at shoulder height so that any part of the store could be seen from anywhere else in the store. A young man stepped inside. His shaggy brown hair hung in his eyes, and he was dressed casually in a t-shirt and jeans.

"Can I help you?" she asked, letting him know she was there.

He glanced at her, studying her for a moment, then shook his head. "Nope. Not yet."

❧❧❧❧

Julie exhaled sharply as she heaved a plastic tub onto one of the small desks lined neatly in a row.

Removing the lid, she peered inside, glad to see her posters and framed pictures that would soon be hung up on her classroom walls. It was strange to be in a new room. She had been in the same one during her entire time at Woodland Middle School.

Pulling out decorations and scattering them on the floor to be gone through later, Julie was relieved to hear Mike Gonzales and his team working maintenance in the quiet building. She wasn't quite ready to be alone there. Eventually she would have to leave the safety of the school and go out to the parking lot.

Julie adjusted her ponytail and brushed her bangs out of her eyes, then took a drink of bottled water. It was going to be a scorcher, and she didn't relish the thought of being stuck in the school all afternoon with the air conditioning turned off for the summer. Leaning back against her new desk, she sighed as the cold liquid slid down her throat.

She smiled as she lowered the bottle and rested it against her upper chest, her thoughts reverting to her and Remmy making love the night before. It had been challenging, trying to stay quiet. That morning, as she made breakfast, it took an effort to not blush every time she looked at their guest. Monica seemed none the wiser, so she assumed they had been quiet enough.

Julie closed her eyes for a moment. She could still feel Remmy inside her, touching her in a way that went beyond the physical. She hoped that Matt could find that kind of love. She half wondered whether he'd been kidding about Monica; his eyes had followed the very attractive woman all through the barbecue. Julie chuckled at the thought. "Wouldn't that be a kick?" she muttered to the empty classroom.

With a sigh, Julie set her water aside and continued unpacking. She was glad that Bob had allowed her into the school so early in the summer. Technically, teachers didn't start preparing their rooms until mid-August at the earliest, but Julie needed to get a curriculum together for her seventh graders, including looking back through her old stuff to see what could be utilized with an older group of kids. The class schedules hadn't yet been made up by the counselor, but Julie looked forward to seeing who she would be teaching. Woodland Middle was a fairly small school, so it was likely she knew most, if not all, of the students assigned to her.

She sighed and grabbed another tub.

☙ ☙ ❧ ❧

Remmy slid the razorblade back into the plastic handle, then slid the utility knife into her back pocket. Scooting the rest of the boxes out of the middle of the aisle and gathering up the deconstructed boxes, she took them into the bullpen and leaned the cardboard against the cigarette shelves. She waited while the customer roamed around the store, fingering a package of candy corn before moving on. He glanced at Remmy from time to time; it made her nervous.

She was totally alone in the store. Joan was off, and her own relief wasn't coming in until after three. Remmy felt a tingle in her spine but couldn't read its origin. "Hot out there, huh?" she said, her words springing more from her nervousness than an attempt to start a conversation with the young man, who looked to be in his early twenties.

"Yep. Pretty hot." He ran a finger along the chill glass of one of the coolers, making a full circuit around the small store until he reached the front doors. He glanced out into the parking lot, noting a man filling up his Bronco. The customer's attention was on the pump meter, not on the store. With a metallic click, the front doors locked with a turn of the man's wrist.

Remmy was very nervous now, her eyes never leaving him as she blindly reached under the counter for the silent alarm button. Josh had casually shown it to her back when she first started, but that was last August, nearly a year ago. Finally she located it, and her finger stabbed at it frantically.

"Look, how can I help you?" she asked, stepping away from the button, trying to avoid raising any suspicion in the calm young man. Finally he walked over to her, his eyes holding a glint that made Remmy's skin crawl.

"Help me?" He casually leaned against the counter as though he was settling in for a chat. "I think you've helped me enough, don't you, Remmy?"

Remmy was surprised to hear her name from his lips. He placed his hand on the counter and her eyes flicked to it. She gasped. On his right ring finger, which was bare, suddenly a shimmer of light appeared. The shimmer slowly formed a shape in her mind: a band, a ring. The stone shone red. Fear gripping her throat and rendering her nearly mute, her gaze flicked back up to his.

❧ ❧ ❧ ❧ ❧

Julie flipped through the pages of her planning notebook. Head resting on her upturned palm, she read her small, neat handwriting. Sighing heavily, she slapped the notebook closed. She felt fidgety, anxious. She wasn't sure whether it was the heat in the room or just because she was so damn bored, but she could barely sit still. Grabbing her third bottle of water, she twisted off the top and took a healthy sip, staring out over her classroom.

Posters and pictures had been hung; the room was nearing the ready point. She supposed it was a good thing. She hadn't meant to hang decorations today, but figured that while she was there—two birds, one stone.

Suddenly, the room around her began to fade; her eyes slipped closed.

The waters of the lake were churning with chaotic waves, the skies swirling with heavy clouds and threatening lightning. The flowers in the field were dancing erratically, the winds nearly beating them down.

Julie stood in the center of the disquiet, looking up into the sky as she spun in a circle. "Remmy?" she called, a chill skittering down her spine and settling in her gut. "Remmy?" She whipped around at the sound of Remmy's voice on the wind, calling her name...

Julie gasped, the air rushing into her lungs nearly choking her. She looked around frantically, the feeling of terror that gripped her still holding tight. Something was wrong. Something was very wrong.

⁂

Dennis Collins pulled a pack of cigarettes out of a pocket in his cargo pants, never taking his eyes off her as he lit the end and took a deep drag. "I heard about what you did with that guy and the bitches he kept all chained up in his basement. Guess he had a pretty good fuck every night, huh?"

Dennis' eyes crinkled as he grinned and blew the cigarette smoke directly into Remmy's face. She did her best not to react to his words, even though inside she was a tempest of growing anger. "What do you want, Dennis?" she said, her voice deadly calm.

Dennis Collins smiled, pointing at her with the

cigarette tucked between two fingers. "You're good."

"I know who you are, and I know what you did. Why are you here?" Remmy slid her hand behind her back.

"I'd really rather you keep your hands where they were," he said, nodding at her hand. "You're smart, too," he said as both hands became visible again. "I'm here today because I'd say I'm pretty much fucked, right?" His eyes turned hard again. "Because of you, you fucking meddling bitch."

Not daring to look away, Remmy kept eye contact. She tried desperately to think of another way to get to the utility knife tucked in her back pocket.

"What have I done to you? You use your...freakish, ability — or whatever the fuck it's called — and pinpoint me. That really pisses me off, Remmy, I gotta tell ya." He pushed away from the counter.

Remmy was very, very anxious. She felt trapped in the bullpen. "Look, Dennis, I was just trying to help out, okay? I have nothing to do with what you did. You did it, man, not me." It was the wrong thing to say.

"Fuck you!" Dennis raised his fist and backhanded Remmy so quickly that her teeth rattled in her head. She fell back against the counter, the edge of it digging into her lower back.

✦ ✦ ✦ ✦

Julie slammed her phone shut. "Damnit!" She tossed the cell onto the passenger seat of her car as she floored the little sports car toward the store. She had felt sick ever since she'd been suddenly thrust into their lake venue. Remmy's cell phone was turned off, as it always was when she was working, but Julie knew that Remmy was trying to send her a message, trying to call for help.

She had tried to get hold of Grace, but she wasn't at the station and her voicemail had picked up on her cell. Julie grabbed the phone again and dialed 911. She gave the address of the store to the officer who answered.

"What seems to be the problem, ma'am?" the officer asked, voice calm and even.

Julie chewed her bottom lip. What, indeed? "I'm not sure. This will sound strange, but it's just a feeling. I don't know." She heard typing. He was probably typing what she told him, as well as the store's address.

"Ma'am, an officer has already been dispatched to that address. She should be there, or will be shortly."

Julie felt her blood run cold. "Who called?" she whispered, voice just this side of shaky.

"Silent alarm, ma'am."

Without another word, Julie flipped her phone closed and tossed it onto the seat, pushing the speed limit as she sped to the store as quickly as she dared.

≈≈≈≈≈

Remmy was still reeling from the blow, and her eye was pulsing. She backed away from Dennis until she reached the swinging door and pushed out of the bullpen. She glanced over her shoulder at the dark hallway which led to the back door. Her attention was drawn back to Collins by the metallic click of a cocking gun.

"You're not going anywhere, bitch," he said, holding the small handgun in front of him, aiming it at Remmy's head.

Her eyes were drawn to the deadly tip before they made their way back to Dennis' face. "This isn't necessary, Dennis," she said, her heart pounding. Cold sweat broke out on her forehead and in her armpits. She wiped her palms on the thighs of her jeans. A flash of Julie appeared before her mind's eye, and she knew she had to find a way out of the deadly situation. "Think about what you're doing, Dennis," she said, her voice as calm as she could manage. "Think about the penalty for this."

Dennis smirked, shaking his head. "You're really fucking stupid, you know that? Do you honestly think I've got a chance? No. And it's all because of you!"

"Wait, hold on." Remmy held up her hands up. "Listen, how about this. I open up the cash register and give you the money. There's more than three grand. Think about it, man. You could get pretty far on three grand, right?"

Dennis hesitated as he tossed that tidbit of information around. His arm began to lower as he seriously considered the offer. In that one moment, Remmy dove behind the shoulder-high shelving unit that held a limited offering of pet products. The phone's shrill ringing heightened the tension.

Remmy landed hard on her shoulder and tried not to cry out in pain. She heard Dennis yell in surprise and anger, followed by the near deafening sound of a gunshot.

☙☙☙☙

Officer Beth Canton arrived at the convenience store, checking out the situation as she came to a stop. The silent alarm had been activated, and no one had answered attempts to call the store. The officer radioed in her position and location, and was told that, additionally, a Julie Wilson had called in to request police presence at the store.

"Ten-four," Officer Canton said, opening the door

of her cruiser, glad for the heft of her gun on her hip. As she stepped out of the car, she looked through the large front windows of the store. There was no clerk at the counter but she could see the back of a man's head. He was facing one of the aisles. Beth's eyes widened as she realized that he held a gun, just an instant before the crack of a gunshot rocked the early afternoon.

⁂

Remmy crawled faster than she would have thought possible, rounding the end of the aisles and coming up against her newest display creation, this one made of cases of Mountain Dew and other Pepsi products. She winced as her injured shoulder objected to a sudden movement. Taking cover behind the soda, she reached into her pocket and grabbed the utility knife, leaving the blade tucked inside the casing so she didn't accidentally cut herself.

Dennis held the gun in both hands, tracking from side to side as he made his way down the aisle, swinging dramatically around at the end but finding nothing. "I'm going to fucking kill you, Remmy!" Suddenly a can of soda hit him, and he was flat on his ass, head banging against the glass door of the cooler behind him. He was also being showered with something wet and sticky. The cans of soda landing near him erupted on impact. "Fucking bitch," he muttered, bringing a hand up to his temple where he'd been hit, then to his forehead. He felt warmth, blood on his fingertips. He got to his feet, fingers re-wrapping around the grip of the gun.

Hunched down, shoes nearly slipping in the soda that had exploded across the floor, Remmy got to her feet and ran toward the other side of the store. She saw the police car parked in front of the store, saw the officer getting out.

"Help!" she yelled, banging on the glass, which she knew was bulletproof, a belief that was validated when a bullet whizzed by her head and slammed into the glass, cracking it but not going through.

Again Remmy dove for cover, crying out as white hot pain shot through her arm as she landed on the same shoulder. She almost couldn't breathe.

⁂

Julie's Miata squealed into the parking lot. As if in a nightmarish world, she saw the police officer exiting the cruiser, saw Remmy banging on the glass, her cries silent screams behind the thick glass. Julie screamed when she heard the gunshot, a sudden crack appearing in the glass less than six inches from Remmy's head. Remmy suddenly disappeared.

The officer heard the scream and turned, hurrying over to intercept Julie, who was running toward the store. "Ma'am! You need to stay back!" she yelled.

Julie fought against the strong arms of the policewoman, the steely voice finally getting through her terrified haze.

"Ma'am!"

Julie stopped fighting. "What's happening in there?" she asked, her voice on the verge of hysteria.

"I don't know yet; I just arrived. I need to do my job, okay? Get back in your car and leave."

"Not a chance." Julie said, jaw set.

Beth Canton sighed, nodding. "Alright. At the very least, either get into your car or go and stand behind it."

Julie nodded numbly, walking back toward her car, where she stood, eyes glued to the store and arms wrapped around herself. "Remmy," she whispered.

❧❧❧❧

Remmy crawled around toward the coffee stand, a fresh pot brewed not ten minutes ago. She eyed it quickly then returned her attention to Dennis Collins, who was cautiously making his way over to her side of the store.

❧❧❧❧

Joan arrived to find the parking lot of the store filling with bystanders and three police cars, the third pulling up as she parked. She had gotten Julie's frantic message. She spotted Julie leaning against the trunk of her car and hurried over to her.

"What the hell is happening?" she asked, placing a hand on Julie's shoulder. She was shocked when she suddenly had an armful of a sobbing Julie Wilson.

❧❧❧❧

Dennis could hear his heartbeat pounding in his ears, which were still ringing from the two gunshots in such confined quarters. He could see the audience they had out in the parking lot, but he didn't care. At this point, none of that mattered. He wasn't going to be taken alive, and he was going to take this bitch with him.

His head whipped around toward the back wall of the store where the softdrink machines were alongside a clear plastic case which held doughnuts and bagels. He was hurrying back there, finger on the trigger, when a metal rack of plastic cups was knocked to the floor.

Remmy held her breath, waiting until Dennis rounded the corner. She had to act quickly or she would get a bullet. As the toe of his tennis shoe became visible, she swung, the steaming liquid flying from its metal container.

Dennis screamed as the scalding coffee streamed down his face and neck. He cried out again when a sharp pain lanced through his gun hand, causing the gun to fall from his grasp.

The utility knife fell to the floor as Remmy launched herself at him, landing them both on the ground. She felt his blood against her skin, the slice on his arm deep. She could imagine how painful it must be, but she didn't care. She was on top of him immediately, landing a punch on his jaw. He punched her back, knocking her off of him with an uppercut to her right eye.

As soon as he was free of her weight, Dennis scrambled toward the gun which had skittered over near the dairy cooler.

✤ ✤ ✤ ✤

The watching crowd was barely able to see the two combatants as they wrestled on the floor. Julie was glued to the glass; officers were trying to peel her away. Joan was fumbling on her key ring for the key to the front door, her hands trembling in her haste. She could feel the heat of restless officers behind her, waiting for her to give them entry.

✤ ✤ ✤ ✤

Remmy shook herself, trying not to surrender to the fuzziness around her vision. When Dennis hit her, she had smacked her head on the cabinet, nearly knocking herself out. She saw Dennis moving and realized he was trying for the gun. She saw that her utility knife was closer than the gun and knew there was no way she would reach him or the gun in time, so she snatched the knife and ran toward the food aisles, ducking as another shot rang out.

�✧✧✧

Julie cried out at the sound, her heart pounding, a steady stream of tears coursing down her cheeks. All non-police personnel had previously been instructed to get back behind the barricade that had been put up and, at the sound of the third shot, they had been forced behind it. Julie fought against the officer that held her, but she was no match for his strength.

"Remmy!" she screamed.

✧✧✧✧

Remmy spared a glance out the wide windows, and found Julie. For a split second she held the terrified green eyes and smiled, trying to let Julie know that no matter what happened, she loved her. Julie was crying, and it broke Remmy's heart.

Their moment was shattered when a box of instant rice exploded next to her head, grains flying everywhere as Remmy ducked again, instinctively covering her head as she sped down another aisle.

✧✧✧✧

Grace removed her jacket and tossed it over the back of her chair. She glanced over at her partner, noting that he was taking furious notes as he listened to what she assumed was his voicemail. He hung up the receiver and turned to her.

"Don't get too comfortable. Your little

dreamwalker just found our suspect for us."

❧❧❧❧

Julie had understood Remmy's message of love, loud and clear, and she couldn't stop crying. She had the horrible feeling that she was going to lose Remmy. If the worst happened, the only thing she would have to hold on to was Remmy's love for her, however short lived; it was the greatest gift she had ever been given. From Remmy, she had learned that it was okay to not only love and be loved, but also to love herself and be a strong woman.

A warm hand against her back startled her from her bleak thoughts. Seeing Matt's compassionate gaze, she lost it. She clung to him as he held her close.

❧❧❧❧

Remmy was trying desperately to keep the blackness at bay. She figured she probably had a bad concussion. If she blacked out, she'd never wake up again. She felt groggy, her stomach nauseous, and her face hurt from the two punches she'd taken.

Her hand was sweating badly as her thumb ran back and forth over the smooth plastic handle of the knife. The blade was still out and deadly sharp. She hadn't heard any movement from Dennis since he had fired at her and had no idea where he was. She tried not to breathe, afraid that any noise would alert him or distract herself.

Ears perked and eyes wide, she listened. Glancing over at the beer cooler, she grinned at being able to see Dennis in a reflection in the glass as he tried to sneak up on her, gun held firmly. She decided to move around to the other aisle, but she slipped on the rice scattered on the floor and landed flat on her back. Dennis' shoes slapped on the tile as he ran toward her.

Remmy watched him round the corner, gun held in both hands, straight out in front of him. The muzzle was pointed at her head. Without thought, she raised her hand and threw the utility knife. She watched in fascination as it tumbled end over end and embedded in his throat.

Dennis' eyes grew wide, a wet gurgling erupting from his throat, the gun falling to the floor with a clang. He grabbed at his throat. Swinging her leg out, Remmy kicked the gun out of his reach, crying out in surprise as she was suddenly grabbed from behind. An officer helped her to her feet.

❧❧❧❧

Trying to run to the store, Julie fought against Matt's arms, but he held her tight.

"No!" he said between gritted teeth as he struggled with her. "Julie, no!"

"Let me go! Matt, let me fucking go!"

She saw the doors pulled open and a dazed Remmy was led out, her t-shirt splattered with blood and blood dripping from a cut beside her eye.

"Remmy!" Julie screamed, shoving Matt away from her and running forward, nearly knocking down two police officers in her haste to reach Remmy.

"Julie," Remmy whispered, taking Julie in her arms and holding her for dear life. She was exhausted, hurt, and wanted nothing more than to sit down, but all of that was forgotten as the warm body pressed against her. "Shh, don't cry," she whispered, Julie sobbing against her.

Chapter 62

After the incident, a police car had taken Remmy to the hospital, where her wounds had been assessed . Her face was horribly bruised, as was her tailbone from where she had landed. Her shoulder had been dislocated and was popped back into place. In short, she was miserable. But now she was sleeping.

Julie spooned her protectively. Her head resting on an upturned palm, Julie studied Remmy's profile, gently tracing around the colorful bruises, her touch feather light. She leaned down and placed a soft kiss on top of Remmy's head then lay her head on the pillow, burrowing as close to Remmy as she could.

It had been a draining day. Though he had lost a great deal of blood, Dennis Collins hadn't died of his injuries. They were able to get him medical treatment in time. Remmy was happy about that. He would stand trial for what he had done to the Bailey family, and what he did to Remmy. He refused to say why he had murdered Yvonne and Tyler, but Julie figured that his motive would come out in time. Perhaps the D.A. would make some sort of deal with him: no death penalty if he confessed and told his story. Who knew.

One thing Julie did know, she was exhausted from her emotions being all over the place over the course of the day. She had never been so grateful for anything as she was when she saw Remmy walk out of the store, alive and in one piece. How much more could Remmy take? Julie wondered. She was strong, but even the strongest could break. What was Remmy's breaking point? When would she have taken enough mental—and physical—abuse, to the point that she would lock down her gift for good, refusing to help. Julie would stand behind her one hundred percent, whatever she chose.

Julie tightened her grasp on Remmy and closed her eyes. There was a lot to think about. A lot to talk about. Tomorrow.

Epilogue: A year later

The sun overhead was hot but there was enough of a breeze that the day was pleasant, beautiful. Hand in hand, Remmy and Julie walked through the thick, well-maintained grass, watching a lone bird take flight. Julie shaded her eyes with her hand, following the bird until it was out of sight.

"I think we've got a good shot at breaking this case," Remmy said, swinging their joined hands.

"Oh, yeah? Think you can catch him, tiger?"

Remmy nodded. "Yes I do." She smiled over at Julie.

"At least the media has been considerate, huh?" Julie said, referring to the agreement after the events of the previous year. Neither the newspapers nor news stations were allowed to know of Remmy's involvements in any cases, nor were they allowed to report it, should they find out. That was Remmy's condition for Grace and the Woodland Police Department if they wanted her help. Julie squeezed Remmy's hand affectionately. "I have no doubt you'll get your man."

They walked among the rows of headstones, following the map Julie had been given at the main office. They stopped and looked at the simple granite marker:

Sergio X. Venti
February 4, 1966 — November 5, 2011

They stood in silence; no words were necessary. Julie searched her brain, and her heart, and realized that she felt nothing. No fear. No terror. No anger. Nothing. Over the intervening year, she had come to realize that he had given her more than he had taken. Without him she would never have had Remmy in her life.

Remmy studied Julie's profile, wondering what was going through her mind. Finally she wrapped her arm around the slender shoulder and gently drew Julie against her. She kissed Julie's cheek. "He can't hurt you anymore."

Julie leaned into Remmy, looking up at her with a gentle smile. "He can't hurt us anymore."

Remmy smiled back. "Let's go home."

About the Author

Kim Pritekel was born and raised in Colorado and still lives there today, in love with the Rockies and simple beauty of home. She began writing at age 9 and has yet to stop, as writing a novel is more fulfilling than therapy. Cheaper, too. Kim embraces all forms of creativity, including filmmaking, which she has done as a writer, producer and director, since 2006. She can be reached on Facebook or by email at XenaNut@hotmail.com

You can also find Kim's other books at -

www.sapphirebooks.com

www.kimpritekel.com

Check out Kim's other books.

After Shadow - ISBN - 978-1-939062-10-9

Clara always knew she was different, but just how different she was was to be seen. She will be forced on a journey to places that, though nightmarish to some, make perfect sense to her. While living a life in darkness and shadow, massaging the ghosts we all want to hide from beneath the covers, she will discover her own light of day. But, can she discover her heart?

Shadow Box - ISBN - 978-1939062-07-9

One 3 a.m. incident would change everything forever.

Tamson Robard spent a childhood with a weak mother, desperate to land a man in order to escape a horrific secret that Tamson can't even fathom. Tamson ran away as a teenager, but is now a grown woman. Other than drugs, her only friend is a guardian angel, Penny, whom she confides in, sharing feeble hopes and unending pain.

Together, the two will discover buried truths that will lead them through tears and to death's door. Can the collision of Erin and Tamson's worlds save them both?